The Unseen Hand of Peter Gyges

R. L. Richards

Copyright © 2015 R. L. Richards

Cover design by James Richards and Joshua Ford

All rights reserved.

ISBN-10: 1490936335
ISBN-13: 978-1490936338

This book is dedicated to my late friend John Kiley. For over forty years our lives were intertwined. We shared an evolving set of interests and activities over the years but one thing always remained constant: our love and commitment to each other. John was the first to read the first draft of this novel over twelve years ago. We all miss him everyday.

R. L. Richards

This novel would not have been possible without the inspiration, guidance, editing, enthusiasm, criticisms and encouragement of my son James Thomas Richards. He has spent uncounted hours working with me to bring this book to publication. No James, no book. It is as simple as that. More co-author than editor.

Carl Herzig gets credit for the final edit and polish. He's the best.

Finally, I would like to say thanks to all of my St. Ambrose University colleagues who make going to work everyday a pleasure.

1

Peter Gyges pulled the dead man's hand close and cut off the right ring finger. He worked deftly, as if cleaning a fish. Then he washed off the blood by the rocky shore of the lake. He freed the ring and threw the severed finger to the catfish.

It had taken two hours of vigorous paddling to reach the Hook and the islands beyond it. It was not a trip a canoeist could make every day on the Whitefish Chain. If there was much wind at all, the waves were too high and the going too rough. Today he had made it, but it had been a struggle. The deep V-hulled Lunds created waves that attacked his canoe from the right flank. When he saw these ubiquitous powerboats coming, he maneuvered the canoe to face the waves head-on so that the bow of the canoe would slice into them. Jockeying around to accommodate the larger, more powerful boats made the trip more difficult. Fortunately, the attacks were rare during the week. On weekends, he would never venture out there.

The Hook jutted out into the middle of the lake, stretching for three fourths of a mile—three small islands cast out like the marks left by a skipped stone. Gyges directed his canoe to the smallest and farthest of the islands. For reasons he did not know, the waves and wind there were often much calmer than on the rest of the big lake. Some years back, he had fallen asleep fishing in a cove and the canoe had drifted out among the islands.

That same piece of sleepy fortune also revealed a hidden underwater pile of smooth round rocks that formed a submerged island about two hundred yards off the last island. Perhaps forty yards across and seventy yards long, it lay in ten feet of water, compared with the rest of the lake's twenty to twenty-five. The current flowed over the top from west to east—a classic hump.

Fish were drawn to the Hump like iron filings to a magnet. Depending on the season, time of day, and weather, you could catch almost anything there. To Gyges's knowledge, no one else was aware of the spot. He'd never seen anyone fish there, and he'd never heard any locals, not even Bob who ran Black Pine Resort, talk about it.

He certainly would never have shared the location with anyone. It was his secret piece of underwater real estate. It was true he'd taken some buddies out that way, but he'd taken them to Big Island and the area just off the Hook, where the fishing was spotty at best.

But never to the Hump. He'd have rather they thought he told fish stories.

The trip down the length of the Hump took him all morning. He caught a dozen smallmouth and also a few scrappy rock bass. It was just after he finished his lunch that the day changed.

Gyges looked up into the western sky. Black clouds were rolling ominously in his direction, claiming half the sky, and were soon accompanied by grumbling thunder. The wind picked up and the temperature dropped. Gyges dug hard against the water, making a straight line for the nearest island. His back and arms ached, but he didn't slow. Lightning flashed in the dark clouds behind him. He reached the island before the full force of the storm broke over the lake, and pulled the canoe out of the water. He snatched his paddle and gear and overturned the canoe. Propping up the front end with the paddle, he crawled underneath for cover. Flashes ripped through the sky. The pine trees at the back edge of the beach moaned in complaint, bent over by the violent wind. A few sprinkles quickly turned into an ice-cold curtain that swept east across the lake and over the island. Everything around him stirred in the torrent.

When a sudden white blast shattered a pine behind him, Gyges tucked his head under his arms. The canoe rocked unsteadily in the wind. He kicked out the paddle, enclosing himself under the canoe, reached up into the portage spars, and pulled tight to keep the canoe from blowing away. The wind beat waves onto the island shore. When water flowed in under the canoe, he scooted his shell backward in fear that he might actually drown.

But the canoe was not washed into the lake. The lightening moved further east, and the wind and the rain eased. Gyges peeked out from under his shell. The sky was still black . . . then another flash and he saw it.

A white form, like the pale flesh of a giant dead fish, had been washed onto the edge of the island. He stared out at the lump, but it was too dark to make out anything but a vague form.

After a few minutes, the storm abated enough for Gyges to prop up the canoe. The sky returned to a dark gray, and the thunder receded into the distance. He crawled from under the canoe and sat next to it for a moment to study the sky. Then he turned his gaze back to the white mass. He carefully moved closer to get a better look.

It was a man.

"Hey, buddy—are you okay?" he called.

No response.

He picked up a rock and tossed it at the body. The rock struck the figure's back. It did not move. He picked up a long stick and poked at its legs. Still no movement.

Cupping his hand over his eyes, he scanned the horizon for any boats.

Nothing.

He looked down again at the body, nudged it with his foot, then knelt down, reached out, and shook its cold shoulder. The body wasn't bloated or discolored. On its right hand he saw a ring.

He reached out and tried to pry the ring from the finger, but it wouldn't move. He rubbed water on it, but the ring was still too tight.

He took out a Swiss army knife from his back pocket and opened it to the largest blade.

When he was done, he stood there on the edge of the shore and held the ring up to his face. Strange. Striking. Compelling.

He put it on his own hand and was surprised—it was a perfect fit.

2

The veins in Elizabeth Heath O'Brien's neck expanded as she yelled into the phone. "Listen, pendejo, if you ever expect to cater another party for the O'Briens, you better get your cabeza out of your culo. We've spent enough dinero at your place to smuggle half your cousins up from Guanajuato. Get it right!"

She went downstairs to find her husband, Danny, and his brother, Tommy, sitting on the deck overlooking Gray's Bay and drinking their usual Turf Mor from the Connemara Distillery. The O'Brien brothers thought that if you were going to drink in the tradition of the Old Sod, the whisky should taste as much like the old sod as possible. Elizabeth stopped at the bottom of the stairs and looked out over the lake. It was a stunning view. Their backyard stretched seventy yards across and another forty down to the docks. She saw the caterers put out the final food, secure the tents, and light the tiki torches. The band was unloading their gear and setting up on the deck by the docks where a multitude would arrive by boats as expensive as houses.

The O'Brien Holdings Annual Labor-Day picnic had achieved a kind of mythic status in the Metro Twin Cities as one of the most lavish and raucous parties of the year. The O'Briens had begun as sons of shanty Irish. They'd crawled and brawled to success as turn-around magicians in the gritty, unforgiving world of Midwest manufacturing. They bought troubled manufacturing firms, broke the unions, kicked out incompetent managers, got them working and productive, and then sold them off as moneymakers. The parties were a reflection of the O'Brien ethos: work hard, drink hard, play hard. These were no genteel Scandinavian affairs at the Minneapolis Institute of Arts with Pinots and finger food. If you didn't drink Guinness and Fitzgerald's, you'd go thirsty. And you'd better not let Danny or Tommy catch you smuggling in anything else. Invites went out to six hundred people—mostly employees and their spouses, retirees, customers, and suppliers. In the early hours, when security's diligence waned, the invited would be joined by more than a few party-crashers.

* * *

"Yeah, Tracy, where's your buddy Gyges?" asked Dave, picking up a walleye burrito with chipotle sauce. "I haven't seen him yet. He never misses an O'Brien Holding's party. Not that I can blame him. Danny and Tommy know how to lay one out."

"Gyges is not my buddy," Tracy declared." He's my sub—or—din—not my buddy."

"Touchy, touchy," said Paul.

"I don't have ass-kissers for friends, and Gyges is King of the Ass-kissers," Tracy said. "He's not my buddy, chum, pal, compadre, or amigo."

"I'm sure he only has good things to say about you," Dave said, more interested in spicing his burrito than in Tracy's caustic remarks.

"That shows you how retarded he is," said Tracy.

Paul sighed. "Okay, moving on . . ."

"Very soon, no more Gyges. The time's they are a changin' my friends," said Tracy, butchering the famous north-country accent.

"You know, Tracy, the guy just wants to be liked," said Paul. "Yeah, sometimes he tries too hard. But there are worse sins. We all have our faults—even you, Teddy. You're infamously self-centered . . ."

"Seriously, Paul? You think he's not? Don't let the fawning façade fool you. He tries to get what he wants by ingratiating himself to people. The little turd has no backbone. He's a coward. He's sneaky and insincere. I hate that shit. I'm just more direct and open."

"Aggression parading as honesty—that's good, Tracy. Disguise your vices as virtues."

Tracy went red. "Watch how you talk to me, Paul. Let's not forget who you work for. A little more deference would be wise. I think you have a performance review coming up."

"Hail, the gang's all here," called Gyges, coming up from behind them.

"Pull up a chair, G-man," said Dave.

"Thanks, don't mind if I do."

"Hey have you tried these walleye burritos?"

Gyges held one up. "My third. Speaking of walleyes, did I tell you guys what happened to me on my fishing trip last week up on the Whitefish Chain?"

"No, and don't," said Tracy. "Your fishing exploits give fishing stories a bad name."

Gyges laughed, missing the point of Tracy's sarcasm.

"No, no. You've really got to hear this," Gyges continued undaunted. "I had canoed out to my favorite spot—a place called the Hook. Yeah, Tracy knows the place. I showed it to him the first time I took him fishing up there. 'Member, Tracy, that huge smallmouth you took on the blue sinking Rapala?"

The memory triggered a smile from Tracy. He nodded.

"Well, I was out there and catching keeper 'eyes on almost every cast. Then out of nowhere I was overtaken by a huge storm. I mean, I was smack in the middle of a maelstrom. I'm telling you guys . . . it was intense. Wind, rain, waves, thunder, lightning—I got blasted by it all. I had to paddle for my life and get off the lake. It's a shame, 'cuz I was on them 'eyes like Minnesota mosquitoes on Alabama campers. So, I crawled under the canoe. It was rocking and rolling in the wind, water coming up from under. I had to hold on for dear life. I was scared. A little . . . I thought I could be blown into the lake or drowned. I'm not ashamed . . ."

"When the storms come rolling through the Whitefish, the Hook's the first place to be hit," said Patrick O'Brien, coming up from behind. "We've been there before. Remember when Michael and us skipped the first day of school our sophomore year and drove up to fish the Chain? We'd discovered the secret of the Hook earlier that summer and headed straight for it."

"Hey, Patrick!" Gyges stopped and gave him a big hug. Patrick shook hands with the rest of the guys.

"Damn, now that you mention it, that was even worse!" Gyges said. "Shit, that storm came on us so fast, it capsized that beat-to-shit fourteen-footer the three of us had jammed into."

Patrick picked up the story from there: "We clung to that upside-down boat for our lives. Of course, we were too young and stupid to be wearing life jackets. But somehow we managed to hold on. And after the storm passed, we got the boat righted again."

"Scariest day of my life," said Gyges, grateful that Patrick had been kind enough not to mention that he had lost his grip. Patrick had needed to swim after him and pull him back to the safety of the boat.

"Yeah, it was scary, but not as scary as when we got back and my old man and Tommy found out what we'd done," Patrick said with a mixture of amusement and anger. "Our old men blew up a helluva storm of their own."

The rest of the guys laughed along with him. They had a pretty good idea what it would have meant to have Danny and Tommy as dads.

Unnoticed by Patrick or Gyges, Tracy rolled his eyes. More Gyges and O'Brien family-lore bullshit—their adventures together growing up, the family outings, the birthday parties, their tedious school antics. It nauseated him. He'd never heard this story before, but the theme was familiar—Gyges as surrogate son to Danny and brother of Patrick.

"Hey, Gyges, where's Angela?" asked Patrick. "I haven't

seen her for a while. She and I need to catch up."

"Let's go find her," said Gyges. "She loves to see you, 'cause next to me, you're the coolest guy she knows."

Patrick laughed and put his arm over his boyhood friend's shoulder and the two went off in search of Gyges's wife.

"If we're lucky, they'll disappear together for the rest of the night," said Tracy. "Can you believe we had to endure yet another Life-with-the-O'Briens bullshit story with Gyges as the co-star? I can't stand it."

"You need to lighten up, Tracy," said Paul. "Cut him some slack." He had tired of Tracy's rants on Gyges.

Tracy paid no attention. "He's absolutely worthless. He's incompetent, and he's constantly screwing up. I just make up projects for him to work on; I can't trust him with the real stuff. That way he stays busy and outta my hair and isn't fucking up anything that matters. You'd think he'd get the hint and quit, but he's too dense. He's a loser, I'm telling you."

"So then fire him, already," said Dave, who'd been quiet for some time.

"I can't. Tommy O hired him. He's tight with his kid, Michael. You heard that fishing story. He practically grew up with the O'Briens. Apparently he was at their house all the time. They went everywhere together, and blah, blah, blah. I'm so tired of hearing about how close he is with them. He acts like he's one of the family."

"And why does that matter?" asked Dave.

"Be—cause I'm not sure Tommy would stand for it. If I made a move on Gyges, no doubt Tommy'd be on the phone with Danny and I'd be out in no time. Those mick brothers are too tight, for my way of thinking. They can be great guys to work for if you are doing what they want. But you don't want to be on the other end. They're merciless if they think the situation calls for it. And it doesn't take much to make them think it does. I'm planning on firing him . . . but I can't risk it right now."

"Yeah, but if he's as bad as you say, wouldn't you have grounds?" Paul interjected.

"Jesus Christ, Paulie, are you serious? Don't ever mess with your boss's buddies. What planet you from? You do what your boss wants. Period. Your sole purpose in life is to him get what he wants."

"Cut the condescending crap, Tracy. Save that shit for someone who doesn't know you like I do. You're over-simplifying this."

"But Tommy will be retiring soon," Tracy kept on, "and you can expect Tommy to recommend me to take his spot. After that, it's my turn to get what I want. I hire my replacement. After a little time has passed, I give my replacement my Gyges fuck-up file. Tell him to add a couple of incidents of his own. Then whack him. My hands will be clean. I can make the case to Danny that I am just backing my own management team's reasonable decisions. Plausible deniability. Without Tommy to protect him, Gyges will have no cover. Even crawling under a canoe won't save him."

Tracy was the only one to laugh. He lifted his glass and toasted in a bad Irish accent, "To the end o' me troubles with Gyges. Drink up, laddies! His end is near at hand, me boys, his end is near at hand."

"I don't know why you can't just talk to Gyges," Paul objected. "Give him a chance. Plotting his downfall in such detail? That's just ruthless."

"You say it's ruthless. I say it's smart."

"Just admit it's ruthless," said Dave. "At least then you'd be honest."

"Have it your way . . . It's ruthless. Call it whatever you want. It's the way of the world—those in power get what they want. The rest do their bidding."

Tracy and the group had been so intent on the conversation that they hadn't noticed Gyges slipping up behind them with a six-pack of Guinness. He'd been close enough to hear most of the conversation, and was stunned. He knew Tracy didn't like him, but he'd never realized the animosity ran so deep. A fire swelled up within him. How could I not have seen this? he thought. Jesus, he's right . . . I am a loser. No, fuck that. Fuck

Tracy. Tommy's not gone yet, and either am I. The flame burned bright, and he gnashed his teeth. He stepped forward next to Dave.

Dave jumped, startled by Gyges's sudden appearance. "Where the hell did you come from?" he gasped. "You scared the crap outta me. . . . Wow, you brought beer!"

"You guys were so busy talking, I thought you might need some hydration," said Gyges.

"Here's to our good fortune," toasted Paul.

Gyges, Dave, and Paul raised their bottles to toast and drank. Tracy stared out into darkness.

* * *

Gyges headed back toward the house in search of Angela and Patrick, navigating his way through islands of boisterous guests. Along the way, he bumped into Danny and Elizabeth talking to a small group of partiers. He didn't recognize them as employees.

"Peter!" said Danny. "Great to see you having a good time!"

"You'd have to be dead not to have a good time tonight," Gyges said. "But you know I am not even sure about that. I saw the ghost of your dad down by the docks."

Danny exploded in laughter and bear-hugged Gyges. "Shit, I thought I saw him, too, but then I figured it was the Turf Mor!"

"Well, if we both saw him, he must be here," said Gyges.

"Elizabeth," said Danny, trying to get his wife's attention, "This is Peter Gyges. I'm sure you remember me talking about him. He practically lived with us when Patrick and Michael were in school. The three of them were inseparable."

Elizabeth acknowledged Danny's comments with a slight nod and a perfunctory smile. She didn't even make eye contact. She was too busy chatting up one of the Pillsbury heirs, who was schmoozing her up for a donation to the Guthrie Theatre.

Danny shrugged his left shoulder and took another drink.

"Girl talk, I guess."

"Speaking of the three of us growing up together," said Gyges, "Patrick and I were just talking about the time we skipped school and got capsized in that storm."

"Jesus Christ. What a dumb fuckin' stunt that was! I was so pissed off," Danny shouted. "And no life jackets! Goddamn, that was fuckin' stupid!"

Elizabeth shot Danny a disapproving scowl, but he didn't see it. Even if he had, it wouldn't have made any difference. If the Pillsbury and Burkhardt clans didn't like his language, they could kiss his Irish immigrant ass.

"Well, I don't want to keep you from your guests," said Gyges. "I'm trying to find Patrick and Angela. They were up near the deck last time I saw them."

"If you see that son of mine, tell him it would be nice if he stopped down to say hello," Danny said, not hiding his irritation.

* * *

Patrick got the message from Gyges and wandered down to put in a guest appearance with his old man. It was purely out of duty, to keep the uneasy peace. Danny's affair and divorce had created a permanent rift between them. Not so big as to drive them out of each other's lives, but wide enough that they could never be close. They were both deeply pained by the lost connection, but words had been said that couldn't be taken back.

Danny wasn't hard to find. Even with the loud music and laughter, Patrick could practically hear his booming profanities from across the lake.

"Havin' a good time, I see," said Patrick, patting Danny on the back.

"Goddammit. Where have you been? Too busy to see the old man, huh?"

"Not too busy," said Patrick. He noticed that Danny was right on the edge of sloppy drunk. And that was saying something. His father could drink anyone under the table—even Tommy.

Elizabeth saw Patrick but ignored him.

Patrick returned the favor. "Hey, listen Dad," he said, "Let's go get some food together. Plus, there're a couple of old buyers near there. I think we might get them drunk and interested in Swenson Lathing."

"Damn right. Nothing like a little lubrication to get a deal going."

3

On the way home from the party, Angela noticed that her husband was unusually quiet. He loved the O'Briens and reveled in being so close to them. Coming back from an OH party, he was typically effusive—Patrick was doing this and Danny said that and Tommy told me . . . But not tonight. She tried to find out what was wrong. "You feeling okay?" she asked.

"Yeah . . . why?"
"You seem kinda quiet."
"Just tired, I guess. A bit past my usual bedtime."

As Angela studied him more closely for signs of distress, she noticed something unusual. He was wearing a ring on his right hand. She was surprised she hadn't noticed it before and even more surprised he was wearing it. He was not given to ornamentation. A wedding band—that was it.

"Gosh, Peter. Where did you get that ring? How long have you been wearing it? I just now noticed it."

For the first time since they'd left the party, Gyges became animated.

"Oh, yeah. I just put it on tonight coming back from the party. I dunno—just felt like wearing it."

"Where did you get it?"

"Off the Hook when I was fishing last week. Been keepin' it in my pocket."

"You found that out there?"

"Remember I told you about the storm? Right on the

island where I hid from the storm."

"Can I see it?"

"Sure."

He took off the ring and handed it to her. "I think those are diamonds on the signet," he said.

"Look like diamonds to me," said Angela, "but then it is hard to tell. What's this emblem they surround?"

"Dunno . . . never noticed it. Maybe a veil or some kind of cloth." He squinted to get a closer look.

"Wow, you just found this out there on the island?"

"It was lying there among the rocks right at the edge of the shore. I couldn't believe my good luck. Here I was trying to escape this storm and I stumbled upon this."

He took it back and put it on.

"I wonder how it got there," she said.

"I guess it just washed up. Who knows how old it is. Maybe it's from a ship or somethin'. You know, from the days when the French explored this place. Who knows how it got there."

* * *

Gyges was up early from a fitful sleep. Tracy's plan to get him fired had triggered a round of worst-case scenarios inside his head, including all manner of personal grief and disruption. He couldn't stop thinking about it, so he headed to the garage.

He worked on cleaning his rods and disassembling and oiling his reels. After about thirty minutes, he went over to the work sink to wash his hands. Despite the distraction of prepping his fishing gear, the Tracy problem came back to pain him like a bad tooth. He doused his face with cold water and sighed. While drying his hands, he accidently turned the ring's signet around to face his palm.

Gyges shook with a surge of . . . something. It was a strange rush.

He returned the signet back to its original position. The powerful billow within disappeared. He shuddered again. What the hell?

Slowly, deliberately now, he turned the signet toward his palm again. The sensation returned. Gyges wasn't well practiced at distinguishing the nuances of his feelings. Nor did he have much to compare it to. The exhilaration was overpowering, for sure, but there was also some deeper release. Something lifted within him to reveal a fire inside, burning with intensity from having been concealed for so long. He stood there for a moment and allowed its heat to flow through his body.

He felt like he could do anything he wanted and nothing could touch him.

When he looked up into the mirror above the sink, panic jolted through his already-charged nerves. He struggled to breathe and broke out in a sweat. Gyges couldn't see himself in the mirror. He waved his arms, hopped up and down. It was as if he weren't there. The mirror reflected only the garage contents behind him.

He turned the ring back. He appeared solid again. The feelings of power and invincibility disappeared. His mind went light and dizzy. Fearful thoughts overtook him, and he couldn't concentrate. He fell against the trash bin, nearly passed out from hyperventilating.

Gyges worked to slow his breathing and regain a measure of calm. Then he looked at the ring for a moment and repeated the experiment. When he turned the ring, the confidence returned and his hand disappeared. He looked again into the mirror, but it was just the garage. His mind locked up, and he barely managed to turn signet. Then he reappeared, sweating and shaking in the mirror.

Gyges sat on a stool next to the mirror for several minutes turning the ring back and forth and feeling the emotional tide and considered what to do.

* * *

Gyges proceeded down the aisle past the herbicides, pesticides, and mole repellents. It was a little after nine a.m. He paced the store aimlessly for twenty minutes and finally summoned the courage to try it. Midway through the aisle, he stopped to double-check that he was alone, closed his eyes, and turned the ring's signet. He squinted and raised his hand. It was transparent again. Then came the rush.

At the end of the aisle, he turned right and struggled to remain standing. He grew frustrated and quickly decided that he had to overcome this initial obstruction if he were to harness the ring's potential. He practiced walking until he could do it with confidence. He changed pace, pivoted, hopped, sat, stood, stooped, and stretched. It wasn't long before he had mastered moving for long periods under the ring's cover. He even skipped. As he practiced, the dizziness subsided and then disappeared altogether.

Now instead of avoiding people, Gyges sought them out. Weaving his way amongst the crowded aisles, he moved undetected through Minnesota shoppers. No one noticed him at all.

He looked to the shelf next to him. A package of d-CON rodent-control tablets disappeared as soon as he picked it up. He put it in his pocket. In the next aisle, a few customers browsed the selection of soaps and detergents. He maneuvered between them and lifted a small bottle of Joy from the shelf. A pudgy blonde looked right through him. He stuffed the dish soap into his jacket. She wrestled with an extra-large box of Mr. Clean.

Gyges wandered up to the checkout counters. He hesitated. He'd never done anything like this in his entire life. He'd never broken the law—not even a speeding ticket. Buckled up before starting the engine. Even kept his hands at ten and two. He'd waited until he was twenty-one to buy liquor. Always drank responsibly. Often volunteered to be designated driver. Never experiment with drugs. He'd been completely faithful to his wife. Took sick days only when actually sick. One ticket, one movie—no sneaking around for a second show. Recycled newspapers and bottles. Never littered. Gave back change when the clerk miscounted. Gyges had always done exactly what was expected of him—as a child, student, husband, employee, and citizen . . . except for skipping school to go fishing. And in his whole existence on this planet, he had never taken something that did not belong to him.

Until now.

He looked up. Twenty yards ahead was the front door—just twenty yards to cross the line he'd been toeing all those years. His unblemished record of obedience to the rules was about to be smudged. His heart pounded, and part of him wanted to take everything back. He glanced at his hand one last time to make sure.

Then he stepped forward. He forged ahead past the checkout lanes and the greeters and out the doors.

The morning sun hung over the parking lot. Gyges burst into uninhibited laughter. He ran to his car, jumping and skipping with wild-child exuberance. He'd done it! He had beaten Wal-Mart. Corporate megalith. Retail Leviathan. Mighty Wal-Mart brought to its knees by Gyges and his ring. He'd actually pulled it off—transgressed the laws of God and man. Undiscovered, unpunished, unrepentant. He had passed through the automatic doors transformed. Liberated. Born again. Superior and unashamed.

A thought seized him then and held him in abject fear: What if the ring was lost? He struggled to breathe. He vowed never to allow that to happen. It must never leave his finger. He repeated this to himself over and over.

Without knowing how he'd gotten there, Gyges found himself back at his car. He turned the signet outward before he opened the door and sat behind the wheel. He took the d-CON and Joy out of his pocket and laid them on the passenger's seat. Looking at them produced an odd mix of sensations. Amidst his glee and exhilaration, he detected an element of disappointment. He stared at his illicit treasure—mouse poison and dishwashing liquid. Not much of a cache, but inconsequential when compared with the potential offered by the ring.

As he exited the Wal-Mart lot, he realized that in all the excitement of the last couple of hours, he had forgotten. He was forty-two.

Happy Birthday, Peter Gyges.

4

Gyges turned on the light over his workbench and unloaded items from his latest trip to Wal-Mart. This time he'd been more discriminating—a new drill, a spinning reel, an iPod, and a camping axe. And an expensive watch. He'd never owned one, and he was especially pleased with himself. Gyges was not given to luxury items, nor were they given to him. Before, such things had seemed frivolous. Looking at the watch now, however, he began to appreciate its value.

He replaced his old drill with the new one. He slid the watch onto his wrist. Even without diamonds, it matched the ring well.

* * *

Angela sat in her usual kitchen chair across from her husband. She served up lamb and rice. He was in an ebullient mood.

"This is really excellent," he said. "Better than mother's."

"I don't know about that. Besides, she taught me."

"Well, you learned your lessons well."

"Glad you like it. . . ." She paused when she noticed his new watch. "Is that new?"

"It is. I bought it from some guy standing outside Wal-Mart this morning."

"It looks expensive, too," she said.

"It does? I dunno. This guy looked like he'd seen better days. He gave me this hard-luck story. You know, the usual stuff—lost his job, house, wife, blah, blah, blah. Who knows if it's bullshit or not, but, anyway, he asked if I wanted to buy it. At first I said no, but he insisted, so I finally offered him twenty bucks. He, of course, assured me it was worth well over that. So we went back and forth until we settled on thirty-five."

He shoved a forkful of food into his mouth. "God, this is so great. I hope there's more."

"Plenty," said Angela. She wondered what to believe. A lifetime fisherman, Peter was prone to exaggeration. But he was not a man given to outright lies. Still, these stories pushed the limits of credulity. Not only that; there was something different about him. She wasn't sure what it was, but she did not like it. It made her nervous. She preferred things steady and predictable. And lately, Peter had been neither. She decided to keep it to herself for now. But she would be more vigilant for any further signs or disturbances.

She wouldn't have to wait long.

5

Gyges showed up to work at O'Brien Holdings as usual.

He sat at his desk and sighed as he rifled listlessly through his current projects. It was clear—slowly but surely, Tracy had definitely maneuvered him into the periphery of the company. And that was putting it kindly. If he disappeared tomorrow, no one would miss him. Tracy could easily push him out when he saw fit.

Gyges felt foolish and angry that he hadn't picked up on it sooner. He didn't have a future at O'Brien unless he protected himself. Maybe he could sit down with Tracy, talk to him, try to straighten things out. But he'd always been the guy who did what he was told, and the prospect of meeting with Tracy was onerous. What would he even say?

"Whatcha thinkin' about, Pete?"

The question startled Gyges from his thoughts. He hadn't noticed Patrick O'Brien approach his desk.

"Hey, Patrick. How you doing?"

"Great. How have the fish been?"

"Haven't been out since just before Labor Day," Gyges said.

"Be careful or you'll miss the fall northerns," said Patrick. "They'll be starting to feed for winter pretty soon."

Gyges liked Patrick. A lot. He never acted like the owner's son. He worked hard and earned his way just as Danny O had with Patrick's grandfather. He was expected to perform, just like every other employee. Loyalty was huge, but no matter what, kith and kin were expected to perform. Or else.

Danny wasn't opposed to putting a shoe up your ass. And that was no metaphor. In the old days, before modern management practices frowned on it, rumor was that Danny had solved his employee problems behind the old building. Some of those guys were still with the company, and Gyges heard their stories. Danny was like that. Settle it man to man and then get back to work. Even though he was in his late sixties, no one doubted that the Old Man could still dish it out. Not that he needed to. Everyone knew you just didn't fuck with him. Even Patrick. But to Patrick that was just Danny's way. You never heard Patrick whine about how tough his father was on him. He did what needed to be done. Period. He was a son who would take over the business and grow it—not run it into the ground.

"Patrick, I need your advice," Gyges blurted, not yet weighing the implications. "I don't mean to impose, but I really need help."

"You know me, Pete. My advice is worth the price you pay for it. But if you're foolish enough to seek it, I'm foolish enough to deliver."

"Not here, if that's okay," said Gyges. He shot a quick look in the direction of Tracy's office.

"Kieran's at one? We'll let the lunch crowd filter out."

"How about I meet you there," said Gyges. He didn't want to be seen leaving the building with Patrick. Tracy might become suspicious.

"Fine. See you then." Patrick was already headed for the door.

"I'll call for reservations. Can I use your name? It's like magic there."

"Oh, yeah—pure magic. The fact that we drop 30k a year there has nothing to do with it. It's my stunning personality." He smiled and then was gone.

As soon as Patrick left, Gyges worried if asking him

for help had been a mistake. He didn't want Patrick to think he was seeking special favors. Gyges realized how far out of the loop he'd been at OH. Tracy did a good job for the company. He researched all negotiating acquisitions and disposals of business units. Gyges wasn't confident he could win a showdown with him. Not only that, he was completely expendable.

He couldn't say what he wanted out of his meeting with Patrick. He just knew he didn't want to lose his job.

Why the hell not? he thought. What's so great about this fucking job? You're nothing more than a useless appendage within this company. Why do you even want to keep this job?

This startled him. The question was absurd. He needed this job. He had debts to pay, a wife to support.

You need money. But you don't need this job. In fact, you need to get out. It's a loser's position. You've been willing to settle for this because you're a fucking loser.

Could this be right? He'd settled for this diminished role because he was afraid to confront Tracy. He hated conflict. Confronting Tracy was bound to be ugly. Maybe there was a way around trying to back Tracy down.

A loser's wish. You want Patrick and the family to bail you out? Be honest, for God's sake. You just want a way to make this disappear, but it isn't going to. Tracy is preparing to make you vanish. You're the only one who's gonna disappear. You'll be a distant memory. You're just gonna take it, though, huh? You're just gonna let that arrogant sonofabitch do this to you. You're too afraid to stand up for yourself. Your only plan is to ask the O'Brien's to save you? Save you from whom?

Tracy, of course.

Bullshit.

It's not bullshit. Tracy wants to fire me. He'll do it as soon as Tommy retires.

Bullshit. Complete bullshit. Tracy wants to fuck Danny's hot young wife, but he can't. Why's that?

He's afraid of Danny.

No, that'd be your chicken-shit reason.

She won't let him.

Bingo, Ringo. What does that tell you about your bullshit reasoning?

I dunno.

That's for sure. Tracy wants a lot of things in life. So what? He ain't gonna get most of 'em. Who cares if he wants to fire you? What are you gonna do to stop him? You're the only thing standing between you and what you want. Tracy ain't the problem; you are. You're letting him push you around. You're letting him make your life miserable. You're letting him decide your future.

The thoughts agitated Gyges. He tried to work but couldn't bring himself to go through the useless gestures. None of it had any value to anyone at all. He hurled his coffee cup against the wall, and it shattered in a shower of blue shards. He looked around to see if anyone was watching. Those at their cubicles seemed oblivious to his fit. They were absorbed in their work. He looked at the pieces for a long time. A sense of emptiness and waves of defeat washed over him.

Then he remembered.

He stood up, walked to his office door, and looked out—no one in sight. He turned the ring. The negative thoughts and feelings left him instantly. He smiled and savored the relief. He breathed slowly, and the tension in his back released. He was invincible now—powerful and unseen. He walked out of his office and left the building. He was done for the day.

Peter Gyges had better things to do with his time.

* * *

Patrick watched Gyges place the order. Gyges was agitated by something—could be work, could be home. More likely work. He couldn't be having problems with Angela, unless he was the cause. That seemed unlikely.

Gyges returned and sat back down.

"So, why the secret confab?" asked Patrick.

"I need advice."

"So you said. You didn't say about what."

"It's work."

"Okay. Shoot."

"I need to know what you think. But before I say anything, I'm just asking for advice. I'm not asking you to do anything."

"I don't have to do anything? Great, you're making this easy. Not doing anything is one thing I have mastered. Go ahead; the doctor is in."

"I'm working on bullshit stuff that doesn't matter to anyone. It's just busy work. I'm wasting my time and your family's money. I dunno what to do. I need help figuring it all out."

"You talk to Tracy about it?"

"Oh, God, no! And don't say anything!"

"Easy there, pard. You said I didn't have to do anything. Talking to Tracy would be doing something. I'm deeply committed to inaction, remember?"

"Sorry. I didn't mean to jump on you. It's just that things at work have me on edge."

"It's fine. Work can be intense at times."

"That's the problem. It's not for me. Tracy's got me off planning recognition supper celebrations and running down meeting minutiae. Obviously I didn't graduate from a big-name school like he did, but I'm capable of contributing a lot more to O'Brien Holdings. And I want to. I don't want to be expendable. I want to be vital."

"Well, you're carrying quite a load," said Patrick.

"I didn't know who else to talk to. I can't talk to Tracy. He really intimidates me. I can't tell Tommy, because then it looks like I'm going around Tracy. I thought you might have ideas."

"On how you can be more important at work?"

"Yeah, I mean . . . how do I work on more important

things?"

"Hmm . . ." Patrick looked at Gyges and paused. He didn't want to upset his friend any further.

" 'Hmm,' what?"

"To be honest, you have a reputation for being a nice guy but . . . well . . . a lightweight."

"Goddammit. I was afraid of that. Nobody takes me seriously. Goddammit!" He pounded the table, stood up and paced a few steps, then sat back down. "What can I do?"

"Get closer to the action."

"Closer to the action?"

"Yeah, closer to what we're doing that's important."

"Like what? Give me an example."

"Right away that should tell you there's a problem," said Patrick. "You aren't sure what's important to us. That's not a good sign."

"Yeah, I know. I guess I thought if I did a good job at what I was given, that would be enough."

"Enough for what?"

"To be a desirable employee. I never thought of myself as a star, just a solid work-a-day guy."

"You probably are. Why does this suddenly matter?"

"I'm afraid that if things get tight, the company won't see any need to keep me on."

"There's little danger of that. We're ahead of projections for growth. But I still think it would be good if you were a little more visible."

"Yes, yes. You've said it exactly right. Better than me. That's my point—visibility. I want higher visibility. For people to see me as important."

"Then you'll have to hook up with hot shots. You know, the projects everyone is talking about, working on. The stuff that's troubling and no one can figure out how to handle. You have to find a niche where you can do something no one else can do as well as you. Then do it so well that everyone can see it."

"Something no one else can do . . . yeah . . . okay . . . I

see what you're saying. I wish I would have thought of that myself."

"And I wish I could find smallies the way you do." Patrick smiled.

Gyges and Patrick spent the rest of their meal talking about fishing. As they got ready to leave, Gyges remembered something else. "Patrick," he said, "I heard a rumor. I wonder if you can confirm it."

"Maybe . . ."

"I heard Tommy's retiring soon. That true?"

Patrick paused to reflect. "Well, I'm not free to talk about it. Let's just say, some conversations have transpired."

"When? I heard it was soon."

"That's a relative term. I don't know what 'soon' means, but he is sixty-five and wants to spend more time back in Ireland. He loves the west coast, and I think he's buying some land in Connemara Peninsula, near Clifden, I think. I suspect once he gets all of that finalized, he'll move quickly. But then, this is just speculation on my part. You didn't hear this from me, okay?"

"I'm the soul of discretion."

6

Several weeks followed Patrick and Gyges's meeting at Kieran's. During that time, Gyges often thought about Patrick's advice, but he did little about it. His old habits were harder to break than he'd thought. But he was more attentive to what people talked about and what they worked on and fretted over.

He used the ring to build up a cache of desirable gadgets. He re-equipped his work area with the best brands and models: new drills, handsaws, sanders, planers. He even got stuff he'd never known existed or could see no practical application for. Why not? He'd indulge his fancy. He also ripped off new fishing gear—rods, reels, lures, outdoor clothing, and some electronics he'd never desired before.

For inside, he replaced any small appliance he could lug off a store shelf. He had to make up some stories to calm Angela's concerns about all the new stuff that was suddenly appearing in the house. He told her he'd gotten a raise. Then it was the stock market. Whenever they watched TV and the host reported a dramatic rise in a stock's value, Gyges would tell her it was one of his hot picks. Then within a few days, a new watch or necklace would appear. Eventually she asked him to stop. She had no place to wear these things.

Soon the rush abated. Shoplifting became too easy. But Gyges missed the sensation the ring imparted, so he looked for new ways to use it. To his surprise, the office provided a new place to explore. For a while he crashed meetings. They were dull, lifeless affairs, though, and he usually didn't stay long. He learned to avoid meetings in the accounting and IT departments. But the ones in marketing were informative. Occasionally he'd find something fascinating. He learned that the company was researching a major corporation, a big name, for possible acquisition. He was surprised that O'Brien Holdings was big enough to pull it off. He'd never thought about the company in those terms.

He also avoided meetings involving Tracy. Even though he couldn't be seen, Gyges was uncomfortable knowing that the man was planning to do him in. He detested Tracy's duplicity.

Gyges frequented what OH called "performance adjustment meetings," PAMS, between employees and their supervisor. Everyone hated to be PAMMED. Theoretically, the meetings were designed to help employees improve performance by identifying weak areas. In practice, they were the corporate equivalent of an old-fashioned trip to the woodshed. PAMS were actually the first step in a progressive disciplinary process that could end in a pink slip. In PAMS, there were chances to see real fireworks—people yelling, getting reprimanded, crying (lots of crying and yelling), and plenty of gut-wrenching emotions on full display. Initially Gyges was ill at ease with these raw exhibitions, but he quickly warmed to them and sought out PAMS at every opportunity. One day after leaving an especially volatile one, he absentmindedly followed Andie Dorken into the woman's bathroom. He panicked when he realized his mistake, and u-turned toward the door. Then remembered he was invisible. So he stayed.

The allure of the taboo behavior drew Gyges back to the women's bathroom, but he never saw much. And he never actually went into the stalls—they were too small. But just entering the bathroom was as irresistibly thrilling as when he had begun shoplifting, and he explored new territories. He tried department store changing rooms, but they had the same space restrictions. Showers at health clubs proved the best places to entertain his new desire. He'd venture to a club not far from work and spend his lunch hour in the women's shower room. He was intoxicated by the sexual stimulation he got from his deviant behavior. Some days he was so overwhelmed he barely made it back to work. Other days he didn't make it back on time or return at all.

Gyges's trips to the health club were also useful in other ways. The clientele associated crime with the underclass, none of whom were members, so they often left their lockers unlocked. Stealing money was even better than shoplifting. He took only what he thought wouldn't be missed. These people didn't know how much cash they carried, and he never took all of it—just a hundred here or there, sometimes two if the wallet was especially fat. And he never took jewelry or credit cards—only cash. The way he saw it, people who ran through money quickly and without special effort could seldom account for where it had gone; missing credit cards, jewelry, and large amounts of cash could trigger that special effort.

The excursions to the club grew longer with every visit—from an hour to an hour and a half to two hours some days, increasing his absenteeism at work. And the longer lunches and absences did not escape Tracy's notice.

7

One Friday when Gyges arrived at the club (he'd been delayed by a PAM with Smitty from shipping that ran long after security was called), he was disappointed to find that the women's locker room was closed for plumbing repairs. He decided to stay and get a steam and relax from a long, boring morning at work. He undressed and locked away his valuables. Mist drifted into the hallway as he opened the steam room door. Another man was already inside. Gyges sat down opposite him on the smooth wooden bench. He leaned back and pulled his towel over his lap while his eyes adjusted to the heat and vapors. The man was middle aged, with a dark complexion and a thick black mustache. He'd wrapped a towel around his head. He must have weighed three hundred pounds. Some of it was fat, but Gyges could tell that a lot of muscle remained under the soft exterior. He guessed that the man had once been a wrestler or football player.

"Feels great," the man said. "Only reason I come here."

"Kinda expensive just for that," remarked Gyges.

The man laughed. "Yeah, it is, but it's the best steam room in the Twin Cities. Trust me, I've tried them all. The best."

"It is nice. I don't often get a chance."

"Every day."

"What?"

"You should get one every day. Gets rid of the

poisons. Cleans out your pores. Wait, I get you something."

The man jumped up and pushed out the door. Gyges didn't recognize the accent, but it seemed familiar and he liked it. The man returned with a bottle, handed it to Gyges.

"Drink, drink. It won't hurt you. Special tea my father taught me how to make." Gyges looked at the man. He looked down and smiled back.

Gyges sniffed the bottle—pungent. He paused.

"Go ahead, it won't hurt. Do you good—more sweating."

He took a small sip. Not too bad. There was a strong mint flavor and some other peculiarities he couldn't identify.

"Oh, more than that. Big drink, take big drink."

So Gyges took a longer drink. He liked it. It was strangely refreshing. "Not bad," he said as he handed back the bottle.

The man still stood over him. "Not bad? Good, very good," he said and wiped the bottle mouth with his large brown hand. Then he drained it in one long drink.

"Bhuto," he said, extending his hand.

"Buddha?" Gyges shook it.

"No, Bhuto," the man corrected.

"Nice to meet you, Mr. Bhuto."

"No, no, no. Not Mr. Bhuto—just Bhuto. Everyone calls me Bhuto."

"Guy Petros," Gyges replied.

"Petros? Is Greek, yes?"

"My father came from Greece."

"Where in Greece?"

"I'm not sure, actually."

"Petros . . . you should find out. How can you know who you are unless you know where you come from?" He sat down next to Gyges.

"What's the difference? They left. If things had been better, they would have stayed. To hell with the bad old days."

"You miss something. Turkey—my family's from Turkey. You know, back home we'd try to kill each other. Here we steam together. I love America!" Bhuto laughed deep, shaking all of his three hundred pounds.

"So, what do you do for a living?"

"I'm self-employed. I am an independent freelance contractor. I tried to work for others, but it never worked out. Now I work for myself. I'm happier this way."

"Contractor?"

"People contract me to resolve difficult problems."

"You mean, like . . . business problems?" Gyges wiped his face with the towel. The tea was starting to kick in. It really worked.

"Sure, like business problems. All kinds of business problems," Bhuto said. "You play chess?"

Gyges thought it was an odd question. "Chess? When I was a kid—not for years."

"I play every day. It helps me resolve business problems for my clients. I teach you to play better. It will help you, too."

"Thanks, but I don't have a lot of free time, and when I do I go fishing."

"You go fishing? Meh. . . . Everyone in Minnesota go crazy for fishing. I don't get fishing. Chess—you should know chess more and fishing less."

"Why? It's just another game."

"I like you, my friend, but—excuse me for being so rude—you say the stupidest thing. If you say chess is a game like any other, you know nothing about it. Play me one time and I will tell you all about yourself. In one game, I can do this. I will know you after one game." The Turk eyed him without a hint of his previous smile.

Gyges remained silent. What could one game hurt? he thought. And this Bhuto character was interesting. It might be fun to get to know him better.

"Okay. One game."

"Yes, after this one game, I will tell and you will be amazed."

Gyges laughed and wiped his face again. "I already am.

You'll have to give me the recipe for that tea."

"Petros, I'm sorry but I could not do this. It is a family secret. But I will bring you a bottle for the next time we sweat together."

* * *

Gyges never would have found Café Morocco without Bhuto's directions. He drove around the block twice before finding a parking spot. Not a single streetlight cast its light on the dark neighborhood. He locked the car, as Bhuto had advised. He just about pushed the cafe door open when he remembered the card. He dug it out of his wallet, went back to his car, and placed it under the driver's wiper, just as the Turk had instructed. It was then that he noticed two men leaning against a car twenty-five yards down the block. He looked down at the card on his windshield. It was red with a yellow scimitar. Bhuto had called it a talisman. It didn't look like it would ward off evil. He laughed.

Strolling back to the cafe, Gyges missed the two men walking toward his Explorer. Nor did he see them examine the card and then return to their watch down the street.

* * *

He seriously thought about turning around to leave.

The room was poorly lit and badly ventilated. He took two tentative steps inside and stopped to survey the place. To his left, a dwarfish man wearing an apron stood behind a short dark bar. Over his face he had a spider tattoo.

Gyges held his ground and looked around for Bhuto. There were chairs around two tables in front of the bar, where seven men drank from very small cups. Backgammon boards were set up on both tables. As he entered, the men's spirited exchanges came to an immediate halt. Everyone turned to look his way. Theirs were not friendly, welcoming looks. The intensity of the faces almost forced him to turn around again.

Then, from the back of the cafe, he heard the unmistakable voice of his new friend.

"Petros—where are you going, my friend?" Through the smoke, Gyges could see Bhuto standing in a doorway, motioning for Gyges to join him. The players' conversations picked up again, and he maneuvered back through the backgammon tables.

"My friend," Bhuto said, giving him a hearty slap on the back. "Welcome to the Café Morocco. Did you have any trouble finding it? Great spot, yes?"

"Your directions were quite good. Drove right to it," said Gyges. He left the second question to answer itself.

"We'll play in here—less noisy. I have coffee ready, and the board is set up. See—I have thought of everything." Bhuto smiled.

Inside it was cleaner, less smoky, and, when Bhuto shut the door, much quieter. They were the only people in the room. There were three tables, each with a chess set and two dark wooden chairs. The only light fell from three lamps suspended above the tables. Bhuto directed Gyges to the farthest table and took the seat facing the door.

"You play white first. I give a bit of advantage in the first game," Bhuto said.

"Now, remember," said Gyges, pulling his chair closer to the table, "I haven't played in a long time and I was never very good. Don't expect much from me."

"Yes, yes, sure. I understand all of this," said Bhuto. "Have a bit of coffee. It helps alert the mind."

Bhuto sipped from his small cup. Gyges followed suit. The coffee was very strong and had a bitter aftertaste. He fought back a cough.

"Okay, we start. You move first."

Gyges looked at the board and tried to remember how to open the game. He slid the king's pawn out two spaces. Bhuto immediately moved his king's pawn out two spaces so their pawns faced each other out in the middle of the board.

Gyges moved his queen diagonally three squares in

front of the king's bishop. Bhuto answered with his king's bishop four squares in front of the queen's bishop.

Gyges noticed but paid the bishop little attention. He moved his queen one square to the left on the black square in front of the knight's pawn. Bhuto slid his queen's pawn in front of the queen's bishop.

Gyges was elated. The Turk had failed to protect his king's knight's pawn. Gyges could seize the pawn and trap the rook. He took the piece quickly, before Bhuto could change his mind. A big smile broke on his face as he set the black pawn on his side of the table. He looked at Bhuto.

With his stoic expression unchanged, Bhuto met Gyges's eyes, revealing nothing. He moved his queen all the way across the board to Gyges's king's rook on the fifth black square.

Gyges focused his attention on his queen, and he used her to capture Bhuto's rook. This also trapped the knight; to move it would put the Bhuto's king in check.

Gyges began to gain confidence. Maybe he was better than he had remembered. He planned several moves ahead. Take the knight, put the king in check. Then the rook's pawn. He'd take four pieces without losing one. All with the queen.

With his queen, Bhuto took Gyges's pawn.

"Check," Bhuto stated.

Gyges looked at the move. It was really stupid. It left the black queen open to Gyges's queen. He started to move but then saw that the black bishop protected the queen. He couldn't attack the queen. His only possibility was to move his king to the right one square. He did, but he could now see its futility.

Bhuto took his bishop.

"Checkmate."

Bhuto's expression did not change.

"Boy, I didn't see that coming," Gyges said.

"Play white again. I can see you're rusty."

"All right. You gotta admit, though, I was doing well. I'd taken a lot of pieces and was moving in on your knight and pawn. I was way ahead in pieces."

"Your move."

Again, Gyges brought out the queen early. Bhuto lured him into taking some pawns while he positioned his bishops and knights. Gyges was sailing along comfortably with three pawns and a knight when Bhuto closed on him and in three deft moves again declared, "Checkmate."

Gyges was even more surprised by the second loss.

"Let's see how you do with black," Bhuto said.

They reset the board. This time it took Bhuto six moves to checkmate Gyges. In a fourth game, he won in eight. They switched colors and Bhuto beat him in ten. Each time, Gyges believed he was doing well and winning pieces and then Bhuto would strike with a succession of moves too quickly and mercilessly end the game.

"I was ahead every game—just a move or two away from winning," Gyges said. He leaned back in his chair.

"You were finished by the fourth move in every game."

"How was that? I was ahead in every game until the very end."

"You were behind in every game, and the end confirmed it."

Gyges didn't know what to say. Bhuto was wrong. He'd been winning. He looked at the Turk in disbelief.

"You think I am mistaken?"

"Bhuto, I was clearly winning. Anyone could see that. It was so obvious."

"You only thought you were ahead, because of what you thought you saw. But you were beaten by what you didn't see. The unseen is often far more important than the seen. Great minds teach us this for thousands of years." Bhuto spoke calmly, without emotion.

"I don't get it."

"Let me start with something simple. Maybe you will see then. Let me ask you—why bring out your queen first time every time?"

"You lead with your most powerful force. Attack with strength, weaken the other side."

"Did it work?"

"Yeah, it worked."

"It did?"

"Sure, look at all the pieces I took."

"How did taking those pieces help you win games?"

"I didn't . . ." Gyges paused, "win any games."

"And is the object of the game to take as many pieces as possible?"

"No, the object is to checkmate your opponent."

"Save your queen until you can use her power and versatility to help checkmate. Don't use your most valuable resource to run fools' errands," Bhuto advised. "At best, you waste your time. At worst, you risk losing her."

"You said you could tell a lot by my game. What did you learn?" Gyges asked. He was curious what his new friend would tell him.

"I just told you," replied Bhuto.

"Not about the game. About me as a person."

"Yes, I understand. I just told you what I learned. Think about it—you'll see."

"That's all?"

"For tonight. Let us drink to your first lesson." Bhuto rose from the table. He opened the door, signaled to the dwarf with the spider tattoo.

"My first lesson? You mean, you want to play again after my pitiful performance?"

"I said I show you how chess will help you think. This will take more than one lesson. Chess more and fishing less."

The dwarf arrived with a tray. Amber liquid filled two shot glasses. He put it on the table.

"Your drinks, Ahmed." The dwarf's voice was deep and wheezy. It took Gyges off-guard, made him nervous.

"Oscar, this is Petros. He'll pay for the drinks tonight. Cheap tuition, no?" Bhuto laughed his deep laugh.

Gyges laughed too. Oscar only nodded and waited.

"He'll pay when he leaves," said Bhuto. Oscar recognized this signal to leave.

Bhuto took a glass from the tray. He gave Gyges the other and raised his in a toast.

"To our ancestors—may they rest in peace and leave us alone." He quickly downed the shot. Gyges was more cautious. He tasted first, then drank slowly.

"I've noticed your ring. Quite unusual. Where did you get it?"

"I found it."

"You found it! That's even more unusual. May I see?"

Gyges extended his hand to show Bhuto the ring. Bhuto looked at it, then at Gyges.

"Could you please take it off so I can get a better look?"

Gyges hesitated. He hadn't taken the ring off since he'd discovered its power in the garage. Bhuto noticed his hesitation and grinned.

"You think I might not give it back? Perhaps I run out the door, have Oscar stab you to keep you from chasing me?"

"No, it's not that. I've just never taken it off."

"You've had it how long now?"

"Several months."

"And you've never once taken it off?"

"No, never."

"Well, then it's not me you are afraid of. You are afraid of the world! You think it that valuable? Where did you find this?"

"On an island. North of here. During a storm while I was fishing. When I came ashore, I found it lying in the rocks."

"And you think these are diamonds on this?"

"Yes, I'm pretty sure they are."

"But this is not why you won't take it off, yes?"

"No, it's my talisman," said Gyges. "I considered it such good luck, I swore to never take it off."

"It has brought you good luck, protected you from evil?"

"Oh, yeah; this ring has helped me get all kinds of good things. I've gotten—" Gyges stopped. He didn't want to say too much. He thought his endorsement might already have revealed too much. "Well, you know, I suppose I'm just superstitious."

"What is this symbol?" Bhuto asked.

"I'm not sure. A piece of cloth." He stuck his hand back out for Bhuto to see.

Bhuto looked it over carefully. He took out his glasses from his shirt pocket, put them on, and studied the symbol even more closely.

"It's a shroud," the big man said after a minute.

"A shroud?"

"To drape over the dead."

Gyges held the ring up to his face for a better look. He caught a glimpse of his watch.

"Oh, shit, look at the time. I must go."

"Petros, we have a steam next week. Then we come here again. I give you another lesson. You buy me a drink."

Gyges agreed and the two men left the room. Bhuto stopped to talk with the men playing backgammon. Gyges settled the bill with Oscar. Oscar didn't say a word; Gyges was thankful.

Gyges stood by the door waiting for Bhuto to finish with the men. He thought it best to leave together. Bhuto looked up, saw him at the door.

"See you next week," Bhuto called out, and waved goodbye.

Gyges waved back, then took a deep breath and walked out onto the street alone.

8

Tracy slid a piece of paper across his large oak desk.

Gyges had enjoyed an especially fun weekend. Angela had gone out of town with her friends, so he'd been able to spend time at the health club. Weekends brought plenty of youthful traffic to the women's shower, and guests with extra cash. But then, first thing Monday morning, he'd gotten a call from Tracy. Even ruder and more abrasive than usual, Tracy had demanded that they meet before lunch. Gyges had tried to postpone the meeting, but Tracy wouldn't have it.

Gyges had spent the past hour and a half trying to figure out what his boss wanted. He had no clue. Then he eyed the paper.

"You know what this is?" Tracy asked before Gyges could even look it over.

Gyges read the top of the page aloud: "Performance Adjustment Meeting."

Shit, he thought. This is a fucking PAM. "Well, sort of . . ." he mumbled.

"This is an official performance adjustment meeting. I'm here to help you."

Gyges noticed the corners of Tracy's mouth betray a malicious little twist. He'd seen the smirk whenever Tracy felt he had someone by the balls. His stomach churned, and sweat broke from under his arms.

"Good, Tracy. . . . I'm always grateful for your help."

"I'm so pleased, Gyges. You're one of my favorite

people, and I really do want you to succeed. Sadly, however, your performance, which has always been remarkably ordinary, has been showing signs of deterioration." Tracy gave a concerned look.

"Not to contradict you, but I don't see it. I mean, I've hit every project deadline, haven't I?"

"I'm looking here at your attendance record. You've missed a lot of work in the last couple months." Tracy handed Gyges a calendar sheet with days marked in red and yellow. "As part of my effort to be helpful, I've marked the days you've missed in red."

"Are you certain these are right? I mean, I don't remember being gone all these days. I know I was here the fifth, eighth, and ninth. I'm pretty sure I was here on some of these other days too."

"If you'll take the time for a closer look, you'll see you were here in the mornings but gone in the afternoons."

"Oh."

"Oh?"

"Oh, yeah, I guess that could be right, then. I've had some trouble lately with migraines. Really tough, unrelenting migraines, you know."

"Gee, sorry to hear that. Have you consulted a doctor?"

"Well, no . . . not really."

"Too bad; that might have been helpful."

"I think they are stress-related. From work."

"Stress-related from work? You're joking, right?"

"No, I'm not joking. I'm under a lot of pressure here."

Tracy broke out laughing. "What pressure? You have the least pressure of anyone here. You've got no pressure at all. Now, these yellow marks are the times you've come back from lunch late."

"Well, again, the migraines . . ."

"Migraines? No, I don't think so, Gyges." Tracy leaned forward and eyed Gyges with mock sympathy. "As your friend and supervisor, can I express my concern? Perhaps the problem is . . . you've been drinking on your breaks. That's why you're late coming back and even failing to return from lunch, isn't it? Maybe you've been drinking on the job too. You disappear from your office and no one can find you."

"You must be the one who's joking. That's ridiculous. I don't eat or drink at lunch. I go to a health club to work out. You can check their records; they'll show I was there. I'm trying to relieve the stress from working for an asshole like you."

These last words exploded into the room. Gyges was as shocked as Tracy to hear them come out of his mouth.

"What did you just say to me?"

"I said I work out my stress at the health club."

"Not that part. Didn't you just call me an asshole?"

"No, I said, 'That's all.' I was working out to relieve stress, that's all. Meaning, that's all I was doing. I wasn't drinking."

"I distinctly heard you say 'asshole.' "

"Oh, no, I'd never call you an asshole. I mean, why would I do that? You're here to help me, right? That would make me pretty ungrateful, wouldn't it?"

"Don't fuck with me, Gyges."

Gyges paused for a few seconds and looked at Tracy as if he were seeing him for the first time. He saw Tracy setting him up for an easy fire after Tommy retired. This PAM was his opening move.

Gyges searched his mind for a defensive counter attack. "Tracy, I'm not fucking with you. I'm not drinking on the job or on my lunch. I'm sorry I didn't realize these headaches were causing such a problem. I'll see a doctor ASAP and have them send a note. Would that be helpful?"

"Yeah, but note or no note, you better clean up this attendance problem. I'm putting this on your permanent record. If I have to bring it to your attention again, it will mean disciplinary action."

"You can be sure I'll get it taken care of. But can I ask you something else? Am I behind on any of my work?"

"Behind? What do you mean?"

"You know, is there anything I was supposed to complete that I haven't?"

"Shit, I don't know. The stuff you're working on isn't exactly high enough priority to draw my attention."

"So, as far as you know, I've gotten all my work done and in on time?"

"Yeah, as far as I know. . . . But that isn't the point of this meeting."

"Oh, no, no, no . . . I wasn't trying to imply anything. I'm just making sure I understand the exact nature of our working relationship."

"The exact nature of our working relationship is that you need to stop missing work and get your ass back here from lunch on time. You'd better get this taken care of or you'll be gone."

"Thank you for being so helpful and considerate. This talk has really been enlightening. It's called my attention to a problem. I guess I let it get the better of me. I'll get right on it. I'll see my family doctor as soon as he can get me in. And you know . . ." Gyges leaned forward. "You're more than a supervisor, Tracy; you're a true friend."

"Yeah, right. Get back to work. But first sign this form, saying we discussed this."

Gyges glanced down at the form. He looked at Tracy and smiled. This was going to be fun.

"Can I write something? I think the company policy states that I can comment on our meeting."

"Yeah, that's the policy. There should be a space for your comments at the bottom. What are you writing?"

"Just that it's a medical problem. You know, stress-related, and that I'm seeing a doctor. Oh, and that you and I agree this is the only issue I'm having trouble with, you know, and that I'm getting my work done—things like that."

"I didn't say you were getting your work done. I said I didn't know if you were or not."

"You're right. So should I put that I'm getting my

work done or that you're not sure if I am or not?"

Gyges looked up from the paper. He let the last question sink in. Tracy started to answer and then stopped. He started again and stopped.

"Which should I put down, then?"

"Put down whatever you want; they're your comments."

"Great. I'll say we agreed these were the only problems I'm having."

Gyges bent over the desk and pushed Tracy's papers and supplies out of the way. In the process, he knocked over a coffee cup. It spilled onto Tracy's lap.

"Goddammit! Look what you did! All over my pants!" Tracy jumped up and stormed out of the room.

Gyges smiled and finished his comments.

Tracy left to go home and change, so Gyges left the paper with Tracy's secretary, Mary, then returned to his desk, no longer sweating, his stomach calm. He wasn't afraid of Tracy anymore. Tracy was a bully, but he was a predictable bully. Gyges had always been terrorized by the bully, but that predictability left Tracy vulnerable. He was clumsy and obvious. Gyges smiled; he'd never realized this before. Up until now, he'd been too dense to figure it out. Tracy was the sitting duck and he was the shotgun.

Patience was a virtue.

Gyges picked up the phone to schedule a doctor's appointment.

* * *

Gyges had no trouble convincing the doctor he was suffering stress at work. It was easy. He just told the truth about Tracy and how hard it was to work for the prick. He even told him about Tracy's plot to fire him. The doctor couldn't decide if Gyges's fear was valid or some kind of paranoid rambling brought on by the stress. But either way, it played into Gyges's claim. The doctor wrote a clinical diagnosis and sent it to the O'Brien Holdings' HR department.

Gyges made sure a copy fell on Tracy's desk. The doctor's report cited pressure and harassment as the major factors in Gyges's stress.

After that, Gyges saw the HR director, Sheila Gerba. He'd dropped in on a few HR meetings and knew she held little regard for Tracy. She'd complained in one meeting that Tracy was a hard guy to work for and that turnover in his department was high.

"Ms. Gerba," Gyges said, tapping lightly on her open door. "May I see you for a minute?"

"Yes, certainly, Mr. Gyges. All employees should feel free to stop by and share concerns with me. I suppose you want to know if I got the report from the doctor?"

"Yeah, I just want it on record that I wasn't messing around. I have real problems. I know Tracy thinks I'm gold bricking but . . . it's just so . . . well, it's just so hard working under . . . I'm sorry . . . I . . . I didn't mean to complain to you." Gyges put his head in his hands and drew a deep breath.

Ms. Gerba got up from her desk, put her arm around Gyges's shoulder, and patted him on the back.

"I just came to see if you got the report from my doctor. I guess you did," he said.

"I did. And let me assure you, I read it carefully. I think I understand what you're going through. We want to help you work out any problems between you and Tracy. I'm going to review the report with him. To make sure he understands."

"Oh, no, please don't bring him into it." Gyges feigned panic. "I mean, can't we just keep this between us? I don't want to get Tracy in trouble. I just want to do my job and not make waves. I don't need any more trouble with him."

She patted him on the back again. "Oh, now, Mr. Gyges, you don't need to be afraid. I'll make that clear when I talk with him."

"I would really prefer you didn't. At least not now. Maybe you could just send him the report with a note that you attached a copy to the PAM for my file? Please? Couldn't we leave it at that? I really want to keep this low key."

Ms. Gerba finally agreed.

Gyges thanked her and waited for the report to reach Tracy. In the meantime, he renewed his daily noon visits to the health-club shower rooms, though now he was more conscious of the time.

* * *

It took two days for the copy to land on Tracy's desk and another day and a half for him to read it. It took twenty seconds for him to locate himself as the source of Gyges's problems, then five more to get Ms. Gerba on the phone.

"Gerba, I just read this doctor's report for Peter Gyges. What a load of bullshit! Your note says you attached this to his PAM? I get that right?"

"I'd prefer if you addressed me as Ms. Gerba," she said. "Or Director Gerba, if you don't mind."

"Yeah, sure, whatever sails your boat. Listen, Ms. Director Gerba, Gyges is pulling some shit on us here. This fucking guy is faking this just to get out of work. Don't we have our own doc to check on this shit?"

"I don't think the use of profanity is called for here. In some circles, that would constitute sexual harassment."

"What the hell are you talking about? Sexual harassment? Sexual harassment? Try listening to me. I'm not asking you out on a date, for Chrissake. I'm talking about stopping Gyges from fuc . . . from screwing this company over. Let's stay in the real world, okay, Ms. Director?"

"I assure you, I am in the real world."

"I think he's drinking over lunch. Maybe even here at work."

"Do you have any evidence?"

"Yeah—he's late and absent a lot."

"That isn't evidence of alcoholism."

"According to that little employee seminar you forced

everyone to go to last year, it is. Absenteeism and lateness are 'classic signs' of alcohol and drug use. I have it in my notes, if you need reminding. You went on for over an hour. Of course, when I accused him he denied it but—"

"You accused him of drinking on the job?"

"Yeah, like I said, he denied it with this lame dodge about how—"

"Apparently, you aren't aware of the legal ramifications of making an accusation like that without any proof."

"No, the legal niceties protecting slackers, whiners, and complainers is your area. Mine is getting shit done so we actually make a little money—you know, just a little, not a lot. Just enough to keep the doors open."

"Other than complaining, is there a point to this phone call?"

"Yeah, I don't want this report going into Gyges's file with the PAM. It makes it look like his work problems are my fault, when they're his responsibility."

"Well, that's actually not your call. It's mine. I'm including it. And I promise to note your reaction to the report."

Tracy slammed the phone down. He wadded up the doctor's report and threw it in the trash. He then turned his attention to more urgent matters, primarily the stalled acquisition of Freeport Enterprises. Tommy was pushing hard, and Tracy's area was under heavy pressure to cut corners and get a report to the executive staff as soon as possible.

* * *

Human Resource Management Director Sheila Gerba hung up the phone. Over the next hour, she recorded notes for Tracy's personnel file regarding Peter Gyges's health report.

9

Gyges logged on to his email the next morning to find a message from Danny O'Brien. Before he even opened it, he knew it was the news he'd dreaded. He stared at the cursor for a moment and then reluctantly clicked on Danny's email. The announcement punched Gyges square in the stomach. His legs weakened and he gasped for air. Anxiety flushed over him as he read:

It's with a mixture of pleasure and sadness we wish to announce that Vice President of Growth and Acquisitions, Thomas O'Brien, will be retiring to Ireland in six months' time. During this period, we will be working with everyone to ensure a smooth transition. Obviously, Tommy, the heart and soul of O'Brien Holdings, is truly irreplaceable, but we can all make an effort to help fill the void.

Here it was—only six months away. The specter of Tracy pacing Tommy's office floated through his mind. Tracy's intent had been clear back on the lawn at the Labor Day party. He'd fire Gyges first chance.

Gyges had to learn more about what Tracy did with his time—and maybe more importantly, what he didn't do with his time. Up until now, Gyges had avoided Tracy and his meetings. Even the thought made his palms clammy, but he had to become Tracy's shadow. Only then could he discover the man's Achilles heel before Tommy left.

Gyges logged on to the company calendar to schedule an appointment with Tracy. He opened Tracy's schedule and noted his meetings for the following week. He also added an appointment with Tracy for that afternoon—promptly at 1:00. No time for the health club; sacrifices were required to get this done right.

Not long after Gyges made the appointment, he received a call from Tracy's secretary.

"Mr. Gyges, this is Mary."

"Hi, Mary. How are you? How's your son's baseball team this summer?"

"Oh, they're not doing so well, but Jeff is leading the team in home runs."

"That's great!" Gyges said. "Well, what can I do for ya, Mary?"

"Tracy wondered what your appointment concerns."

"Just tell him I want to talk about how I might be more helpful to him as Tommy gets ready to leave. I'm sure there will be a lot more work for Tracy and, like the memo said, we must all do what we can to fill the void. So I thought I'd see what I could do to help."

"That's nice of you. Tommy's already moving more stuff to him. Between you and me, I think he's feeling a bit swamped. I'm sure he'll appreciate any help he can get."

"I'm sure," Gyges said with enough sincerity that even he almost believed it. "See you at one. Thanks, Mary."

* * *

Ordinarily, Gyges avoided acquisitions meetings; they bored him. But today he was as alert as if reading water for signs of baitfish. He remained attentive to what Tracy said and tracked his emotional level when each point or topic changed. He took careful notes throughout. When the meeting was over, he went back to his office and entered his notes into his computer. Tracy had two more meetings scheduled. Gyges slipped into those as well and took notes. He created a file for each topic and logged the notes.

By end of the third meeting, Gyges was exhausted. He wasn't used to this kind of sustained focus. He needed a break and seriously considered cutting out to the health club. But he resisted and stayed until his meeting with Tracy.

When he arrived outside Tracy's office, Mary told him to go in—Tracy was expecting him.

"What's this happy horseshit about you wanting to help out?" Tracy challenged as soon as Gyges entered.

"Good to see you, too, Tracy. My day's going well. How's yours?"

"What gives? How come you're back from lunch so soon?"

"Didn't go to lunch—heavy appointment schedule today. Luckily I managed to squeeze you in. You know me—business first." Instead of sitting, Gyges wandered to Tracy's bookshelf.

"Quit screwin' around, Gyges. What do you want?"

"I wanted to offer my help." Gyges flipped through a book on acquisitions strategy. The strategy angle reminded him of his chess lessons with the Turk. "This any good?"

"No pictures; you wouldn't be interested. Put it back."

"Why the hostility? This is a genuine offer. Honestly, what you see is what you get."

Tracy paused to study Gyges, who hadn't moved or replaced the book. "I can't think of a single thing you could do for me," he said.

"Well, think on it; maybe something will come to you. You don't mind if I borrow this, do you?"

"Why would you need to read that?"

"I'm developing an interest in the topic." Gyges moved to the door without waiting for Tracy's permission. "I'll bring it back when I'm done. Thanks."

Gyges stopped at Mary's desk.

"Mary, I'm borrowing one of Tracy's books. I'll bring it back when I'm done, but there're others I want to borrow, too. If I'm going to help Tracy, I have to bone up a bit—kinda rusty on some of this stuff."

"Okay." Mary scrawled a note that Gyges had borrowed the book.

* * *

When Gyges checked Tracy's schedule for the rest of the afternoon, he was happy to see that Tracy would be out of the office for meetings. He read a couple chapters from the book but eventually nodded off. It was tough going. He had graduated with a general business degree but hadn't done much reading since beyond fishing magazines.

Then he remembered he was scheduled to meet Bhuto at the health club for a late steam. He tossed the book into his valise, left a message with Mary to say he was taking a late lunch, and headed downtown to meet Bhuto.

10

Unable to resist the temptation, Gyges used the time before Bhuto arrived at the club to stroll through the women's locker room. Only a few women were present, but what the room lacked in quantity it made up in quality. He lingered awhile and then picked up cash from unattended purses before heading back to the men's room. Bhuto was there undressing. Gyges stepped into one of the stalls and turned the ring around.

"Ah, Petros—I see you beat me here."

"Not by much; I just got here, too." Gyges said, opening his locker and taking off his shirt. "I'm looking forward to this steam. It's been a tough day at work."

"Well, then, a steam is the perfect remedy. Look here—I brought you five liters of my grandfather's tea." Bhuto pulled five plastic bottles from his bag.

Gyges placed four of them in his locker. He drank half of the final one and kept it with him. Another man sat against the far wall when they entered the steam room. Bhuto looked at the man and then moved to the farthest seat. The man had blonde hair, and his face was draped with a wet cloth. He took no notice of the others; his head rested on the wall. Gyges sat next to Bhuto, partially blocking the man's view of the Turk.

"Ahh . . . this is just perfect. Just what the doctor—"

Bhuto raised his hand to stop Gyges from continuing. The blonde man snatched the cloth from his face to get a look. Then he leaned forward to see better.

"I told you to stop following me, Carlos," said the blonde man.

"I go where I please," Bhuto replied.

"I don't want you here at my club," the man shot back. "I thought I made that clear. Your presence here is distasteful."

"I go where I please," repeated Bhuto, taking a drink from his bottle. "And I have no interest in your aesthetic incapacity."

"I think you should leave."

"I think you should go fuck yourself," Bhuto said in a matter-of-fact tone.

The blonde man bolted up and took a long step forward. Gyges flinched, but Bhuto did not budge. He took another drink of his tea. Nearing 6'4", the man peered down on Bhuto with clenched fists, but Bhuto simply stared back.

"I won't be intimidated, even by you," the man said. "If I run into you here again, someone will be hurt. I don't care what happens after that, but I will do something about it."

"That shall be an interesting day for both of us, then," said Bhuto.

The blonde man stormed from the steam room.

"Who the hell was that?" asked Gyges. "Jesus!"

Bhuto shrugged. "I don't know him. Never met him before. Kind of an asshole, though, don't you think?"

"He called you Carlos?"

"Obviously he is crazy. Perhaps he confuses me with someone else. It happens to me all the time. All Mediterraneans look the same to these Swedes. So, you said you had a tough day at work?"

"Yeah, I'm having trouble with my boss." Gyges sighed.

"Doesn't everyone?" Bhuto chuckled.

"Yeah, but this is more than the usual stuff. He wants to fire me."

"This is not good. Why is this?"

"He thinks I'm incompetent."

"Are you?"

"What do you mean by that?"

"I just ask a simple question."

"Why would you ask that? You think I'm not competent at my job?" asked Gyges.

"How the hell would I know?" said Bhuto. "And why would I care about this? You don't work for me."

Gyges paused. It seemed odd that Bhuto never spoke about work. And he'd never asked Gyges what he did for a living. Almost everyone talked about work, complained about it like the weather or the wife. But not Bhuto. He showed no conversational interest in it—Gyges's or his own.

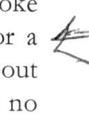

"I don't want to lose my job," Gyges continued. "I need it. I put in my eight and forty and then go do what I want. Maybe I've not been as dedicated as I could be, but I've done what I've been asked to do. I mean, it's work, for God's sake. This guy hates me."

"So, what are you doing about this?"

"Funny you should ask. . . . These chess lessons have helped."

"How so? I am not surprised, just curious."

"I see now what he's trying to do, and I'm countering to stop him. He complained about my absenteeism and tried to write me up, but I—"

"No offense, but I am not interested in details, only strategy. Work talk bores me. Strategy is exciting. Tell me about this." Bhuto smiled.

"It'll be hard without all the details."

"Make them sparse."

"He wrote me up for a work infraction, but I got him to admit in writing that he didn't have a problem with my work itself so it would be clear to anyone else that he was just being petty. Then I got a doctor to back up my side of the story."

"Not bad."

"Then I fixed it so the HR person was on my side."

"Very good. And next?"

"Well, that's the problem. I need to launch some kind

of offense, but I'm not sure how to do it. I'm trying to learn what he's working on so I can find a possible weak spot and get him fired before he fires me."

"You need a gambit."

"Gambit?"

"I'll show you some chess gambits tonight. They are like tricks, sleights of hand—like magician. You watch one hand while they work you with the other. Get him to think and act on one thing when you're really doing something else."

"Yes. That's what I'm looking for. A gambit."

Gyges took a long drink, draped his towel over his shoulders, and settled back against the wall. He closed his eyes and relaxed, letting the steam draw out his worries. All of his problems fell away, his mind empty of everything but heat and sweat and steam.

Bhuto moved to the opposite bench and stretched out his big body. It wasn't long before he closed his eyes, snoring loudly.

* * *

Gyges parked his Explorer in front of Café Morocco. He fingered through his wallet for the red card with the yellow scimitar and placed it under his windshield wiper. A very powerful talisman, indeed, he considered. All the times Gyges had parked there, no one had bothered his car. He felt enough like a regular now to wait for Bhuto inside.

Acrid cigarette smoke hung over the usual backgammon players. Their fervent voices drowned everything out. Their game, unlike chess, was not played in deep silence. The men shouted and cursed at each roll of the dice. At least, Gyges thought they were cursing. He didn't understand the language, but the tone and timing inclined him to think the outbursts where profane.

Oscar scowled from behind the bar as Gyges approached. The dwarf's voice pierced his ears. "Ahmed's not here."

"Yes, I know," Gyges replied. "Bhuto and I are meeting. He should be here shortly." The little man grimaced and began to shuffle away. "Can you get us two coffees, please?"

"You pay first."

"Yes, of course." Gyges dug out a twenty and gave it to Oscar. Oscar examined the bill closely in the light beside the register. He turned it over and examined the back. Then he flipped it upside down and repeated the inspection.

"Jesus, Oscar. Can I just get the coffees, please?"

Oscar's scowl deepened, moving the spider forward on his face. "I check to see if it is fake."

"I know what the fuck you're doing. It's rude and unnecessary." Gyges was losing patience. He ate shit all day from Tracy. He'd be damned if he let this diminutive creature treat him the same. The little prick probably slept in a hole in the wall. Every night they'd throw him a ripped blanket and a few scraps of trash for dinner and chain him up 'til opening hours. "I'm in here all the time. You know I'm honest."

"My boss tell me, Oscar, check all money for falseness. I do as boss say. You not my boss." Oscar made change from the twenty and handed it to Gyges.

"Thank God for that. Huh, Oscar?"

* * *

Gyges was still brooding over the exchange when Bhuto arrived. The sound of the backgammon games briefly passed through the quiet room as he opened and closed the door. Gyges glanced up and raised the coffee tray.

"Oscar sends his best," Gyges muttered.

"He doesn't like you," said Bhuto.

"I noticed."

"Thinks you are a cheat of some kind. A thief."

"When did he tell you this?"

"First night you were here. I assured him you would not cheat him, but he insisted you were not to be trusted. He says it is in your eyes."

"Does he do palm readings too?"

"Enough play. Ready for your lesson?"

Gyges set up the board to let Bhuto sip his coffee and gather his thoughts.

"Like I said this afternoon, the point of a gambit is to convince your opponent you are doing one thing when you are really doing something else. Some end the game as soon as you spring the trap. Your opponent suddenly realizes what you have done to them. Most often, this has an immediate demoralizing effect. When done well, it is a thing of beauty. They are crushed by the recognition you have completely outsmarted them. They are beaten, dejected men who have been humbled by you.

"With other gambits, they may discover the trap, but the end is not quick. If you have made the trap properly—like spider web, yes?—they will not be able to struggle out of it. Their frustration will build as they try to free themselves from your design. Most often here, anger grows, as their efforts are useless. It is humiliating and adds shame for them. An excellent player can construct both."

Bhuto illustrated several examples of both gambits, explaining why they worked and how they utilized misdirection. Gyges soon recognized that he fell into many of these traps when playing Bhuto. Bhuto often allowed him to believe he was close, maybe two moves from winning, maybe only one, but designed the trap to spring before he could execute those moves.

"You convince them they have won something from you—either position or piece. Or that you are careless. Either way, they must believe you are weak and they will be enticed into error. They will press the advantage rather than spot the trap. Gambits work best with impetuous, offensive, aggressive players. This is the gambit's other beauty—you get to punish the arrogant. It is much harder to trap a cautious player; they already think you want to trap them. In fact, they usually set their own traps for you."

Gyges followed every word. He couldn't help imagining Tracy's downfall. The familiar burn that the ring revealed back in the tavern returned, stronger than it had been in some time. He quietly savored the sensation as Bhuto talked.

"Earlier you said your boss wants to fire you. Is this man arrogant and pushy? Does he throw his weight around?"

"Yes, exactly. He's intimidated me until recently. Now I see I must get him fired before he fires me."

"Is that the only reason?"

"Isn't that good enough? I need to keep my job."

"So, if he didn't want to fire you, you wouldn't be trying to get him fired?"

"No, why would I?"

"There is a saying among the desert tribes: If you are not the lead camel in the caravan, the view of the desert never changes."

Gyges thought for a minute and then laughed. "Very funny, but what's that got to do with this?"

"How far back in the caravan do want to be? If you're not looking up your boss's ass, then it'll be someone else. The same view. Why not move up?"

"Oh, wow. The thought never crossed my mind. I never wanted his job. I just wanted him to leave me alone."

"Why is simply keeping your job a better reason than getting him out of the way so you can move up? Do you think this makes you less guilty?"

"Well, I guess . . . I dunno. I suppose it does. You know, like self-defense."

"Bullshit. You must treat this man as an obstacle to what you want. Why not want something more? If you knife the bastard, knife him for something worth it; don't remain in same place."

"That's so ruthless. It's just not me."

"You're about to screw your boss, to set him up to be fired. Period. This is ruthless. The reasons why do not lessen its ruthlessness. If you are not prepared to act ruthlessly, be prepared to get screwed yourself. This is the game you play now, whether you want to or not. He wants to fuck you, yes? If you do not act without conscience, you should just bend over."

The starkness of the image and Bhuto's cold intense delivery struck Gyges into silence.

Bhuto let Gyges's thoughts fill the void.

Finally, after a few minutes, Gyges said, "What difference does it make?"

"What difference does what make?"

"My reason."

"This is what I'm telling you. It does not make any difference at all. If you act ruthlessly, you are still a ruthless bastard."

"No, I see that part. You've convinced me of that. I can accept being a ruthless bastard. But I mean, what difference will the reason have on the plan?"

"The gambit you use?"

"Yes, yes—the gambit."

"A big difference, my friend," said Bhuto. "If you want his job, you must get him in a way that makes you the unsung hero. If you only want to save your job . . ."

"No, I'm interested in more. What do mean by 'the unsung hero'?"

"If you look like you intentionally screwed him, you may get him fired but you will not be picked to take his place. You may even generate sympathy for him. You cannot appear to have done this for selfish reasons. Everyone must think you did this for the health of the organization. For the team, the good of the whole."

"I'm not sure I can do this."

"That makes two of us."

"I need to think this over."

"Oh, yes! I brought you something. I think it will help." Bhuto reached in his back pocket and retrieved a tattered paperback. The cover was half-torn, the pages yellowed by time. He handed Gyges the book.

"The Prince," Gyges read. "I've heard of this. I think

we were supposed to read it in college." He looked up with a sheepish smile. "But I didn't."

"That does not surprise me. Machiavelli wrote it about six hundred years ago. It is a how-to book for rulers."

"Six hundred years old? How is this gonna help me? He doesn't know shit about corporate politics."

"Maybe not," Bhuto shrugged, "but you might be surprised. If you don't want to read it, throw it away. Or maybe you should just give to your boss?"

They put the chess pieces away in their box.

On the way out, Gyges cast a sideways glance at Oscar, who kept a watchful spider's eye on him all the way out the door.

11

Tracy walked briskly toward the meeting room. Gyges followed unseen and slipped in, avoiding the traffic. It didn't take long before the seats were filled with suits. Tracy insisted on prompt start times and made any latecomers regret it.

O'Brien Holdings wanted to buy a company called Freeman Enterprises. It looked like a good deal, but Tracy voiced worry to the attendees. He thought Freeman's owners were hiding problems or costs to make it seem more appealing. Freeman was a larger organization, but it lacked OH's capital and finances. The company had been on the market for four years when the owners finally dropped the price. Immediately, Tommy O'Brien became interested. Tracy went on to say that Freeman had struggled during those four years, but the previous year's numbers showed improvement. And even more promising, the current numbers suggested a record year. Because of the success, the owners had once again increased the selling price. Tracy assigned the attendees to research different aspects of the company. They needed to learn as much as possible as quickly as possible. The acquisition research group had only a couple weeks. Another company was now interested in Freeman, and O'Brien Holdings had to decide.

There wasn't much discussion. Tracy delegated responsibility, and everyone wrote down what they needed to do. There were few questions, and nobody volunteered anything. Tracy was clearly in charge, and no one challenged him. The only time anyone else spoke was when he asked a direct question. Gyges couldn't help but be impressed with the clarity of each assignment.

When the meeting ended, Gyges went back to his office. He thought about how he might help Tracy make a bad recommendation—possible areas where Tracy could slip up and overlook something important. It wouldn't be easy. Tracy was an asshole, but he knew what he was doing. He'd been successful in his position in the three years since Tommy had promoted him to Director of Acquisitions Research. Still, there was a lot riding on his recommendation, and he was under the gun.

Gyges needed something Tracy and his group might not discover. They were all experts in their areas. They knew just what to look for. He did not. What could he possibly learn that Tracy didn't already know himself? It was a fruitless search for leverage. Gyges theoretically understood what was required, but he didn't know enough details to make it happen. He felt overwhelmed by the task. He spent so much time thinking of solutions, he missed Tracy's next meeting.

Tracy believed that Freeman Enterprises was hiding something, Gyges recalled. The company had increased the asking price. They were more profitable now than they had ever been. Had their own management team figured out the problems and fixed them? Or were they making the company appear more profitable than it really was? Were they cooking the books? Tracy's people would have already thought of that; he'd sent an accounting team to look over the books. If something was wrong, they would have picked up on it.

Gyges tried to remember what he had learned back in Operations Management classes. Nothing came to mind. From the outside, there was no way to know what was going on at Freeman. He wished he knew someone inside the company—a mole, someone who could feed him inside information that showed a real picture of the organization. Gyges was so close he could feel it; victory was within reach.

He slammed his hand down on his desk and sat up

with a start. Goddamn it, Gyges, he told himself. It's right here in front you, right here within your grasp.

Then he looked down at his ring and laughed.

***

Gyges rapped lightly on the Sheila Gerba's open door and poked his head inside.

"Got a minute?"

"Of course. I'm never too busy to see one of our valued employees."

"Are you sure? I can always come back later. I could use your help."

"Oh, no; come in and sit down."

"Is it okay if I close the door? I don't want everyone hearing this."

"By all means."

Gyges closed the door. Ms. Gerba pulled two chairs in front of her desk.

"Let's sit here. It's less formal. What can I help you with, Mr. Gyges?"

Gyges sat down next to her. "Well, first off, I wanted to thank you for the way you handled the PAM thing. I thought you acted with professionalism and sensitivity. It's rare to find that combination in a corporate setting. I really appreciate it." Gyges patted her shoulder.

"Why, thank you," the director beamed. "That's why I'm here—to make the work environment more humane and supportive. How's the stress management going?"

"Not as well as I hoped, honestly. That's actually why I'm here. I need some time off to get my medication adjusted and take care of some problems at home."

"I'm sorry to hear that. I'd hoped things were improving for you."

"They have in some ways, yes. I don't want to paint a dark picture. But . . ." he paused and lowered his voice, "this will stay between us, won't it? You won't tell anyone?"

"I do not gossip about what you tell me, Mr. Gyges. But I do have a responsibility to look after the company's interests. You understand that, don't you? I mean, that is to be expected, right?"

"Oh, yes, for sure. It's not the company at all. It's that my wife and I are having serious problems. Or problem, I guess . . . the stress medication is . . . well, this is difficult to say . . . causing me some problems . . . well, umm . . . meeting my, you know, uhhh . . . spousal duties, if you know what I mean."

"Yes, I understand. Let me assure you that this will stay within these walls."

"Thanks; I really appreciate your kind understanding. I have a few vacation weeks coming, and I know it's short notice, but I wonder if it's possible to use them . . . I mean, so I can get all of this squared away. I think two weeks should take care of it."

"Did you discuss this request with Tracy?"

"Oh, no. I couldn't tell him what I've told you. He'd laugh me out of his office. Make mockery of it. Plus he's so indiscreet. Last year, Dave had swelling problems after his vasectomy. It sometimes happens, and he had trouble walking. Tracy let everyone know why. He thought it was hilarious. Dave was a good sport, but with everything going on already, I don't know if I could handle it."

"I completely understand the painful and private nature of your problem and why you'd like to keep it from Tracy. However, it's standard procedure for supervisors to grant vacation."

"Is there any way around that?"

"Maybe. Let me see what I can do. I'll talk to Tracy and see."

"My god, you're not going to tell him about my thing . . . I mean, my problem, are you?" Gyges jumped forward as if panicked.

"No, absolutely not. I'll see if Tracy has substantial objections if you take a vacation for personal reasons on short notice."

Gyges eased back into his chair. "Okay, as long as you don't mention the nature of . . ."

"Mr. Gyges, I'm not going to betray your trust. You can be confident our chat stays between us. Stop by later, at the end of the day. I'll talk to him before then. I know it's important to take care of this right away."

Gyges leaned in and hugged Ms. Gerba. "Thank you, so much. I feel more relieved already."

"I'm just glad I can help."

Gyges went back to his desk to gather his notes together. He didn't want to leave any incriminating evidence for Tracy to find while he was on vacation. Gyges chuckled to himself.

Personal reasons.

Peter Gyges, you are a badass.

* * *

The blonde man charged so swiftly and quietly into the locker room, he almost caught Gyges rifling through a couple of wallets. Fortunately, the man was whistling to himself as he went to his locker. Gyges watched as the Swede took his time, methodically folding his clothes and placing them neatly in his locker. But as attentive as the man seemed, he failed to turn the number wheel after he closed his lock and headed for the steam room. Gyges went to the locker and popped it open. Now a professional, he reached into the locker and lifted the wallet in one smooth motion. Taking money from the man would be a way to score one for his friend Bhuto. The guy was loaded. Gyges took a hundred, a fifty, a couple twenties, and a few tens. As usual, he left most of the contents untouched.

He went to return the wallet when he paused for a moment. His desire to learn something more about Bhuto spurred him to do something he ordinarily wouldn't have considered—he pulled the Swede's driver's license. It read Olaf Swenson 918 Governor's St. St. Paul. Gyges quickly replaced the license and then the wallet. He thought he'd head back to work but changed his mind; Swenson might reveal something about Bhuto.

Gyges opened the door to the steam room. Swenson and two bodybuilders sat inside. They all looked up as he closed the door.

"Guys," said Gyges with a nod. "How's it goin'?"

Swenson gave him a second look. From under his towel, Gyges grabbed his sweat tea and took a long drink. The bodybuilders left. Swenson looked over at him a few more times but said nothing. If he recognized Gyges, he wasn't showing it. Gyges closed his eyes. He wasn't satisfied being just another pawn at O'Brien Holdings. His talk with Bhuto had awakened the desire for Tracy's job.

Tracy expected Tommy's job when he retired. But once he took Tracy's job, he'd be the logical choice for the promotion. Jesus, he could be one of the top three guys at OH. Gyges had never been this excited in his life. Up until this moment, these ideas hadn't even been in his realm of thinking. Yes, he wanted Tommy's job. And more importantly, it was within his grasp. He just had to reach out and take it. First, he'd look into Freeman and set up Tracy for a fall. But his spot would be a mere stepping stone to something far better—VP of O'Brien Holdings in less than six months.

In his excitement, Gyges hadn't noticed Swenson leave. He sat up. He needed to get moving, too, and he hit the shower. Driven by his new desire, he was motivated to move up, to get more than just trinkets and toys. Jesus, what a fool he'd been. He'd wasted his time. He possessed this incredible ring that granted him virtually anything he wanted, yet he was just pissing away every opportunity. He was ashamed of his weak understanding of its potential. He thought too small. A new fucking power drill? He could rise to a position of real power. He could be in charge.

Gyges strode around the corner of the shower to the locker room and bumped into Swenson.

"You people better leave me alone," Swenson said

through clenched teeth.

"What? It was an accident, man," said Gyges. "Maybe you should be more careful yourself."

"Don't threaten me. Your asshole boss knows I'll have the money by Monday. Just leave me alone. He's not as tough as he thinks. And sending you now? I'd break you in five seconds." Swenson pushed Gyges into a locker and stormed from the room.

* * *

Gyges returned to the office and went straight for his voice mail, confident that his new ally, Director Gerba, had gotten him the time off. He figured Tracy might complain, but he wouldn't stand in the way. Bigger worries occupied his mind.

Gyges was right. A message from Gerba granted his request for vacation. He packed his things and headed home.

12

When the Explorer pulled into the drive that afternoon, Angela wondered if Peter had gotten into trouble at work. Maybe his behavior there was mirroring his behavior at home. Not that he had been around, and when she did see him, he said almost nothing. He wouldn't talk to her, and his body language made it clear he didn't want to. What else could she do? She'd simply run out of ideas on ways to connect with him.

Earlier in the day, she had taken a slow walk through the house. On a yellow legal pad, she had listed all the new appliances, electronic gadgets, and other useless crap Peter had brought home over the previous few months. She reviewed the list at the kitchen table. The items were even more than she had realized. The total had to be thousands of dollars. Until these items had showed up, Peter hadn't shown the slightest interest in the stock market. They shared a savings account. No other investments. Now he was Warren Buffet. She knew he must be lying. It just wasn't the Peter she had married. He would never have gotten involved in the stock market; it was too risky.

She loved Peter's caution, his gentleness, his desire in life to not rock the boat. She saw things the same way. Anything else was against his nature. And that was fine with her. He had always been humble and quiet and accepting and thankful. That was the man she loved. She couldn't quite pinpoint this new Peter, but many of those qualities were no longer there. He'd transformed. Now he was withdrawn and less forthcoming. But there was something else too. He was different. Since when, though? She couldn't say exactly, but she kept coming back to the day he returned from that fishing trip.

Without him there or emotionally available to talk when he was, Angela conjured up all kinds of possible reasons. He must be on drugs, she thought. She remembered a magazine article describing a man much like Peter who had lost everything because of his addiction. One day a nice loveable family man, the next a drug-crazed addict running up thousands in credit-card debt. He sold the car. Eventually lost the house. The police caught him after a twelve-day binge masturbating in a dark alley. He was eventually sentenced for a laundry list of crimes, leaving his destitute wife to fend for herself on welfare.

But the more she thought about it, the less she saw a connection between Peter and the man in the article. Peter wasn't running up debt or selling everything in the house. He was adding to it! But still . . . it didn't change his secrecy. Maybe it was even worse than she thought. Maybe he wasn't using drugs; maybe he was selling them. It would explain all the new money and his uncharacteristic behavior. She tried to imagine Peter Gyges, suburban drug dealer. She laughed out loud. It was too great a leap to take seriously.

She'd considered the possibility that Peter was having an affair, that he'd bought her everything to soothe his guilty conscience. Maybe he'd thought these things would keep her happy, silence any suspicions she might develop. It certainly would have explained his clandestine demeanor. He was always checking on this or that, disappearing for hours, coming home late or not at all. He seemed especially pleased when she went away on that trip a few months back. But after she thought about it, the theory didn't explain the extra money to buy all the new things. If Peter were having an affair, he'd be spending money on the mistress.

Perhaps he'd stolen everything, embezzled the money from O'Brien Holdings. But that theory didn't work, either.

Peter didn't have access to company funds. Not in large amounts, anyway. He arranged company parties. He couldn't write checks or authorize payments to suppliers. He'd complained many times that he required Ted's approval to spend more than two hundred dollars.

Angela didn't know what was going on with her husband, but she resolved to make one last attempt to get him to open up. If it failed, she'd leave him. Or ask him to move out. He was hardly there anyway. Why should she find another place?

"You're home?" she asked when he came in from the garage.

"Life is full of surprises," he responded.

"What's in the bag?"

"Gym clothes. Need to do a load of laundry."

"I'll do them."

Gyges didn't respond. He hoisted the bag over his shoulder and stomped downstairs to the basement. Angela opened the refrigerator, took out deli meat, cheese, mustard, and rye. She heard the washer start as she made herself a sandwich.

After a few minutes, Gyges stomped back up.

"Want a sandwich?" she asked.

"Uhh . . . sounds good."

He sat down at the kitchen table. Angela placed a turkey sandwich and beer in front of him. Then she joined him with her own sandwich.

He took a drink. Neither spoke for some time.

"How's the sandwich?" She couldn't think of a better icebreaker.

"Good."

"Is everything okay at work?"

"Yeah, why shouldn't it be?"

"I dunno. Just wondering. You're home so early."

"It's fine. I've been assigned to a special project and I won't be going into the office for a few days."

"Oh, wow—a special project. What is it?"

"Nothing exciting. Just not the usual stuff."

"Peter . . . What's going on? Something's changed, and I'm not happy with the way things are between us."

"Yeah . . ."

"You've become withdrawn. Hostile even. You—"

"Oh, so it's on me now? Yeah, okay, it's me, then. I'm the problem."

"See—I didn't mean it that way. I'm just trying to talk to you and you're—"

"I've changed, right? Is that what this is about?"

"Yes, you have. I miss the old you."

"Well, too bad."

"So you like being hostile all the time?"

"I like getting what I want, not letting people walk all over me."

"But why are you pushing me away? I'm on your side."

"Whatever. You don't mind being a doormat; you don't mind people shitting on you or taking advantage of you or talking about you behind your back. You're weak."

"Peter, I don't understand. Where is all this anger coming from?"

"I've just realized how the world is. I see now that I was too afraid to reach out and take what was mine. You can't get anywhere with kindness and trying to be everybody's pal. I'm going to move up. I'm not gonna be a lackey anymore. I'm gonna take what I want, just like everyone else."

"You know that's not true. You don't really believe you have to be like that to succeed. That's not the way we were raised. Your parents didn't teach you that. We're doing fine."

"We were taught to be losers, to tow the line, be compliant to the people on the top. Well, that's not good enough for me. I'm better than them, and I always have been. Now I'm going to be the one on top, the one in front."

"I don't see how you've been run over by anyone."

"You just don't get it, Angela. You can't see what's right before your eyes. You're blinded by all those lies you inherited. You're happy with whatever crumbs of life you're thrown. Just so long as things are calm and you don't have to rock the boat. No, that would be scary. It makes you uneasy. Good people don't push to the front of the line. Good people don't speak up for themselves. They're courteous and share and help each other out. And good people never lie, do they, honey? They don't cheat or steal. They don't blow through people to get what they want. They're just supposed to be like a goddamn dog begging at the dinner table." Gyges slammed his hand on the kitchen table.

"But what we have is good," Angela countered. "We haven't been given anything. We've worked for our success—this home, this way of life, this relationship, our love."

"Oh, fuck that bullshit! This life is dog shit compared to what we could have. All we have are missed opportunities. Don't get me wrong—I'm not blaming anyone but me. The old me. But that's over now."

Angela's eyes welled up with tears. "But I'm happy with what we have, Peter. I don't think it's bullshit. I have you. If this is all bullshit, then so is our love. You think our love is bullshit? Is that what you're telling me? That our love isn't enough anymore?"

"I guess we're different. And I can't settle for it anymore. You're welcome to it, but I can't let you hold me back."

"I don't know what happened to make you say all this, but it's just gonna make you miserable. I pity you. You truly are alone now."

"Pity me? Please . . . you're brainwashed by weakness and complacency. You can't even imagine having a life people really envy, can you?"

"Why would I want that?"

"Just asking the question makes answering it a waste of time."

Gyges left the table and returned to the basement. He unloaded the washer and moved his clothes to the dryer. Then he started the second load. She was worse than useless, he thought. All this time, she had been an anchor. When he emerged from the basement, she was gone. Good. Fuck her. He gathered essential clothes and personal items. He didn't even bother to leave a note. He left his wedding band on the kitchen counter. Then Peter Gyges hopped into his Explorer and drove away.

Angela never saw him again.

13

Gyges stood in front of the slip at Excelsior Marina and watched the painter stencil the final letters on the back of the white Boston Whaler.

The Ghost.

That morning, he'd driven by the marina hunting for an apartment when he saw the *For Sale* sign. Immediately, he knew he must have it. He'd live on it until he found a more permanent solution to his residency problem. He told the salesman at the marina he'd buy it on the spot, the two stipulations being that they airbrush the name on it and that they had it running by the end of the day. He'd figure out how to meet the payments later. For now, it was his.

He fired up the twin 420 diesel engines and eased away from the marina to his slip at the far end of the docks. For the next few hours, he loaded his belongings. It took two more trips back to the house to collect everything he wanted. He finished after midnight. Then it was finally time for The Ghost's maiden voyage.

He let loose the ropes that bound him to the land.

He left the engines off, instead using a long pole to push the boat out from the dock. He just wanted to drift out into the black quiet of the lake. Only when the lights on the dock had completely faded did he turn on the engines, and then only to a low idle. He switched on the night running lights and steered his way out of the bay into the larger lake. He loved it out there. He was free.

The Ghost cleared the bay mouth and Gyges found the channel buoy marker. Once beyond it, he pushed the engines to three-fourths throttle and The Ghost came into its own. The stern dropped deeper into the water. The props dug in for power and speed. The bow lifted up and cut a swath into the cool night air.

Since childhood, Gyges had paddled across the water in his canoe, slipping quietly in and out of coves, black bays, and private dock areas unnoticed. But this was a completely new experience. He clutched the wheel with white knuckles. The Ghost filled him with invigorating power.

No moon above, the boat floated in pitch black. The only lights came from distant houses and streetlights on the shoreline—Gyges's only anchor to the world. He'd felt an urge and he'd gone with it; he'd no longer deny himself anything in this life. He shed his clothes, stripped everything that had been placed upon him since childhood. If he could, Peter Gyges would have stripped himself of even his name. He didn't need any of it.

He threw The Ghost into full throttle. The flood of exhilaration almost caused him to lose consciousness. He grabbed the steering wheel to keep from toppling over and shouted out from the depths of his belly. Coarse, amorphous emotion unhindered by words or ideas. He never wanted it to stop. On the dark of the lake, The Ghost screamed over the water, no driver behind the wheel.

14

"I'm here to see Dean Tinker," Gyges told the secretary at the Carlson School of Management.

"May I tell him who's here?" she asked.

"Peter Gyges from O'Brien Holdings."

The secretary called the dean and after getting his okay, directed Gyges to his office down the hall.

Gyges knocked on the door.

"Come in," a voice called.

Gyges entered, a confident swagger in his step.

"Dean Tinker, pleasure to meet you." Gyges extended his hand. He never understood a firm handshake. It didn't reveal shit about someone's character. Except one thing, he thought—the firmer the handshake, the bigger the asshole. Tracy had a vice grip, and he was never shy letting Gyges know how delicate his was.

"Great, great. Nice to meet you as well," said Tinker. Gyges detected a slight twitch on the dean's face. "That's quite the handshake you've got there, Mr. Gyges."

That's right. Peter Gyges can play the game too, he thought. However stupid the rituals. He'd be the biggest asshole of them all. This was just the beginning.

"I must confess I'm not familiar with your corporation," Tinker said. He rubbed his hand as he sat back down.

"That's not surprising. We're family owned and run. We don't get much publicity, and that's the way we like it. We buy troubled companies, get them healthy, then sell them."

"Sounds like an interesting operation."

"Oh, it is."

"That's great, just great. . . . So, what can I do for you today?"

"It's better to ask what we can do for each other," said Gyges. "I have a business opportunity I think benefits both our organizations." His voice struck with the cocksure authority of a seasoned pitchman. Shit, Gyges, he told himself, you make this look easy.

"Super. You've come to the right place, Mr. Gyges. We have an excellent reputation partnering with local corporations."

"Of course; that's why I'm here. But I've tried other consulting firms, all of which championed their 'excellent reputations' as well. Quite frankly, they were dogshit, if you'll excuse my language. I need your expertise on a problem we have. I'm on a very short deadline. Money is no issue, but cutting edge 'expertise' is. No bullshit. If you can't do it, don't waste my time."

"All right. What's the problem?"

Gyges was straightforward. He told Tinker everything except the name of the company. When he'd finished, Tinker thought for a minute. "I'd recommend Dr. Brenda Hosbinder. She has a PhD in Operations Management and she's recently developed an interest in forensic assessment."

"Forensic assessment?" Gyges asked. "I must confess I don't know what you mean."

The dean laughed. "Well, honestly, I didn't either until a few years ago. It's a field that looks at company operations. Tries to spot areas where criminal or borderline activity may be taking place. Dr. Hosbinder's the best choice for the job. And she's not teaching this semester. We moved her onto a research project connected to a special grant from NSF."

"I'm sorry, Mr. Tinker. I thought I made it clear that we are under a tight deadline."

"Yes, yes. I think we can shake her free for this." He picked up the phone. "Lemme call her right now."

Dean Tinker got Hosbinder on the phone and quickly explained the situation. Less than two minutes later he hung up. "She's interested in discussing it with you but reserves the right to turn you down."

"Fair enough. So do I." Gyges flashed the dean a toothy grin.

* * *

"Mr. Gyges?" Dr. Brenda Hosbinder said without looking up from her desk. She was in her early thirties, her beauty understated but sophisticated—a brainy, academic kind of sexy.

"Yes." Gyges made a mental note to find out what health club she used.

"I'll just be . . . one sec here. Need to finish this calculation. Sorry."

"No problem. I appreciate you seeing me on such short notice."

He walked over to a glass-topped table in the corner, sat down, and watched her work. She never looked up from her laptop. He was surprised that it was the only thing on her desk. His college professors' offices had looked like paper bombs had exploded and they were content working in the fallout. Not here. Hosbinder worked in a perfectly kept room. It was Spartan—no books, no filing cabinets. There was only her oak desk and the table. The walls were shades of gray and maroon, with only indirect lighting.

After five minutes, Dr. Hosbinder stood up and joined Gyges at the table. "Dean Tinker explained everything, so you don't need to go over it again. Just tell me what you need."

"First, I need your assurance that this won't go beyond your office."

"That goes without saying."

"Maybe, but I need you to promise. Nothing leaves this room, not even back to Tinker."

"Okay. I promise. Now, what can I do for you?"

"We're on a short deadline. I have only ten days to recommend this company or not. My team is looking over the usual financial ratios, but my gut tells me this company's hiding something to skew the picture. My people don't have time to look into everything, and we can't afford to make a mistake here. I need you to direct me to where and what I'm looking for."

"I can definitely help you with this."

"I'd need you to give me a fast analysis on several documents and reports. Stuff beyond what my team is doing."

"No problem. I can do that too. Anything else?"

"That covers it. But I need to get started on it today." Gyges got up and headed for the door.

"If you're willing to do a working supper, I can get you started tonight."

15

Gyges drove straight from Hosbinder's office to a strip mall several blocks from the Freeman Building. He parked and stepped into an alley to turn his ring. Then he walked the short distance and waited outside the building doors.

He didn't have to wait long. When a group of Chatty Cathies returned from a late lunch, he piggybacked on their entrance. The women migrated to the elevator. Gyges stayed on the ground floor, made the rounds through the maintenance and office supply areas and then into the mailroom. None of his recon was likely to yield useful information, but he wanted to be thorough. He wound his way back to the elevators and discretely punched the up arrow.

The fourth floor contained Shadmun and Braddock executive offices but little else—a couple other conference rooms and dark, empty offices. The place was desolate, more like a morgue than the hub of a thriving enterprise. Shadmun and Braddock's offices were closed. The reception desk was abandoned; a computer had been left on, and files were scattered atop the workspace. Gyges didn't want to spend any more time there; it felt eerie. He located the stairwell and quietly escaped the floor.

He strolled around the second and third floors in the same manner. In his memo pad, he crudely drew each floor's general layout. Then he retraced his steps a second and third time, taking notes. When you don't know where the fish might be hiding, he thought, you have to fan cast your line in all directions. He wanted to know every detail of the company.

He made a special point to spy on the director for Management Information Systems. He lurked about her office until she took a coffee break, and then he turned off her computer. When she returned and rebooted the machine, he recorded her passwords and codes in his pad.

He also milled about the second-floor cafeteria and several bathrooms. Gossip was usually a great source of information. Most of it was banal work talk, but he gleaned an overall anxiety from the conversations. Apparently, many employees had recently been let go and those remaining were readying themselves for the other shoe to drop.

It wasn't a bad start, but Gyges still left the Freeman Building feeling unsuccessful. He had failed to uncover where the acquisition information was located. This kind of thing would have disheartened him a year before, but he now saw the urgency of persistence. Finding Tracy's contact was essential.

He checked his watched—nearly five. Just enough time to hit O'Brien to pick up a few things and still make it to his meeting with Hosbinder at seven.

* * *

The offices would be mostly empty, but Gyges used the ring anyway. After all, he was supposed to be on vacation. He went straight to Tracy's office. No one was around. He'd seen Mary hide an office key under the mail tray, and when he slid a hand under the tray, there it was. He double-checked that the area was clear, unlocked the door, and entered.

Tracy often kept his project files stacked on the credenza behind his desk. Gyges located a stack of the Freeman files with notes and reports. To save time, he grabbed them all; he had no idea what Hosbinder would find useful. He needed to get into Capt'n Douchebag's computer. He'd have to pencil in a visit to the office again the next day. He carefully cracked open the door, eyed the hallway, then slipped out, locked the office, and returned the key to its hiding place. He turned to leave but then changed his mind; he'd need the key again. Before leaving, he stopped by his office and downloaded Tracy's schedule for the following week.

* * *

Despite speeding across town, Gyges still didn't get to the restaurant until after seven. He hustled inside to find that Hosbinder had already started eating.

She looked up and, before he could apologize, said, "You're late."

"Yes, I'm sorry. I had to stop at the office for the files."

"I charge for my time whether you're here or not. I want to be upfront so there's no misunderstanding when you get my bill."

"Of course. I wouldn't expect anything else."

The waitress came over for Gyges's order. Hosbinder opened the top file on the stack he'd set on the table. She alternated reading with bites of salad. Gyges wondered if she counted how many times she chewed each bite.

"Good. This is helpful. Okay . . . yes . . . all right," she said between bites without looking up. "Can I keep these?"

"Oh, no . . ." Gyges dug through his jacket, handed her a pad of sticky notes. "Mark what you need and I'll copy them. These have to go back to the office. My team needs them first thing. I would've copied them, but I didn't want to waste time . . ."—Gyges couldn't help himself—"*and* I didn't want to be late."

Hosbinder took the sticky notes and kept reading. She shook her head and pasted notes as she went. Gyges let her go about her business. The waitress returned with his dinner. He ate in silence. Hosbinder finished the work and her meal at exactly same time. Gyges wondered if it was a coincidence or if she had worked it out that way. He'd put money on the latter.

"Okay, I've marked everything I need. When can you

make me copies?"

"They'll be under your door when you get to work in the morning."

"Pfft . . . I doubt it. I start at six sharp."

"They'll be under your door in the morning," he repeated with stern emphasis. Her smug Dr. Efficiency routine was wearing thin.

"Good. You've got us on a tight timeframe. I've already alerted two of my strongest grad assistants to be ready."

Gyges tried to imagine having to work for her. Poor kids. "What kind of things are we looking for here? That might help my team as well."

"Here's the deal. You say the company claims they turned things around. That page of ratios over the last five years suggests the same. But this miraculous turnaround is conveniently timed with the owners selling? Red light. Maybe it's legit, maybe not. My first question would be, Who are the owners? I don't mean their names. I mean background, histories, motives—that sort of thing. Has your team done any work on that angle?"

"Just the usual."

"Well, the usual won't turn up what you need here. Think about this: Are these people even the real owners or just a front for someone else? I've seen that more than a few times."

"How the hell do you find something like that out? This is a privately held company."

"Tax forms, incorporation papers, state filings, court documents from law suits—anything like that."

"What else should we pay attention to that we may be missing?"

"Until I go over the reports, I can't say specifically, but they may be inflating their assets. You said they have multiple plants and locations?"

"Yeah. Headquarters and four manufacturing sites."

"They may be overvaluing them. There are lots of

ways to do that. That's definitely worth looking at. Also, are they listing assets they don't have? Fake inventory? Either they are completely making them up or they have already sold them but are listing them anyway."

"Wouldn't that be illegal?"

Dr. Hosbinder chuckled. "Well, obviously, Mr. Gyges. So what? People do it all the time. Once you own the company, you'll find out. Then you'd have to prove it to a state's attorney who probably doesn't have the interest, resources, or expertise to pursue the case. This isn't the movies. You could try to sue, but that's expensive and time-consuming. So there's plenty incentive to chance flat-out illegal behavior. This is why you want to know who the owners are. Have they pulled this kind of thing before? Are they US citizens, or would you have to pursue them through foreign courts—extradition and all of that?"

Hosbinder was condescending, annoying, anal, and short on personality. She also impressed the hell out of Gyges.

"Is there anyone in your company who's in a position to influence the decision whom they might bribe or influence?"

"No, the decision's the owners'." Then it struck him. Tracy. Capt'n Douchebag was definitely in that position. "Wouldn't that person be exposed after the fraud comes to light?"

"Maybe, but it depends on whether or not the company engaged in blatantly illegal activity. Your person could just turn around and claim he was just as much a victim as everyone else. His reputation might be damaged a bit. I mean, you pay them to spot these problems. But," she shrugged, "if there's no evidence, your person would be in the clear. Or maybe, instead, it isn't blatantly criminal. Your person should have found it but instead takes a bribe and leaves the company after the sale but before the fraud is exposed. By the time you do find out, they have another job and you can't prove they took a bribe. There are a number of variations in how this could play out. In the end, it all amounts to one thing: there's plenty of incentive for one party to attempt a bribery and for your person to accept it."

"How would you find that out?"

"Some kind of smoking gun."

"Like a check."

"Yeah," she laughed, "that would be nice. But it's not usually that obvious. If the parties are smart enough, they'd use cash and launder it through a third party. Lots of these people aren't that smart, though. Again, it depends on what you're trying to do. If you want to prosecute, then you'll need proof beyond reasonable doubt. You'd need evidence—checks, memos, letters, emails, audio. You know, the incontrovertible stuff.

But maybe you don't intend to go that route. You only want to know whether this person was fooled, made an unintentional mistake, or took money under the table. Then the mere suspicion is enough, isn't it? Because, as you know, the corporate world often works on suspicion, not proof."

"So, in that case, what would we look for?"

"Any connection at all. Less-obvious memos, secret meetings, hidden or deleted emails, phone records, unusual notes . . . anything to cast enough suspicion on the person that you can get them out even if you don't have legally admissible evidence. In your case, that's unlikely if the owners are making the call. But . . . bribing you would make sense. You could make a bogus recommendation to buy."

Gyges laughed. "I was just thinking the same thing."

"Has anyone approached you?"

"No, of course not!"

"No need to get indignant, Mr. Gyges; I wasn't accusing you. I just thought you'd know something was fishy if they weren't willing to go with the merits of the deal."

"Oh, okay. I thought for a minute—"

"No, no. You wouldn't be going to all this trouble to find the problems if you were being bribed." She paused and smiled. "Unless, of course, you're figuring out how to hide your tracks. Or . . . you're trying to find the problems, then ask for a bribe."

"Dr. Hosbinder, you have a wicked mind. There's always an angle with you, isn't there?"

"I'll take that as a compliment. In my work, I have to look beyond the obvious to the unseen. But nothing is completely hidden. There are always traces or little clues to what is really going on. You just need to know where and how to look."

"Like seeing fish in the water," Gyges said to himself.

"What?"

"Like learning to see fish in the water. They're invisible unless you know how to look. They've evolved to blend into their environment. It's part of their survival. Most people can look right at them and never see them, as if they were invisible. But I can. I've spent hundreds of hours on the water. I guess it's the same."

"I'd have never thought of it that way. Do you mind if I steal that? Up here in Minnesota, a little metaphor like that might help recruit new clients."

"Sure, if you deduct some of this meeting from my bill." He grinned.

She paused, registered the jibe, and smiled. "Right. Point for you. Fifty bucks sound fair?"

"How 'bout you pick up the tab and we call it even?"

"Deal. I actually should be going. Anything else?"

"That should be good for tonight. Thank you; it's been a real education."

They shook hands and walked out together.

It'd been a long day, and Gyges still needed to finish a few things before heading back to The Ghost. But the meeting with Hosbinder had re-energized him. Adrenaline kicked in—he was enthusiastic instead of tired. He made a quick stop at a hardware store to copy Tracy's office key. Then he drove back to OH. He Xeroxed the pages Hosbinder had requested. It was past midnight when he finished.

He drove back to the Carlson School. Dr. Hosbinder's office building was locked. It took Gyges forty-five minutes to track down a security guard, only to learn that the guy's supervisor on the other side of campus had all the keys. The guard offered to give the files to his supervisor, but Gyges refused. He couldn't trust a dumbass rent-a-watchman to make the handoff without a fumble. He demanded that the guard get his supervisor on his little radio. Gyges would wait all night if he had to; there was no way he'd leave until the files were under Dr. Hosbinder's door.

16

Fifteen minutes into the meeting, Gyges's cell phone rang.

"Goddamn it," Tracy said, "Whose is that? You know the rules."

Everyone checked their phones. No one said anything. They just stared back meekly—a roomful of deer waiting for a deathblow. Then it went off again, and Gyges realized it was his. He felt blood rush to his invisible face. He nearly panicked but then managed to silence it before it rang a third time.

By now, Tracy was livid that no one had copped to it. "It came from the back of the room," he shouted. "Now whose is it? Come on—one of you sonsofbitches better own up."

The people in back all looked at each other, shaking their heads to indicate it wasn't them. Harold Donaway, a guy Gyges didn't know very well, finally said, "I think it was from the other room. I heard it behind me."

"I don't think so, Harold," scolded Tracy. "I know it was in here. I don't want to hear it again. Next time just leave 'em at your desks. I hate that shit! Now get out and do some work."

Gyges hadn't taken a breath since the second ring. He took in some air.

Goddamn it. Get with it. Think about what you're doing.

It seemed he was in for a long day. He'd woken up late

and hadn't even had time to stop for coffee. Then he hadn't been able to park in the company lot and could only find a spot three blocks away. He'd missed the beginning of the meeting. Tracy's people were already giving updates on each of their assignments by the time he'd arrived.

No one raised any red flags or said anything about the owners. There were still some open questions about sales figures, customer base, and manufacturing capacities. Tracy scheduled a team to inspect the four plants over the following two days. "Inspect" might be a little misleading, Tracy admitted; it would be a fast tour of each facility to verify their condition, inventory, machinery, and production and maintenance records.

Gyges sighed and looked at the call number. Some number he didn't know.

He followed Tracy back to his office. The Capt'n was still pissed and gave Mary an earful about the audacity of his crew. She feigned concern, then returned to her work. Gyges followed him into the office. He needed Tracy's pass codes and tried to maneuver himself into a position to turn off the surge protector, when someone knocked hard on the door.

Tommy O in the flesh. "How'd the meeting update go?" he asked Tracy.

"Great, Tommy."

"Got a sec?" Not waiting for an answer, he continued, "Give me the short and sweet. Bob Shadmun called, wanted to remind us there's only seven days to match the other offer. What's the story?"

"What's up with that? I mean, geez, we told him last week we'd be on time with the decision. I hate being upstaged."

"Forget it. He's just thorough. Where are we?"

"So far, everything looks kosher. I'm sending a plant inspection team out this afternoon. We're also looking more closely at the sales figures and customer-base numbers."

"So, if you had to decide today, what would you say?" Tommy hung in the doorway with his arms crossed. Gyges could never tell whether the man was happy or pissed off. He always looked the same—an intimidating SOB. He still carried the solid build Gyges remembered from childhood.

"The numbers definitely look right. I know it's more than we wanted to pay, but if they've turned things around we can assume there'll be less trouble and expense on the restoration."

"That'd be nice for a change."

"We can probably turn this baby around faster than normal. We'll make less in gross, but the net might actually be higher, since we'll have less expenses rollin' 'er into the black again."

"Maybe," said Tommy. "Still, I don't like this kind of deadline and having to match someone else's price." The man was stone. He hadn't moved since he'd appeared.

"Would you rather have lost the deal outright?" Tracy asked more forcefully than he'd probably intended.

"No, but that doesn't mean I like this."

"Right—me neither. But what are you gonna do?" asked Tracy.

"Make sure it's a good deal and we don't get screwed."

"Business as usual, then."

"I hope so. I'd love to have Freeman. A lot can be done there. We can sell one of their manufacturing plants to Stover's straight out the gate. And they have a big contract with GM on plastic fasteners. Danny talked to Philips at Stover—asked him if he'd be interested in a company that did big business with GM, if we had one. He didn't say who, of course. Phillips was really excited. He's got a line of plastic coatings and lubricants he's been pitching to GM, but he's not getting anywhere. If he can get in the door with the fastener business, they'd be more willing to listen."

"Really? I hadn't heard that."

"That's 'cuz it's just between Danny and me. Danny checked their interest right after Freeman raised the price. Selling that piece to Stover would go a long way to making this deal worth our time. We wouldn't even have to fix it up. It's a mess over there, but I think Stover would take it right away and do it all themselves."

"Should I say anything to the team?"

"You're joking, right? No, absolutely not. Freeman hears about it, you can be sure they'll try to deal directly with Stover. Or if Stover catches wind, they might make an offer to Freeman directly. I'm just telling you so you know."

"Yeah, I didn't think you wanted me to . . . ." Tracy trailed off. "But I do appreciate you sharing that with me."

"I gotta run. Danny and Patrick are joining me at Braddock's office this afternoon. I gotta bunch of shit to take care of before then."

Tommy left without another word. He wasn't the kind of guy to stay for small talk, not one to ask about the wife and kids or how the kitchen remodel was going, or offer sympathy for your last prostate exam. It's not that he didn't give a shit about his employees; he just didn't dawdle. Work was work. Time was money.

Or at least, Gyges hoped it wasn't because Tommy didn't give a shit about his employees. Honestly, if he really thought about it, he couldn't be sure. For as long as he had been around the O'Briens, maybe he really didn't know them as well as he thought.

"Good luck," Tracy said.

Tommy was probably already at the elevator, Gyges thought.

Tracy went to the door and told Mary to get him another cup of coffee. Gyges wished Mary would tell Capt'n to get his own goddamn coffee. Seriously, what was this guy's problem? He couldn't walk the twenty feet to the coffee machine? Gyges wondered if Mary wiped Tracy's ass when he took a shit.

Then Gyges realized he was missing his opportunity, and at the last second he flipped the surge protector off and on again. Tracy's computer rebooted.

Tracy turned from the door and made his way back to his desk. "Oh, what the hell? Goddamn piece of shit! Mary did your machine just go down?"

"No, I don't think so. Why?" Mary entered with his majesty's fresh cup and placed it on the desk.

He logged back onto his computer. When Tracy was done, Gyges had the passwords to access his directories and files.

Gyges couldn't resist. He flipped the surge protector off on his way out of the office.

"Goddamn it!" Tracy yelled, hitting the side of the monitor.

* * *

Gyges peeked over Tommy's secretary at the appointment book on her desk. The Freeman meeting was scheduled for 11:00—a couple hours to kill.

He walked back to his car. It was then, while wondering what to do for two hours, that his mind came back to the phone call. He turned the ring around and punched up the number. The phone rang twice before it went to voice mail. It was Hosbinder. Gyges left a message that he'd call back later.

He decided to head over to Freeman before the meeting to nose around and see if anything turned up.

* * *

Concealed by the ring, Gyges climbed the four flights of stairs to Braddock's office. A secretary typed rapidly from behind the desk. He needed to find out where the meeting would be. He tried to spot a calendar or schedule. No luck. He noted the secretary's extension on the bottom of her phone. Then he backtracked to the abandoned offices closer to the elevator. He slipped inside one, called Freeman's mainline, and entered the secretary's extension.

"Mr. Braddock's office. This is Peggy Cooper. How may I help you today?"

"Ms. Cooper. This is . . ." Gyges stumbled and almost gave his own name. He blurted out the only other name that came to mind: "Tracy Mackus at O'Brien Holdings. I'm meeting with Braddock later and just need to verify the location and time."

"Yes, Mr. Mackus. The meeting is at eleven. Just come right up to Mr. Braddock's office on the fourth floor."

They exchanged pleasant goodbyes and hung up. Gyges checked his watch. There was still an hour before the meeting. He called Hosbinder again. After the second ring, it went to her voice mail. He didn't leave another message.

* * *

In the cafeteria, the drones retrieved their coffee and breakfast pastries. Gyges eavesdropped on knots of employees gathered at tables. The weather. Viking talk. Grand kids. Blah, blah, blah. Useless empty babble . . . not even interesting babble.

He was heading back to the fourth floor when he spotted Braddock's secretary sitting with a co-worker. He paused and listened. Work talk.

Praise Jesus.

He carefully squirmed into a nearby chair. The secretary's friend spoke: ". . . Oh, I dunno how you can be so optimistic. My hairdresser Cynthia's aunt worked for a company OH bought out. Most of the employees lost their jobs after the takeover. The O'Brien people are merciless, Peg. But . . . then again, there are so few of us left now, they might not have anybody to let go. I heard another company's interested. Strokers or Slavers—something like that. I hope they buy us, instead."

"Well, you have to keep this to yourself; you can't tell anyone." Peggy leaned forward, dropped her voice just above a whisper. Gyges leaned forward, too. "The other company isn't interested anymore. It's all hush, hush, Martha. You can't be telling—"

"Oh, I won't." Martha dropped her voice to match Peg's. "Why aren't they?"

"I'm not real sure. I just know they aren't. Mr. Braddock doesn't want anyone to know. Not until the deal is done with O'Brien. Like if you sell your house. It's better if two people are fighting for it."

"Yeah, that happened to Sally's mother in Minnetonka. She was selling her place, and three people all wanted to buy it after an open house. She ended up getting five thousand more than the asking price . . ."

The women's voices faded as Gyges walked away. He wasn't interested in the real estate market in the suburbs. He had more than enough—a real plum piece of inside info. This Braddock guy must have a huge pair of balls or a fresh lobotomy, jacking the O'Briens around like that. They weren't anyone to fuck over. Once they found out, and Gyges would guarantee they did, Braddock had better book a one-way flight to Taiwan.

* * *

Braddock sat in one of the leather chairs surrounding a cherry table in the walnut-paneled executive room. Heavy red curtains were drawn over the windows behind him. He was a small man of medium build with slicked-back thinning gray hair. Wire-rim glasses framed his soft jowly face. There was something in the guy's manner that Gyges didn't trust, though he couldn't pinpoint exactly what or why. The O'Briens were justified in their unease. Still, business was business. Tommy wanted Freeman regardless of the turd's character flaws.

"The O'Briens have arrived, Mr. Braddock," Peggy's voice announced from a conference speaker on the center of the table.

"Yeah, okay, send 'em in. Call Bob and send him on over, too." Braddock hopped up and went to the door. "Danny, Tommy. How ya doin'," he said as they approached from the hall.

"Well enough, John," Danny answered. Braddock ushered them in. Patrick was the last to enter. "This is my son Patrick. He's helping us with the decisions."

"Good to meet you, son." Braddock gave him an overly warm handshake. Gyges guessed the guy put a lot of stock in handshakes. 'Come along to help the ol' man, huh?"

"Yeah . . . something like that," Patrick said. Gyges knew his friend had a low tolerance for bullshit. Like his father, Patrick could spot it anywhere.

Bob, another short middle-aged goon, charged into the meeting room, his best smile on display. He shook Danny and Tommy's hands.

"This is my son Patrick. He's helping us with the decision. Patrick, Bob Shadmun," Danny repeated.

"Patrick, good to meet you," Bob said. Another firm handshake. "So, you came along to help out your old man?"

"Seems to be the consensus. Until now, I didn't know how much help the old man needed." Patrick smiled.

Danny shot him a look. He wasn't smiling. Patrick grinned at his father, look or no look. The four men took a seat at the table.

"Would you like me to send Mr. Mackus in when he gets here?" Peggy asked through the conference speaker. Bob and John shot the O'Briens a look from the other side of the table.

"Mr. Mackus?" Tommy echoed.

"Yes, isn't he coming?" Peggy asked.

"Ah . . . no, he's not." Tommy looked at the other men perplexed.

Shit, I should have used another name, Gyges thought. He hadn't been thinking; it had just leapt from his mouth. Hopefully, Tommy would forget.

"Danny, you requested the meeting," said John. "What we can help you with?"

"Perhaps it's more what we can do for each other," Danny replied.

"Even better. What's on your mind?"

"We want to make sure your people are as open as possible with our research team and—"

"Let me assure you," Bob interrupted, "that word's gone out to give any information and assistance your people may need. We've opened our books. We appreciate you're under the gun here and that's why—"

"And then," Danny continued as if he'd not been interrupted, "we want to know if the deadline could be moved back."

"Move back the deadline?" John chimed in. "Danny, we have an offer on the table with this other company. That offer's good only 'til the day after your deadline. After that, they withdraw. If we passed on them, and you decided, for whatever reason, not to buy, where would we be? We'd have to start all over. That's not something we want to do. Bob and I have put a lot of tough years in this business. We're ready to put our feet up and relax. You can understand that, right? I hear Tommy's retiring himself. What would you do in our position?"

"I'd stick to the deadline and sell to the highest bidder, of course. But—"

"So you can see why we can't grant an extension. To be honest, gentlemen, we were just gonna sell to the other company outright, but Bob really insisted we give you a shot to match the offer. I mean, Bob here has really been a huge advocate for you guys."

"I thought it only right," Bob said. "After all, you had shown real interest and put time and money into working out a deal. Business is business, but there's also simple decency and fairness. That's the philosophy to which we've always adhered. So we went back and told the other company the situation."

"The other company knows we're trying to match their bid?" Tommy asked.

"Yes, of course," said Bob. "The Eight Beatitudes have always guided our business. We call that 'The Freeman Way.' John and I are both religious men, so it's natural for us to be as open with them as we are with you. 'WWJD' is also part of 'The Freeman Way.' "

"Wait just a sec." Tommy's patience was wearing thin. "If we match their bid, aren't you just gonna go back to them for a second offer? We're not interested in getting squeezed in a tit-for-tat bidding war, I can tell you that right now!"

"Oh, no. They've made it clear that their offer is final both in terms of money and deadline. Like you, they aren't interested in extended bidding. I mean, why would we tell you this if that was our plan? No, Tommy, you have our word as Christians. This is a one-time, take-it-or-leave-it offer. If you match it, we'll ink the deal on the spot. I'll simply let the deadline pass, and the other deal will be legally off the table."

Danny looked at Tommy for a moment.

Tommy nodded to him. "We're sending a team to look at each of your facilities," he said "You have the schedule, yes?"

"Yes, we forwarded it to our plant managers," said John. "And again, they've been instructed to act as if you were working for us."

"There's been some turnover in some of the managerial positions," Bob added. "We've been as honest with our employees as we have been with you. They are aware of our plans to sell. We asked them to stick it out until the sale. Sadly, many jumped ship right away. Often, there's a price to pay for letting everyone see what you are doing. In any case, I just wanted to let you know that your team may find some new managers who aren't as knowledgeable. If you have any questions they can't answer, just call John or me and we'll get an answer right away."

"Good enough," Danny said, tapping the table.

"I guess that covers our end," Tommy said.

"Where you boys planning on retiring to?" Danny asked cordially.

"I've got land in Arkansas. Bull Shoals. I'm gonna build a new home there. Far enough south to avoid these winters. Bob's signed up for some missionary work in Japan."

"Great. I hope it works out. Well, gentleman, we

should be moving on. No rest for the working man. Thanks for your time. I think we understand your position better now. We'll be in touch a day before the deadline."

There was another round of handshakes, and the O'Briens exited the room. Gyges stayed behind with John and Bob.

John closed the door.

"So?" Bob asked.

"I think they're definitely still interested."

"They damn well better be. We've bet the whole damn farm. If this doesn't work, we're fucked."

"It'll be fine," John said.

"I'm not so sure. Stover backing out and all."

"Well, that had to do with GM dropping the fastener contract. Those Micks have only about a week to uncover what's going on. There's no way they'll find out."

"We're running out of time keeping everything hidden."

"One more week, Bob. That's it. Then it's over and you'll be able to buy what's left for pennies on the dollar."

"By then we'll be basking in the sun in Belize. I almost lost it when you said I was going to Japan for missionary work."

"Yeah, I pulled that out of my ass. I thought it was a nice touch, too. You'll be taking a missionary position all right."

"Those temporary plant managers have to be on board," Bob warned. "We don't want some dumb-fuck fill-in queerin' the deal in the twenty-fifth hour."

"That's why you're heading out this afternoon," said John, handing Bob a packet and airline tickets. "You'll be there a day ahead of OH to make sure everything is in place and appears to be running full-tilt. And make sure our guys are so busy they don't have a lot of time to spend with the team."

"You gonna contact Buchetti, let her know what's up so she can tell the others?"

"Nah, I'm playing it close to the vest with her. No

sense drawing more of her attention. If the deal goes through, I don't give a fuck what she thinks or does. If it doesn't, no amount of making nice will save our asses anyway."

They said their good-byes, and Gyges followed Bob back to his office. He wanted to take a peek at the itinerary. Bob tossed the packet on his desk and headed for the bathroom. Gyges hurried to the desk and flipped open the packet. He couldn't be away for all of the visits. One ought to do it. Freeman had a plant in Austin, Minnesota. Bob was scheduled there in two days. It was a couple hours' drive.

* * *

Gyges called Hosbinder on the way to her office. Voice mail again. Maybe she was screening her calls. He left a message to say he was on the way to see her.

The closest parking space was eight blocks from Hosbinder's building. He squeezed the Explorer into a small space on a side street and walked the rest of the way. She wasn't in, but a note said she'd return in fifteen minutes. He waited.

She showed up exactly fifteen minutes later, wearing the same business dress suit as the first time they had met. Gyges wondered if it was a coincidence. Nah, she probably had a closet full of the same suit—like it's her uniform.

"Mr. Gyges," she said, rushing past to unlock the door, "I've been expecting you. We've learned some interesting things from those reports. Come on in."

She motioned him to take a seat at the table. She powered up her laptop and then took out a remote and pointed it at a box on the wall. A screen descended that linked to her computer, displaying a spreadsheet page.

"Look at this. They've significantly cut expenses." From her laptop, she highlighted a column of numbers. "We wondered where the reductions occurred. We traced the lines back through a series of tables, and it looks like it's almost exclusively in employee wages and salaries. There's been a huge drop in the last two years."

She opened several more reports. They flashed on the screen one after another, each with a few cells highlighted.

"Look here."

Another report opened up on screen.

"And this."

Another.

"And this."

And another.

"And here again."

She moved faster than Gyges could follow. He wasn't sure what he was looking at, but Hosbinder forged ahead, rocketing through several more pages.

"So what do you make of it all?" he finally asked.

"It took us awhile to dig it out, but once we put it all together, it's clear they've been dropping people from payroll like autumn leaves."

"We've learned through rumor that they've made some cutbacks," he said, recalling the cafeteria gossip.

"I'll say. Looks like they've trimmed half their employees in the last eighteen months. Yet, at the same time, their production expenses are down and income is up. It could be they've really learned how to run lean, but that's doubtful. Income is up, too. I'd say they've cut production and are selling off inventory and other assets."

"Okay, but isn't that just sound business practice?"

"It is if you aren't gutting the company's future to make the present quarter look fantastic. Seems to me like they just want to make income look more impressive than it actually is. It would be to their advantage at this point, don't you think? The profit turnaround coincided with a raise in the asking price."

"How do we tell the difference?"

"Look at future orders and contracts, current production numbers. Is there anything coming up the pipeline? You know, what's down the road in terms of income?"

"Funny you should mention contracts. Another rumor

says they just lost a huge contract with a major customer."

"Mmmm . . . How much credence do you put in that?"

"I think it's accurate, but I need real proof."

"There should be correspondence from the marketing department. Tell your team to look in the market correspondence. Of course, you might also check the customer about it. Though they may not tell you. Still, can't hurt to ask."

"Okay, good. We'll see what we can turn up on those fronts. What now for you?"

"Check newspaper articles in the towns they have plants. See if any news turns up about them. You'd be surprised what little nuggets you can glean from the pages of those newspapers. Problems with OHSA, EPA, DOL. Discrimination or other lawsuits. Hiring, lay-offs—that sort of thing. I also have someone looking through the help-wanted ads. And we're accessing the state employment database for unemployment rates in the Minnesota and Wisconsin plants."

"I also picked up on a rumor that there is no other competing company. They pulled out of the deal months ago."

"You're really tapped into the rumor mill, Mr. Gyges. You don't have an informant on the inside, do you?" Hosbinder asked.

"Oh, no. Nothing like that. You just pick up on things here and there. Nothing concrete. But I was wondering how I might verify if that's true."

"Same way as the customer contract. Look for correspondence. If you know the other company, you could try to talk to them."

"Great. Well, thanks again. Lots of ideas for my team. And it looks like yours is busy, too. I'll leave you to it."

Dr. Hosbinder flicked off the display screen. Gyges headed for the door, saying, "Call if you turn up anything else."

17

Gyges's head was swimming in details. He'd been running for days without much sleep, and though he wasn't near exhausted, he needed some time to re-charge his batteries and review his notes. He pulled into the marina parking lot.

As he approached The Ghost, he noticed a younger man leaning against another boat. He seemed to be keeping his eye on Gyges, singling him out for special attention. The man moved from the boat and walked toward him. Gyges slowed. The man closed the gap with long strides. It didn't seem like the man meant him harm, but Gyges was still uneasy. When the man was within ten feet, Gyges stopped and gave an unenthusiastic smile.

"Good afternoon," the man said. "Are you Peter Gyges?"

"Ah . . . yeah. Why?"

"Consider yourself served." The man shoved a manila envelope into his hand, then strode off toward the marina parking lot.

Gyges turned the envelope over in his hands. No markings on the outside. Just his name and a snapshot of him on The Ghost. The picture infuriated him. This kind of thing must be against the law, he thought. Spying on people without their knowledge. He tore open the envelope.

Divorce papers.

He shoved them back into the envelope without reading them. Maybe later. He didn't want the distraction now.

He walked to the boat and climbed aboard.

* * *

Gyges pulled a beer from the mini-frig, twisted off the cap, and downed half the bottle in one long gulp. Really cold, just the way he liked it. He reviewed his notes for forty-five minutes. Then, after another beer, he set about making a list. He combined several items, crossed out a few others, and numbered the list. Then he re-wrote it all in order of importance. He opened the calendar on his touch phone and assigned every item a date and, in some cases, a specific time of day. He read through the list several more times. Pride and relief washed over him.

This was it—the complete action plan.

Yes, Peter Gyges was a man to be reckoned with now. Brilliant. Ruthless. Wrathful. King Shit of Fuck You Mountain.

He fingered the ring appreciatively.

Then he retrieved the brown envelope from below and brought it back on deck. He opened it and read through the legal document. Angela had requested a meeting with him and his lawyer to hammer out the details of the property issues. He set the papers down. He felt no emotion beyond a sense of relief. No kids to complicate things. A nice clean break. No mess. A simple unhooking of property interests. Merely an economic settlement. The house was close to being paid off, and even better for her, the price of property in Excelsior had skyrocketed since they had bought the house fifteen years before. He only cared about his tools, his fishing gear, and The Ghost. She wasn't interested in any of that. It shouldn't be a contentious process.

He thought about Angela for the first time in a long time. Sure, he'd miss her in some ways, but she was part of his old life. That wasn't him anymore. He didn't even know who that was. It was like looking at those childhood photo albums his mother kept. He never felt a connection to the boy in the pictures; that child wasn't him. It didn't even much look like him. And it certainly didn't feel like him. The boy might as well have been a stranger. And just like he had with that foreign bygone childhood, he'd progressed way beyond his life with Angela. It was someone else's boring cardboard world. He could hardly remember it in any detail. It was more of an abstraction, a TV show he'd seen once thirty years ago. And what was there to remember? Or feel? He hadn't even really been alive. They may have been a good match at the time, Gyges conceded, but things changed. She'd be fine, would find a quiet little corner of the world to hide out in. Keep a small garden. Go shopping. A life with no risks and long queues at the supermarket. In bed by ten. Up at six. Living vicariously through TV lives and celebrity gossip. Church on Sunday. Everything safe, secure. Yes, she'd be happy with the small things.

But I'm a bigger fish.

First Tracy. Then Tommy's job. Then who knew what? Right now he had a plan, even if only short term. He was a mover and a shaker. Peter Gyges's long-term elevation to fame, fortune, and power needed time to gestate.

After all, it was only recently that he'd truly been born. And this opening gambit was merely a prelude to his arrival.

* * *

The streets near the Morocco were jam-packed with cars. Gyges had never seen it so full. After circling the block several times, he was forced to park a couple blocks away in an unfamiliar area. As always, he slid the card under the windshield wiper, though he was uncertain its power would reach that far from the cafe. He walked with purpose through the rundown streets, though there wasn't anyone out for him to impress.

When he pushed open the door to the cafe, the place was noisier and smokier than usual. There were men playing backgammon at every table. It was like league night at a bowling alley. No one seemed to notice as he steered his way through to the back. But the chess room was empty. He had hoped to find Bhuto here. With the events at OH, Gyges had forgotten about trips to the Downtown Club and meeting Bhuto for a steam. He felt bad for standing up Bhuto and hoped he wouldn't be offended, but he had no way to contact his friend—no phone number or address. They'd always made plans in person. He wanted to find Bhuto and explain, maybe even share some of the events of the last few days. He knew Bhuto would be interested in his strategic maneuvering.

He wandered back to the bar. He didn't relish the idea of talking with the spider midget, but he wanted to find Bhuto. Oscar was serving beers at the other end of the bar. He looked busy. Another bartender approached. It was strange to see someone other than the Oscar creature behind the counter. Not that this guy didn't give Oscar a run for his money. He was dark brown with a face heavy with pockmarks. An ugly scar snaked from outside his left eye down his cheek. Goddamn, Gyges thought, this place staffs every out-of-work sideshow freak in town.

"What cha wan?" the man mumbled.

"Looking for a friend. Bhuto. You seen him here tonight?"

"Don't know 'im," the man said, and turned and walked away.

Hmmm . . . and just as friendly as the little one, too.

The man went directly to Oscar at the other end of the bar, leaned over, and spoke into his ear. Oscar looked up but didn't acknowledge Gyges.

That little fuck, Gyges thought. Screw it. He stormed over, shoving past men waiting and drinking, until he was directly in front of Oscar.

"He's not here," Oscar said, pulling a beer for a customer.

"I can see that. Do you know when he might be back?"

"Nope," said Oscar, taking money for the beer. He continued to work the bar, avoiding any direct eye contact with

Gyges.

"Do you know where I might get a hold of him?"

"Nope."

"If you see him, will you tell him I'm looking for him? I was supposed to meet him but got held up."

Oscar rinsed out a bar towel in the sink. He didn't speak.

"Hey, Oscar, why are you such an asshole? I'm just trying to get a message to my friend. What's your problem?"

Oscar turned around and glared at Gyges. The spider on his face moved menacingly as he squinted. "Listen, I don't like you. You're a liar and a thief. I wouldn't let you come here, but the boss, he says you can. So I do what the boss says. But he don't say I have to talk to you or help you—just let you come and buy drinks. Now, you want drink? If not, get away from the bar."

"Wait—the boss? Bhuto owns this place?"

"You want a drink?"

"Hold on! You said the boss told you to serve me. Is that Bhuto?"

"You ordering or not?"

"You really *are* a little prick. Next time you see Bhuto, tell him I was in here looking for him."

Oscar turned back to his work. Why'd I bother? Gyges thought. The creature would never tell Bhuto he was looking for him.

Gyges walked out the door and back toward the Explorer. Away from the main street, a group of men milled about, staring at him as he passed. He heard them talking, and though he couldn't tell what they were saying, he was sure it was about him. His thumb instinctively felt for the ring. Two of the men broke off from the group and followed him. He quickened his pace. They matched his steps. He increased his pace, walking as fast as he could without running, thinking he could make it to the Explorer before they caught up. Just as he reached the car door, however, a heavy hand grabbed his shoulder from behind. Gyges spun around into a glancing blow to the top of his head. He staggered to the left of his car. He caught his balance, pulled both feet under him, and righted himself as he faced his attackers.

They hesitated, sizing him up as he stared back, waiting to strike. Without thinking, Gyges turned the ring and moved behind them. They glanced at each other in disbelief. He grabbed the back of one's hair and smashed his face into the Explorer's rear window. He could hear the man's nose break and saw blood redden the window. The man dropped, clutched his face, and writhed on the pavement. The second man froze in stunned confusion. Gyges wasted no time. He whipped a boot heel into the side of the man's knee. The snap echoed into the night. The knee buckled inward, and the man fell on top of his comrade. The two rolled on the ground, crying out. Gyges jumped on them and stomped on both of them over and over, until he was out of breath, his jeans splattered with blood.

* * *

Still shaking from the altercation, Gyges pulled on the handle of the front door of the Freeman Building. It didn't budge. He tried again. Same result—locked. It hadn't occurred to him that they'd lock the building at night.

Duh, dumb ass, he thought. Why would they leave the fucking building open all night? He scolded himself for not coming sooner. He should have hidden on the fourth floor until most of the employees had left for the night. He didn't know what to do; it was essential that he to get in and access the company server.

Jesus, what a night.

He ventured around the building, hoping to find another way in. In the alley, he discovered a loading dock cloaked in shadow. He halfheartedly tugged at the steel door, but it, too, was locked. He continued down the alley until he'd circled the entire building. There were no windows at all on the ground floor, and any doors he found were exit only, no knobs outside.

He cursed himself for the worthless trip to the Morocco. That fucking prick Oscar. Gyges wanted to kick the shit out of the creepy little bastard. Maybe he would. He could go back later, unseen, and unload on him. That derelict Munchkin wouldn't know what hit him. Literally. The image brought a smile to Gyges's serious face. At least that would be satisfying capstone to his day.

He circled the entire building. No way in. He'd have to change plans for the next day. Just then, as he turned to leave, a black van pulled up to the front door. Five Asians—Gyges guessed Cambodians, four men and a woman—got out. One of the men unlocked the door. The others unloaded equipment from the back of the van. Of course, he thought—the cleaning crew.

Gyges turned the ring and hustled back to follow the last two men inside. The crew took the elevator to the top floor. Gyges took the stairs.

When he reached the fourth floor, he heard some kind of Asian music playing from a small stereo. The woman had unlocked all the offices, setting the wastebaskets outside each door. As she made her way down the hall, one of the men entered each office to do the general wipe-down. Another followed behind the woman with a mobile trashcan and emptied each of the smaller wastebaskets. Behind him, the last two men vacuumed. The crew crisscrossed down the hall, alternating offices. When they'd finished each, they returned its wastebasket and locked up. All of them talked and laughed. Gyges admired their efficiency. But he couldn't understand how or why they'd be happy while doing that kind of work.

What a pitiful existence, he thought. They'd be lucky to clock minimum wage. If they wanted more out of their insignificant lives, they'd have to reach out and grab it. Just like he did. But then, not everyone's constitution was constructed from the same metal. Not everyone's destiny was to be envied. Some men were destined to be on top, to be king.

Gyges had to get into the MIS director's office on the

third floor. The crew finished and took the elevator down to the next level. Finally, after forty-five minutes, Gyges followed one of the men into the director's office. After replacing the wastebasket, the man shut the door and locked it. More waiting. Gyges didn't mind; he'd spent many days and nights on water waiting for a bite. He remained still until they finished cleaning the rest of the floor. The roll of their carts and chatter softened as they made their way back to the elevator. Then the distinctive ding that signaled the automated doors.

Gyges turned on the lights and slid into the cushioned chair. He pulled out his notes, booted the computer, and got onto the system without problem. The problem was what to do now. He just stared at the system administrator's screen. It looked nothing like anything he'd used before. He couldn't see any file directories. Nothing even looked familiar.

He knew what he needed: any files between or about Stover, GM, or OH. He couldn't locate a FIND function anywhere. He had no choice but to experiment. At least there was a menu listing. He started with the choices from the administrator's list. An hour later, he found Braddock's directories; then another hour to find his correspondence. He didn't stop to read anything beyond key words. He dumped anything that could be relevant onto a flash drive. There were more than two dozen pieces of correspondence. He couldn't log into Johnny boy's email. Too bad. He repeated the process with Shadmun's directories. Then he moved on through each executive, again downloading whatever looked even remotely relevant. It took hours, but Gyges couldn't figure out a way to search the system globally. It didn't matter. By whatever means, the tortoise beats the hare.

What he really needed were those emails. He was getting ready to cycle back through the top menu when he heard something outside. He hopped up and went to the door to listen. He glanced down at his watch. Six-thirty. Shit, he thought. People were coming to work. He'd been at it for longer than he'd realized. He hurried back to the computer, unplugged his flash drive, and turned off the computer. He cracked the door and then, when he was sure the coast was clear, slipped out of the office.

* * *

He resisted the gentle rocking of The Ghost as long as he could, but after only ten minutes of sifting through the Freeman files, Peter Gyges fell asleep at the keyboard.

18

Bonnie Martel could tell that someone had been on her computer.

Whoever it was had simply exited and powered down without the proper sequence, causing a message window to pop up when she logged on. She'd have thought it impossible, but she couldn't deny the evidence. The records showed that the culprit had logged on in the early morning hours. No one had hacked in from the outside. Moreover, it had been done directly on her machine.

She looked for any sign of a break-in, but nothing looked out of the ordinary. Someone had used a key. Ben, the building manager, kept a master set. He was the only other person to have one. But it didn't make sense that he'd be responsible.

Most unsettling, the person had entered her codes correctly on the first attempt. She was the only one who knew them. There were written copies in John's safe in case of an emergency, but he had no motive to break in and use her codes; he could just ask her for anything he needed. And it was unlikely he'd hack into her computer to look through his own files.

Bonnie spent the morning tracking the hacker's activity—every directory and file, every piece of correspondence and time, everything he or she had downloaded—but she couldn't come up with a common thread or rationale. The administrative file search function hadn't been used, so there wasn't a record of key words. She'd have to read the documents to understand what they were looking for.

She picked up the phone to inform Braddock about the break-in but then put it back down. She didn't know what to tell him—someone had broken into her office and used her password to access dozens of files and documents, but she couldn't find a connection without going through all of them? The little bastard would crucify her. He was always quick to blame others for mistakes and even quicker to steal credit for their successes. John didn't know shit about the computer system, however much he pretended. If she called him now, he'd subject her to a round of ignorant questions and she'd have to explain a bunch of technical stuff he wouldn't get anyway.

She'd find a better explanation for the theft. Maybe then she'd let him know. Right now, she thought, mum was the word.

Then Bonnie changed the passwords and codes.

* * *

Gyges woke up drooling on the computer keyboard. He rubbed the spit from his cheek and checked his watch. One in the afternoon.

He tossed a bag into the Explorer and drove downtown. He dropped off his clothes at a twenty-four-hour cleaner. Then he stopped at a men's clothing store not far from the health club. He was a powerhouse, and it was about time the rest of the world noticed. You gotta dress for success, he told himself. He picked out three suits and some shirts to go with them and left them all to be tailored for a custom-fit. When he paid the bill, well over three thousand dollars, the store tossed in a handful of striking ties.

Gyges headed to the club to pick-up some cash to pay for his new look and get in a quick steam to settle him down for a long night ahead. He changed into his workout clothes and wandered through the club. His attention was drawn immediately to a redheaded woman using the treadmill. He mounted a stationary bike behind her so he could watch her walk. After about thirty minutes, she headed back to the locker room. Gyges followed her, splitting off to enter the men's locker room, only to emerge a moment later unseen.

He watched the woman get undressed and followed her into the shower. She was beautiful and he wanted her. In the past, he would never have considered that he could have a woman like this. But now he saw no reason why he couldn't, or shouldn't. It was all a simple matter of plotting, arranging, maneuvering. Getting her into bed, he thought, wouldn't be that hard.

He followed her back to the dressing area and watched her dress. While she was drying her hair, he cribbed her name and address from her wallet, then hurried back to the men's locker room. He got dressed and checked his notepad for her name and address: Erica Vincent, Far Hill, Wayzata. He rushed out the locker room door but did not see her in the hall or near the front desk. Neither did he find her outside. He checked his watch. He had time to check her neighborhood and then head to Freeman.

He had a general idea of where Erica Vincent lived. He thought he had driven though the area once or twice a couple of years before, when he and Angela had considered moving out of Excelsior into a more fashionable neighborhood. It took him a half hour to get to her neighborhood. He was right; he had been here before. He found her street and then quickly located her house. It didn't appear that anyone was home. He made a single pass so as not to draw attention to himself. Now that he knew where she lived, he could return another time when he didn't have such pressing business.

* * *

Gyges was back at The Ghost by five to review his score from Freeman. He found correspondence between Braddock and some guy at Stover named Phillips regarding a meeting about a possible purchase. He copied the name into his notepad. If he couldn't find what he needed, he'd have to speak to the man. Accompanying the email were several other meaningless reports on Stover's financial backing.ABgyges also found a memo from Braddock to Shadmun that implied that Stover was backing out of the deal.

There were several emails from General Motors. Nearly all concerned the poor quality of Freeman's fasteners. He also found a copy of the companies' original fastener contract. The two-year deal was effective for another two months. The complaints went back a year and had grown in number. Clearly, GM's frustration had grown with Freeman's inattentiveness to the complaints. Three months before, however, the complaints had tapered off. Gyges couldn't tell if GM had given up or if Freeman had finally resolved the problems. He couldn't find anything on GM's decision to not renew the contract, but the end date was useful. He figured GM had simply met with Freeman in person. If there was written notice, he hadn't uncovered it yet.

When he finished going through everything, Gyges sat back with some disappointment. The useful information was pretty meager. He'd have to go back that night and figure out how to access the email files for more stuff on GM and Stover.

Then he remembered that he hadn't checked his phone messages all day. Since Tracy's last meeting, he'd kept his phone on silent and hadn't noticed that Hosbinder had called him several times.

He called her; to his surprise, she answered on the first ring.

"Mr. Gyges—it's about time," Hosbinder said before he could say hello.

"Yeah, I know. My apologies. I've been really busy reviewing my team's information. It looks like Freeman lost one of its biggest customers. I've been running that down."

"Good, good. We talked about the pipeline for future business. Glad to see you're doing something on that. We've checked on the downsizing. They've cut their plants down to skeleton crews—just enough people to get a little product out the door."

"My team is visiting all the plants right now. We should see that when we go on site. I'm going to Austin tomorrow, actually."

"Yes, it should be obvious right away. My guess is these places look like ghost towns. I'm convinced now that they're playing games to make the numbers look good long enough to dump it. Let me know what you find." She hung up without a goodbye.

* * *

Gyges's trip to the Freeman Building to gather more information that night was a complete bust. The MIS director had changed the passwords. He was late getting to the floor with the cleaning crew to get into Braddock and Shadmun's offices. He came away with nothing. His brilliantly conceived plan was not working out the way he had expected. His anxiety rose.

19

Gyges was up, on his third coffee, and heading south on 35 to Austin by six a.m. He wanted to be there waiting when Shadmun arrived. He knew Austin fairly well, as well as the general vicinity of the Freeman plant. The GPS he'd scored within days of finding the ring would lead him to the exact location. Close to an hour south, he passed the mega sporting-goods store Cabella's. He wondered as he passed how long it had been since he'd gone fishing.

The last time was the trip to the Whitefish chain, when he'd found the ring. Had it really been that long? It was an unheard-of lapse for him. He even fished winters, spent Sunday afternoons watching the Vikes and jigging for walleyes at Patrick's icehouse on Minnetonka. A twinge of nostalgia passed through him. He'd definitely have to stop at Cabella's on the way back from Austin. He loved to just walk around and admire all the gear.

He reached the Freeman plant thirty minutes later—no gate, no guard in the lot. Just an open lot with a few cars. At six-forty the first shift trickled in. He waited in his car ten minutes, then followed a short parade into the parking lot. Then he held off another couple of minutes, until the heaviest in-coming traffic slowed a bit, drinking his coffee and pretending to read the paper. He noticed five Explorers scattered about—his would be invisible in its unremarkable visibility. But the number of cars wasn't what Hosbinder had suggested. It wasn't a ghost town. That she'd been wrong worried him.

By seven, cars filled the lot. Gyges's Explorer was tucked away in the middle. He opened his door and stepped out. After taking a slow look around, he bent down to make like he was tying his shoe. Hidden by cars on both sides, he turned the ring and disappeared. He walked up to the building and passed the production workers' entrance. The deadbolt was still locked; no one was in the office yet. He walked back to the empty visitor's spaces to wait for Shadmun's arrival.

Not long after, a rusty pickup rolled into the plant manager's spot. Gyges laughed from his perch on an Accord's fender just behind the reserved spaces. What the hell was this guy doing? he wondered. Maybe he was new or just messing with the manager. But his amusement changed when a man in a suit emerged from driver's side and walked to the front office. Not the usual plant manager's ride. He remembered that Shadmun and Braddock had told the O'Briens that there had been a lot of turnover. He caught up to the manager and edged in behind him. Out of the corner of his eye, he saw a silver Tundra pull into a visitor's spot.

Inside, the manager turned on the lights and started the computers, printers, and copying machines. Gyges gazed out the front windows at Shadmun stepping from the Tundra. Good, he thought, the main players were taking the stage. He stepped back from the door when Shadmun entered.

"Anybody home?" Shadmun called from the atrium.

"Just getting some coffee on. Want some?" came the reply from the back.

"Please. Cream. No sugar."

"Be there in a minute. Just head into my office."

Shadmun shuffled past the receptionist desk to the back of a short hallway. Gyges followed but remained quiet and cautious; he didn't want to be betrayed by the sound of his footsteps on the tile floor. The last office door on the right was open. Shadmun went in. Gyges heard the manager behind him and backed out of the way to allow him to enter. Then he slipped in and tucked himself into a back corner.

"There ya go," the manager said, handing Bob his coffee.

Shadmun took a sip from the steaming cup. "Not bad, Ralph. Geeze, you do everything—open up, turn everything on, make coffee . . ."

"I wouldn't have taken the job if it wasn't so glamorous," said Ralph. He delivered the zinger deadpan, but Gyges detected more than humor in his reply.

He thought Shadmun had noticed, too.

"Where's the office staff?" Bob asked, blowing into his coffee.

"Martha's here at eight," said Ralph. "She has to get her mother settled before she comes in. The rest took other jobs or didn't want to come back from the layoff. I hired two temps to fill in, but they both have child-care arrangements that don't allow them to start before nine."

"You should have gotten someone else," Bob said.

"Right . . . these are such plum jobs, I had so many choices."

"I don't care what gene pool you draw from. The OH people are going to be here the day after tomorrow, and this place has to look staffed."

"Yeah, Bob, I know. I've got it covered."

"Oh, and those three bitches who wouldn't come back from layoff—make sure the unemployment office knows they turned down the work."

"Feel free to make that call yourself," said Ralph. "I'm not screwing them like that."

"What? You forget who pays you?"

Ralph's face and neck turned a splotchy red and his eyes narrowed, "Go ahead and fire me," he challenged. "I dare you. I only came back for this charade because I needed the money. But," said he continued, leaning in closer to Shadmun, "I don't need it bad enough to take any more shit from you. You wanna handle the OH folks yourself? Go right ahead. I'll be sure to let Braddock know why."

"Okay, chill out. I was just kidding. Geeze." Bob

brushed some imaginary lint from his arm. "What's up with the production call-backs? The lot looked pretty full."

"I got enough to run the place and look productive for a couple days. After that, we're out of parts. If you want anything more, I have to order it this morning."

"No, that should do. You know we can't incur any more expenses."

"That's what I thought, but . . ."

"What's inventory look like?"

"Like it did before layoffs. There's a little in the shipping area—not much. After a couple days, there won't be anything left."

"Perfect. Leave the stuff in shipping as it is. Put the rest in the warehouse. I've got ten boxes of printouts and reports for your girls to file and store for OH. You mind helping?"

"I'm going to finish this coffee. I'll call maintenance to bring them in."

"Great. I'm gonna walk the plant and make sure everything looks all right."

"Knock yourself out," said Ralph. He sipped his coffee.

"I'll be back in an hour, and then I'll show Martha and those temps what I want done with the reports and what to say to the OH fucks. You and I still need to go over some stuff, too."

"You know where to find me."

* * *

Gyges followed Shadmun around the plant for over an hour. He didn't know anything about the business of assembling air cleaners and filters, but it looked normal to him. Work was getting done.

At one point, he left Shadmun to follow two employees to the break room and listen in. It was clear they'd been laid off for the previous three months. Freeman had called them back due to a bunch of "new orders." No one knew how long they might work, but the word was that the new orders could see them through for the next six-to-nine months. Other rumors circulated among the men, as well—some company in the east had negotiated a buyout, Freeman was bankrupt, they were adding a second shift for a new product line, the plant would soon close, with the work transferred to their oil filter assembly plant in the south, Freeman would give workers the opportunity to relocate to that plant, and, conversely, workers wouldn't be invited to relocate.

Gyges knew the OH team wouldn't hear any of it. Standard Operating Procedure was to simply observe productivity of the plant. They never talked to workers—only management. They'd check inventory, equipment lists, machinery conditions, and maintenance records. They were trained to examine assets and liabilities, schooled to evaluate customer lists and future orders booked through manual or automated systems. Gathering intelligence through the workers was not part of their MO.

* * *

Back at the main office, three women and Ralph listened to Shadmun's instructions. Gyges assumed the older woman was Martha. The other two were in their twenties, slightly overweight, and had a glaze to their eyes. Shadmun told them the reports he'd brought were the most recent. The computer had broken down, he told them, leaving a backlog of work that had to be bound and filed before the OH visit. If the auditors had questions, they should direct them to Ralph. He'd answer everything, Bob stressed three times. They were to answer no questions themselves; all questions were to be deferred to Ralph. Martha took notes. The other two looked bored or lost. One of them used a paper clip to clean dirt from under her nails while Shadmun instructed them how to label and file each box.

"Are you getting all this?" he asked the girl.

"Me?" She looked around to make sure the question was directed at her.

"Yes, you. You don't seem to be taking notes or anything."

"No need ta," she said, chomping her gum, with an accent considerably farther south than the land of ten thousand lakes. "She doin' all dat," she pointed to Martha. "No need ta have both us doin' the same thang."

"Do you have questions so far?" Bob said, probing for any sign of interest.

"Yeah," the other one interrupted. "Kin I eat at my desk? I gots that hypnoglycomia thang en I gots ta eat every two hours or the sugar in my blood gits low en I pass out."

"Me too," said the paperclip manicurist. "We sisters, and the peoples at the clinic said it was hairdetary. Is thar a snack machine nearby?"

Gyges stifled a laugh but let out an odd noise in the attempt. Shadmun didn't notice. He looked stunned and clearly shaken. The fate of the entire buyout hinged on these two hillbilly sisters. He looked at Ralph for a sign of reassurance, but Ralph just shrugged and muttered something about the temporary-labor pool. Shadmun ended the meeting and sent the sisters in the direction of the snack machine.

When they left, he asked, "God almighty, do those two even know the alphabet?"

"Look," said Ralph, "just tell Martha and me what you want, and we'll get them to do what we need."

"For Chrissake," Shadmun shouted, "do not let them speak to the OH team."

"I'll keep them busy in the back, filing and cleaning up," Martha offered.

"They'll be fine," said Ralph. "The team won't even bother with them. We'll handle everything."

Shadmun wasn't any more relieved, but he finished directing Martha and Ralph. He was reassured by Martha's diligent note-taking. When he finished, he was sure she'd know what to do.

The girls returned with enough candy bars and chips to keep them from passing out for days. Martha picked up a box and escorted the girls to a back office to show them how to run the three-hole punch machine.

Ralph walked with Shadmun to his truck. Gyges followed, but there wasn't anything new to learn. Shadmun had the annoying habit of repeating himself. Ralph obviously knew this, as he stopped listening before they left the building, instinctively shaking his head in agreement when necessary. He didn't bother to wave to Bob Shadmun as he pulled away, and muttered an obscenity to himself before heading back to the office.

* * *

Gyges started the Explorer and drove back to the interstate and north past Cabella's without giving it a second thought. Back to Freeman—he had to get there before Braddock left for the night. There was still work to be done.

20

When Gyges hit town, he phoned Braddock's secretary and pretended to be a friend of John's. Peggy said that John had just left for a meeting. Gyges reached the Freeman Building by mid-afternoon. Parking in his usual spot, he turned the ring in the alley and shadowed a mopey employee into the building and onto the elevator.

Braddock's secretary was typing at her desk. Gyges snuck past her into Braddock's office.

Time was running out; he needed to get into Braddock's email. He'd have to take a risk. He went back to the door and checked the area. Peggy had wandered off somewhere. He quickly closed and locked the door. Braddock's computer was on.

Pure Vanilla.

Despite minor setbacks, Gyges more and more sensed some invisible will on his side moving everything into position. He had never been religious. This wasn't a guardian angel or higher power. "Will" was the best he could describe it. He remembered back to that first night in the garage—that bizarre feeling when he had intuitively understood that reality itself was malleable. Maybe he was willing all this into being and that was the overwhelming physical and emotional power that dizzied him in those initial spurts with the ring. Or maybe, he speculated, the ring's power was different for everyone, simultaneously cloaking its user while unleashing and augmenting whatever inner attributes defined their character.

Fuck, he didn't know. It sounded good. And more importantly, it felt right. Both inside his prideful heart and in the evidence of the reality unfolding before him, the obstacles crumbled.

This shit was easy.

With the recognition came contentment. The universe wanted him to succeed; he was in tune with righteousness. He didn't yet know how the final pieces of his gambit would come together, but he was certain they would. He just had to trust in the process—and in himself. All would be revealed. Que Sera, sera.

Fearlessly, he opened Braddock's email and scanned his Inbox for messages related to O'Brien, GM, or Stover. He found three. He slid a flash drive into the USB port and dumped them there. He'd read them later. He was confident, not stupid. Then he searched the Sent directory and repeated the process. It took a bit longer, but he discovered several messages. Finally, he opened the Trash directory. He smiled. It hadn't been emptied in weeks. There were dozens of subject headings regarding OH, GM, and Stover. He dumped those onto his drive, too. He closed Braddock's email to search the desktop for more correspondence when he heard movement outside the door. On instinct, he pulled the flash drive from the USB, then realized that he had forgotten to eject. He hoped he hadn't lost anything.

He heard a key in the lock. The door opened.

"Why is this door locked?" Braddock asked Peggy.

"I don't know. I thought you did it."

"No, I left it opened. I hate unlocking it every time I get back."

"It locks when you close it."

"Thanks, Peggy. I'm aware of that. Were there any calls?"

"Just one. He said he'd call back."

"Who was it?"

"He didn't say."

"Did you bother to ask?"

Peggy didn't answer.

Braddock just sighed, walked away, and muttered, "Just get Bob on his cell." He entered the office, closed the door, and went to the credenza behind his desk. Behind the right-side door was a mini bar. He retrieved a half-full bottle of bourbon and a snifter, poured a generous amount, slammed it, and poured another. Then he screwed the cap back on the bottle and put it on the desk.

The phone rang.

He hesitated with his arm resting on the back of his chair, staring at the opposite wall. He sighed again and plopped down into the chair and pulled the phone up to his ear like it required his remaining energy.

"All right, put him through." John rubbed his eyes and said, "Bob, where you at? . . . Still? What's the holdup? . . . Shit. Well, how bad are they?" He listened and took another drink. Then another. He swallowed and said, "Shit. What the fuck is the matter with Hodges? He knows how critical this is. He shoulda found someone else. Jesus Christ."

He took another drink.

"All right, but we're really rolling the dice here. I don't like it. If we lose this because he screwed up, I'll open a vein. His. What about the other managers? . . . Good . . . Any other issues? . . . Okay, call me when you get in."

He hung up the phone and slouched in his black ergonomic chair, his head sliding down the padded back. The stem of the snifter dangled lightly between his fingers. Gyges thought he looked like a pensive child king on a throne built for ancient titans.

Heavy is the crown and all that, huh, Johnny boy?

Gyges thought back to the sisters at the Austin plant. They might be a real problem. He realized that he was in the same boat as Shadmun and Braddock, though for different reasons. Regardless, their scam had to work, and these two dimwitted chicks from Alabama might undo all their careful planning. Millions hung on the OH team believing the plant was running at full capacity. Sometimes the lowliest pawn was the key to the entire attack. At the same time, a part of Gyges wished they would screw it up. There would be a kind of cosmic justice in it. Actually, he was almost gleeful at the prospect. But he made a conscious wish that they wouldn't, not wanting to tempt the fates by rooting for the wrong side.

Braddock finished his bourbon and slammed the glass on his desk. He sat up straight and pulled the mouse forward. Gyges seized the opportunity; the red light on the surge protector went out as he switched it off.

"Oh, now what? Fuckin' perfect. This fuckin' machine."

Gyges switched the surge protector back on and heard the computer power up. He moved silently behind Braddock, entering the heavy bourbon and cologne aura that surrounded the small man. When the desktop finished loading, Braddock went back to his email. He entered his password: Screw_em.

Exactly, lil' Johnny boy, Gyges thought. Exactly.

* * *

Gyges sat inside his Explorer two blocks from O'Brien Holdings. He'd been so involved with the day, he'd again forgotten to check his phone messages. Two calls from Hosbinder. He called her back. The phone rang twice before going to voicemail.

"Professor," Gyges said as he got out of the car and slammed the door. "Sorry I missed your calls. I've been in Austin all day. I'm going to be unavailable until late, so I'll talk to you tomorrow. You were right about Freeman—at least, in terms of the Austin plant. It was a shell. They've gutted the operation to look good for the quarter. I saw it for myself. Good job. Talk to you tomorrow when I pick up your final report. Expect a call from me around nine."

He hung up and turned the ring before walking the rest of the way to the building.

It was past five; Gyges headed straight to Tracy's office. Most everyone was gone, and Capt'n D was no exception. He powered up Tracy's computer and entered the password: Drive. He scanned the email for any field reports. He found two attached to emails from team leaders. He read through them quickly and then, wanting to be sure he understood, went back and read them again. Both teams had given clean reports. That left Austin and the fastener plant. There were only two days left; surely they'd be in tonight. But if they didn't come until the morning, Tracy would see them and recommend a pass on Freeman.

Gyges had two hours to kill until he had to head back to Freeman for the last piece of his work there. If the reports didn't come through by then, he'd have to return. It could be a long night. All this driving around was crazy, but he didn't have a choice; it was the only way to see both ends. He did not wait patiently. He fidgeted and fussed. Increasingly agitated, he kept checking the screen, but nothing came across. Then it occurred to him the reports might already have been in. Tracy could have moved them elsewhere. The thought sent a hot flash through his body. He suddenly felt nauseous.

He hopelessly searched Tracy's files and directories for the other two reports. He was no better than Johnny boy. The uncertainty was killing him.

Get it together, pussy. No time left to lose your nerve. Trust in the process.

He stopped and took in a few deep breaths. Without realizing it, he had opened a complete log of all his tardies, absences, conversations, and work assignment assessments—Tracy's arsenal against him. He wanted to delete the file. It could all disappear with one determined push at the key. His finger hovered above the key. More than likely, it would only tip Tracy off. All this work would be in vain. Reluctantly, he closed the file.

Whatever will be, will be.

The computer beeped as a new email arrived. The report from the fastener team. Gyges eagerly read the attached report on the customer base. The team had discovered that Freeman had lost the GM account. It was a simple two-line comment: "A review of the customer database reveals that GM has notified the division that they will not be renewing the contract for the next fiscal year. They are not satisfied with the quality of the product."

Gyges knew what had to be done. If they missed the GM issue, it would be fine. The deal would go through. Luckily, there was still time; Tracy had not seen it. The guillotine would fall. Capt'n Douchebag's fat head would roll.

He deleted the word *not* twice, changing the two lines to read, "A review of the customer database reveals that GM has notified the division that they will be renewing the contract for the next fiscal year. They are satisfied with the quality of the product." Then he saved the file over the original. Now Tracy would read the report, print it out, and include it in the overall documentation.

He had managed to dodge this bullet, but there was another in the chamber. Austin's report had not yet arrived— and it probably wouldn't until late the next afternoon at the earliest. The team was probably putting the finishing touches on it right then. Assuming it was bad, he'd be fucked if it came in while Tracy was in his office. He'd have to think more on it, but maybe there was nothing he could do.

In the meantime, he had to head back to Freeman to move the final piece into position. And then he'd have to return to Tracy's office to hide the coup de grâce.

The guillotine was sharpened and ready to go. One way or another, the blade would drop. Peter Gyges let out a long slow breath.

The future's not ours to see. Que Sera, sera.

21

At eight a.m. the alarm on Gyges's phone went off. He grudgingly opened his eyes. As much as he forced himself to concentrate, the cogs of his mind refused to cooperate, demanding more rest. He downed a cup of coffee and tried to remember everything he needed to do for the day. The damn Austin report had cast a shadow that loomed over his mind. The thought made him sick, and part of him just wanted to climb back into bed and hide under his blanket.

He picked up his phone and called Patrick, instead.

"Peter, how you doing, buddy?" Patrick answered in his usual sociable tone. Gyges rubbed the back of his neck, letting out one last yawn. "I heard you're having some health problems. Why didn't you say something? Maybe I coulda helped."

"Look, I need to see you first thing tomorrow morning," Gyges said, ignoring the question. "It's urgent . . . really urgent. Can we meet for breakfast? I have something you have to see—it's absolutely critical."

"Sure. Are you all right? What's this about?"

"Yeah, I'm fine. Don't worry. If I see you in the morning, everything will be fine."

They made plans to meet at the Mill Race Cafe at seven the next morning. Gyges knew he had his attention; Patrick would show up at the meeting in great anticipation.

He hung up and dialed Hosbinder. They exchanged pleasantries, and then she went on to tell him that the report would be ready for pickup later in the afternoon at a copy store a few blocks from the university. She also said that two copies were included as part of the contract, but each additional one would be another hundred. He ordered four total.

Gyges was starting to feel the coffee now, and his mind shook off the shackles of sleep.

* * *

Tracy's office was vacant.

Gyges searched the floor but couldn't find him. Cloaked by the ring, he walked down to the conference room on the floor below. The door was closed; Tracy was already with his Austin team. Gyges was turning over various schemes to get inside when the meeting broke up and the team emerged from the room. No one said anything as they exited back to their offices and cubicles.

Gyges followed Tracy back up to his office. There, Tracy leaned into his leather chair and grabbed the phone.

"Hey, Tommy. Yeah, it's me."

* * *

Gyges's call had disturbed Patrick. He knew he was having trouble with his supervisor. Patrick didn't like Tracy Mackus. The man might get things done, but Patrick didn't like the way he got there. He was a bully and a self-promoter. Patrick had heard the rumor that Tracy expected to take Tommy's seat when he retired. And Tommy had let it be known that he felt the same. Patrick opposed the idea; it would be a big mistake. But in the end, it would be up to Danny, regardless of Patrick's thoughts. It was easy to see why Gyges had problems under the man, and Patrick completely empathized, but ultimately, that didn't matter next to Gyges's poor performance and reputation.

Patrick decided to nose around before he met with Gyges in the morning. He was surprised, after stopping by

Tracy's department, to learn about the two-week vacation. The department was full of speculation; the abrupt vacation was rumored to be a cover for some other problem in Gyges's life. Tracy offered no help. He refused to speak on the matter and referred him to Gerba.

When Patrick approached her, Gerba maintained that the matter was private and that she was not at liberty to discuss it. Patrick gently reminded her whom she was speaking to. She waffled and he waited, but finally she told him. Nothing he learned made him feel better about the meeting. Gyges had sounded desperate on the phone, and this new information only increased Patrick's worry that his lifelong friend was in trouble. Evidently, he was under a lot of pressure here and at home. Patrick felt guilty—Peter was in a bad way and he hadn't even known about it. It was, he thought, an indication of just how far apart they'd drifted over the years.

Not quite sure what more he could do to prepare for the meeting, Patrick thought of Angela. She'd grown up with them as well and had dated Gyges since high school. He knew he could talk to her friend to friend. But when he called the house, the phone was disconnected with no forwarding number. Then he tried the hospital, but they said she'd accepted a job out of town two weeks before. The more he learned, the more concerned he became. He called a few of Gyges's fishing buddies. No one had seen or heard from him in months; he hadn't called or returned their calls. Sterba said he was seeing a doctor and that the stress had affected his physical health. Patrick wondered if all the stress had driven Gyges to some kind of irrational behavior.

He expected to find Gyges in rough shape and tried to steel himself for the meeting. He wasn't looking forward to it; he feared that Gyges had concocted some desperate scheme to redeem his crumbling life and had called Patrick in to help him fix it. Patrick took a long deep breath and felt a terrible sadness.

Patrick got to breakfast early. He hadn't slept well. He found a booth in the back and told the waitress to direct Gyges there when he arrived. He ordered a coffee and prepared for the worst. When Gyges arrived, Patrick was finishing his second cup. He had expected a disheveled unshaven hobo to show up, so he was surprised to see Gyges in an expensive tailored suit carrying a valise. Gyges never carried a valise. He had even changed his hairstyle—it wasn't long anymore, but cut extremely short. He looked younger and edgier. In fact, he looked so different that at first, Patrick didn't recognize him. It wasn't until Gyges stepped to the table that Patrick finally picked up on who he was.

He couldn't deny that Gyges looked better than ever, but instead of reassuring Patrick, this only made him more anxious. Gyges was not a man given to change, and he was never concerned much with his appearance or fashion. But it looked like he had stepped from the glossy pages of the latest men's magazine.

"Wow, Peter. I haven't seen you since you changed your hair. It really threw me off. I almost didn't recognize you. I don't remember you ever having your hair this short."

"Maybe back in grade school. I needed a change."

"I guess so. New suit?"

"Yeah. Armani."

"Jesus! Well, it looks super on you. Fits perfect."

"Yeah, I had it tailored. I like it, too."

"How's Angela?" Patrick asked, seeing an opening to discuss whatever was really going on with his friend's change. "I haven't seen her for a while."

"No offense, Patrick, but I didn't ask you here to shoot the shit about my personal life. There's something going on at work that you need to know about."

Patrick braced himself. He was afraid Gyges was going to ask him to intercede for him with Tracy. "Okay—shoot."

"It's the Freeman deal."

The Freeman deal? Patrick was caught completely off-guard. Why the hell would Peter call him there to discuss that? He wasn't even involved with the deal. "What about it?" Patrick asked, trying to hide his surprise.

"You're getting a recommendation from Tracy's group this afternoon, right?"

"Yes . . . Tracy is giving us a presentation. What's this about, Peter?"

"I've learned some things."

"Really?"

"I have information that may affect not just the Freeman deal, but OH's future as a viable organization. We are in danger of making a terrible mistake, Patrick."

Peter's way of parceling out the information irritated Patrick. The meeting had turned a corner he did not understand. He didn't like not knowing what was going on. "Look, don't be coy. If you have something to say, let's hear it."

Gyges pulled two half-inch-thick bound documents from his valise. He gave one to Patrick and kept the other. Patrick stared at the cover, reading aloud, "The Shell Game at Freeman, by Peter Gyges."

"I've put together a thorough expose on how Freeman is trying to fool OH into buying," Gyges said. He flipped open his copy. "I'm sure there is more, but I couldn't uncover everything in time. There's plenty of documentation you can study, but the main points are outlined in the executive summary."

Gyges waited patiently while Patrick read the two-page summary. When he finished, Patrick just sat there, stunned. He didn't know what to say, because he didn't know what to think. He went back to the summary and then flipped through a few pages of the report.

"Where did you get this?" he finally asked.

"What do you mean? I told you—I wrote most of it. And there's a supplementary report inside from Dr. Hosbinder. She's an expert on business organization with a specialty in forensic assessment. She and her team documented several areas of concern. I followed their suggestions and gathered other information on my own."

"You investigated Freeman? Why? How? I mean, you

haven't been at work for the last couple weeks. You're supposedly on vacation."

"Officially, yes."

"What? I don't get what's going on, Peter. I'm confused. Was this something Tracy told you to do?"

"Well, Patrick, I guess *I'm* confused. I bring you information on how Freeman is screwing us—real solid information. You aren't concerned about that?"

"That's just it. I don't know what you've done."

"I've shown that following Tracy's buy recommendation will be a mistake."

"How do you know Tracy's going to issue a buy recommendation this afternoon? None of us know that."

"I know it. And Tommy knows, because Tracy's already told him."

"How do you know all this? How do I know this is real?"

"How do you know this is real?" Gyges raised his voice. "Do you think I made all this shit up?"

"Honestly, Peter, I don't know what to think. Out of the blue, you ask to meet, and then you lay this report on me. Evidently you believe you have all this evidence for why the buy would be a mistake. I think it's a fair question. I mean, for God's sake, doesn't all this sound a bit odd?"

Gyges's face went tight. Finally he said, "Patrick, if OH buys Freeman, the O'Brien family will be ruined."

"So then why would Tracy issue a buy recommendation?"

"I didn't put it in the report, because I can't prove it— I included only verifiable evidence—but I strongly suspect that Tracy may be responsible for covering up information that would make the acquisition attractive."

"You can't be serious. I know you have problems with this guy, but that's an incredibly serious charge. Can you prove it?"

"No, I can't. I just said that's why I didn't put it in." Gyges paused and sighed. He gazed beyond Patrick to the pedestrians walking outside. "I'm telling you as a friend of the family, as almost a part of the family—this will take the company under, Patrick. Freeman's fastener division lost the GM account. Tracy's going to conveniently omit that from his presentation."

"Goddammit, how do you know this shit? Have you seen his report?"

"No, not all of it, but I know what he'll leave out. You'll see this afternoon."

Patrick grimaced and reread the summary. He feared this was a man sliding into a breakdown. "Who did you say this Dr. Hosbinder is?" he asked.

"She's a leading expert in forensic accounting and business organizations."

"And what's that?"

"It examines business operations to see if there's criminal activity taking place. I hired her, told her I was in charge of the teams checking out Freeman, and let her analyze the reports."

"Jesus Christ, Peter—you didn't have the authority! You'll lose your job over this. I can't save you from this kind of thing."

"I wouldn't expect you to. Besides, I'm ready to lose my job if I'm wrong. I accept that. But either Tracy has made a big mistake or, worse, he's in cahoots with Freeman. Should I lose my job then? When I risked everything for the O'Briens? If anyone goes, it's gotta be Tracy. I mean, if I'm right."

"Fuck me," Patrick said. "I don't know. Why didn't you come to me with this sooner?"

"I didn't think anyone would believe me. I thought this was the only way to prove it. And I have. I know I'm right about Freeman. What's the worst-case scenario if you pass? Maybe you miss out on an opportunity. But if you go ahead with this and I'm right, the entire O'Brien Empire is done, over. Have your old man call Stover. He probably knows 'em. Danny knows practically everyone in the region. Ask them if they were going to buy Freeman but passed. That's the other company. The one Freeman is holding over your head. There is no other offer on the table. That deadline is there to force us into a rushed decision."

Patrick studied Peter's face as he spoke. His whole approach was off, but Patrick had to admit that his friend was making sense.

Gyges continued, "If your old man finds out that Stover passed on this buy, you'll at least know that Freeman is jacking us around. You'll know there's no real deadline. I'm sure if you asked for another couple days, they'd flinch and find a reason to grant it. I'm telling you, Patrick—they don't have another buyer."

Patrick remained silent. He didn't know what he'd tell the old man about calling Stover.

"What about you? What if you took the risk? Fuck the old man; you call Stover. Tell 'em Danny asked you to call. Then you can ask 'em about this yourself."

"Not all of us jump from planes without a parachute, Peter. Danny wouldn't like that. Not at all."

"Would he like it any better if . . ."

"Enough. I'll figure it out."

"Okay. I just ask that you let Tracy proceed with his presentation without raising the issue. Here's two more copies for your dad and Tommy."

Patrick took the extra copies. Gyges stood up to leave.

"Would you call me later tonight, lemme know what decision you guys come to? Either way, I'd like to know where I stand. In the end, I'll be vindicated, but I'd like to know if you're going to buy Freeman or not."

Patrick nodded. Before leaving, Gyges put a hand on his shoulder and said, "I know you'll figure this out, Patrick. Once you read through my report, you'll see I what I have done for the family."

As Gyges strode back to the entrance, Patrick reflected that though his friend might be completely nuts, he'd never seen him so confident.

***

Patrick sat at his desk and pored over the report. He'd told his secretary to hold all calls except from Tommy and his father. The report began with the professor's report. There was enough in it alone to scuttle the deal. Gyges's section, however, was a different story. He filled in some of the gaps suggested by the professor, but there was no indication of how he knew all the information. There were pages on what Braddock and Shadmun had said and done but no way to tell how he knew it. And all of it fit with the independent report from the professor. It seemed that Gyges had written from more than an educated guess, reporting on what he knew to have taken place. It was as if he had been there. He'd also referenced emails, documents, reports, and phone and personal conversations that could only have come from inside Freeman.

There were only two possibilities: Gyges had either simply made the shit up or had an inside informant. Patrick leaned toward the informant theory. There was no way Gyges could have pulled all this from his head and been so utterly convinced that he'd be vindicated in the end.

He dialed Dr. Hosbinder in hopes of learning more. They spoke for over thirty minutes. She knew nothing about Gyges's additions to the report, but she definitely knew her stuff. She ticked off a list of red flags in rapid-fire succession from the top of her head. Patrick thought OH should be consulting her more often, though he didn't express this to her. By the time the call ended, he was committed to not buying the company.

Patrick was particularly concerned with Gyges's claim that the fastener division had lost the GM account. If true, a major payoff of the deal would be gone. Interesting too, Patrick thought, that Gyges had referred to Stover as "the other company."

After weighing what could go wrong if he called Stover directly, he decided to chance it. There was no reason not to ask Phillips. If Peter was wrong, it didn't matter, because the deadline was the next day. It wasn't like they could join the line to buy Freeman. Besides, he didn't have to tell Phillips his reason for asking. He knew him almost as well as Danny did. He'd played golf with him and had been to his house on many occasions.

He checked his contact list and phoned Phillips's personal cell.

"Phil. Patrick O'Brien."

"Hey, bub—how's the old man?"

"Ornery as always but too tough for me to do anything about it," Patrick said. "Have you fixed that horrid slice of yours yet? I'm running low on cash and thought I could hustle you for a few bucks on the greens."

"You're welcome to try. When?"

"How about Thursday afternoon? Late—five or so."

"You're on, junior. Bring folding money; I don't take checks. Thursday at five. I'm writing it down."

"Great. Say, Phil," Patrick said in a practiced transition, "while I got you on the horn, I have a business question."

"Always willing to educate the youth," Philips replied. "What's up? Not sure what an asset is?"

"Gee, I'm not, but that's not my question. I wondered if you guys ever looked at buying Freeman Industries?"

"Oh, yeah, we looked at them. They had a fastener division with a GM contract, but the dumb bastards fucked it up and lost it. We broke off the talks with them about a month ago. Why? You guys thinking about throwin' money at 'em? God knows they could use the help. The two dipshits in charge couldn't find their asses with both hands."

"Not really. They just sorta popped up on our radar."

"Oh, speaking of GM, Danny said he might have somebody with a contract with them. Any luck on that?"

"Sadly, not yet. We're still working on it. Hey, I gotta let you go. Some of us have to work for a living. See you Thursday."

So, there it was, Patrick thought, hanging up the

phone. Gyges was right after all. Patrick was certain he had someone inside Freeman feeding him information. The deadline was bullshit. They were fucking with the wrong guys, he thought. The O'Brien brothers would always find some way to even the score. Patrick knew the old Micks wouldn't see this as just business; they'd make it personal. He stood up and headed to the meeting with Tracy.

22

Tracy pulled out the notebook with the raw reports and notes from each team. Then he took out his own folder on Freeman. He went over to the printing department to pick up four copies of his report. Just to make sure there weren't any errors in collating, he quickly flipped through each copy, fanning the pages.

He'd been through the routine a couple dozen times and had stopped feeling nervous around the fifth. They were always the same. Still, he couldn't help but feel slightly uneasy this time around. He'd been rushed to meet the deadline, which created a higher possibility for error. He also hated the Freeman boys. He detected insincerity in their dealings with his team. Shadmun and Braddock were a bit too eager to please. And it seemed like they were hiding something. Tracy preferred to go head-to-head with someone fighting for his own interests—no soft-sell bullshit.

But honestly, he couldn't read the O'Briens either. He got mixed signals. They wanted Freeman, to be sure. They'd set the whole thing in motion. But they didn't like the price—it was considerably higher than they wanted to pay. Theoretically, his group's report was meant to be a straightforward information gathering, analysis, and recommendation based solely on the facts of what they found. In practice, as he'd found out early in his career, it was better for everybody if the report confirmed the brothers' intuitions. They really did want the facts, but they also wanted the facts to confirm that they were right. In this case, he didn't know which way to lean, and that made him nervous.

He couldn't wait until Tommy retired. All his hard work would finally pay off. Some else could assemble these reports. He could see the day when he'd be alongside Danny and Patrick, listening and asking question and then agreeing to follow the recommendations. It wasn't long, he told himself. Tommy had made that clear to him in private.

Tracy walked up the flight of stairs to the meeting room. The O'Briens were already there when he entered the room, chatting about family matters. He sat and waited quietly until they were ready for him. It wasn't long.

Tommy said, "We all appreciate the overtime and extra effort you and your people put into this project, Tracy. It was certainly more rushed than what we normally do—circumstances being what they were. So, why don't you take us through the summary, and then I'm sure we'll have a few questions."

Tracy thanked Tommy and read through the summary. It was a down-and-dirty analysis of the nine key ratios OH used to make a buy decision: current ratio, acid test ratio, inventory turnover, accounts-receivable turnover, debt ratio times interest earned, return on net assets, return on total assets, return on common equity, and gross profit analysis. The ratios looked better than what they typically saw, but that was expected. In the end, Tracy recommended the buy. It was more than they usually paid, but the numbers showed that it was worth more than their typical purchase. Tracy concluded that the higher price would be recouped more quickly because of the higher value.

Danny asked about the condition of the machinery in a couple of the plants. Tracy referred him to the parts of the report that covered those issues. Tommy wanted to know about inventories and sales figures. Once again, Tracy took them to the pertinent sections. Danny followed up with some concerns about the veracity of the reports of increased profits for a couple divisions. How had they been able to turn things around so quickly? Did the numbers really check out? Tracy had answers for these questions too.

The two brothers finally looked at each other and shook their heads. Tracy knew this meant the questions were through and they would wrap up the meeting. He exhaled his anxiety.

Then, surprisingly, Patrick spoke up. "I know it wasn't something you were asked specifically to do, Tracy," Patrick began, "but in looking over things at Freeman, did you ever find out the name of the other company whom they said made an offer?"

Tracy felt a small patch of heat on the back of his neck. What the hell was this? he thought. Patrick rarely asked any questions, and Tracy often wondered what the kid's role was in these decisions. He figured they were grooming him for Danny's seat down the road, that sitting in on meetings was like an apprenticeship for him. Well, children should be seen and not heard, he thought, and that old saw applied here. "That wasn't part of my assignment," he replied.

"I know; I said that. That's not what I asked."

"Ah, no, they didn't share that with me."

"Okay. Do you happen to know the fastener division's largest customer?"

The question confused Tracy. It wasn't the sort of thing typically asked in these meetings. Too low-level a detail. Jesus, Tracy thought, the kid had been in enough of these things to know it wasn't appropriate.

Tracy looked at Tommy for help.

"Patrick, what's the interest here?" Tommy said, picking up Tracy's non-verbal prompt.

"It's GM, isn't it?"

Tommy looked back at Tracy in a way that indicated he was interested in the line of questioning. Danny leaned forward as well.

"I believe you're right. Yes, I do recall GM being the largest customer in that division, but I'd have to double-check to be sure."

"Do you know the status of that contract?" Patrick asked.

"Status? I'm not sure, lemme . . ." Tracy said as he dug out his own notes.

"I'm wondering if there've been any problems with that contract."

"If there were, I'm sure my people would have reported them," said Tracy, locating his backup file on the fastener division. "Give me just a minute to look for the customer section." He read through the notes, comments, and emails from the team on customer base. Then he found it. Thank God, he thought. "Great, here it is. I thought it was in here. The notes from the team indicate that GM extended the contract and is satisfied with the quality of the product."

Tracy looked up from his notes in time to catch a small shrug from Danny to Tommy. Patrick looked at him the way an experienced poker player does when he has just doubled down on your bet.

Tracy had no idea what had just transpired. He didn't like not knowing why things were asked in these meetings—it made him edgy.

"Any other questions?" Danny asked Patrick.

"Nope, I'm good," said Patrick. "That's all I needed to know. Thanks."

"Again, Tracy, thank you for your excellent work," Tommy told him. "Please convey my appreciation to your team on the fine work they've done. We'll let you know our decision later today."

"Thanks; I look forward to it," said Tracy.

As Tracy rose to leave, he felt a pressure on his left arm and toppled from the chair, sprawling against the near wall and spilling his notes on the carpet.

"Tracy—are you all right?" asked Tommy, launching up from his chair.

"Damn, yeah. I'm fine—guess I must have caught my sleeve on the chair," Tracy said, looking up from the floor redfaced. He hurried to gather his papers. The other three men just watched him.

"Are you sure you're okay? Nothing broken?" asked Danny. "That was quite a spill."

"No, I'm fine, just fine," he said and stood up. He quickly left without another word.

"I hope he's okay," said Tommy when the door closed.

"His pride might be hurt—not much else," Patrick replied. "I wonder why he tripped. He sure was in a hurry to leave."

"What are you talking about? And what the hell was behind all those questions? You never say anything unless you've got some—"

"Reason to do so," Patrick interrupted. "I do."

"Well, I thought it was inappropriate to ask if he knew who the other buyer was. How's he supposed to know that?" Tommy said.

"There is no other buyer."

"What?" Danny asked.

"Freeman has been lying to us. There *was* another buyer, but they pulled out about a month ago, I'd guess about the same time Freeman gave us that cock-and-bull story about the deadline and the increased price."

"Why didn't you say something earlier?" Danny said.

"I just found out myself this morning. Don't you want to know who the other buyer was?" Patrick could barely restrain himself.

"You seem to know everything. Just fill us in, would you?"

"Stover," Patrick said, unable now to hold back a grin. "They were the other buyer."

"You're shitting me. Who told you that?" his father asked.

"I talked to Phillips less than two hours ago. He said they were interested at one time but pulled the plug over two months ago."

"Cocksuckers!" Tommy said. "How did this come up

in conversation? You weren't talking about the deal, were you? Damn it, Patrick, you know better than that."

"I wasn't talking to him about the deal. I do know better than that. Thanks, but I don't need a lecture on negotiating for OH."

"How did you even know to ask him?" added Tommy.

"A third party. I went down to Danny's office to get him to call, but he wasn't in, so I verified it myself. Made a golf outing the excuse. He might suspect we're thinking about buying them, but I didn't say anything about it."

"So there's no deadline."

"Nope. It's just a ploy by Braddock and Shadmun to make us think it was a take-it-or-leave-it situation."

"Not a bad negotiation strategy. We've done as much. Hard ball but fair ball," said Danny.

"Well, before you decide whether the ball was in or out, you may want to get another angle on the play," said Patrick.

"What are you talking about?" Tommy asked.

"Don't you want to know why Stover pulled out?"

"Phillips told you that too? My, you've been thorough," said Danny.

"Stover found out they'd lost the GM account, which had been their only interest in buying Freeman."

"Shit, we were going to peddle that division to them right away."

"That can't be right," said Tommy. "Tracy said that contract was solid."

"Then either Tracy's mistaken or something more nefarious is going on here," said Patrick.

"You want me to believe he lied to us? Come on, Patty," Tommy said. "He's a straight shooter. Arrogant and pushy sometimes, but honest—too honest for his own good. I don't like the insinuation."

"I didn't say he lied. I said it was a possibility. The other is that his people missed the info on the GM deal. In which case, it's incompetence, not dishonesty. Feel any better?"

"You can ease back on the sarcasm," said Danny. "I guess this puts the deal in a whole new light. We should—"

"I'm not done—there's more, lots more. Braddock and Shadmun basically gutted the company to make it look good. They're gonna sell us an empty shell and take the money and run. Those two caring Christians are trying to fuck us in the ass."

"Goddamn, Patrick," exclaimed Tommy. "How do you know all of this?"

"Like I said, I just found out this morning. I didn't believe it all either until I started checking it out. That's what led me to call Phillips—to confirm what I learned this morning."

"You keep saying you learned about it all this morning. How?" asked Danny.

"Let's just say I was given an alternate report on Freeman." Patrick pulled out Gyges's report.

"From whom?" Tommy asked. "Are you checking on my people without consulting me?"

"Easy—I wasn't doing anything at all. This came out of the blue. I was more surprised than you. In fact, considering the source, I didn't believe it at first, either. I do now, though, after verifying most of it." Patrick paused and took a sip of water from the glass in front of him. "The report was written by Gyges."

"Peter Gyges? No fuckin' way," said Tommy. "He's off—and that might be the right word in a number of ways. The poor bastard's on vacation to cope with a bad stress condition."

"Yeah, I know the whole story. I checked with HR, but he told me this morning that his stress story was just a cover to get the real scope on Freeman. Here's his report. He knew all about the GM contract, and he knew about Stover too. He knew that's why they pulled the plug, but he didn't know it would be so important to us; he just mentioned it as a way for me to check the veracity of his conclusions."

"This is just nuts," muttered Tommy when Patrick handed him the report. He opened it and scanned it. "There's no way he could have done all this by himself."

"I thought the same. Frankly, when he dropped all this on me, I told him I didn't believe him. I thought he'd cracked up. But he didn't do it all by himself. He hired a consulting firm from the university to help. Their report's included there in the appendix. I called the professor who authored it. She confirmed many of Peter's claims."

"Where did he get the money to hire these people?" asked Danny.

"He used ours," said Patrick, smiling. "You'll probably get the bill in a couple days. They ain't cheap, by the way."

"Who the fuck gave him permission to do that?" asked Tommy.

"No one. He did it on his own initiative."

"I knew those employee-empowerment tapes we gave him would bite us in the ass one day," laughed Danny. He'd been reading the summary while Patrick and Tommy sparred. "Patrick, all of this is true, then?"

"Hard to say about all of it. But look—the stuff from the university is all proven and well-documented. And what is only concluded from the evidence is likely to be what we'd surmise as well. So their stuff is definitely solid. But Gyges has all this other information that isn't in the appendix. Like the Stover and GM info. It isn't clear how he knows so much, but I think he has a mole inside Freeman."

"Christ, this sounds like a plot from a LeCarre novel," said Tommy. "I don't understand why he didn't just bring this to Tracy. Why did he do it all so surreptitiously?"

"I'm not sure, either," said Patrick, "but I think it's because he thought Tracy wouldn't listen. Or worse. It looks to me like Tracy wants him fired."

"Well, our friend hasn't been exactly a stellar performer here," replied Tommy, clearly irritated by any criticism of Tracy.

"I know, but that does—at least in part—explain his

reticence to bring this to Tracy . . . or you, for that matter. Honestly, if he had, would you really have listened to him? Would you have given him permission to hire that consulting firm?"

"Absolutely not. Still, Gyges doing all this is a shock. I didn't even know he'd be capable of these sorts of things. It seems so out of character for him. He's usually so . . ."

"Okay, okay. So, what do we do next?" asked Danny.

"Clearly, we don't buy Freeman," Patrick replied.

"Agreed. I'll call and decline. Plus I wanna give the bastards a piece of my mind. Trying to screw us—we'll find a way to pay them back down the road."

"Can I make another suggestion?" Patrick asked.

"Shoot."

"Don't call them. Let the deadline pass. They'll call you. Gyges thinks they'll drop the price. They're betting everything on sneaking this deal past us. The university people have preliminary data on what they're really worth. If you look at the numbers, it's more like something we ordinarily do. Let's wait."

Tommy and Danny looked at each other and grinned.

"I like that idea. Let them make the next move."

"That settles it, then. We wait, let the deadline pass, and if they call us, play coy. Let's see if Gyges is right. First, I think they'll offer to extend the deadline. If they do, we'll know for sure that they've been trying to cheat us. I decline and say the price is out of our range. They'll drop the offer, and then we'll screw 'em to the wall. Tommy, can you take these figures and have your people work up a more precise number on what they think we can get Freeman for?"

"Sure, I'll get Tracy working on it right away."

"Whoa, whoa," said Patrick. "That's a terrible idea. He either missed the call on this by a mile, or worse. If it's worse, he might tip off the folks at Freeman."

"I can't believe Tracy's done this on purpose," Tommy said.

"Why not give the project to Peter?" asked Patrick.

"Have him set up a meeting with the university people and you. Give them whatever other data we have so they can calculate the real value. Sub out the work and don't tell Tracy or our people."

"I don't like that. We've always done our own work on this stuff," said Tommy.

"I like Patrick's idea. Do it. Get a hold of Gyges and set this thing up. Today. I also want to know for sure if Tracy slipped up or if he's in on this. I have some ideas on that. Also, Patrick, you take the calls with Freeman. I'll drop out—it'll send a signal as well."

"Yeah, great signal—the men aren't talking about the deal anymore; deal with the kid," laughed Patrick.

Danny shrugged and smiled. "Hey, sorry. But I think this will work."

23

Gyges followed the three O'Briens out of the meeting room. He was ecstatic—the meeting had worked out even better than he had hoped. Soon he'd be in charge of finding Freeman's real value. Tracy was in deep trouble, no longer a force to be feared. Gyges had neutered the pit bull, and Tracy's days were numbered one way or another. Danny or his surrogates in MIS would find more incriminating nuggets planted in Tracy's emails and files. These would seal his fate.

Gyges thought he should be rewarded for his long and successful campaign, and while it was too early for a real blowout celebration, he could take the afternoon off and loaf for a few days until he was due back from his vacation. Tommy would probably call him later that day or the next.

He headed downtown to the club and arrived after the lunch crowd had returned to work. He opted for a steam—it was senior ladies' aerobics day. Maybe traffic would pick up later when the young professionals filtered in from work. He opened the steam room door to reveal the large brown figure of Bhuto.

"Bhuto—what a surprise! I've been trying to find you. I've missed steaming and scheming with you."

"I heard from Oscar that you were looking for me."

"I wasn't sure he'd pass that on, but I'm glad he did. I've been so busy that I've not been able to shake away, but that's all going to change."

"Good. A man should not be so busy working that he

misses what he's earned. So how *is* work? Your strategy with your boss successful?"

"Funny you should ask—I just came from a meeting about that. It's not finalized, but they're definitely moving in that direction. I took your advice."

"Which piece? I've given you so much!" Bhuto laughed his big laugh.

"The one about maneuvering over his job, not just getting him fired. I think upper management is leaning in that direction, as well."

Bhuto gave him a hearty slap on the back. "Very good, my friend. You have learned well. When will you know for sure about all of this?"

"I would think a week or ten days."

"I'm pleased for you, Petros. You see what thinking strategically can do for you. Thinking several moves ahead in chess is good practice for other things in life as well. Good for you!"

"Do you think we could play again soon?" Gyges asked. "I miss the lessons and the coffee."

"Yes, of course. I miss them, too. How about tonight? I have to change an appointment—a woman." He winked and shrugged. "But I think she can do without me for a night. She'll just have to settle for her husband."

He laughed even louder, slapping Gyges so hard he nearly knocked him off the bench, which only made him laugh harder.

"You don't happen to have any extra steam tea with you? I miss that too."

"No, sorry. I'll bring a big bottle tonight."

"You sure I can't get the recipe? I promise not to tell others or sell it to Coke."

"Some things in life you cannot share even with your friends. You will just have to get it from me. Family secrets are sacred. You understand?"

"Sure, I respect that. But how about sharing your phone number? I realized when I couldn't find you that it would be easier just to call."

Bhuto studied him closely, weighing alternatives. He was clearly hesitant to give out his number. "Only a handful of people have it. I will give it to you, but you must never give it to anyone else. Yes?"

"I promise." Gyges was honored.

"When we dress, we should exchange numbers then. Yes?"

"Yes, of course. I don't know why I haven't given you mine you sooner."

"Good, good. Now we have no excuse for not 'steaming and scheming,' as you say. I like that. Very good."

* * *

On his way out of the locker room, Gyges passed Erica, the redhead whose address he'd cribbed from her license. He'd completely forgotten about her during the ensuing weeks. But now his passion for her stirred him to do more than drive around the block where she lived.

Gyges found her street and quickly located her house. He drove a couple blocks back to a main street, parked in the parking ramp by the lake, and walked back to her house. Before he got there, he turned the ring.

A white Celica was parked in the drive; perhaps it was her car. Maybe her husband's or boyfriend's? He looked inside the only window without a shade pulled but didn't see anyone. At the back of the house were two sets of double windows looking over the yard. None of the shades were drawn. Inside he could see a small dining room and a doorway leading into a kitchen. He heard music and glimpsed a shadow move from one room to the other. It sounded like a woman was humming along to the music.

He waited patiently at the window. Erica soon appeared in the dining room. She was carrying a salad. She set the plate on the table and returned to the kitchen. She was back in the dining room almost instantly with a glass of ice water and a plate of steaming vegetables. When she sat down to eat, he left the window. He continued into the yard and found a screen door between the two sets of windows. The inside door was open to let in the cool evening air. Gently, Gyges turned the handle on the screen door. It popped open with an audible click. He quickly opened the door just enough to get through and silently slid inside the house.

The door opened onto a small landing. To his right were steps leading to the basement. He went straight into the kitchen. He heard footsteps coming his way and moved to his right. Erica appeared and looked at the back door. She closed it, still chewing a mouthful of salad. As she spun around back into the house, Gyges matched his footsteps to hers and followed her in. He saw a wooden board with two sets of keys hanging from wooden pegs. He hesitated a moment, allowing her to get a couple steps ahead, and then carefully wrapped his hand around one of the sets and slid them into his pocket.

He wanted to explore the house, but this was an older house and the floor squeaked in spots. Instead, he waited at the passageway between the kitchen and the dining room and watched her eat.

The phone rang. Erica got up and rushed to a room at the front of the house. Tired from standing, Gyges took a seat at the window. He strained to hear, but he could barely make out her soft voice on the phone. She came back into the room and finished her dinner. When she was done, she took the empty plates into the kitchen and loaded them into the dishwasher. Gyges crept back into the kitchen and watched her start the machine. He smiled to himself. The noise would give him cover.

Erica snatched her gym bag from the floor of the landing and took it with her down into the basement. He took the opportunity to walk through the house. He slipped into her bedroom to look for any pictures or evidence of a man living there with her. Only women's clothes inside the open closet door. None of the pictures on the dresser revealed a man. He returned to the hallway and listened for her. He didn't hear her, so he was surprised to find her sitting in the reading room as he moved down the hall.

Erica sat in a large comfortable chair under a reading lamp. She had put on glasses and looked to be halfway through a romance novel. He wasn't interested in watching her read. He hoped for something more intimate. He remembered the keys he'd taken from the peg. He'd come back soon. He needed to know more before he made his move. He could afford to be patient.

* * *

Gyges was glad to be back at the Morocco even if it meant enduring the dagger stares of the dwarf. He pulled open the beat-up and weathered back door and passed the empty tables usually crowded with backgammon players, straight to the chess room. Although he did not look back toward the bar, he felt the Oscar's rat-like eyes squinting at him. He imagined the spider scowled forward. Someday, Gyges assured himself, he'd catch the little shit unawares and give him and his pet spider a spanking to remember.

Bhuto was waiting for him with the board positioned for Gyges to play white. He smiled; it'd take more than the slight advantage of playing white to beat the fat man. Nonetheless, it was a nice gesture to open the evening.

"Ah, Petros; I thought you might leave me standing again."

"I think you mean 'stand you up,' " laughed Gyges. "No, sorry, there was an accident. I wouldn't miss the chance to be humbled."

"The saints teach us that humility is supposed to be a great virtue," Bhuto said with a grin.

"And you believe them?"

"Oh, no, of course not. This is a stupid idea. I was just wanting to make you feel better." Bhuto laughed his big laugh and slapped Gyges on the back. "Sit down and play. You're getting better all the time. Less made up, more planned. This is good."

Gyges placed himself behind the white pieces. He played carefully, attacking without exposing his king to unnecessary risks, and holding back on his queen. He managed to last longer, but in the end he couldn't keep track of Bhuto's onslaught. He lost again. And again. And again. Each time it was the same. He was not good enough to counter all the possibilities Bhuto unleashed upon him.

The fat man built two or three overlapping attacks that wove in with a defense. Each piece supported another. No freebies, no taking a piece without sacrificing one of his own. What looked like easy conquest, Gyges learned over and over, always turned out to be a ploy to weaken his positional situation, draw him away from defending the point Bhuto wished to attack. It was as if the fat man were orchestrating a violent ballet as graceful to watch as it was devastating and frustrating. Gyges could tell that he had improved, but he still never surprised Bhuto.

After the fourth loss, he said, "I just can't keep track of everything you're doing, so I get surprised. I see you build an attack in one place and react to that, but within that attack, you have concealed another I can't see coming. It seems you have more pieces on your side of the board than I do mine."

"I will give you a little hint, if you like," said Bhuto.

"Oh, please. I'm grateful for any crumbs of advice."

"When you're up against a powerful opponent who plays much better than you, it's wiser to trade as many pieces as possible. Get equal value for equal value. Force a game of attrition."

"Why's that?"

"Someone much superior with a full set of pieces can come at you—you said it yourself—in ways you cannot imagine until you are already defeated. That's because you're not experienced enough to see all possibilities. So the trick is . . ."

"To cut down on the number of possibilities."

"Very good, yes. You will still probably still lose, but

you will last longer and perhaps force a stalemate. At least look for ways to trade queens. Take away his most powerful weapon, even if it means losing yours. Also, trade knights as soon as possible. You can play him to a standstill if you decimate his supporting pieces."

"Why the knights and not the bishops? Bishops have longer range."

"Yes, but it is easier to see what he is up to with the bishops—more limited and hence more predictable. With the knights' crooked moves, it's harder to detect what they are up to. You will be surprised far more often from a knight attack hidden among the other pieces than you will from a bishop. They are the only pieces that can jump others. When you are new to the game, they are hard to use effectively and hard to defend against. Find a way to trade them—your knights for their knights. You'll hang around longer."

"Trade knights early and find a way to trade queens. I'll remember that. Sounds simple enough."

"You can try it next time."

"I suspect you'll have an answer for it."

"Perhaps, but if you focus on trading pieces, you can force a trade whether the other wants to or not."

"Then shall we say same time next week?"

"I won't be available next week. Let's make it two weeks."

"Okay, two weeks. What about a steam?"

"Two weeks for that too."

The two friends walked into the main room together. Then Bhuto stayed behind to talk to Oscar. Gyges didn't even try to make eye contact.

It was only when he pulled the card from the windshield wiper that he remembered Bhuto's promise of a bottle of steam tea.

24

"Mary, did you pick up some of the Freeman files from my office?" Tracy hollered from behind his desk.

"Freeman files? Umm . . . no. I don't think so," Mary stammered. "Are some missing?"

Tracy rose with a sigh and marched to the door. He peered at her with an irritated look. "Yes, I can't find the file with the team reports from the fastener division, or the files on sales and inventory from their Austin plant. Did you take them from my office?"

"No, I didn't take them. Could you have left them at home? Sometimes you work on stuff at home. Maybe they're there. Or in your car."

"Yes, I know I work from home. I don't think so, but I guess I'll have to double-check tonight. You make sure to look around, too. Maybe you've already filed them."

"Oh, that's a good idea," she said. "I hadn't thought of that. Maybe I did."

Mary didn't like lying to Tracy, but she'd been summoned to Mr. O'Brien's office the day before. There were a lot of questions about Tracy and the Freeman deal. Daniel O'Brien made her very nervous; he was a nice man unless he got mad, and he got mad in a hurry. She'd almost quit over it once after being on the receiving end of his temper. Next to him, Tracy looked like a pacifist. Mr. O'Brien had later apologized, but since then, she'd never been at ease around him. The previous day, he'd demanded Tracy's office key and told her that their conversation was not to leave his office. She promised not to tell anyone. She'd bet he had the missing files. She wanted to tell Tracy, but if Mr. O'Brien found out, he'd fire her.

Tracy dropped the rest of his files on her desk. "Go ahead and file these too. If I find the others, I'll bring them in tomorrow. If you find them, just file them with the rest."

"Okay," she said, grateful that the matter was ending there. "I'm sure they'll turn up sooner or later."

"By the way, you see any notice on Freeman?" he asked. "Usually, we've heard by now."

"No, I haven't."

"Hmmm . . . I wonder what the holdup is."

Tracy turned back into his office and dialed Tommy. Tommy's secretary said he was in a meeting and would call him back. While he waited, Tracy made a directory containing all his emails from the Freeman deal. He kept a flash copy for himself and then transferred the directory to the company archives.

His phone rang; it was Tommy.

"Hey, Tommy. Hadn't heard anything on the Freeman deal—wondered if I'd missed it."

"We decided to pass."

"What? We issued a buy recommendation. Why?"

"We had other financial considerations come up at the last minute. We wanted it, but just can't right now."

"I see," said Tracy. "Thanks for the info. I was just curious. Catch you later."

He hung up. He didn't like the news. Tommy had been vague, and Tracy had sensed tenseness in his response. It could be nothing. Tracy hated to see all the work go for nothing, though. Not much he could do about. He had done his job, and that was all anyone could expect from him.

He didn't make those decisions. Yet.

* * *

While Tracy pondered how long it would be before he took over Tommy's job, Gyges sat in Tommy's office. He sat on one side, with Tommy and Patrick on the other. An uneasy silence filled the room.

"We were all shocked by what you discovered, Pete. Shocked, too, by the way you went about this," Tommy said.

"I didn't have a choice. I did what I thought was best for the family. I was concerned something was wrong."

"Why didn't you voice this to Tracy?"

"I did. He's not the easiest guy to talk to. We're not particularly close, and he doesn't respect my abilities. He doesn't use me in a way that benefits the company. Usually I let it slide, but I sensed this deal was a disaster."

"Based on your report, so do we. We want to meet with the university people to assess Freeman's true worth. We'd like you to head the project."

"Great; I'd love to. Finally, something I can sink my teeth into. Tracy's been peddling these made-up jobs to me for so long, I can't express how excited I am for this opportunity to make a real contribution. I've already set up a meeting with Hosbinder—day after tomorrow. Eight in the morning."

"Good—the sooner the better. It'll be the three of us. Then you can run things from there on out."

"Fine by me. Hosbinder needs whatever reliable info you have. She may request that you to send out another round of teams. I take it you're still thinking of buying Freeman?"

"If we can get enough of the division running productively again, it'll be an attractive buy for someone else," said Patrick. "Michael might be interested in the fastener division, but even if he isn't, there are other options. We have to drive the price down as low as possible."

"I think I can help get us a bargain," Gyges said.

Patrick glanced at Tommy, then back to Gyges. "Let's be frank here," he said. "There are things in your report that only someone inside Freeman could know. We need to know if you have someone."

"A mole? No."

"Then how could you know all this?"

"I went there, wandered around, picked up rumors. Amazing what you can learn that way."

"Bullshit! They would have spotted you," Tommy said.

"I have no reason to lie, Tommy. They weren't looking for me, so they didn't see me."

"How's that?"

"I blended in. I'm good at being inconspicuous."

"I don't want us caught up in legal problems with you over there stealing company secrets."

"You mean like the ones they kept in trying to screw you?"

Tommy started to respond but stopped. Gyges's responses puzzled him. He was direct and evasive at the same time. Something was different about him, but he couldn't say what.

Gyges could see Tommy searching for something to say. "Look, I wouldn't do anything to get OH into trouble. I risked everything for this company—for this family. Really, I owe you guys. I'm just grateful I can give back some of what I've gotten."

"All right. We'll leave it at that for today. But let me be clear—I don't want to end up in court."

"You won't. Not from anything I've done. What about next Monday? Am I supposed to report back to Tracy?"

Tommy paused and thought for a minute. Then he said, "Yeah, for now. Just come back like nothing's happened. You'll work directly for me on this project but do whatever normal work Tracy assigns you. Once this Freeman mess is worked out, we'll re-examine what to do with you."

Ten minutes later, Gyges was back in his office. He ran a search for divorce lawyers, picked one at random, and made an appointment for the following day. He called a couple apartment locators from a list and gave them a rundown on what he wanted. He'd get back to them the next day, as well.

* * *

It took Gyges almost a half hour to reach the bank, then only two minutes to spot Erica inside.

She was a loan officer.

He knew this, of course, because he'd spent the better part of the morning inside her house. He'd searched every room slowly and carefully. By the time he'd finished, Gyges knew where she worked, shopped, and banked. He knew what she ate, read, listened to, and watched on TV. He knew how much she owed and to whom. He'd even copied her bank account, credit card numbers, social security number, email, and the numbers of friends and family.

He approached her desk.

"Good afternoon," she said, smiling. "How may I help you?"

"Hello. I'm Guy Petros," he said, using his club identity. "I don't need a loan today, but I might soon—for a condo. I just wanted some info on the types of loans available."

Sly dog you are, Guy Petros, he thought.

"Certainly, Mr. Petros. Have a seat and I'll put together a small packet for you."

Gyges watched intently as she prepared the packet, pulling together sheets from different drawers and printing out papers. He wasn't sure why, but he was strongly attracted to her—from the first time he'd seen her at the club. The more he saw her, the more he wanted her.

When she'd finally gathered all the information, she turned the folder for him to see. As she bent over the desk, he could see into the small opening of her blouse and spy a black bra cupping her breasts. Her perfume made him heady, and he became aroused. She prattled on about the folder. He pretended to listen, but he wasn't thinking about interest rates and down payments.

"Do you currently have a home or condo you'll be selling?" she asked.

He focused. "Yes, a house. I want something smaller. I'm at a stage in my career where I don't have time to maintain it—I've recently been promoted—and I'll be concentrating more energy there. More responsibilities and a lot more money." The last bit came out with more emphasis than Gyges had intended, but it was clear from his trip to her house that Erica enjoyed the finer things in life.

Better to get that in early.

She looked at him, and he smiled. He repressed the overpowering urge to kiss her. He wanted to feel her skin, drown in that perfume, touch . . .

"Well, congratulations; I'm sure you deserve it. Purchasing a condo sounds perfect for you, then. Is there anything else I can help you with?" She closed the folder and handed it to him.

Gyges didn't want to stop talking to her, but he wasn't sure what else to say. "No . . . I don't think so. I'll look this over. If I have questions, can I stop back next week?"

"Certainly, Mr. Petros. That's what I'm here for." She stood and handed him a business card. "And actually, if you think of anything, feel free to call."

He took the card and looked at it before shaking her hand. He loved the feel; he put this other hand on top of it. Then he realized he might be holding it longer than social mores allowed and abruptly let go.

"I'm so grateful for your help," he said. "I'll stop by next week."

"You know where to find me." She smiled again.

"Yes, indeed; I do."

Gyges waited in his Explorer until Erica got off work twenty minutes later. He hoped she'd head to the club for a workout but was disappointed when he followed her to a bar. He was even more disappointed when, unseen, he pushed open the bar door to find her sitting with some guy.

He eased close enough to hear the conversation. The man was definitely a romantic interest. But there had been no evidence of him at her house. He must be new, Gyges thought—there'd been no pictures or any other indication that he'd been part of her life for any amount of time. Gyges was angry with himself. Of course, she'd be attached to someone—just look at her.

After a few minutes, he calmed down. So what if she had a boyfriend? He could change that. So even though it pained him to see them touch and eventually kiss, he remained in the bar to pick up anything he could.

The man's name was Dave. Judging from the conversation, Dave was a hot-shit lawyer with two passions—his car and himself. Erica seemed ignorant to how full of shit he was.

After their second drink, Dave and Erica headed to a movie. Gyges followed them out of the bar and down the street to a parking ramp. On the second floor, Dave's immaculately maintained BMW Z3 midnight-blue coupe was backed into a corner and took up two parking spots. One had his name written on a sign on the concrete wall. Dave Johnson. Seriously, thought Gyges, what a lame name. Could it have been any more blandly Scandanavian? The license plate simply read DAVE. This guy was a piece of work.

Gyges loomed until the couple got into the car. Then, as Dave made some idiotic comment and Erica laughed, Gyges took out his Swiss Army knife and gently placed the blade against the car's rear quarter panel on the passenger's side. When Dave finally started the thing and took off, the blade dragged through the deep-blue paint job, leaving a jagged scratch.

Gyges would have loved to see Dave's face when he found the damage. Hopefully, he'd notice before the movie and it would ruin the couple's whole evening. This guy's car was in for a tough time, Gyges laughed.

God knows what would happen next.

25

The street lights were bright outside Danny O'Brien's office window. He usually enjoyed working late—quiet, no interruptions, time to concentrate. But he didn't enjoy what he had found in the reports and printouts sprawled across his desk. Loyalty was everything, and Tracy Mackus had concealed important facts about the Freeman analysis. Danny couldn't prove it, but it was obvious that Tracy had engaged in inappropriate dealings with Braddock. An email from the day before Tracy's final report sounded especially suspicious. Then there was the field team's report explicitly stating that the fastener division had lost the GM account.

Tracy's final report showed the exact opposite. Under his leadership, the teams had missed key indicators that something was wrong. Indicators picked up by the university consultants Gyges had hired. Gyges of all people.

What had Tracy hoped to gain? His recommendation would have been uncovered as soon as the OH turnaround teams had begun their work. He had to know it would have been the kind of mistake to derail his reputation and career at OH. At first, Danny considered that Tracy had simply made a bad call, but this wasn't the kind of mistake Tracy would make. It was intentional—had to be.

Tracy must have been paid off by Braddock and Shadmun, he reasoned. Siding with those two against OH was beyond despicable and stupid—it was unforgivable.

He swiped the phone and dialed Gerba.

"I'm firing Mackus. Tonight," he said.

"Tonight? Why? What did he do?" she asked.

"I don't want to get into it now. I'll explain tomorrow. When you get in—and I want you in early—get the paperwork completed first thing. His personal items will be in your office when you get there. He'll be directed to see you. Call security and fire him. Give him his personal things, get his keys, and have security escort him to his car." His tone let her know he wasn't in the mood for debate.

"First thing," she said. "I'll go in early. Anything else?"

"No." He hung up.

Next he called head of security, Will Logan.

"Will," he said, "this is—"

"Danny, everything okay at the office?" Logan sounded concerned.

"Everything's fine, Will. But I need you to go in early tomorrow. Empty out all of Mackus's personal shit, change the lock, and put a note on his door—signed by you—to go to HR. Then drop his stuff in Gerba's office. Got it?"

"No problem. Consider it done."

Danny slammed the phone down and poured himself a drink. Tracy was a lucky man. In the old days he might have gone home with broken bones. Or worse.

One down, he thought. Next we'll get those cocksuckers from Freeman..

26

Tracy hung up the phone. He didn't know any more now than he'd known the day OH fired him. He'd never been given a reason beyond "We think this is best for you and the company." Typical bullshit from that bleeding-heart bitch in HR.

In his bones, Tracy knew it was over Freeman. The O'Briens hadn't bought Freeman, and he didn't know why. Neither did his buddies who remained at OH. The lid was tighter than on any other deal at the company.

There wasn't much he could do, either. He'd gone to an attorney the Friday Will Logan had escorted him from the building. He didn't fit into any protected class of workers—too young, too white, too male, and too able—nothing to hang a claim that he'd been victim of discrimination. As his lawyer had put it, "Legally, you're screwed."

But Tracy wasn't the kind of man to give up and walk away. He didn't take kindly to being screwed, especially without knowing why. So he began to backtrack over his notes and reports. The answer had to be there. He also kept up contact with a few of his close friends at work. They'd dredge up whatever info they could to help.

Janet had tried to convince him to let it go and move on. He stopped listening when she ignored his request to "kindly shut the fuck up." Out on the deck between helpings of ribs and vodka, trying to block out Janet's grating voice, he resolved to reconstruct the entire deal. He'd get to the bottom of what had happened, and when he did . . . well, at least he'd know.

Not knowing was almost worse than getting fired.

Tommy wouldn't even return his calls. So much for loyalty. Danny had to be behind it; with the boys, blood was everything. If Danny said "No," Tommy would never cross him. But why the dramatic break? It didn't make sense.

This was something personal—an Irish grudge. He had to know why.

* * *

"Hello," said Gyges, standing at Erica's desk. "Remember me? I stopped by last week."

"Yes. Mr. Petros, isn't it?" she said, smiling.

"That's it. Good memory." It was a positive sign she remembered him.

"Do you have questions about the packet I gave you, Mr. Petros?"

"A couple," Gyges said and took the chair. He pulled out the folder, which he hadn't opened since she had given it to him.

He improvised questions to keep her talking for the next half hour. He stopped at that point, fearing that his questions were becoming so mundane that she might think he was dim.

"I really appreciate your time. You really have a knack for making difficult technical material clear and simple. Not everyone can do that. I'm going to make sure your supervisor knows what a good job you're doing."

She blushed at the attention. "Well, thank you, Mr. Petros, but that's not necessary. I'm just doing my job."

"No, I think it's more than that. I've been to three other banks, and no one else has taken the time to really help me the way you have. As a manager myself, I want to know when the customers are satisfied with my people."

"Well, if you insist—she's over there. In the blue suit.

Her name is Ms. Jones." Erica nodded toward the front counter. "This is awfully kind. I appreciate it."

I wonder how much she appreciates it, Mr. Petros, he thought.

"Not at all. You deserve it, but please . . . call me Guy. Mr. Petros makes me feel like I'm seventy."

"Well, thank you, Guy." She smiled again and shook his hand.

Gyges sauntered over to Ms. Jones and made a big show of his appreciation. He saw Erica watch as he did. He caught her eye before he left and waved.

She waved back.

* * *

Gyges couldn't even tell the scratch on Dave's Beamer had been there. Dave hadn't wasted any time in getting it fixed. Very professional job. It must have cost a pretty penny.

Gyges circled the car a couple times, considering what else he could do. He didn't want to repeat himself—another scratch or flat tire was out.

He opted for simplicity—not too destructive, but highly irritating.

He stood at the driver's door, jammed a toothpick from his pocket into the door lock, and snapped it. As he did, the car's alarm blared through the parking garage. Gyges jumped back. The horn stopped. He stepped to the passenger-side door and pushed the other end of the toothpick into its lock. The horn sounded again.

A black kid in green coveralls hustled up the ramp from the first floor. He tugged a pair of ear buds from his ears, paused, and looked at Dave's car. Gyges didn't recognize him, but the green coveralls were the uniform for all the garage attendants.

Gyges put a hand on the hood of the Beamer. The alarm went off. The attendant looked around to see if anyone was near the car. Gyges took his hand from the hood.

The garage attendant rounded the car, and, not seeing anyone, headed back down the ramp. Gyges let him get about ten yards before he touched the car again.

The kid jumped and glared back at Dave's blaring car. Gyges lifted his hand long enough to stop the horn, then put it back. The kid shook his head and returned to the booth on the first floor.

Gyges dug back into his pocket. This time he produced a quarter, which he shoved into the window slot. It kept the alarm sounding as Gyges followed the kid.

Back at the booth, the kid called Dave and told him about the malfunctioning alarm—he should come down and fix it. The kid couldn't keep bouncing from his duties in the booth to the car. They argued until the kid hung up. He leaned back in his chair with his ear buds, bouncing his head slowly to music Gyges couldn't hear.

Gyges watched the traffic roll past the garage for twenty minutes before Big Time showed up. Dave was upset about having to leave his office. He rushed past the booth and up the ramp toward his car. The kid flipped him the finger as he went.

Gyges walked up behind him. He found Dave at the driver's-side lock, fussing with the handle. Dave huffed as he tried to force his key into the lock. He cursed and tried the other side, with the same results.

He didn't notice that the attendant had walked up behind him. "You gonna fix that thing or what, sir?"

"Fuck you, you lazy bastard. Maybe if you did your job someone couldn't shove shit into the locks. Or are you the one that's been fuckin' with it?"

"Hey, sir, I don't work for you. Get that noise stopped or I'll have to call a tow truck."

"Another wanna-be gangsta—who the hell do you think you're talking to? You're just a scumbag garage attendant. I'm a lawyer. Don't tell me what to do. I'll have your job."

The kid stepped forward. "Don't get into anything you can't handle, sir."

Dave pushed him away. The kid pushed back and dropped into a fighting stance. He threw a right hook that landed on the bridge of Dave's nose, opening a small gash. Dave toppled to the ground, pulling the kid with him.

The two scuffled on the dirty concrete. Dave's gonna stain his expensive suit, Gyges observed. He laughed out loud, but the two men were too busy exchanging blows to notice.

He returned to the entrance and called the police from the attendant's office phone.

* * *

At five o' clock, after spending the afternoon bored and attempting to look busy, Gyges stopped at the club.

Hidden by the ring, he leaned against the front of the building. He waited until Erica exited the front doors, then followed her two blocks to a small parking lot. He worried she'd get in her car and leave, but she only stopped to drop her bag in the trunk.

She continued on foot to a nearby restaurant, went inside, and took a booth near the front window. Gyges walked to the bathroom, where he turned the ring so he could be seen when he emerged. He sat at the bar in clear view of Erica if she happened to look over. He wanted her to think he'd been there ahead of her.

Erica's eyes stayed on the window. She checked her watch. She was probably waiting for Dave. No doubt he would have much to tell her. Gyges chuckled to himself when he thought back to the lawyer rolling on the ground with the parking attendant. Tormenting Dave could become one of his favorite pastimes. He ranked right up there with Tracy. The guy was such a pompous ass. Gyges was doing the world a favor, the way he saw it.

Erica became agitated. Gyges knew from her house that she loved Merlot. He called to the bartender and ordered the most expensive bottle from the menu.

Gyges approached Erica with the wine.

"My guess is you're a Merlot kinda gal," he said.

She turned her gaze from the window.

"Oh, Mr. Petros—what are you doing here?"

He laughed off the comment. "Actually I was having a beer when I noticed you over here all by yourself. I figured you must be waiting for someone, but no one showed. I thought you might like something to drink."

She quickly glanced out the window and then back to Gyges. "You're right. I love Merlot."

Gyges paused for a moment, waiting for an invitation to sit. When it didn't come, he put the bottle on the table and said, "Well, I'll let you get back to your waiting."

"Uhh . . . would you want to join me 'til my friend arrives?"

"I don't want to impose."

"It's fine," she said." Please, sit."

"Okay, great." He slid into the seat opposite Erica. "Who are you waiting for, if you don't mind my asking?"

"Dave—my boyfriend. He's late and didn't call."

"Is that typical?"

"Let's just say it's not untypical. He's a very important lawyer. Sometimes he gets caught up in meetings and can't call. I just try to be patient."

"He's lucky to have someone so understanding."

"I hope he thinks so, too," she said. "You come here a lot?"

"Never been here. I had a long day at the office, and one of my co-workers is always talking this place up, so I thought it'd check it out. Kinda nice. You?"

"Yeah, it's a pretty reasonable place for downtown, and it's open late."

"So, did you grow up in the Twin Cities?" Gyges asked.

"Oh, there he is!" she said.

Dave blasted past the window, his face flush. There was a cut on his nose. Yep, there he is, Gyges thought.

Dave charged through the door but didn't see Erica.

She called his name, and he turned to her voice. He didn't look particularly happy to see her, and when he spotted Gyges, he looked even less enthused.

Gyges didn't get up; he simply smiled as if nothing was out of the ordinary.

"Who's this guy?" Dave thumbed toward Gyges, who kept his pleasant smile. He reached out to shake Dave's hand.

"Guy Petros. Nice to meet you."

Dave didn't take his hand. He looked at Erica. "What's up with him?"

"Nothing," she said, "Guy's a customer. I just ran into him here. He offered to wait with me until you got here."

"Well, I'm here now," he said. He glared at Gyges. "You mind, pal? I've had a shit day and would like some private time here."

"Not at all. Perfectly understandable. Erica, you have a nice night. It was nice talking to you. Dave, it's been real."

Gyges headed back to the bar. Back at the table, Dave was animated, his arms flying all over, and he raised his voice a few times. Gyges wondered how he had fared with the police. Probably not too cool to be a hot-shit attorney caught in a street fight with a minimum-wage garage attendant. Of course, the kid wouldn't get the benefit of the doubt on that one.

Still, it couldn't be good for Big Time.

Gyges paid his tab and got up to leave. On his way out, he caught Erica's eye and nodded. She waved back at him. Dave didn't even notice.

Outside, Gyges looked around for Dave's Beamer but couldn't spot it. No matter, he thought; he knew where to find it.

27

The week after Tracy's firing passed quickly for Gyges.

Early Friday, he, Danny, and Patrick met with Hosbinder. She was just as curt and down to business as usual. But despite her lack of social nuance, or maybe because of it, the O'Briens were impressed. She'd have the real value of Freeman in a week.

After the meeting, he met with his new divorce attorney. Harrison Klackau, the first divorce lawyer to pop up on his internet search, was moderately optimistic that a settlement could be reached quickly with few bumps. Gyges hoped so—he had imposed almost no restrictions on the settlement—they'd split the value of the house and maintain their own retirement plans, and he'd keep all his fishing gear.

That was it; what more could she ask for? He was the perfect husband to be divorcing.

He spent the rest of the weekend moving into his new apartment in Minnetonka. As much as he loved The Ghost, he'd grown tired of living on her. He needed more room for his stuff, but what had seemed crowded on the boat was less than minimal in the new place. He had nothing really. No bed; no kitchen essentials; no towels or sheets; not a single chair, table, or couch. He went on a spending spree to lavish his new apartment with the best of even the most inconsequential and extraneous possessions. By Sunday, he'd transformed the place through sheer buying power and theft into a small fantasy from one of those glossy home magazines Angie always had lying around.

When he got to the office Monday, small pockets of co-workers had gathered throughout his floor whispering about Tracy's dramatic departure. Capt'n D had been gone in sixty seconds Friday morning. He'd found a note directing him to HR and then been shown the door. Even Gyges was awed by the speed of the decision—and a little disappointed he hadn't been there to witness it firsthand.

Depending on which of the various rumors one wanted to believe, Tracy had screwed Danny's hot young wife, who'd worked for him before she'd gotten married, screwed Daisy in accounting and his wife found out and gone to Tommy, embezzled money, had an enormous coke habit, fucked up the Freeman deal, or used a racial slur within earshot of Gerba (the last having been contributed by Gyges).

Tracy rubbed most people the wrong way and turnover in his department was higher than anywhere else in the company. Still, when a thing like this happened, Gyges observed, even the most despicable person elicited sympathy. It wasn't unlike hearing about a pervy uncle getting hit by lightning. But to Gyges's pleasure, Tracy got less than the usual benefit of the doubt. The reaction eased what little tension he had. It would make his job easier once he took over.

Tracy did, however, have a few ardent supporters. Overall, they knew more about what really went down, because they had talked to Tracy. The way they told it, Tracy wasn't given a reason but was positive it had something to do with the Freeman deal. A few of these folks went to Tommy, who stated only that OH's top management (read the O'Briens) had rejected the buy recommendation because of "deficient information."

By the end of the week, the rumor mill was still cranking out theories but the waters were calming, and people fell back into their regular routine. Just like always.

Gyges met with Patrick and Tommy several times. In one meeting, Patrick told them about how a day before the deadline, Braddock had called Danny and Danny had transferred it to Patrick. Braddock had been livid about OH's decision and asked if they needed more time to decide. Patrick had told him the deal was simply too expensive. Braddock had hung up.

Shadmun was just as angry about being relegated to dealing with "the boy." Just as Danny had refused Braddock's call, Tommy had also transferred Shadmun to Patrick. Shadmun had hung up when he heard Patrick's voice. Both had left several messages on Danny's phone. Neither brother had returned the messages. Gyges imagined the panic at Freeman. Their bluff had been called. The entire house of cards was about to collapse, and those two assholes had gone all-in. He thought of them a lot throughout the week. And every time they came to mind, so did the ring. He'd always have considerable advantage over his opponents.

While Gyges was eager to press Tommy for Tracy's job, he decided that subtlety was better for the time being. He continued to convey that he was willing to take up any slack and prove he was a major contributor to the company. Tommy's lukewarm non-answers didn't dishearten him; he could feel the momentum moving in his favor.

Besides, Gyges now welcomed being underestimated.

When he arrived to work the following Thursday, Hosbinder's report was in his mailbox. The report showed that Freeman's worth was less than the price they wanted six months before—fewer assets now. They'd sold off some patents, depleted inventories, even sold equipment they continued to list as owning. Gyges wanted to be the one to deliver the news to the O'Briens, and on Friday afternoon he made a presentation to the three of them.

Danny could not have been more delighted; he laughed during parts of the presentation and often nodded in agreement. OH could dictate the price, which vindicated his initial interest. And he loved it when his instincts were proven right. When Gyges finished, Danny clapped and praised his effort.

After the presentation, he gave the go-ahead for

Patrick to open negotiations but for less than the report's estimate. He also wanted Gyges in on the negotiations.

Later, in his office, Patrick punched the number for Freeman Industries and motioned Gyges to the chair next to his desk.

"John Braddock, please. This is Patrick O'Brien from OH. I'm returning his call." The receptionist put him on hold. Patrick hit the speaker button, winking at Gyges.

"Hello. Toni Buchetti speaking." A woman's voice.

"Sorry, I was trying to speak with John Braddock. The receptionist must have—"

"Mr. Braddock no longer works here, sir. I'm running Freeman Industries," she said. "Mr. Shadmun is gone as well."

Patrick shot Gyges a confused glance. "Gone? I don't understand," he stumbled.

"Yes, can I help you in some way?" she asked.

"Well, I'm Patrick O'Brien from OH. We were negotiating with them to buy your company. I guess I'm a little confused. Did you buy the company?"

"No, I represent the other owners."

"Other owners? We were under the impression—"

"Yes, Braddock and Shadmun were only part owners. I represent the others. I've reviewed the files. Give me a couple days and I should be able to re-open the negotiations."

"That sounds fair, but the price was way too high. Braddock and Shadmun weren't operating in good faith. They tried to hide the real value of your company. We now have a more accurate understanding of your worth and what's been going on over there."

"You aren't the only ones, Mr. O'Brien. Sadly, we weren't aware of their machinations, either. And they have disappeared with considerable cash and securities. We're trying to track them down."

Gyges sat up in his chair.

"They embezzled company funds?" Patrick asked.

"Yes, it's been . . . we believe they've left the country. We aren't sure where."

"I'm sorry to hear that. Good luck in finding them. I hope you do."

"Oh, we will. It's only a matter of time. The other owners aren't the kind of people to let this sort of thing go. I'll call you as soon as I can."

She hung up.

Gyges turned to Patrick. "I think I know where they are."

"Seriously? How could you know that?"

"I overheard them talking about going to Belize once the deal was done."

"Jesus, Peter; you're quite the expert on Freeman."

"I could be quite the expert on any company . . . given the chance," he said. "Patrick, I'm not going to be coy. I want Tracy's job. I deserve it. We all know I saved the family from near ruin. I can handle it."

Patrick was quiet. Finally, he said, "Until last week, we didn't think much of your abilities or performance here, Peter. You've never taken advantage of the opportunities we've given you."

"I wouldn't quarrel with that assessment. To be frank, I did just enough to get by. I admit it. But that changed some time back. I saw what Tracy and the guys at Freeman were trying to do to the family, and it shook me from my lethargy. I realized how much I owed OH and put everything on the line. If it didn't work . . ." He paused for effect. "Well, we can all be glad it did. I want to do more, Patrick. Will you speak to your dad about it?"

"It's not my decision. It's Tommy and Danny's."

"Do I have your support?"

Patrick paused again, then he sighed and said, "Yes; I think you've shown what you can do. You did save us. You've earned a shot."

"That's all I'm asking for. When will you talk to them?"

"Today."

"Thanks, Patrick. As usual, I owe you."

"If you get the job, you will. Big time!" Patrick laughed.

Gyges laughed, too, and Patrick gave him a locker-room slap on the back.

Gyges returned to his office smiling. He closed the door and dialed Toni Buchetti.

"Ms. Buchetti, my name is Peter Gyges. I'm working on the negotiation team with Patrick O'Brien. I have some information about the possible whereabouts of your boys, Braddock and Shadmun."

"Oh, do you? And how is it you came by this information, Mister—what did you say your name was?"

"Gyges. Peter Gyges. I believe your guys are in Belize."

"Why's that?"

"Let's just say I have inside information on it."

"Thank you, Mr. Gyges. We'll put one of our associates on it right away. You wouldn't happen to know where in Belize, would you?"

"No, sorry. But two white boys with big mouths and lots of money shouldn't be too hard to spot. I'd say your real problem is extradition back to America."

"Oh, well . . . we aren't interested in extraditing them. Thank you for your help, Mr. Gyges. I owe you one."

28

Patrick kept his word and spoke to Tommy and Danny about the promotion that afternoon. Also true to his word, he did more than just bring it up; he advocated for him. He told them what Gyges had said. Patrick was persuasive and impassioned for his longtime friend. The elder O'Brien's needed considerable convincing. They both thought the Freeman discoveries were a one-shot deal—a lucky pinch-hit. Patrick pointed out how much had gone into uncovering the scam. Gyges had shown initiative, resourcefulness, cunning, risk-taking, drive, and commitment—all against huge odds and little faith. What more could they want from a leader? Patrick asked. In the end, he carried the day for Gyges, moving his elders and surprising even himself with his own words. For the first time in his adult life, he understood the qualities of his childhood friend.

Gyges move into his new office was easy. Housekeeping did it for him. One day the supervisor showed up with a clipboard, Gyges told her what to move and where he wanted it in the new office, and the next morning it was exactly the way he had asked. Later that night, while thinking of his new office, he concluded that it missed one more thing. The next morning he came in with an expensive chess set for the end table.

The memo announcing Gyges as Tracy's replacement sent a shockwave through the company. It surprised those who didn't know him, because it was such an important position and they'd never heard of him. But it was an even greater shock to those who did. Rumors cranked up, the most persistent being that Patrick had gotten the job for him.

These rumors circulated back to the O'Briens. The last thing they wanted was for their employees to think promotions were for whom you knew rather than for what you did. They feared that this mindset could create a culture of sycophants rather than hard-workers. They were also concerned that Gyges wouldn't get the respect or support he needed and deserved. On a personal level, they were angered by the rumors; they'd always held their family to higher standards than others.

Ordinarily, they let gossip work itself out. But this time they decided to counter the rumors with a series of talks with department heads. They'd let the rumor mill work in their direction rather than against them. For the next couple days, the brothers and Patrick sat down with key people and told them what Gyges had done on Freeman.

The plan extinguished the rumors, and the story took on a life of its own; details changed depending on who told it. Over the next week, a small legend grew around Gyges's exploits—a man who had saved the company by risking everything. Like Freddie Smith, who bet Fed Ex's fortune on one dice roll at a craps table in Vegas, Gyges's name developed an aura and cache.

Gyges catapulted from obscure office lackey to corporate hero. Other employees sought his advice, and he reveled in his new status. He loved when others solicited his opinion. When he walked through the office, people turned to greet him. He basked in the attention, often walking around as if he had a destination just to feed on the admiration. He knew they all thought he was a great man.

Gyges recognized that he now stood for something in people's eyes. He'd become a symbol of achievement. Hope for the underdog. An everyman to admire.

People finally saw that he was destined for great things.

29

Walter Burke pulled into the driveway and parked. He'd visited the house a handful of times over the years and wondered how his friend could make mortgage in such an opulent neighborhood. Janet hadn't worked since they married and their two kids were both at college.

He knocked on the side door. Janet answered, looking worried.

"Hello, Walter," she said. "Come in." She wasn't happy to see him.

He stepped inside and wiped his feet on the welcome mat. Her eyes dropped to the file in his right hand.

"How's he doing?" he asked.

"I don't know. He won't talk to me. He spends all his time in that study. You know, if you want to be his friend, you'd encourage him to move on and let this go. He needs to get out and find another job—one with a company that values his worth."

Walt didn't know how to respond. "Katherine wanted me to tell you she sends her regards. If you guys need anything—"

"Yes, well, thank you. You're very kind and helpful."

He hesitated for a second and decided it best to move on. He continued through the house to the study.

He knocked. When there wasn't an answer, he tried again.

"Oh, goddamn it, Janet!" Tracy yelled from inside.

"Go away. I told you not to bother me."

"It's Walt," he said, a little embarrassed.

Tracy opened the door. "Walt! My man—so glad to see you." He looked like shit, like he hadn't shaved since the day he was fired. His hair was disheveled and greasy. Walter wondered if he had even showered. He wore sweatpants and a Vikings jersey, and he reeked of booze. "Come in. Come in."

As soon as Walter entered the study, Tracy shut the door. The place looked even worse than Tracy—papers, post-it notes, dirty dishes, and empty bottles everywhere. Tracy had erected a kind of map on the wall. Words were circled or crossed out, papers pinned up, page numbers and names scrawled in a hurried hand—it seemed to form an odd coded pathway that only Tracy could decipher.

What had happened to Tracy had been bullshit, but he couldn't help wondering if Tracy was losing it.

"So what's up?" Tracy said.

"I've got something to tell you. It's pretty unbelievable."

"The brothers want me back and wanna give me a raise?" Tracy laughed.

"Ahh . . . they announced your replacement this week. I thought I'd let you know in person."

"Oh, yeah, who's that?"

"Peter Gyges."

"This some kinda joke, Walt?"

"Some of us thought it was. But sadly, no. The rumor floating around is that he got the job 'cuz he's pals with the Golden Boy."

"Gyges? Gyges got my job? That sneaky little ass kisser. He shoulda been fired years ago. This is must be a joke!"

"Yeah, I know. Exactly what we thought. The brothers met with department heads and painted him as some kind of savior. Somehow, and the details are vague, he put everything on the line to save the company. The entire thing is laughable and no doubt completely designed to defuse any idea of favoritism. But it worked, and now the majority of OH is up his ass. And you should see him, the way he prances around the office like King Shit."

Tracy fell quiet.

"I don't know, Walt," he said after a few minutes. "Tommy and Danny are a lot of things, but they've never acted on the basis of anything other than what was most beneficial for the company. They weren't big fans—at least Tommy wasn't—of Gyges's performance. They wouldn't roll the dice on someone like this. Not even for that piece of shit."

"You sure about that, Tracy? Seems to make sense to me. In the end, they've always been about family. And Gyges is family. More or less."

"Nah, it can't be that. As easy as that is to think. These are not sentimental men, Walt. They're old-school tough-minded SOB's who value getting things done and done right. Period. As much as I hate Patrick, you can't say that guy doesn't earn his keep. And you can bet if he didn't, Danny would have booted his ass to the curb long ago. That's why I loved working for OH. If Gyges has moved up, it's because he did something, something to convince them he saved their ass on the Freeman deal. That's the only rational explanation."

"So you're completely convinced your firing was over the Freeman deal?"

"It's the only reason possible. There's nothing else."

"You know, they did say that Gyges was working on the Freeman deal when he was supposed to be on that vacation."

"That's almost completely unfathomable to me. Gyges didn't work on the shit I gave him, and it was bitch work. Why would he use his vacation?" Then Tracy's eyes lit up like someone had replaced his batteries. He laughed. "Maybe Gyges was more than an inept little shit. Clearly, he's an ass kisser, but maybe he's far more than that. He must be capable of scheming in some very sophisticated ways, Walt. Ways I never even considered."

He reached into his desk, grabbed a bottle of vodka,

and poured himself a healthy glass.

"How could I have missed the call on Freeman and Gyges gotten it right?"

"I dunno, Tracy. It seems so unlikely. We're talking about Gyges here."

"What did he know that I didn't?" Tracy was talking to himself more than to Walter.

"Listen, I should probably get going. Here are those files you wanted."

Tracy sat up in the chair. "Oh, yeah, shit, I forgot. Thanks, Walt. Don't go now. Stay. Have a drink."

Walter sighed and checked his watch. He was supposed to meet Katherine for dinner.

"Come on, one drink." Tracy dug out another glass from the desk and poured one for his friend. He handed it to Walter.

Walter took it reluctantly. He'd be pushing it to make it on time. "Okay, one drink." Walter decided to change the subject, lighten the air. "So how're Jake and Annie?"

Lost in thought, Tracy leaned back in his chair and stared at the ceiling. It was like Walter wasn't there anymore.

30

Gyges planned to meet Bhuto for a steam and chess, but Bhuto had left a message on his cell that he'd been called out of town on business.

He went to the club after work anyway, hoping to run into Erica. It was time to make a bolder move. She was only with Dave because she saw no other options. He'd give her one to consider.

He found her in her usual spot on her favorite bike, with, to his delight, an open one next to her.

"Hi, Guy," she said. "Seems like I bump into you almost everywhere now."

"It's funny how once you meet someone, you cross paths a lot—just didn't notice each other," he said, pedaling slowly.

She withdrew back into her workout, listening to music on her MP3 player. She finished, to Gyges's disappointment, five minutes later.

"See you later," she said.

"Yeah, okay. Good to see you."

"You, too. Bye now," she said and went to shower and get dressed.

Gyges quickly ducked into the men's bathroom, disappeared, then went to the women's locker room. He watched as Erica undressed and showered. He had to have her, and he resolved to ask her out.

He returned to the men's locker room to dress, then

waited for Erica in the lobby.

"Say, are you doing anything for dinner?" he asked when she came out of the women's locker room. "I'm going over to Gilhooley's and I thought you might like to join me."

"I'm sorry—I can't. I mean, you know . . . well, I'm dating Dave and . . ."

"Oh, it wouldn't be a date—just dinner so we don't have to eat alone."

She hesitated.

"Yeah, I shouldn't. I have some work around the house. Maybe some other time."

"Are you sure? I promise not to keep you all night."

"I'd like to, really, but . . . no . . . I can't. Thanks, though." She patted him on the back. "I've got to run. See you somewhere, I'm sure."

Gyges's spirits sank as she left. He'd truly believed she'd say yes. She wanted to, he was certain. It was that prick Dave. He'd have a chance if it weren't for him.

Well, he told himself, he could still be around her tonight. He'd just drive over to her house.

* * *

Gyges drove out to Erica's neighborhood, parked in his usual spot, and walked the short distance to her house. He went around to the back and gingerly tried the door. It was unlocked.

He was sliding through the doorway when the driveway lit up with headlights. He entered and stood on the landing, out of the way.

A car door slammed. Dave stumbled in and tripped on the steps heading to the kitchen.

"God*damn* it!"

Gyges smelled whiskey.

"Dave, is that you?" Erica called from the other room.

"Who the hell else would it be?" he shouted back.

She came to the back door with him still sprawled out.

"Oh, Dave, are you okay? What happened?"

"What the fuck does it look like? I fell. Help me up, goddamn it—don't just stand there."

Erica grabbed him by an arm and helped him to his feet.

"I thought you had to work late," she said.

"Client canceled. I thought I'd stop by for a little play time." He drunkenly fondled her breasts. "Let's do it right here on the stairs." He unbuttoned his pants, pulled down his underwear. "Suck me off on the table."

"No, Dave. You know I don't like it when you're drunk."

He grabbed her by the hair. "Yeah, but I do. I need it right here, right now."

Dave pushed her to her knees and pulled her head to his groin.

"Suck me," he demanded.

"Dave, no, I don't . . ."

"Now, suck now!"

Erica relented and did as Dave demanded.

He moaned, pulling her head harder in.

"Harder . . . yeah, harder."

Gyges was repulsed.

"Oh, yeah—I'm coming. I'm coming. Nowww." He jerked and then slumped against the table. Erica remained kneeling and put her hand over her mouth. "Did you come too?" He laughed.

She got up and ran crying to the bathroom.

"Hey, I was just joking. Can't you take a fuckin' joke? Jesus. I was joking. Come on back. Let's do it again—this time I'll wait for you to get off." He laughed again.

Gyges's heart fired burning blood into every vein of his body. He ran up the steps. Dave was still leaning against the table with his pants down and his dick out, his eyes half-closed.

Gyges kicked his legs out from under him. Dave crashed down, banging his head hard on the floor.

"Fuckin' A," groaned Dave.

Gyges grabbed him by his legs and pulled him over to the landing stairs.

"What the fuck?" Dave kicked to get his legs free from the unseen force pulling them.

Gyges leaned down and whispered menacingly into Dave's ear, "See if your dick likes how this feels, motherfucker."

In one swift move, he flipped Dave face down on the tiled floor and pulled him down the four steps to the landing. Dave screamed and tried to grab his balls.

Gyges wasn't done. He stomped his foot against Dave's bare ass, crushing his groin against the bottom step one more time.

Dave howled.

Gyges left him on the steps curled up with his pants around his knees, his hands clutching his balls. Dave whined, a wounded little rodent.

In the driveway, Gyges kicked out both taillights.

The brisk walk back to his car did little to settle him down. He regretted not staying to work Dave over more seriously.

He should have broken his arms. A block from his car, he stopped and almost returned. He shook with adrenaline and rage.

Against his will, he kept going. His keys jingled in his hand, and it took him several attempts to unlock the door. He had an equally difficult time getting them in the ignition. He careened home at ninety miles an hour.

When he reached his apartment, he collapsed at the kitchen table and tried to calm his shaking. He began to count. One, two, three, four, five . . .

When his heart had slowed, Gyges went to the refrigerator and opened a beer. He downed it, then he got a second. Then a third.

His thoughts idled long enough for him to register them as they passed. He got up to get a another beer. As he opened the refrigerator, he caught a glimpse of his ring, the signet still turned inward.

Jesus Christ, he was still invisible. He had driven home that way.

* * *

Gyges was still shaken when he awoke the next morning. His rage surprised him. He'd never lost control like that. It couldn't happen again. He could never forget to distinguish between when he could be seen from when he couldn't. That kind of slip-up could ruin everything.

Still, he had relished pummeling Dave. The power and control he felt was immense even now, recalling it. He hated Dave. Obviously, last night's scene hadn't been the first time. Erica was staying with him despite the way he treated her. Was it his money? His car? His position in life? Gyges couldn't understand. But now he had all those things, too. He was better than Dave in every way.

He wondered what had happened after he'd left. Dave may have taken it out on Erica. But Dave hadn't been in a condition to do much of anything. Even if he had, it would have only been better for Gyges.

He also worried that Dave might have recognized his voice. But, he concluded, that was unlikely too. Dave was wretched, and besides, he wasn't the kind of person who paid much attention to others.

He couldn't let on that he knew what happened, but he had to capitalize on the night's incident, use it to his advantage with Erica. He needed her to see him as more desirable than Dave.

He needed to be the complete opposite—cute, romantic.

On his way to work, he stopped by a floral shop and bought flowers and a card. On a piece of paper, he drew a rain check redeemable for one dinner. He signed it and added his phone number. He shoved his homemade check into the card and handed it to the clerk. They scheduled the delivery for later that morning.

    Gyges guessed that after the shitty night Erica had suffered, this would stand out as a welcome relief. It was enough to show his interest, but not too pushy.

31

Tracy rubbed his blurry eyes with the back of his hand.

He'd been up for hours; he was hungry, excited, and tired, but it had paid off. He'd found the smoking gun. He only needed to prove who'd pulled the trigger. Someone had tampered with his team's findings and emails. There were also two emails to Freeman that he never sent. He was certain it was Gyges. No one else had profited from his demise. Tracy felt it in his gut.

He yawned and got up from his desk. He was starting to stink.

After taking the pile of dirty dishes to the kitchen sink, he put on some coffee.

Tommy wouldn't see him. Even if he did, it would be his word against Gyges. At this point, there was no way he could win that fight. Gyges had been elevated up the ladder. Hard evidence was thin. Or non-existent. He needed something objective. After long reexamination, Tracy saw that he'd missed Freeman's con.

Fools rush in. Tracy would wait. He'd gather more evidence and try to rattle Gyges into a mistake or admission. Maybe it was better that he couldn't prove it just yet. He wanted to tarnish the shiny image of Gyges the Savior. And later, if it came down to word against word, Gyges wouldn't be on such a high horse.

Walt and a few others would unleash rumors,

hopefully shake the little shit into making a mistake. In the meantime, he needed more intel.

This was war.

* * *

Gyges heard the rumors by mid-morning. Supposedly, Tracy had evidence that Gyges had tampered with his files and computer.

Publicly, he laughed it off and just shook his head to indicate the ridiculousness of the idea. He expressed sympathy for Tracy's plight—it was only natural for a person to blame another for his failures.

But privately, he was concerned. He went back to his office and looked through everything he'd tampered with. There was no way Tracy could prove a thing.

Still, he didn't like the rumor. Later he heard it again from two other employees. If he was hearing it, everyone else would, too. Most people, he reasoned, would come to the conclusion he offered. The O'Briens would read it that way, too.

Gyges finished out the day late due to another meeting with the brothers and Patrick. He hated working late, but there wasn't a choice. He'd missed Erica's time at the club. She hadn't called since he'd sent the card. He wanted to make sure she'd gotten it. The late meeting meant he'd have to call her at work the next day to find out.

Gyges walked the half block to the OH parking lot. He thought about spending the night at home. Maybe he'd watch a movie. He'd been on the move and hadn't been able to enjoy his new place. Like Bhuto said, what was the point of working if you couldn't enjoy the fruits of your labor? When Gyges got to his car, Tracy stepped from the shadows.

"How you like my job?" he asked.

Gyges jumped at his appearance. "Jesus Christ," he said. "What the hell are you doing here?"

"Answer my question."

"What?"

"Are you enjoying my job?" Tracy repeated.

Gyges just stared at his ex-boss. He barely recognized him. He looked more like an unkempt hobo. And he smelled like one, too. There was a crazy look in Tracy's eyes.

Gyges fingered his ring for reassurance. "What are you doing?"

"I'm looking at the sonofabitch that ruined my life."

"Oh, please. You fucked it up yourself. I'm a little disappointed in you, Tracy. This isn't usually your style. Blaming others for your failures doesn't really make sense for a hardass like yourself."

"My failures? You fuckin' bagged me, and I got the evidence to prove it. You're a little rat—that's all you are. And I know your little secret. I know how you sneak around and get into things you shouldn't."

A cold chill ran up Gyges's back. Tracy couldn't be talking about the ring, could he?

"You don't know shit. There's nothing to know. You smell like you've had a few. Why don't you go home and clean up. You're gonna get more than you bargained for here."

"What's that? Are you threatening me, you ass-kissing little shit?"

Tracy launched forward and grabbed Gyges's lapels. Gyges jerked away his hands and pushed him back into his car.

"Tracy, you're messing with the wrong guy. I don't have to take shit from you anymore. Remember? You're not my boss. You're nothing but a stinking bum now. Go home, before I call the cops."

"Oh, I'm a lot more than that. I'm the man who's gonna bring you down. I've still got plenty of friends at OH, and I'm watching you. I'll expose your little secret, and you'll fall lower than you've ever been in your life. And me . . . I'll be back on top."

Tracy stumbled away from Gyges's car toward the street but turned around once more. "You're fucked, buddy. Really fucked. There's nothing you can do about it."

Then he disappeared into the dark of the sidewalk.

As Gyges drove home, he couldn't get the threat out of his mind. He tried to reassure himself that Tracy didn't know anything, that he was a broken man with a grudge. That's all this was.

His thoughts were on a loop—going back to the beginning, playing over again and again. He arrived at his apartment with no recollection of the drive.

* * *

Gyges sat on his couch and tried to watch a movie, but his mind wouldn't allow him to focus long enough to follow the plot. It faded into the background like banal elevator muzak.

He had assumed that Tracy would walk off with his tail between his legs, disappear from his life forever. He should have known better. Capt'n D was intent to screw his good thing. But Gyges was equally intent not to let that happen. He wasn't going to lose everything he'd worked so hard to gain. He assured himself that he could fix it just as he had Tracy's firing.

Besides, now he held all the pieces: the manager's position, the O'Briens's confidence, the respect of the company. And he had the most important piece. He gently rubbed the ring with his thumb.

Tracy didn't have shit. A few scraps of paper were nothing compared to Gyges's arsenal. He would swat away any attack like a mosquito on his neck. And that's exactly what Tracy was—a bloodsucking mosquito.

He turned the movie off and went to the kitchen. A box on the table caught his eye. It was full of odds and ends he'd brought over from The Ghost. He figured he might as well put it away. Standing over the table, he began extracting the items from the box. Halfway through, he came to the book Bhuto had given him when they'd first met. He'd forgotten about it.

He'd been unimpressed with the gift at the time, and holding it now in his hands didn't change his opinion. He turned it over. The smell of an old library drifted up. It was dirty and dog-eared. The bottom of the front cover was gone and he could tell that the back had been used as a coffee coaster. He flipped through a few pages, then hovered over a few lines:

The wish to acquire is in truth very natural and common, and men always do so when they can, and for this they will be praised not blamed; but when they cannot do so, yet wish to do so by any means, then there is folly and blame.

Gyges sat down and reread the passage a couple more times. It made perfect sense.

Everyone wishes to get ahead. That's what he'd done at work. What's more natural than that? Angela didn't get it. She thought there was something wrong with it, but that was bullshit. For years, he'd hidden the idea from himself because he'd thought it unattainable. He'd finally convinced himself that the unattainable was wrong. But when he'd realized that he could get whatever he wanted in this world, he'd seized the opportunity.

This, Machiavelli said, should be praised, not blamed.

Intrigued now, he flipped to another section.

Everyone sees what you appear to be, few really know what you are, and those few dare not oppose themselves to the opinion of the many, who have the majesty of the state to defend them.

He read farther down.

For that reason, let a prince have the credit of conquering and holding his state, the means will always be considered honest, and he will be praised by everybody because the vulgar are always taken by what a thing seems to be and by what comes of it; and in the world there are only the vulgar, for the few find a place there only when the many have no guard to rest on.

And then again.

Hence it is necessary for a prince wishing to hold his own to know how to do wrong, and to make use of it or not according to necessity.

And again.

> *Everyone admits how praiseworthy it is in a prince to keep faith, and to live with integrity and not with craft. Nevertheless our experience has been that those princes who have done great things have held good faith of little account, and have known how to circumvent the intellect of men by craft, and in the end have overcome those who have relied on their word.*

Gyges set the book down and went to the refrigerator for a beer. He returned and reread the passages. He set the book down. And then after staring at it for a few minutes, he reread the passages a third time. The profound truth of the words struck him as if he were a bell.

He had clearly misjudged what Bhuto had gifted him. Curiously, the fat man had never asked if Gyges had read the book. He wondered why. Bhuto was hard to read. He liked and admired his friend for his easy-going style, sense of humor, and kindness, but he realized there was a lot more to the man.

He picked up the book and got another beer. He sat down in his most comfortable chair and started *The Prince* from the beginning. He'd not read a book since college. Truth be known, he'd not read many in college either. He'd made do with CliffsNotes and what others said about the book. That had been enough to carry him through his courses. Actually reading a book had been an unnecessary burden to pass any of them. And passing was all that mattered.

So it was difficult for him to read for an extended period of time. All the references to names and places confused him. But just when he was frustrated enough to give up, he would come across another passage profound enough to read again. In this way, he was motivated to continue.

While he read, Gyges marked passages with a pen so he could easily return to them. Sometimes he'd go for pages without marking anything. Then there were sections in which he underlined page after page.

Assisted by six beers, Gyges finished the book in one sitting. He went back through it again and read only the passages he'd marked.

Finally, he closed the book and his eyes. He was exhausted, but he knew now what he must do about Tracy.

The course of action was clear—so clear, he was surprised he had not seen it before.

32

Gyges had almost no work waiting for him when he arrived in his office. The Freeman negotiations were scheduled for the end of the week. Hosbinder's group had completed the majority of the prep. Tommy and Danny were in Duluth looking into a couple faltering firms in the Iron Range.

He read from *The Prince* until his mind drifted to Erica. Maybe his note had pushed things too far.

There was only one way to find out. He reached inside his jacket for his cell, and as he did, it rang. It was Erica. He could hardly believe it. She'd called.

"Hello, Guy? Is that you?"

"Hey, Erica. This is wild. I was wondering how you were doing. I was just getting ready to call. No kidding—I had my hand on the phone."

"I got your note. It was very sweet."

"Well, that's why I was going to call. I wanted to make sure you got it."

"Yeah, it was waiting for me on my desk when I got in today." She paused, seeming to weigh what she wanted to say. "I took yesterday off because I had to help Dave."

She paused again, and Gyges waited for her to continue. "Uhh . . . Dave kinda had an accident at my house and needed my help to get around yesterday."

"An accident? Gee, I hope it wasn't too serious. What happened?"

"He slipped and fell down the steps from my kitchen

and . . . injured his back. His face was bruised as well. I had to take him to the ER."

"Boy, what a lucky guy Dave is. I hope he appreciates all you do for him."

"Oh, I think he does. But Dave's not really the kind of man who . . . well . . .

"I'm going to the club after work," said Gyges. "I thought you might want to redeem your rain check. If you're going, we could have dinner after."

"I'd really like that, but I'm fixing dinner for Dave. He's still laid up from work at home."

"Oh, I understand. Well, no deadline on the rain check. It's good for as long as you want."

"I'm gonna use it," she said. "Soon. I should get back to work. I just wanted to call and tell you how much I appreciated your thoughtfulness."

They said their goodbyes and hung up. Overall, it was a positive development. He just wished it wouldn't take so long.

The rest of the morning, Gyges visited his employees. Generally, he found people warm and enthusiastic to see him. He sensed that a few, including at least one team leader, remained loyal to Tracy. He suspected they were funneling information to him.

The visits took most of the morning; Gyges took his time. When he got back to his office, he made a list of suspects. He'd watch them more closely and, if he could prove they were helping Tracy, he'd fire them and replace them with people who would be loyal.

* * *

After lunch, he disappeared and went to Stan's office—the team leader he most suspected of aligning with Tracy. Stan had headed the team investigation at the Austin plant. Tracy had hired Stan when he'd first gotten the job, and they'd seen a lot of each other socially when Tracy had been his boss. Gyges wondered if Stan was stupid enough to leave a trail back to Tracy.

He was going to pull his old password trick, but he thought of the MIS director instead. He had other pieces he could put into play.

With that in mind, he reappeared in the hall outside the director's office. He peeked his head in.

"Ms. Washington, can I bother you for a minute?"

"Sure, what can I do for you?" Bonita Washington said with a hint of a Georgia accent.

Gyges closed the door behind him. "This is sensitive," he said in a low voice. "I don't want others to hear. I need your help and discretion on something."

"What's that?" She matched his tone and volume.

"I've found an employee who may be revealing company information to outsiders and former employees."

"I can't believe that. I know people do that sort of thing, but I'm always shocked by it. Like when Mr. O found out that Mr. M had sent secret emails to people at Freeman."

He was buoyed by her slip of confidence. She'd done this before for Danny. She'd be sympathetic, but Gyges warned himself to be careful using her in the future.

"Yes, we were all shocked by that. Who would have guessed? It saddens me to tell you it might still be going on. I need you to check email messages to and from a few employees. Check for correspondence with Mr. Mackus."

"Do you need these checked from now into the future or do you need their past records?"

"Preferably both."

"That shouldn't be a problem. We can filter email by source. Do you know Mr. Makus's home email?"

He wrote it down and slid it across the desk. "Also, here's a list of names to check against."

She picked up the paper and studied it. "I'll get one of my people on it," she said.

"This is a very sensitive manner. I don't want anyone finding out about this. It may tip them off that we suspect something. Do you have people you trust?"

"I see your point. Would you like me to do it myself?"

"I trust your judgment. Do it the way you think best. I'm just alerting you to the confidential nature of this. I know you'll protect the interests of the company."

"Thank you, Mr. Gyges. I appreciate your confidence."

"Not at all. Danny has told me you are one of the most competent people here."

"I do my best," she said with a broad smile.

Gyges busied himself with putting together a file on Stan. If he was going to replace him with someone more loyal, he'd need the evidence ready. He included a copy of the botched report from the Austin visit, when Stan's team had missed what was going on. Stan would be first, but Gyges suspected he wasn't the only one. He realized after reading The Prince that he had to be ruthless in rooting out the Tracy sympathizers. It was the only way to solidify power in the department; it would build a cadre of loyalist and strike fear in those who thought about opposing him in the future.

Late in the afternoon, his cell phone rang. It was Erica.

"Hi, Guy. It's Erica. I was wondering if I might cash in that rain check after all."

* * *

Gyges and Erica agreed to bypass the workout, and he suggested they meet at The Park Tavern. It wasn't too far from his apartment, and he thought that if things went well, she might come over. He gave her directions.

After they ordered, he made small talk about her work and continued to lie about his interest in a condo. Erica was pleasant but not talkative. She answered his inquires but didn't initiate any conversation herself. She seemed uneasy and nervous.

"I was surprised to get your first call, but even more

so to get the second," he said, hoping to prompt her into revealing what had changed her mind.

"Dave called. He's going out with his legal assistant; she's catching him up on cases. He said she'd pick him up."

"I thought he was only out a couple days?"

"Yeah, but he says that in an important job like his, being out even a short time puts him way behind. That's why he needed Ellen to meet him tonight."

"Does he do evening meetings very often?" Gyges was probing for weak spots.

"Not too often," she said. "Maybe once a week."

"Sounds like a lot to me," he replied, pushing the needle in a bit farther.

"Did I tell you someone's been vandalizing his car?"

"Oh, no. What happened?"

"They've put a scratch in it and broken something off in the locks. The other day someone knocked out his taillight. It's really upsetting him."

"Does he know who's doing it?"

"He thinks maybe a disgruntled client or someone who lost a case to him."

"Has he been to the police?"

"He talked to them, but they didn't show much interest. They said if he can prove who's doing it, they'll arrest them, but they can't watch his car all the time."

"I suppose they're busy doing other things," Gyges said. He imagined Dave didn't have many friends at the police department.

"Yeah, I just worry that some crazy person is following him. But Dave's got a plan to catch the guy. He installed two tiny video cameras on the car—one on each side. They send pictures back to a private security guard. I think they're motion sensitive or something."

"Well, I hope he catches the guy." Gyges was grateful for the information but well past the point of wanting to hear about Dave.

"Me too. It really upsets Dave."

Gyges tried to steer the conversation to Erica's interests. He found out mostly what he already knew from his trips to her apartment. She enjoyed working out and reading romance novels. Decorating her house was important to her. She did some gardening—mostly flowers. She liked drying and pressing them to make gifts for friends.

Gyges found almost all of what she said to be extremely boring. He didn't have the slightest interest in decorating or gardening or dried flowers. He feigned interest and asked questions. After some time, she became more relaxed and opened up. He was grateful he didn't have to hear about Dave anymore. As she talked about changing the color of her living room and buying new curtains, he couldn't stop his mind from wandering to scenes of her long legs and big breasts. Gyges wondered how long until Dave was out of the picture or, at least, he got her into his bed.

The dinner ended well, and Gyges felt they'd connected. Any hopes of getting her back to her place were dashed, however, after he paid the check. Without prompting, she stated that she should get home in case Dave called—he might need her help. Gyges didn't push the issue.

He walked her back to her car. He thought things might be building to a kiss when he heard a voice from behind them.

"Hey, lady—do you know who this asshole is?" he heard someone shout. "Do you know what an absolute prick he is?"

Gyges wheeled around to see Tracy waving his arms.

Erica was frightened by Tracy's approach and leaned against Gyges for protection. He instinctively put his arm around her.

"Tracy, get the hell out of here!" Gyges yelled.

"Did he tell you he's married? Yeah, that's right. Gyges here is a married. He just wants to fuck you—that's all."

Erica abruptly pushed away from Gyges's embrace, eying him strangely.

"Who is this guy?" she asked. "Is he telling the truth?"

"No, of course not. He's a drunk loser!"

"And you're a lying asshole. You tried to ruin my life, Gyges. I told you I'd be watching. I don't know who you are, lady, but you're hooked up with a bad man. You better get away from him while you can."

Gyges could see Erica distance herself from him in fear and confusion. He raced around the end of her car and lunged at Tracy, but Tracy saw him coming and started running. Gyges chased him through the parking lot. He stopped when he remembered Erica alone at her car.

He turned back just in time to see her screech out of the parking lot and down the street.

33

The next day, Gyges called in sick. Tracy threatened everything. He needed to act. Now. His anger had built to a rage, but in the end, it was his own fault. He had miscalculated Tracy's tenacity and resolve. He couldn't afford to let that happen again. As he had learned from *The Prince*, men ought to be treated well or be crushed, because they can avenge themselves of lighter injuries. There was no middle ground.

He'd been to Tracy's house a number of times. He parked a mile away in a shopping center. He turned his ring as he slammed the car door shut. The day was sunny and cool, the leaves turning in the trees on the outskirts of the parking lot. Yet he enjoyed none of this. Gyges was absorbed in his plan.

Twenty minutes later, he checked Tracy's drive and garage. His car was there; Janet's was gone. He would be alone in the house. At the backdoor, Gyges swallowed hard. He twisted the doorknob. Unlocked. He pulled his knife from his jacket and opened the largest blade.

He stepped inside and pulled the door closed. The house was quiet except for the ticking a grandfather clock. He wished a radio or TV were on to cover his footsteps.

He slid through the living room and kitchen. Tracy was in neither. He made his way through the other rooms—they, too, were lifeless and silent.

From the front foyer, he ascended the carpeted stairs to the bedrooms. Halfway up, he paused and listened. Nothing.

He climbed the rest of the way to a long hall. He guessed the left bedroom, but Tracy wasn't there either. The two other rooms were empty, too. He descended back to the front foyer.

Standing in a large family room, he listened as the grandfather clock ticked. Normally the sound relaxed him, but now it only increased the pace of his heartbeat. There was a short hall that broke off from the room. He approached slowly. Two doors. One opened to a bathroom.

The other door was shut.

He rested his ear against it. He couldn't hear anything. He glanced down and spotted a faint light from the gap. He took a deep breath, held it.

The smell of smoke and alcohol rushed into the hallway as he opened the door. He almost coughed. In the glow of the computer screen, Tracy slept at the desk—his cheek in a small pool of saliva, one hand on an empty glass. Gyges slipped in. The room was a mess. Papers were stacked everywhere. Bottles littered the floor, and the ashtray hadn't been emptied in days.

To the right of what Gyges could only describe as a conspiracy chart, a large trophy bass was mounted on the wall.

He stopped.

He had been with Tracy the day he had caught it. It was before Tracy developed his animosity toward Gyges. Tracy had just started at OH that winter and Gyges had asked him to join him and his friends. Tracy hadn't fished much. They had gone down the narrow canal, just off the channel between Lower Whitefish and Rush Lakes into Hidden Lake, and fished a beaver damn off a large bank of lily pads. The water had been a clear green.

Gyges remembered the fish dart at Tracy's worm from beneath the edge of the beaver lodge. Tracy had seen it, too—almost panicked into setting the hook too soon. But Gyges had calmed him, told him to set the hook just as the bass swam away with the worm in its mouth.

Tracy had played the fish just right, keeping him out of the pads near the deeper water. When he had finally boated it, he had been beyond excited. Gyges had unhooked the fish from the line and moved to lower it back into the water.

Tracy had gotten angry. He had wanted a trophy. Gyges had tried to dissuade him but Tracy had insisted. And so Gyges had relented. It was Tracy's catch—he could do with it as he pleased.

Seeing the fish now, Gyges felt an old emotion well up inside. He wished it could have been different.

On the computer screen was the fastener division's report. Tracy was on the right track. Gyges wondered how much he'd puzzled out. It was then, standing over Tracy with the knife, that he first admired his longtime bully and adversary.

Gyges raised the knife. His old boss hadn't budged.

The grandfather cloak continued to tick from the other room. He looked up at the mounted fish.

Then again at the computer screen.

Goddamn it, Gyges. You pussy—just do it! Now! You know he'd do it to you.

He hated Tracy. But he couldn't slit his throat. He just couldn't make himself do it. He cursed his weakness, but it didn't matter how much he berated himself—he just couldn't plunge the knife into Tracy's neck.

He closed the blade and stepped back into the hall.

He almost left but couldn't do that either. He stared into the room at Tracy snoring from the table. The ticking seemed to speed up. But for Gyges, time slowed, and then he was outside his body. He saw himself looming in the doorway.

Then he watched as his body returned to the room. He grabbed a pack of cigarettes from the desk, took one out, and lit it with Tracy's lighter. Then he put the lit cigarette next to a pile of papers.

Within a moment, there was a vicious blaze. Gyges added more paper—Freeman files. Flames caught them. The fire grew.

Smoke filled the room.

Gyges closed the door behind him.

34

Gyges led the way in sentiment for Tracy. He told people, "Sure, Tracy was let go, but that doesn't mean we should be callous or unfeeling toward him or his family." He initiated a company collection for flowers, personally taking it around to each department and recounting stories of happier days when he and Tracy and his buddies had taken fishing trips to Whitefish Chain. After circulating a memo for the funeral arrangements, he gave everyone in his department the morning off to attend the service.

Most of the people there were OH employees. The brothers and Patrick had sent a card and a large wreath, but they didn't make it to the visitation or funeral. Their absence surprised no one. An untimely death didn't erase Tracy's disloyalty. In truth, Tracy was dead to them the day he was escorted to his car. Janet cursed the O'Brien name and had the wreath removed by the funeral director.

A few days rolled by before Gyges returned to Bonita Washington.

"Do you really need these records now?" she asked when he approached her.

Gyges was in a delicate situation—he needed the evidence to purge the department of Tracy's supporters. Tracy's death hadn't changed that. If anything, it was more imperative. These people would always harbor a grudge. They might, despite the lack of evidence, even blame him for the fire. Their spite could only lead to trouble. They had to be crushed.

"I wish I could say I didn't. I wish it was water under the bridge. I really do. If it were just about me, no, I wouldn't. But the gravity of their transgression cannot be ignored. They put this company at risk and by doing so showed they don't truly believe in what we are doing here, or in the opportunities OH has given them." He sighed as if unloading a heavy burden. He waited for her to respond. She didn't, so he continued pounding his theme. "You know, if we could be sure it was a one-time thing—an inadvertent mistake or lapse of judgment—we might let it go. But this is obviously something more. It was an intentional act that placed the private agenda of these individuals above the good of the whole. If they did it once, they'd do it again. Do you think we can afford to work with that hanging over us?"

He could still impress himself. He was like a white-collar Rumpelstiltskin, spinning bullshit to gold. He smiled and looked at her intently. He'd wait all morning for agreement if he had to.

She looked back, then down at the folder in front of her. She shook her head and slid the folder across the desk. Gyges nodded in approval.

"I won't forget your sensitivity and commitment to the company," he said. "I'll personally make sure the O'Briens are aware of your help."

Gyges carried the papers back to his office. Stan's emails were laid out in chronological order. There was no interpretation needed—the cocksucker had been feeding Tracy information. Stan was toast. So was his assistant, Fred, and another team leader, Walter. They weren't as complicit as Stan, but it was necessary to fire them as well. It was unclear if Elvin, Steve's assistant, should be dropped, too. Better safe than sorry, Gyges thought.

He spent the rest of the afternoon preparing the case against the five employees. Gerba would side with them. It was in her nature to champion the underdog. That had worked for him before, but it would work against him now. He didn't need her help or approval; it was better if she sat this one out.

Instead, he went straight to Tommy. He spun it the same way with Tommy that he had with Bonita Washington. Tommy was shaken and disappointed. The old man was worn out and tired, but he agreed that the men had to go. Gyges insisted that he ax them personally. Tommy was grateful and agreed to take the matter up with Gerba. Gyges remained firm and resolute during the entire exchange. Tommy had to believe he was sure of what to do.

Tommy's heart was no longer in the fight. Mentally, he was distracted, ready to retire. Gyges knew it was time for Tommy to get out, but he didn't want or need to get rid of him. Tommy was doing that himself. What he needed to do was demonstrate to Patrick and Danny—mostly Danny—that he was the man to slide into the free spot. He didn't have a lot of time. In the future, he'd find ways to work past Tommy and deal directly with Danny.

He called the stalwarts from the former regime to his office and made them wait outside. Then he called them in one at a time. He started with Elvin and worked his way up to Stan. The men were crushed by Gyges's resoluteness. They'd thought of him as a wavering, indecisive person who wanted to be everyone's friend. Tracy had only re-enforced that view after he'd been let go. Gyges had lulled them into complacency when he'd taken over, and they were not prepared for the blistering attack. He reduced Elvin and Walter to tears and Stan into a confused silence. Each time, he fired the person and then phoned security to escort him from the building. It was in full view of the rest of the department—execution style. He wanted to humiliate them in a public so they would never want to be seen again by their former colleagues. He wanted to make sure they never caused more trouble. It was also a lesson for everyone else.

Gyges relished the task. It was like getting another shot at Tracy. A farewell present for his old fishing buddy.

35

Finding replacements for the fired men took up most of the rest of Gyges's week. He convinced Tommy that he had to be included in the hiring process. Gerba wouldn't ensure he got the kind of people he was looking for—technically competent, organizationally compliant. Gyges also wanted the new hires to feel personally indebted to him. He made a great show of marching through the company and encouraging people to apply for the positions. He told them he'd promote from within if possible.

He devoted the rest of his time to becoming more visible to Danny. He found reasons to consult him on a variety of matters, but he was careful not to overdo it—he didn't want to convey incompetence. He kept the questions on big-picture stuff—the company's strategy and direction. He wanted to know what kind of companies Danny pursued.

The extra effort paid off, and Danny became more comfortable with him. Gyges never sensed impatience, and Danny never rushed him out of the office.

But none of this activity kept Gyges from thinking about Erica. When he made repeated attempts to see her at the club, she stopped going. He assumed she had simply joined another club, but he didn't have the time to follow her. He made usual drives past her house, but she was always gone. He wondered if she was spending the time with Dave. Maybe she was seeing someone else. Not knowing gnawed at him, filling his mind in his bed at night and sometimes distracting him at work. He didn't understand why she wouldn't give him the chance to explain. She owed him that much. It was inconsiderate of her not to consider his feelings.

Finally, one Wednesday afternoon, he drove to the bank. Several other employees were getting in their cars, leaving for the day. He parked near her car in the back of the lot. Within ten minutes, he saw her come out the door. She did not notice him until she was almost to her car.

"Erica," he said, stepping out from the driver's side. "I've been trying to talk to you. I want to explain what happened that night."

"I told you I don't want to talk. I don't want to get involved with a person who has so much drama in his life." She took out her keys and unlocked her door. "Plus, there's something about you that makes me uncomfortable."

"It's not my fault . . . that guy was crazy," he stammered. "He—"

"I don't care. I don't want to get involved with something like that. Stop bothering me."

"But I need to see you," he hollered. "I find you extremely attractive and exciting."

He stepped toward her. He reached out and draped a hand on her shoulder.

She pushed it away. "What are you doing?" she shouted. "What kind of creep are you? Get away from me. And stay away! Dave says that if you keep bothering me, I can have you arrested for stalking. So do yourself a favor and find someone else."

Gyges's eyes narrowed and his voice lowered. "Dave says that, does he? So you get free legal advice for sucking him off?"

"You're disgusting! If I ever see you around, if I even see your car, I'm calling the police." She hurried into her car and sped out of the lot.

He watched her drive off.

Well, that fuckin' cunt won't have to worry about seeing me the next time we meet, he thought. The unfairness was heartbreaking. Tracy had ruined his chances with her. And Dave! She'd chosen Dave over him. Dave was a piece of shit. He abused her. She probably even knew he cheated on her, and still she stayed by his side. Gyges couldn't tolerate it.

He should just let her alone, he knew. It would be the smart thing. But he couldn't stand not getting what he wanted.

* * *

When Gyges arrived, it was already after ten. Erica's car was in the drive. He didn't see any lights on. He let himself in and moved through the dark house. He heard the bathroom shower. In the reading room, he sat and waited.

The water stopped—he imagined her wet, naked, nipples hard, drawing back the shower curtain. After a few minutes, he heard the bathroom door open, then Erica's steps on the way down the hall toward her bedroom. He continued to wait, sitting there for over an hour.

When he was certain she was asleep, he crept to her room and stood in the doorway. He could hear her rhythmic breathing. When his eyes adjusted to the dim light, he could make her out on the bed. He leaned over her, took a deep breath. She stirred slightly but didn't wake. He slid his hand inside her pajama top and rubbed her breasts. He felt himself grow hard.

Then, as if being stabbed with a hot poker, she bolted upright. She snatched his hand as he tried to pull it away.

"Dave, is that you?"

Gyges shook his hand free and stepped back.

"Dave?" she called. "Who's there? Dave, don't mess around." She rolled to the other side of the bed and turned on the light.

Gyges could see that she was truly frightened and backed slowly out of the room. It felt as though she was staring straight into his eyes.

Erica jumped from the bed, then slammed and locked the bedroom door.

* * *

Gyges waited a week before he returned to the house—this time not out of lust, but cruelty. Again, as Erica slept, he fondled her. And again she awoke abruptly, but this time he did not jump back. He continued to touch her.

Erica screamed, flailing her arms to stop him. He retreated to the corner of the room. She switched on the light and stared wildly this way and that, her head darting back and forth in hysteria. Soon she was in tears. Like a child, she pulled the sheets up to her neck and cried.

Poor girl, he noted. The monster under the bed was real.

He hurried to the reading room and slammed books against the table. He could hear her phone the police and lock the bedroom door.

They arrived five minutes later. One banged on the front door while his partner checked around back. Erica unlocked the bedroom door and sprinted to the front of the house. She let the officer in—his gun already drawn.

He motioned for her to step back and swept the house. His partner joined him inside.

The first officer called for Erica, who had retreated back to the bedroom.

"We can't find anyone here, Miss. The back door's locked. All the windows are secure, as well. You remember what time you got home?"

"About eight-thirty," she said, still shaking. "I stopped for dinner and shopping after work."

"Both doors locked when you arrived?"

"Yes. I came in the back. I had to get the mail from the front, so I remember unlocking it."

"Did you hear anything?"

"No, I just read for awhile. I already told the dispatcher all this."

"Yes. Who else has a key?" asked the second cop.

"Only my mother and my boyfriend, Dave Johnson."

"You haven't had any arguments with him lately, have you?"

"No."

"You say you were asleep and then you woke up and thought someone was in the house?" asked the first officer.

"Not just in the house—in my room! He was groping me! That's why I woke up." Her voice wavered and she began to cry. "I didn't dream this," she said, almost shouting. "There was really someone here."

"Miss, please stay calm. We're just trying to figure out what happened here."

"Someone broke into my house—that's what happened here."

"Miss, I'm gonna have to ask you again to calm down. We'll make one more check. If someone was here, they must have gotten in somehow."

Gyges backed away from Erica and the officers. He'd heard enough. As she continued to protest, he sneaked out the back, silently escaping into the night, a weight lifted from his heart.

36

"Petros, you sorry excuse for a Greek," Bhuto boomed from the doorway, two large plastic bottles of his tea by his side. "It's good to see you, my friend."

"It's good to see you, too, Bhuto, even though you're a Turk," Gyges chided back.

Bhuto belted out his big laugh. He looked like he had lost weight and gotten a tan while he was away.

"You look great. Tanned, rested, and slimmer."

Bhuto slapped his ample stomach, "Yes, my friend, here did not find the cuisine to his liking."

"Tough assignment?"

Bhuto joined Gyges in the steam room. "Yes, tough assignment. I didn't think so when I took it, but solving the client's problems was harder than either of us had thought it would be. There were actually two problems. The first I solved right away when I got there. The other was more elusive. But Petros, don't fear; your friend solved that one in the end, too. And how are you? You still have to work for that asshole who is trying to fire you?"

"Oh, no," Gyges replied. "I'm pleased to report he's been sacked and I've been promoted in his place." He tried to play it cool, but he couldn't help beaming.

"What great news, my friend! Let us drink! I have just the libation for such an occasion. Here, I have brought you your own." The fat man handed Gyges a bottle of his tea.

"To our success!" said Gyges.

"To our failures—may they be great teachers," added Bhuto.

Gyges drank deep. It was great to taste the tea again—even better than he remembered.

"I've missed this," he said, tipping the bottle.

"And I have missed this," replied Bhuto. He swept his hand across the room. "Steaming is such a civilized custom. You know, in some places they've never heard of this? Third-world barbarians! Not like us, Petros—the finest stock from ancient Mediterranean cultures." Bhuto let out a rumble.

"Some months back you gave me a copy of *The Prince*."

"Of course, yes. You never read it, did you? Here I give you my own copy and you go and lose it."

"No, I did read it. While you were gone. Remarkable. I wish I would have read it the night you gave it to me."

"Yes, I know. You should listen to me more. I knew you hadn't read it, because you said nothing. But I also knew you would be caught like one of your silly fishes once you did. It fits right in with your chess and strategy work. I give good gifts, yes? 'Just what the doctor ordered,' as you say."

"You are the master," said Gyges. "I bow to your wisdom." He extended his hands and arms in mock bow. "Actually, I'm doing more than just reading it. I'm studying it, trying to absorb its lessons. And I've been applying it at work. Taking his suggestions, I fired the ardent supporters of my old boss. It was clear they'd always be looking to undercut me, so I got rid of them all at once."

Bhuto leaned back and took a drink of tea. "Of course you did. This is very good. When you oust the former prince by force or guile, you must crush his supporters so they no longer pose a threat. What did you do when your old boss tried to mount a campaign to win back his job?"

"I'm impressed—how'd you know he tried that?"

"This is normal," Bhuto said.

"I didn't have to do much," Gyges said with as little emotion as he could manage. "He died in a fire at his home."

Bhuto sat straight up. He peered at his friend through the heavy air. "Died in a fire? Was this a suspicious fire, Petros?" Bhuto's voice shed its usual mirth. He pronounced each word slowly.

The question hung in the air without reply. Gyges's eyes fell to his bottle. He drank and pondered his answer. Bhuto did not break the silence. His eyes were fixed on Gyges.

Finally, after clearing his throat, Gyges spoke. "He died of smoke inhalation after he fell asleep in his study. The fire department ruled it accidental. A cigarette dropped on a pile of papers."

"I see," said Bhuto. "How unfortunate for him." He hadn't blinked.

"Yes, unfortunate. He let himself become obsessed with blaming . . . uhh . . . me, I mean, my company, for his downfall. He let himself go, drinking and whatnot. I didn't expect him to take it as hard as he did. He shoulda just walked away. You know, forgotten it and moved on. He was beaten, but he couldn't accept it. He conspired with friends, pored over reports and shit his buddies smuggled out for him. If he woulda just taken his losses and walked away, he'd probably still be alive today."

"When you're so focused on getting or keeping something, Petros, it's hard to walk away. Impossible sometimes."

"I guess. In the past, I never minded losing. At least, I didn't notice if it bothered me. Now I hate losing. Once it was my boss or me, I would have done anything, risked everything so that it was him."

"Looks like he felt the same way."

Gyges took another drink, "As Machiavelli says, it's natural to desire to acquire things. It's praiseworthy to pursue them. The only shame is in failure."

"Amen to that," said Bhuto. "Let us dress and go to the cafe."

37

For the next few months, Gyges's life settled into a routine while he vied to take over for Tommy. Once he had Tommy's job, he could relax and enjoy life on the top—fewer late hours, fewer headaches. No longer would he continually stress over the pressure and intrigue. He could get back to doing what he truly loved—fishing. Until then, all his gear went into storage. The fish and blue skies would have to wait.

Once the details had been worked out, he signed the divorce papers and it was finished. The rest was anticlimactic, and he was glad to be done with it. By the time of the settlement, she'd sold the house and stored the money in escrow. Neither he nor Angie attended the final divorce hearing.

He and Bhuto continued their Wednesday-afternoon steams. Over the winter months, Gyges gained confidence and understanding. He came to view himself less as Bhuto's pupil and more as his equal—not in chess but in his use and understanding of power. He was still grateful for what Bhuto had taught him—without Bhuto's guidance, he'd probably never be where he was—but Gyges believed he no longer needed Bhuto's strategic commentary. He even grew to resent it. He had killed to achieve his goals. In his mind, this made him superior. He occupied a higher level than Bhuto.

He stopped discussing these matters with the fat man. It created a rift in the relationship that both men felt under the surface. By the end of winter, both found more frequent reasons to cancel their weekly get-togethers. And not long after the ice melted, the meets were dropped altogether.

It didn't take long for Gyges to become bored with the day-to-day grind of OH. The seemingly endless rounds of meetings were especially cumbersome. His concentration would lapse when his team driveled on about the details of inventory, machine-life spans, maintenance schedules, non-tangible assets, or customer databases and retention planning. Through disinterest, he became a manager who delegated almost everything. "Solve it yourself; that's why I pay you" became his mantra. "Bring me solutions, not problems" was another.

He longed for the high-wire intrigue of his coup. He wanted to be working on the fringe—if not on the edge of acceptability, then over it. His adrenals just didn't get the workout with the banal machinations of everyday corporate management. He wanted rock and roll, not the slow waltz of another week of reports, meetings, and data analysis. So Gyges stopped doing the business of business.

Understanding that all business was simply a matter of power relationships and the use of power to acquire what you wanted liberated Gyges; he no longer worried about any of the boring technical or financial details. That garbage was for the lesser lights for whom such matters held a kind of adolescent fascination.

He concentrated on what he had learned from his coup, his conversations with Bhuto, chess, and the hardheaded real politic of *The Prince*. His focus on power relationships and the psychology of power turned him into a formidable force within OH. The fact that he could go anywhere and observe anyone pushed him from formidable into unassailable. Once he decided what had to be accomplished, he was never thwarted.

Tommy was too busy with the details of his move to Ireland to notice Gyges's inattentiveness. And Tommy's frequent absences from work allowed Gyges to court Danny's favor. He was careful, though. Danny, the cagey old bass, could spot a phony even in the murky corporate waters. Gyges remembered Danny's suspicion of the Freeman boys. They had been so obvious in their goodie, goodie act. The man was a realist on people's motivations: they usually wanted something or they wouldn't be talking to you.

Gyges used his time to study Danny, become an expert on the man's behavior and thinking. He spent part of every day following Danny around—observing him in his office, listening to his calls, sitting in on meetings, and reading his emails. He adjusted his days to Danny's calendar.

By the end of the season, he knew more about Danny than everyone except Danny's brother and son. But with only a month until Tommy's retirement, they still had not announced a replacement. The fact that they failed to recognize Gyges's genius and acumen lowered his opinion of all three men. Danny was supposed to be the epitome of business savvy; he was good, but not as good as his reputation. Overrated by the uninformed, Gyges concluded. He could do better with the company. Sure, it made money, but it could be even more prosperous with a man like himself in the driver's seat. The old man was cautious by nature. A real leader put everything on the line if he had to. Lucrative deals were being lost every day. "Missed opportunities" became code for what he considered Danny's failure of nerve.

Criticism of the O'Briens aside, however, Gyges knew he hadn't yet found the pitch he needed to get the promotion, that one big deal that would secure him the job. If he couldn't find one, he'd have to create one.

* * *

"Tommy, how's the construction going?" Patrick asked as he sat down next to his uncle.

"Your dad and I were just discussing it," Tommy said. "Running behind, of course. It doesn't matter what country you're in; it's the same shit everywhere. If we ran our business like those construction bastards run theirs, we'd be broke in a year."

"What's the hold-up?"

"Oh, the damn finish carpenters. First group showed up drunk and the work suffered. But the general contractor refused to fire the guys. I told him, 'Either they go or you go.' So he fired his sons from the job."

The three O'Briens laughed.

From the corner of Danny's office, Gyges glanced down at the street below. Spring had finally arrived, and it was a glorious day.

He attended all their meetings now. Today he hadn't been invited—not that it mattered.

"But now he says he can't find anyone else in Clifden to do the work. Says he'll have to pull in some guys from Galway. Pure bullshit, of course. It's also gonna cost more. He's got me by the balls."

"Can you still move as planned?"

Gyges glanced from the window back to Tommy.

"We could, but Margaret wants to wait. She doesn't want to live in the dust and noise. Can't fault her for that. We've rented a little house for a month on the road just north of Galway. I leave in less than four weeks."

"I'm really excited for you, Tommy," said Patrick with genuine affection for his uncle. "I know this is something you've wanted for a long time. Plus, we'll have a place to stay for free when we visit."

"That's why we put in the small wing with two extra bedrooms. It won't be free, though, Patty."

Patrick smiled at his uncle, but Gyges truly wondered if the old ballbuster was joking.

"Speaking of you leaving brings us to the topic of today's meeting," interjected Danny. "What're we doing about the position?"

"I talked with Michael," Tommy said. "I didn't ask directly, but I opened the door for him by talking about how hard it's been to figure out my replacement. He knew what I was getting at. But he didn't express any interest in returning.

He loves what he's doing."

"Too bad. It would have been great to have him back," Patrick said.

It didn't surprise Gyges. Michael and Danny didn't get along. Michael didn't like Danny's style—too direct and abrupt. That's why he'd left the first time. In fact, it was likely to get worse. Tommy had a calming effect on his brother. God knows, Patrick doesn't. It would be a lot stormier.

"So where does that leave us?" asked Danny.

"Can Pete do the job?" prompted Tommy.

"That's one I was thinking," replied Patrick. "He's worked for you now since Tracy's departure—what's your sense of his abilities?"

"Like both of you, before the Freeman deal I wouldn't have thought he had the drive. Too laid back. *Disinterested* might be a better word. He had an uncanny knack for finding the minimum necessary and letting that be his maximum performance. Great kid. Can't think of anyone I'd rather go fishing or hunting with. Do anything for you. But work just didn't excite him. Having said that, my perception changed after the Freeman deal. What he did there was miraculous."

"Yes, yes, we're all in agreement there," said Danny, impatient with Tommy's habit of recounting known history. "What we need to know is your performance evaluation since."

"I was getting to that." Tommy winked at Patrick. "He's shown some real leadership skills. He has a way of motivating people to get things done. It's not my way, but it works for him. We all have our own styles, I guess."

"What do you mean?" asked Patrick.

"He's definitely got an edge. A sharp one. Not with me, but I've watched him with his people. He can be brutal if he thinks he needs to be. And he thinks he needs to be more often than not. The way he handled those firings was chilling."

"They deserved it," said Danny. "They were part of that bastard's—God rest his soul—treachery here. I was glad he did it. He went out and got the goods on 'em and took action."

"I'm not saying they didn't deserve it. My point is the way he went about it. It made people afraid of him. Afraid to displease him. Plus, I don't know how he does it, but he knows things there's no way you can figure out how he knows them. It's kinda spooky, really. I can't figure it out. Like the Freeman deal. How the hell did he know all that shit was going on? After we took over, we found notes from Braddock to Tracy in his private emails. Gyges knew all about that. How?"

"He says he just went over there and hung out unnoticed," said Patrick.

"Bullshit. You believe that?" asked Tommy.

"No, I still think he had a mole."

"We've been over this before. What the hell difference does it make now?" asked Danny.

"I was getting to that as well—Christ, you're getting impatient in your old age," Tommy chided. "He does that all the time here too. He knows shit he shouldn't. I've noticed on several occasions that he'll say something about what someone said or did that he had no way of knowing about. But he does. I don't know how he does it. It's unnerving. It only adds to the people's feeling of fear."

"Okay," said Danny. "So the guy has an uncanny sense for figuring out what's going on. Maybe he just has great instincts and intuition. Isn't that a good thing?"

"It is in the sense of knowing what's going on," Patrick put in, "but I think Tommy is wondering about its effect on those around him. I don't know about that; I don't work with him on a daily basis. But it's important to note how he works with the people under him. There isn't a real danger of him intimidating us, but I don't think a culture of fear shows solid leadership. That's not the kind of environment we want here, is it?"

"A little fear is good," answered Danny. "Keeps people on their toes."

"Maybe and maybe not; it depends. But let's not get sidetracked into a debate about the supposed benefits of fear. Tommy, Gyges has hired some replacements. What are they like?"

"They're technically very competent. He's picked people who know their shit. Which is great. But I think they're yes-men types, which isn't."

"Bottom line," said Danny. "Do we promote him or not?"

"Yes, with reservations," said Tommy.

"Can I abstain? I don't know enough to say either way," said Patrick.

"Well, I need a recommendation; that's why you're here," Danny reprimanded.

Patrick looked at him. The tone bothered him more than the words. "Then no. I say we leave the position open. Have Peter report directly to you and then decide if he should be upped."

Gyges shot a long look at Patrick. Unbelievable, he thought.

"How long can we leave it open? We don't have any new companies we're ready to pick up. That's what we need; that's what Tommy was out there doing. You can't—you're busy with the Freeman divisions now. We have to keep product in the pipeline. We need someone in the field rooting out new companies to buy."

"Then promote him," said Patrick, growing angry. "It's your call anyway."

"I'm aware of that. I'm looking for your recommendation," Danny shot back. He was getting red in the face.

"I gave you two. You didn't like either. Maybe if you'd let me know what recommendation you're looking for, I could—"

"Why not put Gyges in place on temporary assignment?" Tommy cut in. "A probationary run. Make it clear he's getting a fair shot. If it works after six months, then he gets it permanently. If not, he goes back to his current job."

"That's an interesting idea," said Danny. "I like it. It's fair, gets someone to drum up new business, and we can see how Pete fits into our little family."

"I wasn't asked, but I apparently voted yes," said Patrick. "In case anyone is counting, that makes it unanimous."

38

Danny O'Brien entered the room ahead of Gyges and turned on the lights. He stepped to the windows and opened the curtains to a lovely view of downtown Minneapolis facing the Mississippi. Gyges had to laugh—Danny acted like he was unveiling a previously hidden Monet.

"Well, here it is, Pete, me boy. Welcome to the top floor," said Danny.

Gyges trailed behind him and hovered in the doorway. After many visits to the office, he was still awed by the view. He'd have rather had this office than any other in the building. Even more than Danny's, which was twice as large.

Danny didn't linger over the view. He turned to Gyges at the door, reached into his pocket, pulled out a key, and dropped it in Gyges's hand. The old man gave him a gentle pat on the back and then shook his hand.

"It's all yours now," said Danny.

"Thank you, sir. It's an honor for me to be up here with the rest of the O'Briens." He turned the key in his hand before putting it in his jacket pocket.

"You deserve it after all you've accomplished for us," said Danny. "You can have this done over more to your style. But don't be goin' wild, now. Be sensible, but make it your own. I trust your judgment."

"That's not necessary, Mr. O'Brien. I love it the way it is. No need to change a thing. Why waste money on cosmetics?"

Danny grinned broadly. It was the kind of thing the old man liked to hear. He often said how in all his years of flipping companies, he'd never seen a modest office. He marveled that the company heads never considered cutting back on their own frivolous expenses.

"I appreciate your concern for the family, Pete. I know you have our real interests at heart."

"Something to be treasured, sir. You and Tommy and Patrick have built it into something special. I remember those old photos of your dad and you standing in front of that little office in New York, and all the stories at family dinners about the early days. I've always wanted to work here. I'm sure your father would be proud."

"God bless my old man—he worked at that old shit hole 'til the day he died. Never took a day off in his life. And I spent more time on damn Flaherty Row than at any school. Learned more than if I would have paid for the business education kids think they need."

"Well, you made all this possible," said Gyges, motioning to the office. "Patrick and I are lucky to learn from a teacher who's really done it rather than from someone at the U who could only talk about it."

"There's no substitute for street smarts," Danny agreed. "I have to give it to my old man. He had that in spades. Now it's your turn to continue his legacy. I have to tell you that you have certainly surprised us with your performance in the last six months."

"Thank you, sir. It's great you three believed in me enough to give me this opportunity. I appreciate your confidence and trust."

"We were in a tough spot with the Freeman deal. You were the only one to see that. You saved us from that sonofabitch Tracy and his two bastard buddies."

"They really were pricks," laughed Gyges. "What happened to them? I heard they took the money and ran to Belize."

"Yeah, they did. Until we renegotiated our offer, we

didn't know that they weren't the sole owners. They were just the front guys for some Italian family in Chicago. But I heard through the grapevine that the other owners sent a man down there to find them. From what I gathered, he was able to recover most of it."

"What about Braddock and Shadmun?"

"Not much is known about their current whereabouts." Danny smiled and shrugged. "But enough about them; we're here to talk about you. You've done great in Tracy's seat. Tommy says you have amazing intuition when it comes to strategy. 'Uncanny' is the word he uses when talking about how you get access to information."

"Nothing uncanny about hard work, sir. I learned that from watching you and Tommy. I just do my homework. Thorough prep—that's all it really is. A very underestimated quality these days."

"Tommy thinks you've done an even better job than Tracy. You've hired talented people, and you're committed to getting things done."

"That's gracious of him. I knew it was finally my chance to show what I could do. Tommy hired me originally, and I wanted to show him that he hadn't been mistaken. I was always in Tracy's shadow, behind the scenes, so I know he didn't think I could pull this off."

"To be frank, Pete, none of us did. No offense, son, but none of us gave you a chance."

"None taken. I understand. If I were in your place I would have thought the same. I'm sure I looked like Tracy's gofer, but it wouldn't have been right for me to try to outshine him. He was my boss. I just did my work and waited for the right opportunity. Of course, I never imagined it would come about in the strange way it did."

"You know, Pete, we were all impressed by how you approached those difficult circumstances—and since then, too. But I'm not gonna sugarcoat this for you. We're still not sure you're cut out for this job. It's completely up to you to make it work. Patrick and I will do everything we can to help you succeed, and we want you to, but, in the end, it's your responsibility to get the job done."

Gyges hid his disdain as best he could. On one hand, he couldn't let Danny believe he was ungrateful. On the other, he knew Danny would sense any phoniness. "As long as we're being honest, sir, may I speak openly as well?"

"I expect it," Danny replied. "Not just now, but always."

"Good. Well, as I've said, I'm grateful for the opportunity. But, at the same time, I would be less than honest if I said I wasn't disappointed at the 'temporary' in front of my position. I understand, but it's doesn't make it easier. But, I want to say, the disappointment is in myself, that I evidently waited too long to show my worth. I was too passive. I won't let that happen again."

"I suppose I'd feel no different. But now you have the chance. We want you to be aggressive in pursuing your new responsibilities."

"You can be assured of that. I realize now that I have to seize the opportunities in life regardless of how they come. I've promised myself that I'll take advantage of every situation."

"When my father died from his heart attack," Danny said, "I had to scramble to make it work. I had my own ideas on how to get outta that dump on Flaherty Row, but the old man opposed them all. While he was alive, it was his call. It's a hard thing to say, but honesty requires it—his death gave me the chance to make the business my own. Son, life is uncertain. Who knows what the fates have in store for us. Whatever it is, we must always be prepared to seize the moment."

"My feelings exactly, sir," said Gyges. "Sometimes the most amazing opportunities lie right at our feet. We just have to muster the courage to reach down—"

"Mr. O'Brien," the soft buzz of the intercom cut in. "Your wife is here for lunch."

"Send her in," Danny replied. Again, he patted Gyges on the back.

Elizabeth Heath O'Brien rushed through the door, not hiding her irritation. Gyges could tell she hated having to wait for anything. She was also strikingly beautiful—dark brown hair, blue eyes, classic shape, and a stunning face accented by high cheekbones.

"Dan," she began with barely one foot in the door. "You know how crowded it gets for lunch. Let's go. I'm famished."

"Hello, Elizabeth," Danny said. "It's good to see you, too. Aren't you going to say hello to Peter Gyges? I believe you've met."

Elizabeth spun around and spotted Gyges standing off to the side, almost hidden by the door.

"Sorry, I didn't see you there. You're a bit hidden back by the door." She reached out to shake his hand. "It's nice to meet you. Again."

"And you as well, Mrs. O'Brien. It's been awhile."

She was about as warm as January concrete. She took a moment to study him carefully, trying to place him. Gyges could tell she couldn't recall ever meeting him before.

"Ah, yes . . . yes, it has. Not to be rude, but we're late for lunch. Danny, can we go?"

"You are being rude," Danny said. "We have a moment to converse. Peter here is taking over Tommy's job. He worked for Tracy before . . . Tracy left us. He's been doing a helluva job for us. This is the man who saved us from the Freeman deal."

"Oh, well, yes—the Freeman deal. I can't tell you how many times I've heard about the Freeman deal. Congratulations, Mister . . ."

"Gyges."

"Gyges? That's not Irish, is it?"

"No. Greek."

Gyges could see that this was a bitter revelation for her. She didn't even attempt to hide the malicious smile. He took note.

"Not an O'Brien. Or even Irish. Yet you're taking

Tommy's chair. You must be very good, then, Mr. Gyges"—she stressed it hard this time—"to break the Shamrock Ceiling here at OH. Quite an achievement. When I was here, the rule was that only the Irish moved up."

"Elizabeth Ellen!" Danny blurted out. "What a terrible thing to say. You know that's not true."

But it was clear she believed every word.

"Do I?" she asked, turning her gaze slowly away from Gyges. "Say, are you ready or not? I'm starved, and I don't want to stand in line. Let's go. I'm sure Mr. Gyges won't mind. A man who has just been given Tommy's seat has a learning curve to overcome."

"All right. I'm almost ready. I've gotta get my coat and make a quick call. Wait here and talk to Pete." Without waiting for an answer, he was out the door and down the hall.

"Very shortly, Dan. Very shortly," she called down the hall, not taking her eyes from Gyges.

There was a moment of awkward silence. Elizabeth went to the window and looked irreverently out on the city. She fidgeted, shifting her weight from one leg to the other. She let out a low sigh.

"You don't remember me, do you, Ms. O'Brien?" said Gyges.

Elizabeth took out a cigarette without looking away from the window. She started to light it but stopped and turned back toward him. "What do you mean? Of course I do."

"Really? Where was it then?"

Elizabeth paused, studied him again. Nothing.

"All right, Mr. Gyges. You caught me. I don't remember meeting you. I'm sorry, but I just don't."

"Your house last year. Company picnic."

"If you say so," she said. "I'll have to take your word for it. I'm sorry, but I honestly don't remember your face."

"No need to apologize. You aren't the first person to not remember meeting me. In those days, I wasn't very noticeable. But you certainly were. You were wearing a lovely black dress and a beautiful string of white pearls. You turned the head of every man at the party."

"Why, Mr. Gyges, you are a most observant man." Her voice had lost its icy tone.

"Observing people is one of the things I do best," he said. His voice matched hers.

"Is it really?" she said. A smile crept from the corner of her mouth. She lit her cigarette. "Tell me what else you've *observed* about me."

"You were angry when you heard I got Tommy's job."

"Not angry—surprised." The icy edge returned. "That's all. The O'Brien clan is very tight. I'm just surprised. Besides, I don't recall Danny ever speaking about you."

"I think there's more to it than that, Mrs. O'Brien; you're not being honest with me," he said, smiling.

"What did you say to me?" she scowled.

He could tell she wasn't used to being talked to in this way. "There was more than surprise in your reaction." Gyges continued to smile.

Elizabeth tried to maintain her composure. "Angry—why in the world would I be angry? I don't even know you, Mr. Gyges."

"Yes, I immediately wondered why Danny's wife would be angry—you don't, as you say, even know me. Judging now, though—from the remarks you've made—I'd guess you were on the wrong side of the Shamrock Ceiling when you worked here." Gyges kept up his pleasant demeanor. "But then I'm puzzled. After all, you did end up as Mr. O'Brien's partner."

"Wife," she shot back. "I'm his wife, not his partner."

"Oh, yes, I'm sorry. His wife. Not. His partner. I'll bet you had more in mind for yourself than trophy wife. Yes?"

"Trophy wife! Go to hell. I hate that term."

Gyges laughed. "I'm sure you do. I'm just commenting on what everyone can see. Don't shoot the messenger."

"Well, everyone can just go to hell right along with you. I've got a degree from the London School of Economics.

I'm no one's trophy wife." She blew a thick trail of smoke from her mouth.

"London School or not, you're still Mrs. Daniel O'Brien, trophy wife." He paused for a moment, changing to a more sympathetic tone. "Too bad—from what I hear, you could have made a name for yourself." Gyges let the smile fade. "I mean, a name other than Mrs. O'Brien."

"You're damn right about that. I was moving up in this place. People were starting to note my superior work. I would have gone further except for this damn Irish family bullshit."

"Instead of the O'Brien boardroom, you ended up in the O'Brien bedroom. I'd say you must have gone plenty far to end up there."

"You have a funny way of trying to impress the boss's wife, Mr. Gyges."

"I wasn't trying," he answered. "Not that it would be hard. You asked me what observations I had made. I was merely complying with your request. If you want me to impress you, I can do that too, but now is probably not—"

"You still haven't told me how a Greek passed the Paddy Preference."

"To be honest, I think they were more surprised than you. I came out of nowhere on a white horse. No one saw me coming. I surprised them, and I've kept surprising them ever since. That's how a Greek got the job," he said, taking a few steps just inside too close.

He leaned forward and lowered his voice. "I'll pass along something I've learned that they may not have taught you at the London School of Economics, Ms. O'Brien."

"Go ahead, Mr. Gyges; I'm listening," Elizabeth said, a smile breaking free once again.

"It's easier to get the better of people when they underestimate you. If they don't see you coming, you can overtake them before they realize what's upon them. Then it's too late. Try to get people to underestimate you, Ms. O'Brien. You'll find it much easier to get what you want."

"And you're sharing your how-to philosophy because . . . ?" She leaned in closer.

"I think in your . . . current situation, you're being underestimated. I think you resent it. I'm suggesting it's actually better that way. You just have to know how to exploit it. I have a feeling it will come in handy soon."

"Really? That's intriguing. Are your feelings usually accurate in matters of unexpected opportunity, Mr. Gyges?"

"Almost always. In this case, it's more than a feeling. I may have just an opportunity for a woman of your talents and position. If I did, would you be interested in hearing about it?"

"Probably. But I couldn't say for sure until I knew more."

"Then I should stop by the house sometime, reveal my business proposition for you."

"Would this proposition be for just me, or would Dan be involved?" she asked.

"Danny's very busy these days. I don't think he'd be interested."

"In that case, perhaps you should call first before you just show up at the house. After all, we wouldn't want to cause Dan any extra anxiety."

"No, we would not. Such a thoughtful wife."

"Thank you, Peter. You don't mind if I call you Peter, do you?"

"If you like. Although everyone just calls me Gyges."

"We'll, I wouldn't want to be like everyone. I like Peter better."

"Then for you, Peter it will be."

Gyges heard Danny's door open down the hall. Both Elizabeth and he put more space between them before Danny returned.

They heard him tell the secretary, "I'll be back in a couple hours." Then he stuck his head inside the door. "Okay, Elizabeth. Let's go. Peter, I hope she wasn't too much trouble. When I get back let's talk more about what you should work on while I'm on the coast."

"No trouble at all, sir."

Elizabeth stuck out her hand. Gyges shook it.

"Nice to see you again, Mr. Gyges. I'm sure we'll be seeing more of you now that you're on the family floor."

Gyges smiled. "I'm sure you will."

39

Gyges stalked up the long red-brick drive. Danny's gold Lexus was parked next to what he supposed was Elizabeth's Audi. He'd dropped the old man off at the airport after he'd returned from lunch. With Danny in Florida for a few days, it was the perfect time to find out what the trophy wife was up to.

He scouted the house, checking windows, but he couldn't see her anywhere. All the doors were locked. After cursing his luck and circling around to the front, he found the door to the garage unlocked.

He paused inside to listen. Nothing. He continued to the house door and put his ear to it. Then, satisfied that the other side was clear, he turned the handle just enough to release the latch and gave the door a delicate push. It opened to a laundry room. He crossed the room to a hallway. The thick carpet silenced his steps.

He heard Elizabeth talking on the phone. He moved through the house toward her voice.

She sat on the edge of her bed. "No, he's in Florida for three days. Or that's what he says, anyway." She turned her head and put in an earring. "Yes, of course, we should."

She stood up and went to the wardrobe, where she grabbed a perfume bottle and sprayed two quick shots to her neck. "That sounds great. I've missed you, too. Yeah, the usual place. Don't be late; you know I can't stand waiting."

She hung up the phone and tossed it on the bed. She

finished applying her makeup, then put on her coat, pocketed the phone, and strode to the garage.

Gyges hesitated. He could stay in the house and see what he could surface or he could find out whom she was meeting. Without thinking, he followed her outside to the Audi. Then he realized that he wouldn't get to his car in time to follow. When he turned to go back into the garage, he found the door locked.

He cursed his stupidity and threw his hands up as she pulled down the drive and out of sight.

His anger subsided by the time he reached the Explorer. He'd learned something, at least. It was pretty obvious she was meeting a companion. He just needed to find out who.

* * *

Gyges met Patrick the next morning at Mill Race Cafe. They arrived at the same time, and the waitress escorted them to a table.

"Good to see you," Gyges said.

"You, too. How's the new office? Great view, huh?"

"I think it must be the best in the building," said Gyges. "Why didn't you take it when Tommy left?"

"I actually thought about it, but it would have been a hassle to move everything. Plus, the view. I'm not sure I could concentrate. I'd be likely to spend the day gazing at the city. I think that might be why Tommy always had the drapes pulled."

"I love the view, but it really should be yours." Gyges took a drink of ice water. "I tell you what—if you want the office, say the word and I'll trade you."

Patrick laughed, "No, that's kind, but it's yours now. Enjoy it."

The waitress came back and they ordered the Working Man's Special.

"How are you doing on the job? Or is it too early to

tell?" asked Patrick.

"Yes and no. That's why I wanted to meet. I thought it'd give us more privacy."

"Those doors are pretty thick, Pete," Patrick grinned. "But I know what you mean. What's up?"

"I'm worried about your and Danny's expectations. I get the feeling I'm supposed to be Tommy and be him *now*. I don't think I can be Tommy—I mean, not just now, but ever."

"Tommy's a hard act to follow; I give you that. He and Dad worked together for so many years, they could anticipate what each wanted from the other."

"I have no idea how to anticipate what your dad wants. That's what worries me. And then there's this 'temporary position' hanging over me. I'm feeling the pressure."

"You're just going to have to get Danny to be more explicit about what he wants from you. Make him explain it. I'll warn you, though; he doesn't like doing that. He didn't have to with Tommy."

"I don't mean to pry, but did you ever feel like a third wheel on a two-wheel cart?"

"Oh, sure. Often. They're just so close. No one could come between them. Lots of times, they would discuss stuff between the two of them, decide what they wanted to do, then let me know what I thought. I was supposed to be in on the decision, but they'd already made up their minds."

"That didn't piss you off?"

"Yeah, but you have to remember who they are, and what they went through growing up. They were just two shanty Micks trying to carve out their fortunes in a world dominated by WASP bankers, Wop muscle, and Jewish financiers. They only had each other to depend on. Even later after they'd made their reputations and the Jews and WASPs finally cut 'em some slack and they all made shitloads of money together, the O'Brien boys held themselves apart. Out of sheer force of habit, I guess. They're not the kind of guys who forget. Anything. They keep score. It matters who did what to whom and who owes whom what."

"I get the sense that your dad keeps score with you too, Patrick," said Gyges.

"In a way, but it's a different kind of scorekeeping. Not so much what I owe, but a constant judgmental attitude about what I've done or failed to do."

"That's what I'm afraid of—being judged that I'm not meeting some standard I don't know about. Tommy knew and so do you."

"In one sense, it's simple," said Patrick. "Do whatever you must for the success of the firm. Period. Results matter—a lot. If you don't find new companies—ones that make us money—you won't last."

"I know that."

"I'll also tell you—and I'm being frank here—that you have long odds. Tommy could do it; he knew all those old bankers and financiers. They'd tip him off when they'd see one of their clients getting into trouble. Very clubby. They all knew each other and made each other money. It all goes back to relationships, see? You'll have to cultivate them. Get Danny to introduce you to those guys."

The waitress brought two big plates of ham, eggs, potatoes, toast, and pancakes.

"No one said anything about that. I wish Tommy would've done that before he left. He wasn't around much. Too busy with his house in Ireland."

"I know. I'm sorry. I talked to him about it and he promised to do it, but . . . in the end, his heart just wasn't in it anymore."

"There was a rumor that Michael would come back and take Tommy's place. You don't have to say, but I wondered if he was offered it." Gyges pushed a piece of egg across his plate and onto his toast.

Patrick paused. "He wasn't offered it straight up. Tommy knew he wouldn't take it."

"Why? Because of Danny?"

"Yeah, it's not really a secret. I'm sure you know how

it is from the rumors. Michael likes being the top guy. He doesn't have to answer to anyone or conform to anyone's style. He would have to give that up to come back—do it Danny's way. Why would he wanna give that up?" Patrick spoke between bites of pancakes.

"Do you envy that?" asked Gyges.

Patrick smiled. It was a smile of a longtime friend on the verge of expressing something very personal. "Between me and you?"

"Of course. Shit, who else is interested in this?" Gyges laughed.

"I envy that a lot. Michael has considerably more freedom than I do. It's less restrictive, and there's less pressure."

"I always thought you did pretty much what you wanted."

"Yeah, I know. Everything's rosy from the other side. I'm sure most OH folks think I've got it made 'cause I'm the boss's son. I can feel it every day. But that's okay. None of them know, nor do I want them to know, the pressure of that. I'm just telling you because we're friends and you should know what you've gotten yourself into. You're in a real tough spot, Pete. Working directly for Danny O'Brien—and make no mistake, you are working *for*, not *with* Danny—is no walk in the park. You thought Tracy was bad; the old man is a sonofabitch to please. He doesn't like failure, and reasons why things don't work always sound like excuses to him. I'm not sure—and I don't mean any disrespect—you've got the skills or contacts to pull it off. I hope you do, and I'll do what I can to help, but I can only do so much."

"Well, this is sobering," said Gyges. "Thanks."

"At least you know how things stand. This way you won't be surprised. Isn't that why you asked me to breakfast?"

"It is. But I was hoping for a more optimistic tone."

"I don't have pretty lies here, Pete. I'm being straight with you, and that's the most helpful thing I can do for a friend."

40

By the third hour, Gyges was about to give up and drive home. The stakeout was more of an endurance test than he had expected. He'd hoped to trail Elizabeth, but her car hadn't left the driveway. He would have thought she wasn't there at all if it weren't for the one time he'd spotted her getting the mail, even though it had already been mid-afternoon. It had been two and a half hours since then.

His frustration with the day only grew as he sat there. He'd even forgotten *The Prince*. Most of the previous day had been wasted on trying to run down information on the company list Danny had left for him. Admittedly, it was harder than he had anticipated; as the companies were private, there were no public report filings. He'd talked to Hosbinder briefly to give her the names. It would be a week before she got back to him.

He wondered if Danny wasn't just testing him in some way. The old man never gave him any more guidance than a quick "Look into these places." That was the sum total of his directions. Tommy may have known what that meant, but it was all Greek to Gyges. Har, har. He sighed and rubbed his temple.

How could he be so tired when he hadn't done anything all day? He dug into the open bag of potato chips on passenger's seat. No wonder detectives were so fat.

If what he was going through at work was some kind of O'Brien test, Gyges thought, Danny could shove it up his ass. The more he thought about it, the more pissed off he became. Until breakfast the day before, when Patrick had told him, he hadn't even been aware there *were* banker pals. Seemed like pretty fucking pertinent knowledge that should have come with the torch. It made no sense.

And to top it off, Patrick had gone MIA for the rest of the day.

"Fuck these old-school Micks," Gyges said aloud.

It was getting late. He turned on the ignition and threw the car into drive. But as he was about to turn on his headlights, a light-blue Volvo pulled into the driveway. Gyges paused. He couldn't get a good look at the driver, but he could tell it was a male. No sooner had the car stopped than Elizabeth came running out of the house and jumped into the Volvo on the passenger side.

Bingo.

He followed them easily at first, hanging back a block. The Volvo turned onto 495 and merged into the flow of an evening shopper's rush. Too many cars got between him and the lovers. They took exit 169, but he was boxed in by a slow-moving truck. When he finally made the exit, he could barely make out the Volvo ahead. He weaved through traffic, but the blue car was gone.

A perfect end to the perfect fucking day. He slammed his hand into the steering wheel with an incoherent guttural groan.

* * *

Elizabeth took off her shoes and slid them next to a dozen other pairs in her walk-in closet. She plopped on the bed and removed her earrings.

She unzipped the top of her dress.

"Would you like help with that?" said Gyges, standing in the doorway.

"Jesus Christ! What the hell are you doing here?"

"I saw your car outside. I rang the bell, but no one

answered. The front door was open, so I just walked in."

"No it wasn't. I remember locking it," she said.

"Yeah, you got me. I lied. I came in before you locked it," grinned Gyges.

"Bullshit. You shouldn't be here."

"Because Danny's out of town? If you're expecting company, I'll just come back."

"What? I don't know what you're trying to imply, but—"

"I'm not implying anything," said Gyges. "I'm just here for business."

"Well, I'm not interested in hearing about it tonight."

"No? Too tired after spending the evening on your back, I suppose."

"I've had just about enough—"

"Do you often say things you don't mean?" he asked.

"What?"

"Did you mean it when you said you'd like to make a name for yourself, Ms. O'Brien?" he asked.

"What are you getting at?"

"I'm just checking your integrity level."

"Integrity level?"

"Yeah; do you mean what you say? Or . . . do you just say things to keep the conversation rolling, you know, to help entertain Danny's clients?"

"That's not my role here," she snapped.

"Hmmm. I guess everyone's mistaken about what you do, then. I wonder why." Gyges paused for effect, then said, "Or maybe we're not the ones who are mistaken about your role?"

"You should leave now. What if I told Dan you'd come uninvited while I was here all alone?" she threatened.

"I'd have to tell him about your interests in pastel Swedish automobiles. Frankly, Danny would make a very convincing jealous husband. He's not the kind of man that likes to share his toys. I know I wouldn't want to be the other guy," Gyges said, shrugging. "But I can leave. I wouldn't want to force anything on you. I've learned what I needed to know."

"What do you think you've learned?" she shot back.

"All that woe-is-me poor-rich-bitch bullshit is more alluring to you than your talk about being something more. You don't mind being a trophy wife after all. You get extra sex on the side of your fringe benefit package and allowance." He backed away from the door, not taking his eyes from her. "So I'll be going. Don't worry. I won't mention this to Danny if you don't. I think our secrets can be safe with each other, yes? I'll remember this the next time we deal with each other."

"Remember what? Gyges, are you trying to blackmail me?"

"I thought you were going to call me Peter," he said. He dropped his face in a mock frown. "No, I'm not trying to blackmail you—how boring. No, what I'll remember is that I don't have to take anything you say seriously. You're just around to keep the conversation going—something buoyant and beautiful. An entertaining pet."

"So, what's this business proposition?"

"Let's go through some hypotheticals."

She took a cigarette from her purse and lit it. Exhaled upward.

"What if Dan had a heart attack? Like his old man. Who'd get the business?" He was certain of the answer, but hearing it was entertaining.

"Patrick, of course," she said and rolled her eyes.

"Why not you?"

"The oldest son gets the business. He's in the will to take over the company. I'm not in the company part of the family—remember?"

"If you were to get the company, would you be interested in a partnership with me?"

"Such as?"

"I'd be the Chief Operating Officer; you'd be the Chief Financial Officer and President. We'd run the compan as joint decision-makers, each having authority over r respective areas. You could make a name for yourself—r than Mrs. Danny O'Brien. You could be President Elizabeth Heath. How does that sound?"

"It sounds intriguing."

"Well, would you be interested in such a partnership?"

"That's just fantasy."

"Look, Danny boy is a heart attack waiting to happen—overweight, no exercise, cholesterol through the roof, smokes, drinks heavily, high-stress job, family history of heart disease. He could go any minute. His heart's a landmine."

"He pays no attention to his health."

"So it's a matter of when, not if, he has a heart attack. If he had it tomorrow, Patrick would run OH, yes?"

"Of course," she said.

"And you think he's gonna offer you a deal like this?" he asked.

"That bastard's the reason I'm not at OH anymore," she blurted out.

"Everybody knows that. They know you were doing a great job but had to leave because Patrick put his feelings before the good of the company. OH has suffered because of it."

"Why are you doing this? I mean, you're already V.P."

"I'm great at operations and acquisitions, but I know shit about finances and accounting. You do. From what I hear, you're a phenom. The two of us could get OH roaring. The old fucks run the place like you'd expect a couple small-time Micks would. They never had a bigger vision than passing the family business on to their sons. I've seen 'em turn down deals and pass over things because they fell outside of that limited vision. But you and I," Gyges suggested, "could get OH on the map with a couple of big newsworthy deals. Then we'd be in a position to take the company public. The money they're making now is okay, if you're just caretaking a little nest egg for the kiddies, but it's chump change to what we could make going public. We'd both be set for the good life."

Elizabeth paced back and forth, becoming more excited as he went on. "I've been telling Dan the exact same thing for years. Take OH public. He won't do it. He always [has] these lame excuses. You know, he's afraid of the risk. And [he] doesn't want to lose control to a board and stockholders. S[o] if he'd have listen to me—"

"But he didn't. He won't change, and you stan[d a] snowball's chance in hell once Patrick's in charge. If Patr[ick] takes over, we're both out. He's not one of my bigg[est] supporters, either. At best, he'd demote me. He's jealous [of] what I've done to save the company. He would bring [in] Michael, and it would be the O'Brien Show part two. No o[ne] else would have any influence at all."

"I agree with everything you're saying, but there['s] nothing we can do. I guess we're both going to have to fi[nd] happiness in being screwed."

"We're screwed if we wait by the sidelines and let [it] happen. You either grab what you want in this life or you sh[ut] the fuck up about it. I'm offering you help. The question [is] how bad you really want it."

"I want it bad enough. I just don't see any way to ge[t] it. I thought I'd already gotten it with Dan, but it just didn['t] turn out that way."

"You caved into a guy who just wanted you a[s] property. You let him dictate your satisfaction on his terms[.] I'm only interested in a deal where we both get what we want."

"I haven't heard anything that convinces me we stan[d] a chance," she said.

"Danny would have to change his will. If that doesn'[t] change, there's no reason for me to help move Danny's departure along and you'll remain nothing but an aging trophy wife." Gyges paused. "Has it ever occurred to you that Danny swapped an older wife for a younger one once? It's not going to be harder the second time."

"Of course it has."

"Then you have to make sure Patrick doesn't inherit the company."

"There's no way to change Danny's mind," she said.

"Maybe you're not as clever as you think. Unless you

find an answer, I can't help you. I can only do so much at OH to drive a wedge between them. I'm still a mere mortal. You have to get him out of the will."

"Even if we manage to get Patrick out of the picture, Dan's still in charge. You say he's a heart attack waiting to happen, but he's also stronger than a bull. It could be years."

"Unless something happened to speed up the natural course of things."

"And if that happened, I'd be the first person the police would suspect. I have the most risk here."

"And the most to gain. This is exactly why you need me."

"How can you be so sure?"

"That's my problem. I can assure you it will be seen as an accident. In any accident, there are always witnesses. You'll be nowhere in sight, with a clear alibi."

"And you? Where will you be during this . . . accident?"

"I won't be anywhere in sight, either. Neither of us will be linked to his death. But none of this does us any good until you get Danny to change the will."

"You might as well ask me to change water to wine. There's no reason for him to listen to me," she reiterated.

"You have to figure that out. Work the ancient angles—jealousy, envy, greed, betrayal, lust. You'll think of something; you're smart, right? London School of Economics and all that. Just let me know when Patrick's out."

"I need to think about it."

"Don't think too long," said Gyges as he turned to leave. "The window won't be open forever. Call when you're ready to take charge of your life and get what you want."

"Where are you going?" Elizabeth dropped her hand to her bare shoulder. "No one is watching. Why don't you stay?"

"That's my philosophy exactly. What can't be seen can't be done. I'd like nothing better than to have sex with you, but it would only complicate things and make you doubt why I came. There's plenty time for that. Right now you need to think about how to get Patrick out of the will."

41

Patrick and Gyges finished their last meeting with Domino Textiles. The preliminary work was complete. Before returning to work, Gyges suggested they stop for a beer at a nearby bar. Patrick readily agreed.

"I've learned a lot these past couple weeks working with you," Gyges said. "I have a much clearer idea of what to look for on the acquisition side now that I see what you need to know and do on the reorganization and restoration side. Thanks."

"Don't mention it," said Patrick. "None of us can prosper unless we all work together. Glad to help an old friend, too." He raised his beer. "Here's to mutual prosperity."

"Mutual prosperity," repeated Gyges and drank to the toast. "Say, speaking of old friends, I've been reminiscing lately about all the times you, me, and Michael spent hunting and fishing."

"Yeah, those were great times. How many times did we skip class so we could go fishing? You know, if my kids did that, I'd have their hides, but I'd do it again in a heartbeat. What I got out of being in the outdoors was vastly more valuable than anything I learned in school."

" 'When I think back on all the crap I learned in high school, it's a wonder I can think at all,' " Gyges quoted.

"Cheers to that," said Patrick.

They both drank.

"Well, it got me thinking how nice a little reunion

fishing trip would be—just the three of us. I don't know if I ever told you, but after the divorce I bought a Boston Whaler. It's—"

"You bought a Boston Whaler?" Patrick interrupted. "Damn, I would never have guessed. Did it come with a motor, or do you just paddle it around?"

Gyges burst into laughter. "It's got twin 420 Yamas on it. Really pushes through the water. It's dry-docked now out at St. Alban's Bay Marina in Excelsior. We should get up to the Whitefish. Call Michael and get him to fly in and take a long weekend up there. Just like the old days."

"Goddamn, that's a great idea. Let's go now."

"Why don't you call Michael and see if he can make it for the weekend after Memorial Day?" Gyges suggested. "Bass season will be open, and the traffic on the lakes shouldn't be too bad."

"Unless we play hooky from work, it won't be as much fun. So no telling the old man what we're up to. We'll take off after work Thursday, stay at Black Pines, and fish Friday through Monday morning. We can come back Monday night and head back to work Tuesday."

"Man, that's a plan. Think Michael can get the time off? It wouldn't be the same without him."

"Jesus H. Christ, Pete; he owns the fucking company. He can take off anytime he wants. He's got no excuse to turn us down. I'm callin' him now."

Patrick pulled his cell from his suit and punched in Michael's number. It rang twice. "Michael, you sorry sonofabitch," he hollered into the phone. Gyges could hear Michael's laugh on the other end. "I'm sitting with Gyges cryin' in our beers like some sorry-ass old men about the good ol' days when we used to skip class and go fishing. Now we live the sad broken lives of corporate slaves. As an act of liberation, we've decided to do it again—skip work and go fish. But we can't go unless you fly in and go with. We can't go unless you go, too."

Patrick smiled at Gyges and then laughed again into

the phone. "No, it won't be anything like *Deliverance*—promise."

Gyges joined the laughter.

"Weekend after Memorial Day. You fly in Thursday night and we fish 'til Monday morning. You fly back Monday night. We all go back to work Tuesday and no one's the wiser. Whaddaya say?" Patrick eyed Gyges with raised eyebrows. "I knew you would—that's great! Gyges said you were too much of a pussy to drop everything and take off, but I told him he was wrong. And hey—get this—Mr. Paddles bought a Boston Whaler. Yeah, no shit."

42

Gyges gazed out at the city with his feet up on the sill and his arms behind his head. His cell rang from inside his jacket. He answered.

"Peter?" came the voice on the other end.

"Ms. O'Brien. I wondered if I was ever gonna hear from you."

"I'm in."

"Of course you are. That's good news. So you've gone ahead with your end of the deal?" Gyges lifted his feet from the sill and spun around to the laptop on his desk.

"I'm still working on an angle. Have patience and faith."

"There's time for neither. We need results."

"Yes, I understand but—"

"I'm working on a plan."

"And what's that?" she said with a bit of relief.

"I'll let you know when it's done. Don't call my personal line again." Gyges hung up without another word.

* * *

Thursday afternoon Patrick and Gyges picked up Michael from the airport. They'd left word at OH that they were investigating a new acquisition and weren't to be contacted.

From the airport it was four hours to Whitefish Chain.

Route 45 passed Brainerd's Bunyan statue on 371, and they turned onto 16 just the other side of Pequot Lake. Another five miles down and they pulled into Black Pines just before ten p.m. Lynn had left the cabin keys in an envelope on the porch office. They carried food and beer into the back of the cabin and claimed bedrooms. Bob had stacked ample firewood on the back porch. While Michael and Patrick unpacked, Gyges built a fire and set up a round of beers in the living room.

It had been over ten years since the men had been together like this, but it might as well have only been ten days. Michael and Patrick were more brothers than cousins. Most people mistook them for such anyway.

Drinking beers near the fireplace, the three men recalled how much they'd been a part of each other's lives and how, sadly, they'd neglected their bonds. They made drunken promises to start a new tradition.

The spirit of friendship so moved him that Gyges temporarily forgot why he'd engineered the meeting in the first place.

The three days of fishing passed quickly. The Ghost was on the water every day from sunup until well past sundown. Gyges took them to his favorite hump spot off the Hook. The weather was ideal, and they caught bass all day—so many, they lost track. They kept only enough for dinner each night.

All Gyges's careful planning and skillful manipulation came to fruition on Sunday night around the fireplace and several rounds of beers.

"Michael," Patrick said, "we all know you didn't want to come back to OH and take your dad's spot. I made no secret of it, and Gyges, this is no rap against you, but I was really sorry you didn't take the job."

Michael stared into the fire as he spoke. "I knew if I said I wanted the job, Dad would have gone to Danny and it would have happened. Danny may not have liked it—he's still a bit pissed I left in the first place—but Dad wouldn't have denied Tommy. Besides, my return would have been a kind of told-you-so. But to be honest, I wasn't the slightest bit interested. I love being in charge of the whole shebang. It's such a challenge to stay on top of everything. My team is really wonderful, too. We mesh perfectly. I enjoy going to work every day. I never felt that at OH."

Gyges listened from the kitchen area.

"I love the idea of creating something of lasting value. At OH you get things running well and then you sell the company. Sure, it was exciting to fix someone's mess, and it proves you have skills. But . . . it always felt like the kids were leaving home. I just didn't like it after a while."

"Yeah, I understand. I envy you going to work happy. Honestly, it's a chore for me now. It's gotten worse now that your dad's gone. He helped keep my old man's rough edges from scratching so hard. He could lighten Danny up." Patrick took a drink and belched. "I can't do that. Danny won't allow it. I used to try, but . . ."

"Why don't you work for me?" asked Michael. "We'd have a great time. I'd love having you around. You could be an internal consultant, help us spot and fix problems. Find new opportunities for products and markets. You're great at that."

"Working for an O'Brien once is enough! Nah, if I ever left, I'd want my own place, like you."

"Then why don't you do what I did? Take one of the companies that you fix and OH is going to sell. Shit, you'd already have done most of the work. Plus, by the time you've got things straightened out, you'd know the main aspects of the business. That's why I got off the ground so fast and made so few mistakes. It's a great way to start a company and lessen the risk in the first two years. I don't know why you've waited so long."

Gyges perked up. He couldn't have done a better job if he'd sent Michael a script. He joined the guys at the fire.

" 'Cuz I always thought of OH as a family business," Patrick said. "I'm supposed to take over after the old man is done."

"Patrick, I have my own family business, and it's an O'Brien family business, too. OH is no longer the only one. If you went off on your own, then there'd be three. You'd still have a family business. No offense to your old man, but OH always was, is, and will be Danny's show. You'll get it when he doesn't want it or can't run it anymore. Shit, Danny didn't get it until Grandpa keeled over with a heart attack. You'll get it when it makes sense to him, not when it's best for you. Why not make the decision when you think it best for yourself?"

"There'd be a shit storm through Minnesota," Patrick answered.

"So what? He'll get over it."

"I'm not so sure about that."

"Maybe not—I don't know. I just think your expertise and talents would blossom at your own company. Think about it. Really, you'd be a wizard out on your own. Until then, you're just the wizard's apprentice."

Patrick fell quiet and stared into the fire. Gyges saw that Michael's words had had an impact.

The three sat for awhile in silence.

"I know it's not my place," Gyges broke in, "but Michael has a good point. You could look at this as expanding the O'Brien legacy. What if you took the fastener division from Freeman and that plastics-forming business we're ready to sell? They might make a good place to start. You could get things in the black, eventually win back the GM account. The old man would be upset at first, but he'd get used to it. There's not much he could do about you leaving."

"You overlook one thing," said Patrick somberly. "He couldn't stop me from leaving, but he could refuse to sell me the companies for me to get started."

"That's the sad truth," Michael agreed. "Tommy had a long talk with him when I made an offer on one of the rehabs. Without his intervention, Danny wouldn't have done it. Shit, and I'm Tommy's son, not his. You're right—he ain't gonna let you do it."

After a minute, Gyges was struck with a clever

scheme. He decided to take his chance. "Your old man won't sell them to you, but . . . he would for sure sell them to Michael," he said with a grin.

The other men looked at him, and all three burst into laughter.

Michael sat up. "Holy shit, Gyges! You're brilliant!"

Gyges beamed.

"Of course he would," Michael agreed. "He'd probably give me a pretty reasonable deal, too. That's a great idea, Pete! Then Patrick could come work for me!"

Gyges laughed.

"No, then you could turn around and sell them to me," Patrick said. He punched Michael in the arm. "Asshole."

"Well, shit, that'll piss him off even more," Michael said.

"He's going to be through the roof anyway," Gyges added. "What's an extra few thousand feet? What goes up must come down."

"You're right. It's really sneaky, hiding what we're doing from him. But this way I'm assured of getting what I want."

"Well, if he were more reasonable, you wouldn't have to trick him into it," Gyges said.

Patrick's entire demeanor changed. "I'm not cheating him. He'll get a fair price. I'm just disappointing him. So, what else is new? It's the natural order of fathers and sons. He can tell his cronies about his ungrateful son. They can shake their heads and commiserate. Then they can tell him stories about how ungrateful their own scions have been."

"Maybe you should sleep on it," Michael said.

"Maybe, but now I'm really excited. I didn't realize how unhappy I was in the situation until listening to you talk."

"Hey, don't blame me for this. We're drunk, and I'm sticking to that story," said Michael.

"No, I take responsibility for the whole thing."

Michael looked at Gyges, then back to Patrick. He smiled, "What do you want me to do?"

43

Danny O'Brien was furious. Patrick and Gyges had taken off and hadn't said shit about where they were going. He didn't believe their weak story about a new acquisition. Those two never changed. He'd bet a month's profits they were off fishing somewhere. Probably up on the Whitefish.

They weren't kids anymore. Patrick should have known better, especially luring Gyges away when he was so wet behind the ears. He'd have a serious talk with his son when they got back. Whenever that was. This better not last another day, he thought.

Danny didn't have to wait long. An hour later, Patrick walked into the office.

"Where the hell have you been?" Danny demanded before Patrick's heel even hit the carpet.

"Out. On business."

"Bullshit. You and Gyges went fishing, didn't you?"

"It was a business trip. There was some fishing."

"What a load of shit," said Danny, getting more riled up. "Business, my ass. It was a fishing trip."

"Hey, cut the crap, Danny. How much time you spend in Florida playin' golf? Or whatever else you do with your balls. You didn't get that tan under a set of florescent office lights. If we're going to start looking at the load of shit around here, let's start with the biggest pile. I mean, did OH pay for our trip? We didn't charge a nickel to the company."

"OH is my company," Danny objected. "If I want—"

"And I sold Freeman Fasteners and Plastic Formations while we were gone. It was a package deal—business and fishing. A classic deal, really—the perfect amount of social lubrication before the sell. Just like you taught me," Patrick said with a touch of irony.

Danny stopped. "You sold them? To whom? How much?"

"Didn't agree on a price. What the fuck, do I have to do all the work on these deals? You can negotiate that. The guy knows you'll treat him fair. He's an old customer."

"So, am I supposed to spend my day trying to guess, or are you gonna tell me who it is?"

"Michael."

"Michael O'Brien?"

"Yes, Danny—the one and only. Blood of our blood. Your nephew. A true son of the old sod."

"When does he want 'em?"

"Soon as possible. He'll call you later this morning with an offer. I faxed him the particulars. He's arranging the financing now. It's a done deal . . . if you don't screw up the negotiations."

"No, this is yours. You work it out with him."

"I'd prefer if you did. I'm way behind from this trip. I hate being out of the office this long. Even if I am making us shitloads of cash."

Patrick turned to leave.

"You should have told me what you guys were up to," Danny said as Patrick crossed into the hall.

"Shouldn't have to," snapped Patrick without turning around. "I don't check on what you're doing."

* * *

Two hours later, Michael called Danny and negotiated a price. Danny seemed genuinely excited to talk with him. They hadn't spoken in months. He asked about business. Michael heard admiration in the old man's voice, and pride at his nephew's success. They both knew that Michael was a true product of the OH system. Tommy and Danny had taught him how to be successful. Michael had always acknowledged his debt to them, but it hadn't kept him from moving on. He didn't know how Patrick had lasted as long as he had.

Michael didn't like fooling his uncle. The guilt had eaten at him since Sunday night. Maybe he shouldn't have suggested that Patrick strike out on his own. But Patrick was right, of course—Danny would never have sold him the companies. He owed Danny everything, but Patrick was his brother-in-arms. He'd do anything for him, even scam his uncle. And like Patrick had said, they weren't cheating Danny. He took Danny's first offer. He could have gotten it for less, but he thought Patrick should pay a surcharge for his little charade—like a penance, but instead of the obligatory Hail Mary's, Patrick would cough up an extra quarter million.

Danny would be sore about this for a long time. He might not ever get over it. Michael knew he'd call his dad when he found out the news. His dad would chew his ass out, too but wouldn't be as pissed as Danny. Maybe Tommy could talk to him, Michael thought, get Danny to see why they'd done it this way. He'd never met a more inflexible man. If the guy weren't so set in his ways, Patrick could have been more honest about it. The way Michael saw it, Danny should have encouraged his son to do it years before.

* * *

Danny phoned Patrick immediately after getting off the phone with Michael.

"We closed the deal," he said without a hello. "I'm gonna overnight the papers for him to sign. Stay with the fastener division for a couple more weeks—make sure they transition properly."

"Yes, sir."

Danny hung up.

Patrick felt a swirl of emotion. He was excited, for

sure—he'd be out running his own show, making his own mark outside his father's shadow. But then guilt overtook all positive feeling about the plan. His dad was an asshole, but Patrick knew that the way he'd accomplished it had been dishonorable. The two emotions melded together 'til he could no longer separate them. He hadn't told anyone else about it. Not even Laura.

Needing to talk to someone, he dialed Michael. They went over the next steps. Once Michael signed the papers, he'd draw up another set to sell Patrick the companies. Michael's company would carry the note and act as banker for Patrick. He would pass through the same terms as the ones he'd gotten through his financing. In fact, they set it up so Patrick paid directly into Michael's loan.

"Am I doing the right thing, Michael? I feel guilty," Patrick blurted out at the end of the conversation.

"There's still time to pull the plug. You can call the old man to tell him the truth—try and convince him to sell you the companies directly."

"You think that's the better way to go?"

"Man, this isn't easy any way you look at it. Yeah, it's better to be straight with your intentions in all relationships. So yeah, it's the more honest way. But we both know that it isn't gonna get you what you want. I love your dad, too, but Danny's too much of a hard-ass. I know I don't envy you being his son. So the real question, I guess, is if you're willing to go through with this or you want to forget about the whole thing and bide your time. But again, we both know you're miserable. And that's the bottom line—you need to do what's right for you. Even with all his talk about loyalty and family, you think your old man works any other way?"

"You're right. Danny O'Brien never pulled any punches for anybody—not even for my ma, who stood in his corner for thirty-five years. Motherfucker is the most selfish man I ever met. . . . I'm gonna do it. Fuck it. This is what I want. This is what will make me happy."

"Well, there's your answer."

"Thanks, Michael. I'm lucky to have family like you."

"Right back at cha, but don't forget whose idea this was in the first place."

"What do you mean?"

"Gyges, dumbass."

"Yeah, you're right, I guess."

"What do you mean, you guess? The man loves you. He'd do anything for this family. He saved you and Danny and my old man. You should cut him some slack, Patrick."

"You're right, Michael. Peter is a good man."

* * *

Danny called Gyges into his office a week later. The old man paced the floor, his face ruddier than usual.

"So, I take it you know that Patrick is leaving OH to start a company of his own," he said, skipping the pleasantries with a glare.

"No, sir; I didn't know that. Wow. I can't believe it," Gyges said in a naïve tone. "Why would he want to leave?"

"You went fishing with them last week, didn't you?" Danny shot back.

"Yes, we all went up to the—"

"You're tellin' me the three of you didn't talk about Michael buying two companies from us?"

"No, of course not. Not that I know of. I was under the impression it was a fishing trip. I mean, that's all we did. We caught tons of bass; it was—"

"I don't give a shit about the fishing, Gyges!"

"I'm sorry, sir," Gyges said. "But I'm in the dark on this. I mean, wow. Wow. Patrick leaving? You think this has something to do with Michael buying the companies?"

"Why the hell do you think I'm asking you about it? I better not find out you were in on their little scheme. You'll be leaving with Patrick."

"You have my word, sir; I knew nothing. I can't believe Patrick is going to work for Michael."

"He's not going to work for Michael! Michael bought the companies from me, then turned around and sold 'em to Patrick." Spit shot from his mouth.

"And why's that?" asked Gyges. "It doesn't make any sense."

"Oh, for God's sake. Don't be obtuse, Gyges. Patrick wanted out and figured I wouldn't sell him the companies, so he went to Michael to help him out."

"They never discussed any of it with me. If they made plans on the trip, it was in private. Have you discussed this with him?"

"We spent the last hour shouting at each other before he left. Those boys can expect no more help from me. If they think they can pull this shit and I'll just forget it, they're sadly mistaken. If this were anybody else, I'd . . ." Danny looked away and let the statement die.

"Yeah, fuck that. It's absolutely ungrateful. You deserve better. Why would he do it?"

"He said he was afraid I wouldn't sell him the companies."

"I love Patrick," said Gyges. "We've been friends a long time. But if he's done this, something's snapped. I'm disappointed."

"Not nearly as much as I am."

"Is there anything I can do, you know, to take care of things in his area?"

"I don't know. I haven't thought about it yet. I'll let you know."

Gyges got up to leave. "Pete," Danny said. Gyges looked up at the old man. "Thanks. You're a good man."

"Thank you, sir. You, too."

Gyges left and returned to his office. He shut the door and called Elizabeth.

"You're not going to believe this," he said when she answered. "Patrick O'Brien just filled our inside straight."

"What the hell does that mean?" she asked. The reception on her end was bad. Gyges thought he heard a man's

voice in the background.
"He quit."
"You're joking, right?"

44

Elizabeth gave Gyges the go-ahead—Danny had changed his will. He had to move quickly before Danny changed his mind. Three weeks had passed since Danny had sent Patrick's stuff down to the parking lot. The locks had been changed, and he had sent word for Patrick to never come back.

Patrick had tried to call his father, but Danny had refused his calls. Patrick had sent a cab to pick up his stuff.

Gyges took over parts of Patrick's job. He didn't know anything about the rehab end, so he relied heavily on Patrick's team. They were sad to see Patrick go, but no one left with him. Gyges convinced Danny into giving them a bonus for taking on the extra work, and he let it be known that he was responsible for the extra pay. He moved quickly to show himself as the power OH needed in its time of crisis, and many of Patrick's former employees saw him as the only remaining bright star in the organization. People gravitated to his calm and reassuring demeanor.

In his final days, Danny became moodier. It took less to trigger his infamous temper, and the smell of whiskey was always on him. He'd alternate between confusion and dogmatic assertions. He forgot appointments and missed deadlines. He issued orders without asking Gyges's opinion.

Gyges had never seen Danny like this. He always thought the old man invincible, but this was the moment he'd been waiting for. He'd never have a better chance. Sooner or later, Danny would get off the canvas and regroup.

In this time of emotional vulnerability and intellectual torpor, Gyges struck.

* * *

Gyges's intercom buzzed. "Mr. Gyges, Detective Alfred Hill is here to speak with you."

"Thank you, Mary; send him in," said Gyges. He got up from his desk and straightened his hair in the mirror, waiting for the knock. In a few seconds, there was a gentle rap on the door. Gyges swung the door open to a tall brown-haired man with icy blue eyes. He had a round face and a neck like a tree trunk.

"Detective, come in." Gyges extended his hand.

Hill shook it vigorously, entered, and walked to the window.

"How do you get any work done?" he asked.

"I pull the drapes. It's a trick I learned from Tommy O'Brien before he retired. Can I get you something, Mr. Underhill? Coffee?"

"Hill. It's just Hill, and no thank you; I've already had enough today. Probably be up all night as it is."

"Please sit down." Gyges motioned to the empty chair in front of his desk. Hill took the seat. Gyges pulled his chair out from behind his desk. He wanted to be as helpful as he could, after all.

"I have some questions regarding the death of Daniel O'Brien," Hill began. "I wondering if—"

"What a nightmare," Gyges interrupted. "I can't believe he's gone. He was such a vital and intense man. You have no idea what a void he left in passing." Gyges lowered his eyes and shook his head.

"You accompanied him to the Walker Building on Monday—is that right?" asked the detective.

"Yes, I went with him."

Hill had a small notebook in which he scribbled as Gyges spoke.

"And what was the purpose of your visit?"

"We wanted to look over some new office space. Danny had heard there might be some spaces opening up, and he wanted to see if they were appropriate for our expansion. He is . . . ah . . . *was* quite particular about the company's image."

"What time did you arrive?"

"I'd have to check my calendar to be certain, but I think it was about 11:30," said Gyges. He got up and went to his desk and flipped dramatically through his appointment book.

"Yes. It was 11:30."

"What did you do there?"

"We toured the ground floor. He believed that a building should convey a certain impression. It was his philosophy that—"

"How long did it take?"

"Maybe thirty to forty minutes. He liked what he saw and wanted to see more."

"Then what?"

"Danny was hungry. He decided to eat at El Issa, the Jordanian restaurant on the first floor. Danny enjoyed lots of different ethnic food."

"Did you two have anything to drink at the restaurant?"

"When you ate with Daniel O'Brien, you always had something to drink. It was part of the ritual."

"What do you mean?"

"Danny drank. Irish whisky, neat. And he expected you to drink, as well. You didn't have to keep up, thank God, but he saw men drinking together over business as a kind of civility."

"Were you drinking, too?"

"Of course. As I said, Danny expected you to drink, too. I don't drink spirits, though. Strictly beer."

"How much did he drink?"

"I don't recall. I wasn't paying attention. It's not my role to count his drinks. The usual, I guess."

"The usual?"

"Probably three of four. Five maybe. Depends."

"How long where you there?" the detective asked, glancing up from his scribbling.

"Where?"

"In the bar."

"Oh, I'd guess an hour. Maybe an hour and a half."

"The coroner said he had a blood alcohol level of point one four. That's well over legally intoxicated. Did he usually get drunk over lunch?"

"It may make you or me legally drunk, but not Danny. He didn't get drunk over lunch. Not that day or any other."

"When you left El Issa, what did you do next?" asked Hill.

"Danny wanted to see the roof. He sent me to get a maintenance guy."

"And why would he want to see the roof?"

"He was thorough."

"Okay, but that seems odd. Your clients would never see the roof."

"Maybe not, but the condition of the roof tells you a lot about how well the building's maintained and what kind of landlord you have. Danny didn't want to get into a situation that would possibly become a headache down the line. This would have been our first office site away from our own building. It's odd, at first glance, I suppose, but Danny was concerned with his investments. That's why the guy was successful."

"So, you get the maintenance man," Hill said before flipping through his notebook. "Mr. Lincoln Walby showed you the roof."

"The elderly black gentleman with silver hair escorted us up to unlock the door—yes. I didn't know his name."

"Then what?"

"Danny asked the guy questions, and they walked around a bit. Danny pointed out this and that."

"Where were you at that point?"

"Following behind. I don't know shit about that stuff, so I just kept outta the way."

"Mr. Walby said you left just before the accident."

"Yeah, I had to piss. Those beers hit my bladder more than my head. I went down to the floor below. When I got back, Mr. Walby was very upset. He was shaking uncontrollably. Said Danny had fallen over the edge. I couldn't believe it. I mean, I was only gone for a couple minutes and then Danny was gone. I couldn't register it at the time. I must have been in shock. Danny was like a father to me. I'd known him since I was a kid. It's still hard to wrap my head around what happened. What are the odds? It was just one of these freak accidents. Just totally random and senseless." Gyges's eyes welled up with tears.

"Mr. Walby said he was showing him repair work near the edge. He turned to walk away and heard Mr. O'Brien yell. He turned in time to see him go over the edge. Mr. Walby said he must have tripped. Perhaps Mr. O'Brien felt those drinks more than you thought."

"I keep playing those moments over in my head. I wish . . . you know, I wish I would have been there, waited to piss. I might have caught him—saved him. I mean, I was right behind them." Gyges dropped his head into his hands. He didn't know if they were real tears, but it was clear Detective Hill believed them to be.

"Maybe. Is there anything else you can tell us?"

"I can't think of anything." Gyges wiped his eyes. "If I do, I'll call. You have a card?"

Detective Hill stood up and handed it to Gyges, who took the card and then stood up to show him to the door.

"Oh, there was one other thing." The detective sat back down and re-opened his notebook. Gyges sat down, too.

"Do you know Mrs. O'Brien?"

"Not well. I've met her at company party once or

twice. I knew her enough to say hello. I mean, before she took over."

"Did you know that Mr. O'Brien recently changed his will to leave the company to her and not his son?" asked Detective Hill.

"No, Danny didn't talk to me about the family part of the business."

"Well, it wasn't. Patrick O'Brien had left the company."

"Of course, right. Danny never said a word to me about it, though. One day Patrick was here; the next day he wasn't. He left to start his own company. I don't know anything more than that. If Danny had wanted me to know, he would have told me."

"Were you surprised?"

"Yes, I was. Patrick was a great success here. We were all surprised."

"But not surprised enough to ask why he left?"

"Surprised enough to ask, smart enough not to, Detective."

"Well, were you surprised to find out that Mrs. O'Brien was going to be your boss?"

"Not too. This is a family business," said Gyges.

"Until a month ago, Patrick would have been your new boss."

"So you say. I have no knowledge of that. Detective Hill, I'm in charge of growth and acquisitions—that's the only part of this business that's my business."

"M'kay. Well, Patrick came to us. He's very disturbed by his father's death and deeply suspicious at the timing. He's out of the will, the new wife gets the company, and the old man dies in a sudden freak accident."

"I guess I'd be suspicious in his position, too. Why are telling me this? I don't want to get involved with that side of things."

"You may think of something later that didn't mean anything at the time but might be important in hindsight," the detective said.

"I don't see anything except a terrible accident. What more could it possibly be?"

"It does appear that way, yes. But I've learned in my line of work that appearances are rarely all there is. They can be deceiving, as they say."

Gyges accompanied Detective Hill to the elevator. When he returned to his office, Elizabeth was there. He closed the door.

"So?" she asked.

She was nervous. He barely glanced at her on his way to sit down. He rifled through papers on his desk and read them as he spoke. "Not much. Basically the same stuff I went over the day of the accident. They're just wrapping things up, making sure there are no loose ends."

"They came to me last night," she said.

"Yes, of course they did. They're supposed to, Elizabeth. It's their job. We've been over this. I trust you acted suitably bereaved? Were you dressed in black?"

"They asked a lot of questions about Dan changing his will. It made me nervous."

"None of this is a surprise. That's why we rehearsed it," he sighed.

"I know we did, but I was still nervous. He said Patrick went to them with a lot of accusations."

She's too shaky, Gyges thought. She had talked like she was ready to help push Danny over the edge, but when it came down to it she hadn't had the stomach for it. He'd have to keep an eye on her and keep her focused on getting the company ready to go public.

"Yes, I guess he did. What did you tell the good Detective Hill?"

"I told him Dan wanted him out of the will because Patrick left after scamming him."

"Well, that's true, isn't it?"

"Yes, yes. I pushed the agenda, but it's true."

He looked up from his reading. "Did you kill Danny?"

"Of course not! Don't be ridiculous."

"Do you have an alibi?" he asked.

"You know I do. The dedication ceremony at the art museum."

"Then you have lots of witnesses that can verify you were there. You weren't anywhere near the Wilson Building. There's also a witness to the accident who has no connection with you. Why are you nervous?"

"Because we talked about helping nature take her inevitable course sooner rather than later. Then Dan died. That's why I'm nervous. And you said . . . you'd take care of it. And then—"

"I said that Danny was a heart attack waiting to happen and that I could hurry that along. But as it turned out, I didn't have to."

"You didn't have anything to do with it?"

"I wasn't there when it happened. Remember, I left for the bathroom. The janitor saw the whole thing, and he didn't see me because it *was* an accident." He thought it best to hide the truth about Danny's fall. What she didn't know she couldn't testify to. If she cracked, all she could tell the police was that they had discussed Danny's poor health practices. He'd been a poster boy for a coronary. That was a fact. Discussing it wasn't a crime. Even his remark about hurrying things along could be explained away by the stress from his new position. It may have been tasteless, but it was just talk. And besides, Danny hadn't had a heart attack.

"It's just such a coincidence," she said.

"It is, isn't it? You know, Danny was prescient about these things. He was fond of saying that life is uncertain. Who would have thought he'd fall to his death? Life doesn't get more uncertain than that." Gyges's voice carried venom.

"But the police think it's odd he died right after he changed his will."

"Yes, I'm sure they do. But they have nowhere to go with it. The only thing that can change that is you or me telling them different. And neither of us has a reason to do that, do we?"

"No, no we don't," Elizabeth sighed.

"Okay, so let's not get panicky when the police are doing exactly what we expected them to. We prepared well. Now, please leave. I have work to do. I'm sure you do, too."

She turned and left the room.

Only a fool would share more information with her. He'd have to watch her closely. He just needed her to hang in there until OH went public. After that, he didn't give a shit about her or OH. He'd never have to work again.

Maybe he'd head down to the Caribbean, spend his days mastering deep-sea fishing and learn Spanish. Maybe he'd look up Shadmun and Braddock in Belize.

45

The emotional riptide of his father's death nearly sucked Patrick under. He was still swimming in a sea of anger from his dad's rejection after he and Michael had hatched the Freeman Fasteners' plot. He was not capable of separating out the anger, resentment, guilt, everything else dragging him into the depths in the aftermath of his father's death. It didn't help that the arrangements had been handled by Elizabeth without his consideration.

She had decided on a very private invitation—High Mass at the Cathedral of Saint Paul celebrated by the bishop. Only a few of the O'Brien family and business associates. Patrick's mother, Danny's first wife, was not on the short list.

Tommy, back from the Connemara, had tried to reason with her, but she had refused to listen. She wouldn't even take Patrick's call. She was in total control, and there was nothing they could do about it. At least, not the High Mass funeral arrangements. But that was not to be the end of it.

The three remaining O'Briens decide to stage their own wake for Danny, as much out of love as spite. Tommy had not yet sold his place on Chrystal Bay off Bohn's Point Rd. They would wake it out there. His old compound was private, secluded, and sprawling. When the OH Labor Day parties weren't at Danny's on Gray's Bay, they were out at Tommy's. Scheduled on the eve of the High Mass, they launched a massive blowout to wake from the dead not only Danny but any other corpses that might be in the vicinity. Two Irish bands were hired. Hundreds of invites went out. One caterer was hired and another volunteered for free. Open bar.

So many people arrived the night of the wake, they had to park the cars at the nearby Minnesota Center for the Arts and run shuttle buses to Tommy's. Patrick, Tommy, and Michael set up a greeting line at the front of the house. Tommy was uncanny. He remembered every single former retiree from OH. He asked about their families and told Michael and Patrick stories about each of them. Surprisingly, many of them had brought old photos taken in the old days with Tommy and Danny. There were pictures of the brothers at employees' weddings and baptisms. They told stories of off-the-book loans. There were even pictures of Tommy and Danny as pallbearers. One old-timer flashed a grin missing a few teeth and claimed he'd lost them in a fistfight one afternoon with Danny. Tommy shrugged and laughed at that story.

Patrick and Michael were taken aback by the intimate connection these old employees had with the two brothers. They had always seen their fathers as hardass business guys and headstrong patriarchs. The other side of their fathers' lives was hidden from them.

After three hours of greeting and with all of the guests feasting and drinking behind the house, Tommy and the two younger men went inside and sat at the kitchen table. Tommy poured each a tumbler with four fingers of Danny's favorite whiskey.

"To Danny O'Brien," toasted Tommy. "After all we have seen and heard tonight, that's all we need to say." The three touched glasses and then simultaneously downed the whiskey. Tommy's wife brought in a shoe box and set it on the table. More pictures. Family pictures. Black-and-white Kodaks. Burr-headed skinny boys and their dads camping, riding bikes, working in the yard, boating. Patrick noted that Gyges was there in most of them. Another round of drinks. Michael excused himself to run an errand. Patrick scooped up a picture of Michael, Gyges, himself, and Danny fishing from the docks at an old fishing camp at Crosslake. He went outside to look for Gyges to give it to him as a gift. He had not seen him go through the welcome line.

Patrick didn't get very far in his search for Gyges. He was swarmed again by the guests who wanted to tell him more Danny O'Brien stories. Patrick knew that Danny had made a lot of money for himself and the family, but now he saw how he had also enriched hundreds of other lives along the way. Many people were markedly better off for having known Danny. They had showed up to wake him into the next life with an outpouring of love and hundreds of affectionate stories. No one wanted to leave. And Patrick didn't want them to go.

Around midnight, a long black limo pulled up. Out of the back popped Michael, drunk and grinning. He commandeered Patrick and Tommy and a couple of their burly cousins. From the back of the limo, they pulled out a dark mahogany box. It was Danny's casket. They put it on the back of Tommy's Gator, popped open the lid, and drove it around the grounds to endless choruses of "Danny Boy." Later, the police arrived and forced the return of the casket to the funeral home.

Gyges watched the events from the edges of the night. Patrick never found him.

46

The next six months at OH were a blur of activity. Technically, Gyges was only the VP of Acquisitions, but Elizabeth let him run the operations end, as they had agreed. Gyges hired all the people needed to cover the gaps left by the O'Briens' departure, and he put Hosbinder's group on permanent retainer to help with acquisition research. He promoted three employees internally and hired three new people with expertise in other turn-around firms. He assigned day-to-day operations to Jane Volker, whom he promoted to the new position of Assistant VP of Operations. He let it be known that she was in charge—whatever she said was law. Anyone trying to go around her directly to him would be promptly dismissed.

He was most interested in rooting out anyone who posed even the slightest danger to taking OH public. Neither he nor Elizabeth made a secret of their desire; in fact, they let it be known that it was the company's new direction. He resumed his unobservable trips around the office—sitting in on meetings, conversations in offices, gossiping in the break room. He thought it important to keep up a continuing surveillance of any possible conspiracies. On a couple occasions, Gyges overheard employees speculate about his rise to power and what he may have done to get there. They expressed suspicions about his sleeping with Elizabeth and the two of them getting rid of Danny. That night, security guards boxed those employees' personal effects, brought them to their homes, collected their keys, and delivered a one-line termination notice. The only official release on their status was that they would not be back. Gyges leaked rumors that these employees had been overly critical of him and the way he did things. Punishment for crossing—or even criticizing—him would be swift and brutal. It was unclear how he knew things, and that created a paranoid environment where people stopped speaking honestly to each other in fear that their co-workers would turn them in. Exactly the environment Gyges wanted. It chilled any chance of organized dissent. Better to be feared than loved, as the master had written.

Gyges orchestrated a subtle campaign of attracting employee allegiance through a combination of rewards and promotions. Gyges had Elizabeth put together a simple bonus plan based on years of service, salary, and the selling price of the IPO. It became everybody's best interest to take OH public. The plan would benefit all—not just the few members of the O'Brien family, as it had been in the old days. Gyges presented the O'Briens as a clan of small-minded people interested only in enriching themselves, even if it was at the expense of the employees. Loyalty to the O'Brien regime flagged. Employee recollections of prosperous growth; fair treatment; generous salaries; concern for families; appearances at employee weddings, baptisms, wakes, and hospitalizations, and off-the-book emergency loans—all trademarks of OH under the O'Brien Brothers—evaporated completely.

Gyges spent most of his time hunting for acquisitions to give OH a national reputation as a hot private firm. He expanded the search for companies beyond the Midwest. He had banks in Chicago and Los Angeles and brokerage houses in New York look for possible candidates. Gyges gained a reputation as a savvy negotiator and partner. His ability to anticipate what the other parties were going to do was the subject of conversation in all the financial institutions with which he did business.

After one particularly powerful performance, a CEO became convinced that Gyges had planted listening devices in his headquarters. He paid a private security firm to sweep the place. They found nothing. A Chicago bank figured he'd paid an inside informant. The company launched a surprise polygraph test one morning as key employees came to work. They didn't turn up any connection to Gyges, but they did discover a minor case of embezzlement and several office affairs. On his trips to New York and LA, Gyges started wearing all black, with reflective sunglasses even indoors, to increase the aura of mystery.

Through these efforts, Gyges unearthed a handful of larger acquisitions. None of them were blockbusters or headline-grabbing deals on their own, but together they called attention to the name of O'Brien Holdings. OH's only problem was that it wasn't staffed to handle the volume of business Gyges was trying to acquire and flip. The O'Briens had a simple, effective method—Tommy would carefully look into a few prospects and then focus on one for more in-depth analysis, Patrick's group would rehab acquired divisions to generate profit, and Danny would sell the healthy units. They seldom had more than three companies at a time. OH didn't acquire new companies until Danny had sold the rehabbed units. He didn't believe in inventory. Since the three O'Briens worked so closely together every day, they coordinated through conversation.

Gyges found that the method inhibited growth. But the O'Briens were never focused on growth per se. Gyges was. He couldn't flip the necessary companies fast enough using their method. He needed more volume. When he and Elizabeth looked over their system, the sticking point in ratcheting up volume turned out to be the rehab units. It took time to fix the failing organizations. Danny hadn't kept units once they were fixed, but that had more to do with the way he liked to run the business—keep it simple, he used to say—than with any particular business standpoint. Once fixed, the companies generated profit. They didn't cost OH a thing. Once Gyges stopped treating the companies like live hand grenades, identifying and analyzing prospects wasn't a problem. Tommy and Danny had acquired companies to a large degree based on whether Danny had thought he could find a buyer when they were fixed. Since they held the units longer, Elizabeth pointed out, OH could acquire firms faster and they could expand their options. The real problem was fixing them.

As Gyges's contacts identified more prospects and he acquired them, he couldn't get the old regime out and his rehab management in until they had finished the previous job. The new firms were losing money, which created a cash-flow problem. It took too long to recruit enough people with the skills to turn the companies around. To solve the problem, OH purchased another turn-around firm with a strong rehab department. Gyges cut loose their acquisitions and research divisions and kept only the rehab and marketing people. This quickly allowed OH to increase the volume of companies they could buy.

On her end, Elizabeth barely kept up with managing cash flow and preparing to take the company public. OH had to be seen as a company with a strong bottom line, but investing in Gyges's colonialism made it difficult, leading to a constant tug of war between the two. Gyges tried to grow the company fast enough to draw attention to the OH name when the IPO launched. Elizabeth battled to keep profit margins big enough so that when the IPO was announced, people would want to buy stock. She argued that it wasn't good to be known unless you were known to make money.

The constant push and pull between them produced a zigzag path of improvement. First one and then the other would have his, or her, way. But despite all the tension and fights, they kept moving OH toward going public. After six months, they had doubled the company's holdings and made more money than before Danny's death.

Gyges was sure another six months would be enough.

And as it turned out, the rumors about him and Elizabeth became true. For Gyges, the temptation to sleep with her was just too strong. With Danny no longer in the picture, and with the amount of time traveling and working together, there was hardly a reason not to. It just kind of happened. She was available and more than willing. He insisted she stop seeing anybody else, though no matter what she said, he didn't trust her about that or anything else.

* * *

"I bought you something," Elizabeth said as she came through the door.

Gyges had grown to dislike the sound of her voice; it made the corner of his lip unconsciously curl. "Thanks. What is it?"

She held up a stone statue. It was a sandstone sun with rays of light irradiating from a large eye at its center. "It's ancient Persian," she said. "I found it in an antique store in New York last week. Like it?"

He wondered why she was so chipper. "Yes, especially the color. The eye is a little disconcerting right there in the middle of the sun. It is a sun, right?"

"Very good. It's Ahura Mazda, God of Light. He was the chief god of the ancient Persians. At least, that's what the dealer said."

"What's the occasion? My birthday?"

"No . . . well, I dunno. It could be, I guess. I don't even know when your birthday is."

"It was three months ago. We were on a trip to LA," he said, returning to his reading.

"I had no idea. Why didn't you say something?"

"We had more important fish to fry."

"Well, you can think of this as a birthday present if you like, but I got it as an anniversary gift."

"Anniversary?" asked Gyges, puzzled enough to again look up from his reading.

"Six months of being in business together," she said. "It's been the most stimulating and exciting six months of my life, and I have you to thank for it. So this is my thank-you gift."

"I'm not one for keeping track of those kinds of things, but I appreciate it. It's been . . . an exciting six months for me too. You've turned out to be a great business partner. Your dad's money wasn't wasted at the London School of Economics."

"How about you put it here?" Elizabeth pointed to the credenza opposite Gyges's desk.

He looked at the credenza and then stared at the statue for a minute.

"Yeah, that's fine. We can keep an eye on each other." He mustered up a laugh.

Elizabeth positioned the statue so Gyges could see the front of it from his desk. She moved behind the desk to get his POV of the Persian god. "How's that?"

"It's fine. Do I need to do anything to it? Burn incense? Sacrifice a goat? Violate a virgin? I'm not caught up on pleasing pagan gods these days." He looked at the eye staring straight at him. "This may come as a surprise to you, but in Catholic school worshiping pagan gods was somewhat discouraged."

"You are so funny," she laughed. "Just have the cleaning crew dust it off whenever they're here."

"Great—a low-maintenance god. I like it. I was always puzzled in school about why Gideon's god needed so much attention. Now there's your classic high-maintenance deity. The guy was absolutely obsessed with getting enough attention from those nomadic Semites. I never got that. Here's the Absolute Lord of the Universe—all knowing, all powerful—and he gets all worked up over these hapless losers." Gyges leaned back in his chair. "Plus, he was so demanding—Don't do this, don't do that. If it was fun and you got something you wanted, it pissed the guy off and you'd burn forever in the fires of hell. I mean, how insecure was he? And didn't he have anything better to do? Jesus. For a long time, I paid close attention to the Thou Shalt Nots. But then I discovered I no longer had to worry about anyone watching me—not even

God. It took a while to sink in, but once I stopped worrying about that shit, things have been better for me."

"Well, you've put quite a lot of thought into this. I never did, growing up," she said.

"You didn't grow up Catholic," laughed Gyges.

"Well, I've found you a more compatible god," she said. She bent over and kissed him.

* * *

Gyges picked up the phone and quick-dialed Elizabeth. "Elizabeth, could you come here?" he said as calmly as possible. "Now would be best, please."

He paced the office waiting for her to arrive. Losing patience, he swung around to his desk and picked up the phone again. He'd started to call when he heard a knock at the door.

"It's open," he called out.

Elizabeth entered smiling.

She must think I'm some kind of idiot, he thought.

"You wanted to see me?"

His eyes narrowed. His voice betrayed cold anger. "There's something we need to discuss."

Her eyes widened slightly. It wasn't going to be a pleasant conversation. "Okay . . . what's that?"

"This." Gyges snatched the Mazda statue from the credenza and held it out toward her.

"What about it?"

"It's more than a gift, Elizabeth." He spit her name out like a new curse word. "I think it's less a Persian sun god than a Trojan Horse." He shook the statue furiously.

"What?"

Gyges saw she was stalling for time, hoping to think of an appropriate lie. "Just stop! I was looking at it more closely yesterday after I got back from . . . the break room. It's hollow on the inside. Did you know that?"

She remained silent.

"Of course you did, goddamn it! That's why you bought it," he shouted. "Perfect place to hide something, isn't it?" Gyges reached behind the statue and pulled out a micro camera.

Her face went white. "I can explain," she stammered. "Just give me a chance."

Gyges continued to shout: "You've been spying on me." He grabbed her by the shoulders and tugged her toward him. "What have you seen? You've seen it, haven't you?"

Elizabeth tried to squirm free.

He tightened his grip. "Answer me!" A violent shake snapped her head back and then forward again. "You've seen it, haven't you? Tell me the truth; I know you have."

"Stop it. Get your hands off me," Elizabeth growled.

She ripped free and stepped back. "Yes, I've seen it. If 'it' means the ring. I didn't believe it, but I've watched you do it three times. There's no other explanation."

Gyges threw the camera to the floor and smashed it with his shoe heel.

"Goddamn you, Elizabeth. No one was ever supposed to see that. You really fucked things up now." He paused and rubbed his jaw. "Who else saw it?"

"I'm the only one."

Gyges grabbed her again. "Don't lie to me. Who else knows? Tell me!"

Elizabeth pitched her voice to a low soothing tone. "Peter, let go. You're hurting me. No one else knows . . . I swear. You've got to believe me."

He relaxed his grip. "Is it on tape?" He spaced the words out and pronounced each with an exaggerated distinctness.

"No, I didn't tape it. I just watched when you were in the office. I was just playing a little voyeuristic game, that's all."

"Where's the tape?" he demanded.

"There's no tape."

"Elizabeth, this is vitally important. I want the tape. Tell me where it is and we'll find a way to get past this." Gyges tried to ease his voice.

"Peter, I swear there's no tape. You've got to believe me." She was nearly in tears.

"You want me to trust you after this?" He pointed to the broken camera on the floor.

"I don't understand it. How can you just . . . How is it even possible?" she asked, no longer able to control her curiosity.

"I don't know. I just know it works. That's all that matters."

"Where did you get it?"

"I found it in Lake Minnetonka when I was fishing. It was on beach, in the rocks." His initial wave of anger and panic subsided. He knew that whatever problems he now faced could easily be fixed. He just had to stay calm.

"I wonder where it came from. Do you think there are others?"

"I don't know. Does it matter?"

"No, just curious. May I see it?" Elizabeth tilted her head slightly to the left. A tactic she must have used on Danny to get what she wanted, Gyges thought.

He extended his hand. She inspected it.

"It's quite beautiful. So how's it work? Show me."

Gyges stepped back and turned the ring. Elizabeth couldn't help but gasp. He was indeed invisible. Then he turned it back. She gasped again.

"Wow. Can I try it?" She stepped closer.

Gyges recoiled at the suggestion and involuntarily cupped his opposite hand over the ring.

"Absolutely not!" he shouted.

"I didn't mean for you to give it to me. I just wanted to try it on. What does it feel like? Oh, just once. Lemme try it. Please?"

She was like a damn child—always had to get her way. He became upset again, clenching not only his fist and teeth, but his entire body.

"No. Never. It's too valuable for me to let go . . . even

for an instant. It's never left my finger. I'm the only one who can use it. I'd rather die than give it up."

"Okay, okay. I was just curious, that's all. No need to get so upset."

"I want that tape," he said, returning to his original concern.

"Peter, there's no tape. Period. End of story."

"I'm only going to tell you one last time—give me the tape."

"And this is the last time I'm telling you. There. Is. No. Tape. I didn't set it up for that; I wouldn't even know how." She did the voice again, Gyges noted—the sweet one. The one she used when she was hiding something. The one she used when she was working an angle. "I did it so I could pull those little tricks on you that you pull on me. Which by the way, I now know how you do them."

Wasn't she a cute one?

"All right, I believe you. But now you know," he said.

"So what? How could I tell anyone? Who would believe me? I hardly believed it myself, and I just witnessed it." She crossed her legs; her hand went to the side of her neck. "Are . . . you . . . sure you won't let me try it on?"

So predictable. Sad, really, thought Gyges. He'd hoped she'd be more formidable. Her talents were so pedestrian for a woman as bright and elite as she was. "You weren't listening. I'm the only one who can use it."

"Fine. I guess I'll get back to work, then." She instantly shed the sexy temptress shtick. "I have lots of work to do. So do you. Can I go now? Is the interrogation over?"

"It's over."

Elizabeth turned to leave, then stopped. She went over to the credenza. "I'll just take Mr. Mazda back. You obviously don't appreciate him. And well . . . I'm very fond of him."

She picked up the statue and left.

Gyges shook his head and stared at the directory of raw flash footage on his desktop. Over forty hours altogether. He'd given her every chance to come clean. Elizabeth Heath

O'Brien wanted the ring; Gyges was sure of it. But she also had to know that Gyges wouldn't let that happen.

* * *

Elizabeth poured herself a drink from the mini-fridge in the hotel room. She was shaken by the events of the day. They'd forced her hand before she was ready. She thought she'd have more time to work it out. She realized that she was in imminent danger. Gyges had discovered her subterfuge. She had to work through her situation systematically.

Gyges was sure to come after her. He had a tremendous advantage—she would never see him coming. So she had to be super vigilant—not let anyone know of her private whereabouts, find ways to keep track of Gyges as best she could, be seen in public and always be in the presence of others. But she knew she could only elude him for so long; he would have to be stopped. But she couldn't do this alone. She would need help to get him before he got her.

Elizabeth got another drink from the mini-bar. Time to make a call.

* * *

Gyges sat in the dark at a seat below deck on The Ghost. There was only a single inexorable choice. The logic was unassailable.

Elizabeth was not stupid. She would work out the logic of the situation herself. It was a zero-sum game—only one winner. Lethal checkmate. Death to the king.

The endgame was now clear. Next he just had to work out the way to get there.

47

When Gyges didn't find Elizabeth in her office the next morning, he knew she'd gone into hiding. She'd left immediately after their conversation and was smart enough to see what was coming. He saw how formidable she was when the gloves were off.

If she came out of hiding, she'd have to be in a public place, he considered. She might hire a bodyguard.

Her best strategy would be to tell people that he'd threatened her and she was afraid for her life. She'd probably go to the police. Then if anything happened to her, Gyges would be the obvious suspect. It was her only legitimate play. It definitely put a snag in his plan, but he'd just have to be more creative. It would do him no good to kill her if he was nailed for it.

It took less than an hour to work out a backdoor solution. When he was done, he smiled and looked out his window. It didn't matter what her next move was now. Elizabeth Heath O'Brien was finished, and he was going to end up with all the marbles.

He wasn't surprised when there was a knock at the door.

"Come in," he said.

A pinch-faced female cop entered.

"Mr. Gyges, I'm Robbie Gist. I'm with the domestic violence unit. I have a complaint from Elizabeth Heath O'Brien that you threatened her." She spoke in monotone.

"Please, officer, have a seat." He smiled congenially, pointed to the free chair.

"Ah . . . I'm not here to sit down, Mr. Gyges. I'm here to warn you that in Minneapolis we take domestic-violence threats seriously. We don't wait for an incident to actually occur before taking action." Officer Gist spoke as if she were reading off the clipboard she carried.

"It doesn't matter whether the accused is guilty or not? A mere accusation is enough?" he asked, making sure to watch his tone.

"We think an accusation warrants a visit. That's why I'm here."

"Mmmm . . . I see. I must tell you, however, Officer Gist, Elizabeth Heath is a very disturbed young woman. She lost her husband six months ago and was forced to go back to work before she was ready. She's been overwhelmed by the complexity of the job. It put too much pressure on her, I'm afraid. I should also tell you that we became romantically involved. I had just gotten divorced . . . and, well . . . I guess I was a little vulnerable. In retrospect, I can see it was a bad idea. It has negatively affected her. I have tried to make her see that it has just made things harder for her here. I told her we should break it off, at least for a while, but since then she's been increasingly unstable and strident. I'm quite worried about her."

"I'm here to inform you that you are not to contact Elizabeth Heath O'Brien," Officer Gist said in the same monotone voice.

"Which one of us do you suggest not go to work?" He wasn't trying to sound like a smartass—it just came out that way. He was genuinely curious. "We have a major company to run. I think if Elizabeth got some professional help, she might recover fairly quickly."

"You should not be threatening her in words, deeds, or innuendo," Gist said.

In words? Not *with* words. She was a delight, Gyges thought.

"Officer, are you listening to anything I've said? I'm denying any wrongdoing whatsoever. If you want to protect Elizabeth, you'll advise her to get some help. Did she tell you that she thinks I can become invisible through my magic ring?"

"What?" That got her attention.

"She thinks I have a magic ring that makes me invisible. That's how out of touch she is. She's been secretly taping me in my office to prove I can disappear. I'm sure all the tapes show is me working. There may be shots of me picking my nose or scratching my nuts, but you never see me disappear."

"It is inappropriate to use sexual slang in my presence," Gist said. "I repeat, Mr. Gyges, you are not to contact Elizabeth Heath O'Brien."

"That's fine. I won't. I'm going out of town for a well-deserved fishing trip. I'll be back in five days. In the meantime, maybe you can suggest that Ms. Heath O'Brien get some help with her delusions. When I get back, I'll have time to sort this out in a saner manner. I assure you, Officer Gist, the last thing I want to do is cause Elizabeth any troubles. God knows the poor woman has a heavy enough burden to bear."

Officer Gist handed Gyges a formal warning note. He took it graciously and thanked her as she left.

* * *

"Detective Hill, please," Gyges said into the phone. He sat at his desk, flicking the detective's business card between his fingers.

"Speaking," came the voice on the other end.

"Yes, Detective Hill, this is Peter Gyges over at O'Brien Holdings. You came to see me after the death of Daniel O'Brien—do you remember?" Gyges set the card down.

"Of course I do, Mr. Gyges," replied the detective. "You were the guy with him before he fell. Big office, great view."

The Unseen Hand of Peter Gyges

"That's me," said Gyges. "You said if I remembered anything that I should call. I'm not sure if this is important, but I was cleaning out my desk and found some notes. They made me think about what you said about Mrs. O'Brien being the heir to OH."

"As I recall, you didn't know anything about that. Is that right?"

"Yes, yes, that's right. I told you I didn't know anything about it . . . and I didn't. But it got me thinking when I found these notes. Now, maybe they don't mean anything—you'll have to decide. Do you remember I said that Danny had heard there might be office space open at the Wilson Building?"

"Yeah, so what do they say?"

"Well, we went to that specific building on Elizabeth's recommendation. My notes read: 'Danny wants to see W. Blding for new space. EHO says some openings over there soon.' I forgot when we talked the first time because it seemed so unremarkable. Seeing it again, I wonder."

"Is there any other EHO?" the detective asked.

"No, I'm positive it's her. I use that abbreviation for her all the time."

"And is it dated?"

"Yes, two days before the accident," said Gyges.

"Two days before the accident?" Detective Hill repeated.

"Yes, that's right. But . . . there's something else, too. Under this entry is another. Before I went, I put in a call to the building manager to see what openings there might have been. He was out but called back to say there were no openings. He said that all the current tenants were locked into multiple-year leases. I'm not sure why Mrs. O'Brien would have sent Danny there if that was the case. Maybe she knew someone was going to break their lease; I don't know. Like I said, I'm not sure if it helps or not, but I figured you should know. I thought I'd better give you a call before I threw away the notes."

"Don't throw them away. I'd like to stop by and pick

them up. Is there anything else?" asked the detective.

"No, I hope this is helpful."

"We'll see. Thanks for your conscientiousness, Mr. Gyges."

Gyges hung up the phone. He pulled a pair of plastic gloves from his jacket pocket and put them on. He opened the desk drawer and gathered a yellow legal pad, a blue vial, a lipstick tube, and a small stack of money.

On the legal pad he wrote up the two notes that he had just convinced Detective Hill he had found. He filled the rest of the page with odds and ends: numbers, doodles, company names. When he finished, he went to the credenza, retrieved his valise, and placed all the items into it.

Then he went out to Mary's desk. "Mary, I just wanted to remind you that I'm leaving today for the week," he said. "Fishing on the Whitefish."

"Good for you, Mr. Gyges. You deserve a break with all the hard work you've done these last several months. Have a great time."

"Thank you. Honestly, I think I deserve a break, too," he said, cupping his hand to the side of his mouth like he was telling her a secret. "You have my cell. Don't bother unless the building burns down."

"I'll be sure not to call until I smell smoke," she joked back. "If you get any extra walleyes, I'll take a few."

"You got it, Mary." Gyges smiled a big car-salesman grin and gave her a thumbs-up.

* * *

Gyges was on his way to his car when he noticed the black Mercedes with figures hidden behind its heavily tinted windows parked on the north edge of the lot. The motor was running. He slid into his Explorer and eased it onto the street. He drove slowly, checking his rear-view mirror to make sure the Mercedes was following him. He was impressed that Elizabeth had moved so quickly against him. He'd been expecting something, just not something so fast. He guessed that they would be thinking they had the element of surprise. He wanted to make sure that illusion was intact. He drove normally through traffic on his way north toward the wooded area around Elm Creek Park. He knew the area well, having fished both Lemans Lake and Hayden Lake nearby.

He drove to the park down the long, winding Elm Creek Road. There was a small parking lot with an abandoned outbuilding. Gyges pulled the Explorer into the small lot. He exited the car, popped the back hatch, and pulled out one of his fishing rods as if he were going fishing after work. The Mercedes was hanging back down the road. He made an effort not to notice them. Along with his rod, he pulled his sheathed hunting knife out of the tackle box. Gyges sauntered down a little-used the path toward Hayden Lake. Once he was out of sight down the path, the Mercedes pulled slowly into the lot.

Gyges walked down the narrow path about twenty-five yards. He leaned his fishing rod against a small oak in easy view on the edge of the path. Then he turned the signet, unsheathed the hunting knife, and waited on the side of the path near his rod. He could hear the men's footsteps crunching dried moss and twigs as they came down the path. His heart was pounding, and he struggled to control his breathing.

The men came into view—two Somalians wearing Addidas pull-overs and running pants. They both had guns. They saw the fishing rod and slowed. The one on the right said something that Gyges could not understand, and the other one nodded. The man on the right nearest Gyges stopped to examine the fishing rod while the second man walked ahead a few steps.

Gyges did not hesitate. He thrust the knife forward from his hip with a punching motion into the man's stomach, just below his rib cage. Blood gushed from his wound, and for a moment he made no sound. Then he fell to the ground screaming in pain. Gyges stomped his face with the heel of his foot, breaking his nose. More blood. The second man turned around to see what had happened. He was panicked by what he saw. He spun around wildly, searching for his assailant. Gyges just waited near the fallen man. The second man shouted at his partner, who screamed back at him. He stepped over and knelt down to help him. Gyges struck again. This time he stabbed the knife downward into the man's neck. Blood fountained from the wound, covering the man's face and spraying Gyges's hands and arms. The man fell over on top of his partner. Gyges was frenzied; he screamed obscenities, split flying from his mouth. He stabbed both men repeatedly until they no longer moved.

* * *

Gyges strode confidently, elated, unhurried through the lobby of the Wilson Building just before the security guards were to lock up for the night. He passed by them to the elevator, and though he was invisible, it wouldn't have mattered—they were chatting at the security desk, oblivious to their surroundings. A squad of cheerleaders brandishing semi-automatic assault rifles and yelling "Go Team, Go!" could have paraded through the lobby without notice.

Gyges laughed at the thought as he climbed into the elevator. He pressed the button for the basement.

The doors chimed open twenty seconds later, and Gyges stepped into a corridor. The sound of a TV ricocheted off the concrete walls. He moved down the passage to a small room.

There, Lincoln Walby sipped a cup of coffee and watched the evening news.

48

Elizabeth returned to work mid-afternoon of the following day. She had stopped at the bank and made a large cash withdrawal from the company account. Once she received word that the job was done, she was to drive to the Ramada Inn and wait there with the cash.

She'd never make it there. Shortly after she arrived, her intercom buzzed. "Mrs. O'Brien, there's a Detective Hill here for you."

She didn't even have time to get up from her desk. The detective and two uniformed officers entered the room without knocking.

"Mrs. O'Brien," Hill announced, "we have a warrant for your office and home." He handed her the warrant.

"A search warrant? For what?" she demanded.

"Can we please have the keys to the desk and cabinets?"

"Nothing is locked. But what are you looking for? I don't understand . . . what is this about?"

The two uniformed officers set about their task. One went for the file cabinet, the other for the credenza and closet.

Looking up from the warrant, Elizabeth said, "Detective Hill, I don't understand this at all. Who the hell is Lincoln Walby?"

"Mr. Walby was found dead in his basement office," Hill said calmly. "We're looking for evidence of your role in his death."

"This is nuts!" she exclaimed. "I don't even know this man. You've must have made a mistake."

"He was the maintenance man at the Wilson Building. The only witness to your late husband's death. The last person"—he paused and looked her sternly in the eye—"to see him alive."

"Well, I've never known him. What does this have to do with me?" She threw her hands up in frustration.

"We now know you were the one to send Mr. O'Brien to that building. Perhaps you and Mr. Walby were partners?"

"What? That doesn't even make sense. This is absolutely ridiculous. I didn't know anything about Dan going over there until I got the news about the accident."

"We understand you told him there was space opening up that he may have wanted to check out."

"I didn't know anything about office space at the Wilson Building. Where are you getting this stuff?" She was breathing heavily now.

"We can't discuss our sources at this time, Mrs. O'Brien."

"This is just crazy," she said. She picked up the phone and dialed Mary. "Mary, call our attorney, James Conway, right away."

"You've never been to the Wilson Building?" Hill asked as she put the phone down.

"Of course; Dan loved El Issa. We went often." She pulled the bottom of her suit coat.

"Have you been there recently?"

"Not since a couple weeks before the accident. We went for dinner, I think."

"Did you know Mr. Walby?"

Mary's voice on the intercom interrupted: "Mr. Conway is in court, Mrs. O'Brien. His office said they would have him call as soon as he's done."

"Send it through right away," Elizabeth instructed.

"Did you know Lincoln Walby?" Hill repeated.

"I've already told you I didn't know him. Why would I

have any business with a janitor at a building across town? Detective, you—"

"You never met him? Or spoke with him over the phone? Never made a call to his office? The warrant covers phone records."

"How many times and in how many different ways do I have to tell you? I never met or talked to this man." Her fear was turning to anger.

Detective Hill reached in his pocket and pulled out a plastic bag containing a tube of lipstick. "And do you recognize this?"

"You need me to tell you that?"

"No, but maybe you can tell me why we found it under Mr. Walby's desk? We're checking it for prints. Yours wouldn't be on it, would they, Mrs. O'Brien?"

"Why would my prints be on it?" she asked. She looked at the bag for another moment. "Wait. That does look like the kind I use. But it's not mine . . . mine is home in my . . ." she paused and then blurted out, "Oh, my God. Gyges, you sonofabitch!"

"Gyges. You mean Peter Gyges?" A smile crossed the detective's lips.

"Detective, I'm afraid I haven't been completely frank with you. I should have mentioned this before, but . . ."

"Yeah?"

"I think Peter Gyges may have been involved in my husband's death, and he's trying to frame *me* for it. That's the only explanation for the lipstick."

"You're just now sharing this with us, after six months? And only after we have evidence that you may have been in the office of the last person to see your husband alive? I've not missed anything, have I, Mrs. O'Brien?"

"Yes, yes. I know I should have said something earlier, but . . . I know he's involved. He may have cooked it up with this Mr. Walby."

"Why's that?"

"Well . . . ah . . . because of something he said to me

the day after Dan's death. He said I should be grateful to him for the accident."

"That's your proof? How would Peter Gyges have access to the lipstick you keep at home in your evening purse?" Hill asked.

"Well . . . he must have . . ." Elizabeth didn't know what to say.

"Have you invited Peter Gyges to visit the house since Mr. O'Brien died?" The detective raised his eyebrows.

Elizabeth remained silent. She feared she may have said too much already.

"Have you invited Peter Gyges to visit the house since Mr. O'Brien died?" the detective repeated, raising his voice for the first time.

"Detective Hill, you're an insulting bastard!" she yelled back.

"Frankly, Peter Gyges had nothing to gain from your husband's death," Hill said. "But you . . . you had a lot to gain. You inherited the company."

"I wasn't anywhere near the building when Dan fell. Gyges was there! He was even on the roof with Daniel and that janitor."

"Yes, but Gyges said he'd left right before the accident, and Mr. Walby corroborated his story—that is, when he was still alive. Either your husband fell or Mr. Walby pushed him. Until recently, there was no motive for Walby."

"I didn't do this. Ask anyone who saw me at—"

"The museum? We did. No, you weren't on the roof. But Mr. Walby was doing your dirty work for you. Hidden away in his office drawer was a bag with two thousand dollars and a newspaper clipping about your husband's wealth and company. That's a lot of money for a janitor to have laying around, Mrs. O'Brien."

"So, he kept a little slush fund at work. Maybe he'd hit the lottery, or won over at Mystic Lakes and was keeping it from the Mrs. I don't know."

"Hill," one of the uniformed officers cut in, "You'll

want to see this." The officer handed him the statue of Ahura Mazda, turned it upside down. "It's hollow—look inside."

The detective peered into the back of the statue. "Whoa, whoa, what do we have here? The proverbial smoking gun." He looked up at Elizabeth.

Hill snapped on a latex glove and from the back of the statue pulled a blue vial. He held it up for Elizabeth.

"Doesn't look much like a gun to me, Detective, let alone a smoking one," Elizabeth quipped. "I don't think that's what shot Mr. Walby."

"Well, that might be true . . . if he was shot. But I was only speaking metaphorically, Mrs. O'Brien. He was poisoned." He nodded to the two officers. They moved toward Elizabeth and handcuffed her.

"You have the right to remain silent," one officer began as they led her to the door.

"I . . . didn't . . . do . . . this, goddamn it!" Elizabeth protested, tears now forming in the corner of her eyes. "God damn you, Gyges!"

Detective Hill tapped one of the officers on the elbow and leaned over to say, "Check with the receptionist. We need to sit him down when he gets back from his trip. I think we may get a two-for-one here."

49

The sun hung above The Ghost, and Gyges lay back in a lawn chair half naked, gazing at the sky through a pair of two-hundred-dollar sunglasses. It was a gorgeous day, and he felt like one of the lucky few to experience it; being mid-week, the lake was nearly deserted. He took a swig from a fresh beer and let the can rest on his navel. The sky was such an expansive blue, he almost felt like he was no longer tied down by gravity, no longer weighted by the concerns that had been plaguing him or by the name he'd carried his entire life.

But it was then, looking up at the sun, Ahura Mazda, that Gyges was reminded of his place in the universe. He was still there on Fishhook Point. He was, indeed, still Peter Gyges. He couldn't disappear completely.

Thinking about the sun led his mind back to Elizabeth. She should have been in police custody by that point. He imagined her face behind bars and laughed out loud. She was resourceful and cunning; she'd be all right.

He felt a pull on his line—a hard jerk that almost took the pole out of his left hand. He sprang up from the chair, put his beer down, and gripped the pole tight with both hands. He lifted the rod tip firmly and set the hook with a quick snap of his wrist. The top of the pole bent down toward the water, and for a second, he was afraid it would break. This was a big lunker. The line ran out to his left as the fish swam for the protection of deeper water. But Gyges guided it skillfully back toward the boat. Then lunging skyward out of the water and glinting in the sun, the bronze-and-green fish shook its head in a vigorous attempt to dislodge the hook from its mouth. Gyges had expected this and raised the rod over his head, keeping the line taught. The fish dropped back into the water. Two more jumps later, each less aggressive, Gyges pulled the fish close to the boat, reached into the water, and locked his thumb and forefinger onto the smallmouth's lip.

On deck, he used a pair of needle-nose pliers to loosen the hook from its mouth. He weighed it—five pounds, twenty-three inches—and took a picture with his phone. A beautiful fish. He smiled and released it back into the water.

* * *

Gyges woke to the sound of a boat motor. He looked up from his lawn chair to see a fourteen-foot Lund rental idling next to The Ghost. Still dazed from his nap, he stood up and tried to make out what asshole was driving the piece of shit against his boat.

"Hey, pal," Gyges hollered over to the boat. "You mind? There's miles of open water out here!" He lumbered to the side of his boat to get a better look.

"Petros, my friend!" Bhuto yelled back. "So good to see you! What are the chances we should meet out here?"

"Bhuto—I can't believe it!" Gyges broke out into a small fit of laughter at the sight of his friend on the open water. "You were the last person I expected to see out here."

"Well, if you'd rather be alone, we can leave you be," Bhuto joked.

"No, absolutely not. Please, come aboard. It's a pleasant surprise." Gyges motioned with his hand.

"Great." Bhuto patted his belly. "Petros, you can make your voice very unwelcoming. I wouldn't want to get behind your bad side." The fat man laughed deep.

Gyges laughed too. "We?" he asked. "Is someone with you?" But before Bhuto could answer, Gyges caught sight of the little bald head with the spider tattoo. "Oh . . . I see . . .

Oscar. Great."

"You remember my friend Oscar, yes? He's bartender at the cafe where we played the chess." Bhuto spoke as if Gyges wouldn't remember.

"How could I forget?" Gyges nodded at Oscar. "Oscar."

Oscar nodded back. The small man was in khaki shorts and a Hawaiian shirt. He held two bamboo poles.

The two men climbed from their boat onto the deck of The Ghost.

"So, you've taken up a new hobby, I see," Gyges said, pointing to the poles.

Bhuto laughed, shook his head. "We are trying, I guess. I have business deal next week. They are big fishing people. I do not get it."

"Well, you're not gonna catch much with those," Gyges chuckled.

"So, the big fisherman laughs," Bhuto said. "Actually, this is why we came over. I saw you sleeping there"—he lifted up the binoculars around his neck—"and I said to Oscar, 'We are in luck, here is just the man to help us.' " Bhuto raised his eyes.

"Certainly," said Gyges. "I'd love to teach you. I have plenty of poles here. Let's use those."

"Yes, yes. This is good." Bhuto nudged his small friend. "See, I told you he'd be happy to teach. And after all," he said, turning to Gyges, "I did teach you so much."

"Yes, you did," Gyges agreed. "Can I offer you guys a beer?" Gyges went over to his cooler and grabbed himself one.

Bhuto's mouth dropped into a scowl. "I hate this . . . American beer. Tastes like camel piss." Then, as if remembering his manners, "But it is kind, Petros. It is kind." Bhuto turned to Oscar and nodded behind them to the boat. "But we are in luck. We have cooler full of steam tea!"

Oscar climbed back over to their boat and fetched the cooler. It was almost as big as him, and he struggled to get it over. Bhuto helped him once he got it to the edge, pulling it over and setting it down on the deck of The Ghost. Oscar hopped over and re-joined them.

"So lead the way, Master," said Bhuto. "We are all ears."

Oscar stared hard at Gyges.

* * *

The three men fished for over two hours. Gyges taught them how to cast, and both took to it quickly. Bhuto enjoyed himself, laughing and joking the whole time. Gyges even caught Oscar smiling at one point despite himself. The two newcomers had a successful first lesson; Bhuto caught two small-sized bass, and Oscar caught one at six pounds.

But their interest waned as quickly as it had come, and Bhuto finally said, "Yes, Petros, I can see why some men might enjoy this. But this fishing is for peasants. It does not compare to the chess." This seemed to jar his memory, and he smiled. "Oh, I also forgot, we brought chessboard with us! Let us play for old time sake, yes?"

"You brought a chess set?"

"Sure, Oscar and I take one wherever we go."

"Oscar plays?" asked Gyges.

Bhuto laughed. "Oscar taught me to play. His mother's brother, Mijo, was the first Croatian Grand Master."

"Damn, I had no idea."

"So, do you want to play, or what?"

"I don't know, Bhuto. I'm just kinda enjoying the day. Besides, I think you've handed me my ass enough times."

"Just enjoying the day? What does this even mean? Petros, don't be like this. These are not the words for a man of your worth. Let us play and have some tea." Bhuto's face clinched into a soft fatherly scold.

"All right. One game." Gyges couldn't resist his friend. Though he felt he'd grown beyond Bhuto's instruction, he still enjoyed his company, especially there on the boat in the beautiful surroundings.

Bhuto made a strange whistling noise to Oscar, who instantly scuttled back to their boat.

"Have you been practicing?" Bhuto asked as they moved over to the deck table.

"No, I haven't—not chess."

"Ah, Petros is head honcho now. Mr. VP is too busy to keep up his game." Something about Bhuto's words struck Gyges' as strange, but he couldn't figure out what.

Oscar came back with the board, and they set it up on the deck table.

"Let's have some tea," Bhuto said after his black pieces were ready to go.

Oscar went over to their cooler and opened it up.

"With ice, Oscar. It is goddamn hot. Best ice cold, yes?"

"Indeed." Gyges nodded in agreement.

At the cooler, Oscar took out an ice pick and started stabbing the block of ice.

Gyges couldn't help himself—he burst into laughter. Oscar stopped and turned to give him the cold eye. "I'm sorry," Gyges said, still giggling. "It's just that you're killing that thing."

Bhuto's erupted with laughter. "He's very enthusiastic, yes?" Bhuto said. Then looking to his friend, "Oh, Oscar, Petros only jokes. You do a fine job at killing ice."

Oscar filled three cups with the ice and Bhuto's family recipe and brought them to the table.

Gyges played white. He and Bhuto battled for control over the center of the board. Both men castled to strengthen their defensive positions. The game evolved first in Bhuto's favor and then to Gyges's. At a critical moment, Bhuto's attention seemed to flag and he made a mistake. He allowed his queen to be pinned by a knight, who checked the king. Gyges saw it but couldn't believe it. He stared at it for five minutes to make sure Bhuto had not set a trap for him. He didn't see the trap, so he moved to pin the queen and king with his knight.

"Check."

Bhuto had seen it, too. He knew the loss of his queen meant the final outcome was inevitable. He turned over his king on its side. He looked up at Gyges.

"Your game," he said.

He'd won—he couldn't believe it. He'd beaten Bhuto.

"Ah, Petros, you played a fine game," Bhuto said. He was smiling, but Gyges could see that he wasn't happy. "Perhaps being VP hasn't softened your game after all."

Then it hit him. Gyges knew what was strange about what Bhuto had said before. He'd called him VP. How had he known to call him that? The last time Gyges had seen Bhuto, Danny was still alive. He was about to ask Bhuto about it when his phone rang.

Gyges took it from his pocket and checked the caller. Why was Mary calling? He'd given her specific instructions not to call him. He seriously doubted the building was on fire.

"Mary, tell me your calling from the ashes of the OH building," he said when he answered.

Bhuto shot Oscar a look.

"I'm sorry to call you, Mr. Gyges. But . . . I felt you should know," Mary began in a shaky voice.

"What's up?"

"Well, Mrs. O'Brien was arrested two days ago. She's been charged in the death of Mr. O'Brien. And the cops—they've been asking all kinds of questions."

"Really, like what?"

"I don't know. They wanted to know where you were, and I didn't want to lie to them. I'm sorry, Mr. Gyges, but I think they think you had something to do with Danny's accident, too. I just . . ."

"It's okay, Mary. You didn't do anything wrong."

"Well, you've always been good to me, Mr. Gyges. But . . . but they know you're at Black Pines. I think they might be coming for you."

"All right, Mary; it's okay. Thank you for calling."

"But that's not all, Mr. Gyges. Another man came

looking for you yesterday. He said he was a detective, but I don't know now . . . something about him just didn't seem right, so I thought I should call and let you know."

"What did he look like?"

"He was a large, heavy man. Maybe Mexican? Not sure." Mary's words threw Gyges's heart into overdrive; its beating drowned everything else out.

He looked at Bhuto, who stared at him blankly.

"Listen, Mary. . ." Pain shot up his other arm before he could get out what he was going to say, and he screamed. He dropped the phone, could hear Mary's voice as it fell—"Mr. Gyges? Mr. Gyges, are you all right?"

The chess pieces fell and scattered. Gyges looked down at the table, toward the pain. The ice pick was stuck through the center of his hand and into the tabletop. Blood gurgled up from the wound onto the chessboard. Bhuto stared at him, a grisly smirk at the corner of his mouth. "Petros . . . or should I say Mr. Gyges . . . I'm sorry." He paused. "I liked you."

"Why?" Gyges spat out, squinting from the pain.

"You turned out to be a clever one. You've dispatched the other men I sent. Elizabeth demanded that I see this through to the end this time."

"Elizabeth?"

"Yes, an old friend. She and I used to . . . get close back when her husband was alive."

Gyges's eyes widened through the pain. The blue Volvo. "It was you."

"Small world. She wanted me to make sure you knew she hired me."

"So, this is what you do?"

"Ah, Petros," Bhuto shook his head. "Only part of what I do. I resolve problems, yes? I didn't know Mr. Gyges was Petros until this morning when I saw you napping on your boat. I'm sorry. You are a man like me, Petros. We have both killed for business. You understand . . . it's only business. Nothing personal."

Gyges lunged for the icepick, but Bhuto was faster. He grabbed Gyges's wrist and pushed it down to the table. Bhuto was strong. He just stared into Gyges's eyes, holding him there.

From behind, Oscar pulled his head back and slid a blade across Gyges's throat. It happened so fast, Gyges had no time to register or fight. He gurgled and tried to reach up with his hands. His head dropped to the side as blood ran down his bare chest, and then . . . Peter Gyges was gone.

Bhuto eased his grip. He took a drink of tea. Then he stood up and picked up the phone from the deck.

He threw it into the water, Mary still screaming on the other end.

* * *

Bhuto stripped the body—wallet, keys, necklace, watch, sunglasses, and the ring. Then they slid the body into a black bag. Bhuto dragged the bag to the edge of the boat, lifted it, and with some effort, hoisted it onto the rental. Oscar doused the cabin with gas from a can, then poured the rest all over the motor and deck. When they returned to their boat, Bhuto tossed a lit rag onto The Ghost. Within seconds, the Boston Whaler went up in flames.

Oscar gunned the Lund toward land. Bhuto watched silently as the burning vessel became smaller. When it was but a speck of red on the horizon, he turned and looked down at the body bag. From his pocket, he retrieved the ring. Elizabeth had demanded that he bring her this one item. He knew she had lied about it being her ex-husband's. Petros—Gyges just didn't sound right—had worn it as long as Bhuto had known him. He would keep it—a memento of their friendship. The way Bhuto saw it, she wouldn't need it in prison.

Oscar noticed the fat man staring at the ring, turning it between his thumb and index finger. "Ahmed, you grow sentimental with age."

Bhuto didn't answer. Instead, he put the ring on his right hand.

He was surprised—it was a perfect fit.

EPILOGUE

The elevator opened on the fourth floor, and Patrick O'Brien strolled out, whistling. He made his way down the tiled hallway and swung open the glass door to the reception area.

"Good morning, Mr. O'Brien," said Mary, looking up from her computer.

"Mary, how are you this morning?" He smiled.

"I'm good. Michael beat you in. He asked that you buzz him when you get settled."

"I'm not in trouble, am I?" Patrick joked.

She giggled.

Patrick turned and went to Michael's office. No sense in buzzing him; Patrick could manage the forty feet to his door.

It was open.

"Hey, partner," Michael said when he saw Patrick.

"How's my old office treating you? Looks like the maintenance department did a fine job."

"The previous owner had shitty taste, but I'm settling in." Michael sat behind his desk with an O'Brien Holdings mug full of coffee.

After Elizabeth's conviction for Lincoln Walby's murder, the three O'Briens—Patrick, Michael, and Tommy—had filed suit in probate court. The will was voided and Patrick won the company. Patrick and Michael merged their organizations under the OH umbrella and operated together as joint CEO's. They scrapped the plan to take it public.

"So, you just want to bust my balls, or do you have something for me?" Patrick asked.

"Yeah—we got a meeting with the McKenzie Group at one."

"Okay, great."

"Donneville gave me a call last night. Sorry for the late notice. I guess they freed up some time and are booked solid for the rest of the week."

"No, that's fine. I'll see you then. I'm gonna go pretend like I'm doing something."

"Oh, hey—the wife just let me know we're having dinner with Angela on Friday. You guys are welcome to join us. Actually, I think it would be good if you made it, too." Michael raised his right shoulder in a half-shrug.

"Really? I thought she moved away."

"I guess she's in town visiting. Apparently she has a new man in her life. He's supposed to be a super-nice guy."

"Wow. Okay. Do you think she knows?"

"How could she not?"

"You're right; it's been all over the news," Patrick said. "I'm sure she wouldn't be having dinner with his old friends if she didn't. I don't know . . . maybe she would. Bottom line—yeah, we'll definitely be there. Angela's almost family, too. It'll be good to catch up."

"Great. I'll see you at one."

Patrick turned and backtracked to his office.

He entered and opened the drapes. The view of the city was marvelous. As he looked out Tommy's old office window, his mind wandered back to his missing friend. The police and news reports said that his whaler had been a burned-out shell when they'd found it off the Hook. There had been speculation that Gyges had gone into hiding, that maybe he'd had something to do with Danny's death. Patrick wouldn't even listen to that horseshit. Mary had spoken to him last; the conversation had been strange and the phone had gone dead after some silence. And who was this swarthy fat man posing as a detective? It was obvious to Patrick that Gyges had uncovered the truth about Elizabeth's acquisition of OH and paid the ultimate price. Certainly she was responsible. It just didn't add up—Gyges had had nothing to gain in the death of his father. He'd loved the O'Brien family like it was his own.

Gyges's final moments may have been grisly, but Patrick took solace that his life-long friend had died out on the water doing the purest, holiest thing he was meant to do.

ABOUT THE AUTHOR

R. L. Richards lives in Rock Island, Illinois. He and his wife Dolores have four children and ten grandchildren. When he is not writing or teaching, he is fishing, playing tennis and gardening.

Made in the USA
Lexington, KY
31 March 2015